Kate O'Riordan was brought up in the West of Ireland. She is the award–winning, acclaimed author of three novels, which have been translated into many languages. Kate contributed to the bestselling *Ladies Night at Finbar's Hotel* and has also written for stage and screen. She lives in London with her husband and two children.

Praise for Kate O'Riordan

THE ANGEL IN THE HOUSE
'A book lover's dream. Hugely enjoyable, beautifully written, funny and moving' *Sunday Tribune*

'Highly agreeable . . . with a multitude of twists and turns' *The Times*

'A sublime comedy, with wit and frolics that will make you laugh out loud' *Good Book Guide*

'A slice of reading heaven . . . quite simply, a divine comedy' *Irish Times*

THE BOY IN THE MOON
'A relentless opening of wounds which have scarred in childhood and can still twist body and spirit . . . There is a sting in her writing' HELEN DUNMORE

'A real cliffhanger . . . exquisitely spare in execution, a haunting examination of human strength and frailty' *Time Out*

'Gripping and powerful . . . delight and surprise at every turn' *Sunday Tribune*

'O'Riordan's work is concerned with hidden things, the unsettling secrets of the past that seep into the present. That revelatory quality is evident in all her work, as well as a strain of violence, visceral and disturbingly realistic' *Irish Post*

INVOLVED
'O'Riordan's powerful storytelling icily conveys the horrible ordinariness of evil' *The Times*

'Magical . . . O'Riordan's real skill is in th
approximations that, even between lovers,
for communication' *Scotland on Sunday*

Also by Kate O'Riordan

THE ANGEL IN THE HOUSE
THE BOY IN THE MOON
INVOLVED

THE MEMORY STONES

KATE O'RIORDAN

POCKET
BOOKS

LONDON • SYDNEY • NEW YORK • TOKYO • SINGAPORE • TORONTO

First published in Great Britain by Pocket Books, 2003
An imprint of Simon & Schuster UK Ltd
A Viacom Company

5 7 9 10 8 6

Simon & Schuster UK Ltd
Africa House
64–78 Kingsway
London WC2B 6AH

www.simonsays.co.uk

Simon & Schuster Australia Sydney

A CIP catalogue record for this book is available from the British Library

ISBN 0-7434-5017-5

Typeset by M Rules
Printed and bound in Great Britain by
Cox & Wyman Ltd, Reading, Berkshire

For Paschale

At half-past three a single bird
Unto a silent sky
Propounded but a single term
Of cautious melody.

At half-past four, experiment
Had subjugated test,
And lo! her silver principle
Supplanted all the rest.

At half-past seven, element
Nor implement was seen,
And place was where the presence was,
Circumference between.

Emily Dickinson

CHAPTER ONE

Half-past three in the morning. The phone rings. A birth or a death.

A head turns, a hand snakes out from beneath a pillow. Captured in a moon shadow grotesquely magnified against a white wall, the hand is a tarantula suspended above a ringing phone. Second ring. Lulu yaps from her basket by the end of the bed. Nell is fully alert now. She has seven more trills before the answering machine picks up. A moment to choose limp acceptance of whatever is to come, which unquestionably will be undesirable, or she can elect to hard focus on already acquired knowledge, as a buffer, a coat of arms. She chooses to wrap herself in the armoury of the day just past. Saturday. In Paris.

Third ring. And time has curved, bent round itself, a day sealed in a bubble. Every second and hour encapsulated, poised on her tongue like a taste not yet swallowed. She will have this to hold on to, once the tarantula has pounced.

Saturday morning. While her bath runs, Nell feeds Lulu in the kitchen. She wishes the little poodle didn't have that ridiculous poodly name, wishes Lulu wasn't in fact a poodle at all, but it wasn't her choice. The elderly mutt was an unwanted legacy from her friend Meredith. Lulu wasn't exactly impressed with her new owner from the outset, either. She sulked and snapped and insisted on drawing her incontinent curly ass along the arms of cream sofas and the edges of the Persian rug in the living room. Owner and orphan maintained a mutual if somewhat mechanical loathing for the first year. They were both missing Meredith, after all, and the sight of each other compounded their loss. However, through the passage of time, absence of options and the natural bonding of two ageing females thrown together under one roof, they have grown used to the arrangement. A deal has been struck up. Nell feeds, Lulu eats. Nell walks, Lulu grumbles. Nell grooms, Lulu snaps. Nell rubs Lulu's head as Lulu's leaking behind rubs cream cushions. All told, it is a pretty good deal for an old dog with cataracts and a disobliging temperament.

Nell rubs down the sheets of plastic protecting her sofas, gauging the fullness of the bath from the sound of falling water. It is an old cast-iron bath with trickling brass faucets so there are minutes yet. She opens the living-room shutters to let in a stream of diffuse September light. The window opens onto a wrought-iron balconette filled with autumnal pansies. Five storeys below, weekend traffic moves fluidly along boulevard Raspail. Achingly expensive shops reflect mellow, understated light across the street. The air is unseasonally crisp. Above the mansard roofs, the sky is luminous, neither white nor yellow, more a spillage of light through a sheath of gauze.

Satisfied, licking her chops, Lulu pads into the room, blatantly seeking an unprotected spot on which to rub herself.

She eyes the brown suede chaise longue longingly. Even with Lulu there are boundaries. 'Dream on,' Nell says.

The room is spacious, white-panelled walls, honey parquet floor with a Persian rug in muted duck-egg blue and ivory. Cream bloc-like sofas face a low, ebony lacquered coffee table in front of an enormous grey marble fireplace. White lilies in a cut-glass vase on the table's surface. Discreet, set back shelving lines one wall with books. The wall opposite is covered in old black-framed prints of Paris. Above, a crystal chandelier winks and tinkles from the centre of the elaborately corniced ceiling. It costs a small fortune to have the damn thing polished once a year but it came with the apartment when first rented twelve years ago and cannot be removed, much as Nell would like to get rid of it. Too much, too showy in the otherwise minimalist, neutral room.

After the bath, she dresses loosely in black jersey. Wide flowing pants, swing top with a scoop neck. Soft calfskin pumps for walking. She plunges her head forward and runs a hard bristle brush through the ash-blonde, shoulder-length layers until they crackle and billow out in a cloud of electricity. Folded over, she has a scratchy, uncomfortable feeling, a thought trying to rise to the surface against her will. If she lets the thought through, it will stalk her for the rest of the day. For the moment, she would rather it remained at some distance. An inchoate, formless worry. Something akin to the inexplicable queasiness she experiences when cutting toenails.

Her face in the mirror holds a pinkish bloom for seconds when she stands up straight again, the deepest lines plumped out. For a brief moment she has a memory of a youthful Nell. She is still surprised that she is surprised by the relentless, stealthy creep of age. Didn't she know this would happen? Don't you *know* as a young girl that this is what it turns into? But you don't, not really, she thinks. Not really.

The flush of blood slips back down her neck, leaving empty channels and grooves on her forty-eight-year-old face once more. They are here to stay. Like the dulled edges her corneas have taken on and the faint scalloping along a jaw-line no longer as sharp and distinct as it used to be. Every year, a new drill joining the battalions marching across her epidermis.

What she observes happening to her face reminds her of an apple she once allowed fully to decay out of mild curiosity. First, the skin softened, sagged into tiny folds as the fruit's colour dissolved into jaundice. Second, brown age spots. Third and final stage of maceration, skin seeped inwards to pulped flesh, a ring of white, crusted ash round the stalk. A compulsion to taste the rotten fruit took her over. She plunged a finger into wet, sucking decay and licked. It tasted surprisingly sweet and fermented.

Skin slipping from bone, years giving to putrefaction. Pulp. She saw herself as a sentient apple. Though she was sure her own aftertaste would be bitter.

Woman and dog step out onto the boulevard. Lulu is already protesting at the walk ahead. She wears a tartan tailor-made coat which is as ridiculous as her name and breed, but it too was part of the legacy. Petite, sharp-bobbed Parisienne women pass by with their own manicured pets. Coats on the dogs, expensive shawls on the owners, thrown carelessly over shoulders at first glance, draped, folded and pinned on second look. On boulevard Raspail these are, in the main, women of considerable wealth. While their dogs stop to sniff one another's backsides, their owners do the Parisienne equivalent – eyes begin at another woman's shoes, flicking their way up to take in bag, state of nails, waistline, designer of jacket, until final ruthless, slit-eyed age toll of face. A flashlike reckoning, batting of eyelids again, then the dog is addressed soothingly, coaxingly, and they move on. Whenever and wherever the little dogs choose to shit, the women stand, tap their feet, gaze into the nearest shop window, buff their fingernails. The pavements are littered with heaped triangles of multi-coloured turds.

Nell does not allow Lulu to shit where she likes, though Lulu is not entirely in agreement with this. She widens her back legs and pretends to strain her bowels on occasion, just to annoy Nell. But they both know she will end up going by the usual tree for all her theatrics. Recently, there has been a series of punchy television commercials attempting reverse psychology. To the effect of 'Why worry about where your dog shits? Someone will pick it up.' Then a wheelchair rolls over the mess, or a baby dumps a turd in its playbucket. Punchy and visual, certainly. Effective, no, Nell thinks as she weaves around mounds. Mounds Lulu is desperate to sniff, so she whines plaintively.

Irritated by the constant, persistent whingeing, Nell tucks the poodle under her arm and slips into a side street. Lulu likes to gaze at the place where she once lived. It silences her. There is an old, stunted plane tree with a metal grid round the base where the dog manages to evacuate her bowels properly.

While she waits, Nell gazes up at Meredith's old apartment building. The feeling never goes away that if she looks long enough, hard enough, she will see that aquinine profile in the flung-open casement window of the third floor. Only Lulu would be tucked under Meredith's arm instead, the other arm flapping Nell up, wreaths of spectral smoke slipping in and out of her auburn hair. They met when Nell was commissioned by Meredith to draw up the wine list for her eponymous café-cum-bistro on the Left Bank. It was a roaring success, serving bangers and mash, fry-ups and fish and chips to the French. But she insisted on palatable, safe wines with exorbitant prices for her English clientele. A canny businesswoman. The women immediately struck up one of those peculiar friendships that seem foredestined yet in reality rely upon a slew of arbitrary factors in order to happen; chance, circumstance, timing. The Irishwoman and the Yorkshirewoman. In Paris.

Every day she passes the apartment and each time experiences a throb, a yank at her heart, at the knowledge that she will never again hear the big, blowsy Yorkshire woman's call down to her. *Up, up – now!* The background sound of a cork popping from a bottle. The glass already poured for her. Meredith pacing, slurping, halfway through her first monologue of the evening. Pretending to be angry about things that didn't bother her in the least. Shy in her own way, holding forth as a method of communication, of skirting silences.

Nell skeetering out some time in the early hours of the morning. Trying to act sober. Doing fine until a little telltale crossover of ankles at the corner of the building. Knowing that Meredith was breaking her ass laughing from the open window behind. Waiting for the loud accompanying commentary as she tried to negotiate the pavement in a reasonably straight line. Lights flicking on, angry half-asleep heads thrust out of windows, shouting to Meredith to shut the fuck up. Making her shout all the louder: *don't you understand, you fools, what this woman has done for you? The sacrifices she's made? The years of study and travel and dedication to her . . . Look, look I tell you! There walks what can only be described as a —*

a palate on legs. What that woman hasn't gone through to prove what we have all long suspected: wine makes you DRUNK.

That loud, fag-rattled laugh. Right up to the end, the laugh was bold and defiant, though Meredith herself was a hairless shadow lost in the creases of her hospital bed. She laughed so hard one of the final days when she bequeathed Lulu to her best friend, that she brought on a fit of coughing and choking. It was entirely in keeping with her sense of humour that Nell should end up caring for a poodle she despised. But it was hard not to feel sorry for the silly little thing when it howled and yapped its loss for weeks after Meredith's death. Nell just left Lulu to her vocal mourning, though the apartments above and below complained bitterly. In a way the dog expressed grief for her, too. At a certain age, you can no more afford to lose a good friend than your last good tooth. Nothing fills the void.

They move along toward the Jardins de Luxembourg, one of the few parks in Paris to permit dogs, for a city so full of them. The layout of the park is strictly formal, with straight lines of trees, a canopied bandstand and a central pond. Flower beds conform to the same rectangular linearity. It appeals to Nell's eye. As do the wide, far-reaching boulevards of Paris with their buildings of even height, rarely above six storeys. Order, careful planning, uniform straightness: there is a soft symmetry to this city, underscored by horizontal, rigid lines, which she finds reassuring.

Sometimes, on crisp, leafy autumnal days in particular, she heads down a wide, gravelled path through the Tuilleries with a pleasant feeling akin to ownership. As though she is where she belongs, and what she sees belongs, in part, to her. Other times, very occasionally, it strikes her with force: why here? Why now? How entirely arbitrary it seems, the circumstances that contrive to place one person in one place, rather than another. A job, a brief holiday which extends to a lifetime, a love affair, a missed flight connection, a misread map, a wrong turning on a road leading elsewhere.

Once they have completed circling the pond, Lulu's protests grow ever more vociferous. She yips and whines and sits back on her behind so that Nell has to drag her along.

'C'mon Lulu. You know the vet says your limbs will seize up. Come on. There's a girl. Two biscuits – how about that?'

Nothing will persuade Lulu to move. Her cloudy brown eyes send waves of smouldering hatred along the length of leash. Some days, Nell hasn't got the patience for the on-going battle so she none too gently scoops the dog into her arms and stomps home. They whine and bitch at each other all the way. Clearly, Lulu is pushing for this denouement sooner rather than later, today. But Nell has that itchy scratchy thing going on underneath her top layer of skin, and the longer the time in the apartment the sooner it will rise to the surface. Besides, it's nice to put one over on the mangy little beast every now and then. Show her who's *really* the boss. 'A doggy dog,' Nell repeats the old mantra, 'something with hair, not curls. A lolloping tongue and a long thumping tail. That's what I'd have chosen. If I had to choose a dog. A retriever maybe. Or a spaniel with silky ears. You're a pain in the ass, Lulu.'

Lulu sniffs and gazes away.

'Right', Nell snaps. She bends down about to pick up the recalcitrant poodle, about to give in, when the little excited yip of triumph gets to her. Instead she straightens and quickly, deftly gives the slightest of kicks to Lulu's seated rump. The howl of outrage is very gratifying and Lulu is up, prepared to move again.

'I saw that!' a woman says in English, quickstepping toward them. 'How could you do such a thing? Is that how French people manage their dogs?'

Nell flushes. People are looking. She mumbles something in French, pretending not to understand. Lulu looks up mournfully at the Englishwoman. Her head cocks to the side. *Save me. Save me.*

'Poor little thing,' the woman says. She bends to stroke Lulu's head but that is one step towards intimacy too far for Lulu. Her pointed black head flashes out and the woman receives a quick nip on the thumb for her trouble.

Nell and Lulu walk away, leaving the woman to her exclamations. The dog walks perfectly willingly now. She glances up sideways at Nell, as if to confirm their tryst remains unbroken. There is even a tiny wag to her stump of tail. If Nell had a tail she would wag it, too. But at this moment her main concern is the furnace red of her face. The flush that started with the interfering woman has developed into a full-blown five-minuter and the heat issuing from every pore is enough to sear birds from their branches. She puts her hands to her cheeks, willing the ferocity to calm. A tartan poodle, a puce face: the ignominy gets to Nell and she sits on a bench with her head lowered for a few moments. Lulu eyes her with a tot of sympathy.

The night flushes are the worst. Nell wakes feeling her entire body is on fire. Sweat drenches the sheets. She tosses them off. Rolls to a dry section of bed, desperately seeking a cool pocket of linen to take her temperature down. When she manages to drift back to sleep, the coolness takes over and she wakes up freezing. Back go the covers until she wakes in a frenzy of sweat again. There are nights when she might glean two hours of unbroken sleep at most. Followed by mornings spent staggering around drinking black coffee to jolt a measure of alertness into her aching limbs. In turn, followed by gallons of Evian to help swallow the three dozen or so herbal concoctions she takes in a vain attempt to make menopause endurable without HRT. But she is on the point of succumbing. A by-product of horse sweat glands – or is it horse piss? – seems an ignoble way to get you through to the end. There are times, though, when it seems curiously appropriate. Nature's final nosethumb. A reminder that no cycle can end without a measure of pain, leavetaking and urinal indignity.

When her face is calm again, they leave the park and move along boulevard Saint-Germaine. They cross the first bridge where the Seine divaricates round Île de la Cité. At the second bridge, a tall, black transvestite in short skirt and fishnet stockings sells disposable lighters and postcards from a tray, with Notre Dame as his backdrop. He recognizes Nell.

'Hello, Madame Irish. How are you and the lovely Lulu today?'

'Well, thank you, Simone. And you?'

He pulls a long face. Taps his left hip. 'Not so good. Osteoporosis, I think. My bones are crumbling.'

Nell tuts sympathetically, chooses a red lighter and pays for it. A couple of elderly ladies pass by. One of them emits a disapproving grunt from the back of her throat. The grunt turns into a harumph as she ostentatiously spits on the ground by Simone's feet. The women move on. Simone shouts after them.

When he turns to Nell again, he has tears in his eyes. 'Did you see that? Did you see that?' he keeps repeating.

Yes, Nell assures him, she did see that. She tells him to take no notice; as a matter of fact, he is looking particularly attractive today. She likes the red skirt. Mollified, he bends to stroke Lulu and Nell holds her breath. Lulu grumbles but doesn't nip. The day is looking up.

The dog is panting a little. Nell carries her to the end of the bridge. From the cradle of her arms Lulu's head cranes over the parapet to look down at the brackish, surly waters of the Seine. It is this image of Lulu that Nell conjures when she's away. The back of the small head with the ears slightly raised fills her with tenderness. On impulse, Nell kisses the top curls and is rewarded with a lick. There is a feeling of kindness between them, like an old married couple over the wars, retired generals together, decamped for the final haul. The unexpected kindness dislodges the nagging dread Nell's managed to keep tamped down all morning. Sweat-like, it seeps to the surface. She imagines the back of her daughter's head, the pearly pink of her slightly sticking-out ears, constant elevation of bony shoulders as though in permanent shrug, or permanent apology – and it's not tenderness, more a sharp spasm of irritation that rushes through Nell at the prospect of the long day's worry about Ali, now that she has broken through.

'Ah, Lulu.' Nell nuzzles the upturned face. 'Let's just try to enjoy the rest of the day. We'll be friends. We'll be good to each other.'

The poodle is tired so Nell hails a taxi to take them to Angelina's on the rue du Rivoli. Queues have already formed outside for the small section of takeaway patisserie within. People walk away with their delicately bowed white boxes. The serving area is much too small for the vastness of space within. But, no matter how great the demand, the quantity of cakes and tarts on offer remains the same. By twelve o'clock on a Saturday, usually, the millefeuilles are gone and no amount of disappointment – and every Saturday it is huge – will make the management increase their output. It is one of the peculiarities of life in Paris that both amuse and incense Nell in equal measure. They could of course bake and sell sufficient millefeuilles to satisfy demand, but that would make it too easy on the punter. A whetted appetite is reasonable enough reward, unsatisfied desire the greatest compliment of all. She manages to find a small empty table and orders a hot chocolate and macaroon from the elderly waitress dressed in old-fashioned black and white. The service is always impeccable.

The macaroon is for Lulu, who conducts herself in exemplary fashion. It is as if the little animal knows or senses that in Angelina's she completes a tableau. Solitary, well-dressed woman with her miniature dog. To be found all over this city. Nell is aware of the cursory glances from younger women making up histories for her. She mustn't look as though anything is troubling her. The French are addicted to melancholia, and far more nosy and less self-absorbed than given credit. So she tickles Lulu under the chin and smiles. The poodle accepts titbits of macaroon like an empress.

Yes, to an extent she has quite contentedly slipped into this clichéd version of herself. It's become no more than a suit she shunts on in the morning. Something reliable and well-tailored, travel-friendly, won't let you down. At what point does the suit become your life? Was there a day when she woke up to find the thing she'd been wearing had melded with her skin?

Somewhere in the deepest recesses of her mind, she's even given herself a parallel French history. Short, plumpish, bustling parents, a tiny Loire village with a pointed church spire, a lake with ducks that freezes over in winter. She's imagined herself skating on that lake, gracefully of course, with a skein of red scarf unfurling in the air behind her. Matching lambswool muff concealing her hands. White crusts of impeccably executed figures of eight, scoring the ice in her wake. A perfect match for the adult image she's grown into.

Nevertheless, an invention. She will never be French. No matter how immaculately her tongue wraps round vowels, she is essentially a foreigner. In all the years she has lived here, there is no getting away from that. She looks the part well enough in a sub-Deneuve diluted way – petite, trim figure, navy-blue eyes with deep sockets, cinched and tucked a number of years back, full, well-defined lips, a pointed chin on a pleasing face, symmetrical enough to be pretty, bland enough to be unthreatening. But as soon as she opens her mouth to speak, a swell of pupil in an eye or a slight twitch to a head tells her that she is 'other'.

The hot chocolate is served in a jug with a glass in a silver holder. It is so thick she has to spoon it out. The sensation is an explosion of taste. Thick, glutinous and one hundred per cent pure, it glides down the throat like silk, leaving a muculent coating around the tonsils. All about, behind the elaborately scrolled pillars and beneath the high, gilded dome of ceiling, spoons tinkle the last delicious mouthfuls from glass goblets. People rustle newspapers or fingers drum on large, shiny carrier bags. Conversation is muted, exclamatory facial gestures taking the place of raised voices. Arched eyebrows, mouths curled downwards, shoulders pitched up to ear level. Delicate frond-like fingers of women constantly make shapes in the air. Men in navy wool overcoats appear unshaven, hair unkempt at the backs of their heads, as if they have just tumbled out of bed.

Nell locates a notebook and picks out the rest of the day. She likes to map it all out. Besides, her memory is not quite so acute as it used to be. She has the advance draft of a student's dissertation for the Institute of Masters of Wine programme to look over. Nell is her Master of Wine mentor. She takes someone on any year she can manage for a great deal of time and effort on her part, with no remuneration, but she believes in paying back an industry which has been good to her. It also keeps her abreast of new and fresh developments in viticulture, especially in the area of organically grown crops. This student intends a dissertation on a bio-dynamic cultivation method which is relatively experimental.

Once she has skimmed the outline, she'll make her annotations and suggestions and e-mail the student, who happens to be fifty five years old and on her third attempt to become a member of the Institute. There are only two hundred and fifty members worldwide. Nell is one of only forty women, one of the youngest of either sex to receive the coveted title of Master of Wine, and a rare creature who passed both the theoretical and practical sections of the examinations on first attempt.

The remainder of the day will be devoted to two essays for wine journals which she can do at a leisurely pace. She has been asked, yet again, to give a current overview of the advantages and disadvantages of filtration. And there is a paper to complete on vine diseases and physiological disorders. Later, if there is time and if she still feels inclined, she will work on her itinerary for next season's wine tastings and a series of lectures which at last appraisal seemed to take in just about every member country of the European Community. Except Ireland.

She has not been home in over thirty years.

She realizes, before the door opens, that Henri is inside the apartment. She can smell toasted tobacco. He is in the kitchen pouring wine. The sleeves of his black sweater are rolled up, there is a scrim of dust along the edges of his faded denim jeans. It looks as if he's come straight from the Domaine. His hair is swept back from his high forehead, but a lank rope of peppered black swings loose. He badly needs a haircut. An untipped cigarette hangs out of one corner of his mouth, a writhing snake of blue smoke forces his dark eyes into a squinch. He grins and closes the lids once by way of greeting. Lulu sniffs at his ankles, offers an obligatory yip followed by a disdainful glance, then curls up in her basket for a snooze.

'No, you're not wrong,' Henri says, catching Nell's confused look. 'I *am* a weekend early.' He holds the bottle in midair, having second thoughts. 'Is that a problem?'

'Of course not.' But she doesn't move to kiss him immediately.

Henri continues pouring. It still intrigues her the way Burgundians eschew decanting, handling their wines in almost cavalier manner compared to other regions. In Bordeaux the youngest vintage is given the full treatment, and growers there never come out to meet her in anything but a suit and tie. Perhaps it is a legacy from the formal British influence in the region for so many centuries. By contrast, the first time she turned up at Henri's domaine, he greeted the party in jeans caked with dried mud and had to wipe his palms on his ass pockets before he could shake hands.

Nell puts her nose to the bottle to inhale the bottle-stink, which is so heady it nearly blows her away. He registers her surprise when she looks at the label. Not a particularly good vintage, she would have thought, and old for an unexceptional burgundy at ten years. She swills the paleish ruby liquid round the balloon glass. Even the depth of colour surprises her. The bouquet is intense, both sweet and spicy with a dank, vegetal underlayer almost to the point of decay; rotting banana skins. She sniffs again, thinking she must have misunderstood the aromatic complexity.

'I know,' he says, trying to suppress enthusiasm, not wishing to colour her opinion. 'At most five years – that's what everyone figured. It wasn't even particularly robust two years on. But something, I don't quite remember – you know how it is with me – made me think, let me give this a chance. I only partially destemmed that year, yields were low, soil good, hundred per cent new oak – I was expecting *more*. But there was something . . . something in the nose that just didn't come up in the taste. So I put a case away. As an experiment, if you like, a test to myself. Go on. Tell me I was right.'

He waits, head cocked to the side as she sips, taking the first taste straight down. She takes another, letting the liquid roll round her mouth for seconds. There are layers and layers of black and red fruits. Adequate acidity rather than tannin, and a smooth, silken quality to the texture. Her eyes widen appreciatively. Henri smiles, sucks the last of the butt, flicks it into the sink and tastes for himself. His head nods in quiet modesty.

'I'm really surprised. Exceptional,' she says, aerating

another sip. It sucks through her teeth leaving perfect middle length in her mouth.

'That good, eh?' He pulls his mouth down at the corners, pleased with the praise. She likes the way he inhales the wine's scent, roughly. He doesn't do a number on it, no elaborate hand movements or facial tics. She's seen them all, from little tap dance routines to compulsive throat-clearings. Each producer determined that she will find this, this cup of nectar in his hand here, a taste experience so monumentally exquisite that she will clutch her throat and shed rueful, bitter tears because good things must end. There have been two occasions when she has come close to that – both of them Henri's wine.

He has always been fanatical about the tenor of his produce, in some years, to his own financial detriment, rejecting significant proportions of the harvest so that only the finest-quality wine is sold under his name. In an age of gross over-production, Nell thinks the personalities, concentration and character of many Burgundies and Bordeaux, are in jeopardy. Abusive acidification and excessive fining and filtration have compromised too many vineyards. When she tastes something as good as this, she falls in love with Henri all over again each time.

'Are we celebrating something?' She undulates the glass, watches the liquid cling heavily to the inside.

'We're celebrating that I'm here *this* weekend. But a mistake, I think.'

Nell dismisses this with a cluck and slides her lips along his. But her displeasure is apparent from the way she avoids prolonged touch. She has still to get over that first little frisson of disappointment at having to say goodbye to her carefully planned afternoon. The shivery silence she longed for in an empty, tidy apartment has been supplanted by noise, smoke – busyness.

'I should have called,' Henri says, his lignite eyes conveying his own disappointment.

And now she feels sorry for him. Sorry that she is such a creature of habit, of self-containment, of intrusion by invitation only. Sorry that she is not more of what he needs and deserves, sorry, too, that he needs what he doesn't deserve. No, not love at first sight. More two pathologies going pinggg. It is his burden he must forever crave intimacy from women who offer it with difficulty. Her burden that she must crave intimacy at all. She kisses him again, this time allowing her lips to linger on his. She licks wine rind from his lower lip.

'That's better,' he says, pressing against her, already erect.

'You'll have a nasty headache tomorrow.'

'I will?' He looks down at his flies. 'Oh yes. The Viagra, you mean. You shouldn't mock a poor old man, Nell.' But he is chuckling. Sometimes it troubles him, the insurance policy aspect, dictated a couple of years back by prostate trouble.

'Have you been carrying that thing around all morning? All the way up here? I hope the train wasn't full.'

'You know it doesn't work like that. I saw you and . . .' He flips his hands open at the groin.

'I'm flattered.'

'So you should be.'

Nell cuts some cheese for them to eat with the wine. She is tasting damson at the back of her throat. And a hint of eucalyptus.

'Actually, I came up to see Marie-Louise,' Henri says. Marie-Louise is the elder of his two daughters. Nell considers her a perpetual student. Twenty-eight, currently at the

Sorbonne. Currently studying linguistics. Latterly studying philosophy. Seven months pregnant.

'What's the crisis this time?'

'She's been dumped. Again.'

'Oh, I'm sorry.'

'She was crying last night on the phone. Hysterical, actually. I promised I'd come and spend this evening with her.'

'You're a good father.'

'So be nice to me. I can't stay long and I have a heartbroken daughter to contend with.' Henri grins and pulls her to him. 'D'you want to make love?'

'No.' Nell grins back. 'But I'll have sex with you.'

'How generous.'

'As long as you're not expecting gymnastics.'

'No, no. Just breathe.'

In the bedroom they undress at a leisurely pace. There is no fear or panic on his part: he has taken his Viagra. Nell is the one who suffers a tiny pang of trepidation. She never knows these days if she will produce sufficient lubrication or if her vaginal walls will remain sandpaper dry. Another summons to HRT.

It is fifteen years since they first met at Henri's small vineyard near Beaune. She knew they would have an affair practically from the moment he wiped his dirty hands on his jeans pockets and guided her group towards the cellar. Although she couldn't possibly have foretold that fifteen years later they would still be spending sweat, semen and huge tracts of weekends together in an attempt at falling in love. No, the word attempt isn't fair. They do love. However, not always at the same time.

'I want to leave her. I want to be here, with you,' Henri says as he casually pulls a sock off.

'No, you don't. It's not my fault you have a horrible wife.'

'She is horrible.' He concedes with a face.

'I didn't mean that,' Nell says truthfully. She has met his wife on a number of occasions. The woman is indisputably cold. She is perfectly aware of Nell's existence. She is also perfectly unperturbed by Nell's existence. To Lucienne, with her dulled eyes and cupid mouth, Nell represents a hermetically established bargain without the requisite payout. Nell fucks her husband. Lucienne does not. Lucienne is half-owner of the vineyard. Nell is not. It is a perfectly French affair.

'You couldn't live here in the city,' Nell says.

'Meaning you don't want me to.'

'That's not what I mean. Don't tell me you wouldn't miss the vineyard, the big house, even the horrible wife. You must have some feelings for her.'

'I have. Mostly unspeakable. But I miss you. Maybe it's age. I don't want to die alone.'

'Don't be ridiculous. How will you be alone? You've got two adoring daughters. A wife who'll put up with anything as long as it doesn't mean being on her own. I mean, why should we complicate things?'

'Complicate?' He spits the word.

'I didn't mean it that way,' she says after a while, aware that his glittering eyes are still demanding a response.

'Yes, you did.' He says it quietly, with a note of defeat.

She swivels to look at him, stung by that defeated note. He's contemplating the floor, a black sock dangling ridiculously from one hand, almost like a manifestation of the downturn in his spirits. She is speared by remorse and gently touches the bunched knottiness of muscle along his shoulders. The skin is sallow and seems permanently tanned. He has a creased, handsome face, with little pouches of lived-in skin that stand out when he smiles. A deep vertical groove bisects his forehead. It wasn't such a big thing to say 'complicate', yet he seems genuinely disturbed.

A little spurt of love shoots through her. The warm, familiar love of someone who has come to epitomize the meaning of that word and yet who, in his absence, can mean nothing at all. The absolute nothingness of love once the portions of pain and regret are over. Its airy lightness once it becomes indistinguishable as one breath from the next. She looks at Henri and knows that she loves him. She looks at Henri and knows that she has come close to hating him. So now come familiarity, occasional recriminations and the gentle, persistent afterglow of mutual kindnesses.

'Stop sulking.'

'No. I like sulking.'

'Well, it's sex or a sulk. Which is it to be?'

He flings the sock and pulls her across the bed. She breathes in deeply at the side of his neck. The texture is at once smoky and oily, and bitter to the taste like skin on walnut. Her initial irritation at his unexpected arrival dissolves entirely and she holds him to her tightly, glad that it's a Saturday afternoon and she is being held.

He takes his time, tracing her body with his hands. Pressing against her to prove desire. One hand clamped to her buttock, while the other moves back and forth across her breasts, kneading, tweaking nipples into reluctant peaks. She waits for a warm, liquid feeling to take over her groin but it's the Gobi desert between her legs. Part of her yearns to say, 'C'mon, climb aboard, let's just get it *done*. Don't worry about me.'

She's thinking of fetching Vaseline from the bathroom

cabinet when his teeth catch her lower lip and bite harder than he intended. Nell yelps and he immediately rolls to the side.

'Sorry.'

'No, I'm sorry.' Nell smooths his rumpled hair. And she is. She doesn't know whether to laugh or to cry at the sight of his forlorn, rejected face – the paean to Viagra still thrusting out from his loins, though somewhat subdued.

He touches her swelling lip.

'We're falling apart.' Nell gently kisses the tips of his fingers. He won't say it, but he knows it wasn't just her body that let them down.

It used to be that she would hear the old-fashioned wrought-iron doors of the lift close in the corridor, hear Henri's familiar tread coming towards her front door, and she would grow wet just at the prospect of seeing him. They would talk, drink wine, deliberately brush against one another while preparing food which might never get eaten. She would feel hot little shoots of desire as they exchanged laden, anticipatory smiles. There was a pleasure in prolonging further pleasure. The evening would stretch out ahead full of promise.

It hasn't been like that for some time. There are occasions when she's with him, she can blank him out and pretend that she is alone. Though he says nothing, his gaze is full of silent reproach. He knows. He does know. And his tacit acceptance spurs her to be cruel. She stays even longer in the bath, with the door locked when it was always open before. She feels his absence from Monday through Thursday, thinks of him with kindness. Perversely, on Friday, before he shows up for the weekend, an exhausted irritation overrides any tingle of anticipation, that shortly he will be invading her apartment, invading her life, expecting something from her – though what, she can't imagine. Lately, she has offered him so very little.

Suddenly, she slides down along his short, tight frame. She takes him in her mouth and holds a pearl of extruded semen in her mouth between tongue and roof. Where her lip has cracked, the iron tang of her blood mixes with the salty teardrop. It swells in her mouth. The taste brings her alive. And now there is wetness. Oozing like rich syrup stored by the banks of a river long dried up. She slides up along his torso again so that he may feel it too. A long smudge of red carries over his chest, along his neck, up to his mouth. He hesitates, fearing rejection, then quickly rolls over on top of her. He enters, braced for resistance, shoulders relaxing as he encounters none, only smooth liquefaction. Later, when they have showered and finished the Burgundy, she will catch him looking at her, eyes gleaming with his own thankfulness.

When he has pulled out and spilled himself along the crease of her abdomen, she rubs the viscous liquid in until it curls and peels away like flakes of exfoliance. It's still too risky with her erratic periods to let him come inside, but, if she cannot receive the concentration of protein internally, she can at least allow her parched skin to drink him in.

Henri kisses her forehead and slides off, walking – no, strutting – to the bathroom following his defiant tumescence like a dog happily going for walkies. He catches her appreciative glance and grunts his approval. She has noticed. It's all right. He's not dead yet.

Nell smooths the sheets and opens both casement windows. She lies on the bed again, enjoying a slight, desultory breeze as it sifts through white muslin draped above the shutters. The bedroom gives onto a small courtyard with a cherub fountain in the middle. A few stunted fruit trees surrounded by iron railings. A child's discarded tricycle thrown in an overgrown corner. In the apartments opposite she can pick out figures commencing preparations for the evening meal. A dog barks repeatedly and someone shouts to it. Church bells toll nearby. Shadows are beginning to chase across the far wall.

There is this, Nell thinks. The remainder of a sleepy, sated afternoon ahead, a tender, trickling wind through muslin. September air spicy with promise. A child's sense of good things about to happen, a feeling of inexplicable excitement and happy apprehensiveness. The scent of a man on her sheets. Another person she has made momentarily happy and the reminder of warm, sticky, mature love in the folds of her belly. It might not have sufficed at twenty-eight; at forty-eight it is as close to bliss as she can endure.

She wishes this, in time to come, for her daughter and granddaughter. Henri returns and asks why she is smiling.

'Because of you.'

He hovers a finger over her cracked lip. 'Is it sore?'

'Oh werry.'

There is something wrong. A discordance she can't quite put her finger on immediately. 'Henri?'

'I meant what I said. About leaving Lucienne.'

'But she—'

'No. She didn't seem surprised in the least.'

Nell sits up wrapping her arms round her knees. 'You've *talked* to her? When?'

'Last night. After Marie-Louise's call. It's been coming a long time. Too long. The strangest thing is, she was looking at me with that crooked little smile on her lips, as if she'd been waiting for this; she almost looked relieved. Wouldn't be in the least surprised if she's been seeing someone. But she'd want the finances sorted out first. That would be her way.' His shoulders go up in an exaggerated shrug. 'So I think it can be quite grown-up and amicable after all.'

'But the Domaine?'

'We've even got that far. It'll remain jointly owned. She keeps the house, of course. But I'll still run things. It's my name on the bottles, after all. She can't take my name, but yes, it might have been sticky if she'd decided to be vindictive. I can rent on a nearby estate – buy in time, once I've had a chance to look around – or I can divide my time between here and there.' He looks at her. 'For that matter, so could you.'

For moments Nell can't think of a thing to say. She swallows hard. 'But . . .'

'That's the third sentence you've begun with "but".'

'Why didn't you tell me straight away?'

'Because of your face when you walked in and found me here earlier. The jaw.' He pulls a long face. 'Because I wanted to wait until after we'd made love. So we might feel closer or something. Oh, I don't know. These days, it's hard to know with you, Nell.'

This saddens but doesn't surprise her. He must wrestle with his own contradictory feelings. Only the newborn, she thinks, don't have to wrestle with contradictions. Only the newborn can be that ruthless.

'So, no elation, then?' His lips clamp in a grim, self-mocking smile.

'It's a lot to take in.'

'Not such a lot.' He slides off the bed. 'I'll get the wine.'

His disappointment throbs in the air between them. He slips into a robe she keeps for him on a chair by the bed.

While he gets the wine, Nell lies back and stares at the ceiling. Absurdly, the only honest feeling she can connect with is anger. And a rising panic. The walls are wide in the bedroom, fresh air circulates from the open windows, there is plenty of space, yet her throat feels dry and constricted. She swallows a deep breath, then another and another, until her racing heart and a thousand flashing pinpricks of light dancing before her eyes, tell her she's in danger of hyper-ventilating.

The fire is lit in the huge grate when Nell creeps into the living room to find him. Henri holds the wine by the neck. He is unaware that she is standing there, watching his stooped back, his free arm extended, resting his weight on the overmantel. Knuckles whiten then fill with blood again on the hand that clutches and releases cool marble. She thinks she sees him shudder for an instant, but when he turns his eyes are bright and he has forced his mouth into a rictus of smile. A finger taps an empty space on the mantel where his photograph used to be among the others.

Nell hasn't got the heart to tell him, in the light of his revelation, that the frame fell a couple of nights ago and smashed into a dozen pieces. At the time she'd thought about putting up a more recent photograph of him, in any case – but she hasn't got round to it.

'The frame broke and I took the photo out. I keep it in a drawer by my bed.' She threw it away.

He nods, but there is a trace of bitterness at the edge of his lips. He lifts the photo of Ali smiling self-consciously for the camera, her arms wrapped round an equally uncomfortable Grace. As though they know this is how it should be in mother–daughter images but somehow can't quite make it.

'Ali didn't call last weekend, either,' Nell says, taking the photo from him. 'I keep trying but they haven't fixed the damn phone yet and I've left dozens of messages on her mobile.'

'You think she might be on something again?'

He always does that, she thinks with a twist of irritation. Pins her worst fears to the wall without any preamble. Leaves them wriggling up there, raw and liverish, before she's got the cotton wool out.

'She hasn't touched that stuff in years. There's no reason to think the worst.'

'Except you do. Because you can't get in touch with her.'

'It may be nothing,' Nell says, a touch defensively.

'You could call that neighbour. Get him to pass a message on.'

'He's an elderly man. I don't like to bother him.'

'But he drinks in the pub anyway, you told me. So how bother him? Just call, say you're a little concerned – with reason, after all – the phone in a public house should be working. Ask him to speak to Ali on your behalf.'

'I did that once. She thought I was interfering. She goes quiet, Henri. It's her way. I don't want for her to be rude to her poor old neighbour, especially as he's my only lifeline for emergencies.'

'Maybe you should—'

'Maybe you should tell me why now, Henri,' she cuts across flintily, softening her tone at the end.

He refills their glasses and hands her hers. She's never forced the issue, never once asked him to leave his wife. It's worked perfectly, hasn't it? Why the grand gesture now? She knows her eyes are silently conveying all this, and hates herself for it. They've both known for years that it wasn't Henri hiding behind his wife's existence, it was Nell. He takes a long swig, lowering his eyes into the glass to hide the trace of disgust at her duplicity that shadows them.

'Last week' – he turns his back to her – 'I went shopping with Marie-Louise. Nesting stuff for the baby. She wanted things to make a proper home of the apartment. We had a lovely day, just like old times – before she set up with this moron who keeps breaking her heart. I think, for the first time, it really hit me that very soon I'm going to be a grandfather. I tried to imagine what that will be like. This tiny person coming to visit me, still stuck in the same life, the same old lie. Doting grandparents who can hardly stand to be in the same room. No, I thought, I can't do that. I must have said something aloud because Marie-Louise started laughing and shaking her head. She said I was going senile.

We were in the Galleries Lafayette buying a toaster, knives and forks, that kind of thing, when I noticed that everything had a lifetime guarantee. Don't ask me why, but it made me sad. Here was this stupid spoon in my hand, I could see my own grey face in the bowl, shapeless and distorted like those mirrors in fairgrounds – it felt as if the spoon was mocking me. What lifetime? Whose? I'm fifty-three years old. We say middle age, but who lives to be a hundred and six? Who is this old guy holding a spoon? I thought. Where's his guarantee? For the rest of the day, the damn thing haunted me. Then, last night, Marie-Louise, the same girl who'd laughed and tucked her arm through mine only days past, sobbing, broken up because the moron had left her again. What good lifetime guarantees for your cutlery then?' He pauses to light a cigarette, cupping his hands round the flame in a gesture so familiar that it contracts her heart. He blows out, phitting a loose flake of tobacco from the tip of his tongue.

'After I put the phone down. I went and found Lucienne in the garden. She must have known from my face what was coming. The way she immediately sat down, hands perfectly placed one on top of the other, on her lap, the way she does, lips in that measured smile – this much and no more. I said, "I'm leaving you". That's all. She nodded after a while, then she patted the bench for me to sit down beside her. We sat in silence for . . . an hour, longer maybe, stars were showing in the sky. Then we started discussing the best way to go about this. How to divide things up, when to tell the girls. We might have been debating funeral arrangements. One of those conversations which have to take place, though no one wants to talk. Then I kissed her cheek and went to bed.' He tops up their glasses, taking care not to spill the loose sediment at the bottom of the bottle. 'That part is done,' he adds with a twist of lips. 'The rest is up to you.'

'Move your things in next week if you like.' She knows her smile is fixed, too bright, like light refracting on stagnant water. But she hasn't had time to prepare for this. *Only fifteen years.*

'No.'

'No?'

'Look, Nell, I didn't do this to force your hand or anything. To force *us*. If anything, it was that stupid spoon.' A light chuckle, then he raises a hand before she can say more. 'Let's just leave it for now. Look, I got something for you, too, while I was shopping with Marie-Louise.' She follows his gaze to a small, square box on one of the shelves by the fire. 'No, it's not a ring – Please, I'm not that stupid,' he adds softly, seeing her startled face.

She unwraps carefully, untying knotted string and peeling cellophane so that the thick paper holds its shape – a delaying tactic but also the way she would unwrap anything, mindful of the structure of containers. The arbitrary symbiosis of receptacle and content. Paper holding the impression of something long removed. A skull emptied of thoughts. Skin holding a silenced heart.

'Careful, it's delicate,' Henri says as she extracts a white cube. Beneath layers of scrunched-up tissue paper lies a silver wine stopper with a glittering crystal on top.

Nell cups it in her hands. 'It's beautiful.'

'Thought you'd like it.' He smiles. 'I saw it in an antiques shop and thought it was the perfect antidote to things with guarantees.'

He doesn't have to say it. If she wants, this will be his leaving present to her. Nell strokes the delicate filigree work scrolled into claws holding the crystal.

She moves to the window, holding up the stopper to the fading light. It flashes, sending out fractured beams which seem to laser through her fingers. There is a hint of early dusk behind the petal-hued sky. A slender shaving of moon winks down upon the city, diffident, tremulous, as though it has slipped onto the stage too soon. A few last straining flickers of sunlight sidle across the top storeys of the buildings opposite, turning the light-tan stone to white. The blanched sandstone of Paris, streaked traffic-black here and there. Long, six-paned casement windows, close together, fronted by black elaborate grilles. Busy roofs with inverted crescent fenestrations jutting randomly, frequently, piled one above the other. A sense of hum, ebb and flow amidst the rooftops.

People moving up and down the boulevard Raspail, cars gliding, the seen and the unseen alike, blur in one feeling of continuous movement. Could she really look on all that and not see Henri as part of it?

Behind her, he speaks quietly to his daughter on his mobile.

'I've got to go,' he says when Nell turns. His face has paled. 'She thinks she may be having pains.'

'The baby, you mean?'

'Yes. On the other hand, she says it may be that all the crying has brought on false contractions. At any rate, I'd better check. I don't think I've ever heard her this upset before. I could stab that bastard.'

Nell understands that he is glad of the distraction. Now he can shower and dress swiftly. With purpose. As though he is any preoccupied father on any Saturday, leaving with haste to provide comfort to any heartbroken daughter. And not a man who has just told his lover that she is free to leave him.

They share the last of the wine before Henri goes. His skin is stretched tight and drawn-looking. Nell opens her mouth to say something, anything, but hastily closes it again when he shoots her a warning glance. Talk to him when she's had time to mull things over; he's crushed enough by her reaction, or non-reaction. Talk to him when she knows what she wants.

'Will you drop in tomorrow, on your way home?' Nell asks, remembering to keep her voice light and inflection-free. Buying into this new game of ellipsis.

'Of course.'

But she can't do it. 'Henri—'

'Don't,' he snaps back. 'Just don't, Nell.'

'I am sorry,' she perseveres.

'For what, precisely.' But it's not a question. Because he is a good-natured, gentle man and vindictiveness doesn't come easily to him, he doesn't catalogue her distant behaviour toward him over the past couple of years. The long baths eating into their precious time together, the newspapers read in silence from cover to cover, then read all over again on their Sunday mornings, the way she hums, turning from him, as if he isn't standing there waiting. How can she find the words to explain to him what she doesn't fully understand herself? That he is waiting for nothing. *There is nothing more. You've had all there is.*

His words eat into the silence. 'What's the worst that could happen, hmm?' he says with a trace of sadness. 'You leave me. I leave you. It doesn't work, what?'

'That. All of that. Maybe. I don't know. I don't know, Henri.'

She calls to his retreating back. He stops still. She can tell from the way his shoulders bunch up that she's blown it.

'I do love you,' she says, hating herself.

He turns slowly. The light in his eyes comes from a million galaxies away. 'The thing is, I know you do. 'Bye, Nell.'

Sixth ring. Nell's hand circles the receiver. She lifts. 'Hello?' She responds instinctively in English. Because she knows it's her daughter's neighbour calling from Ireland. Because she knows that time's circumference has caught her up and the frothy capsule of her bubbled day has burst on her tongue. She is certain that time can be stilled, but not for long.

And she is certain that her daughter is dead.

CHAPTER TWO

'Are you all right there?' A matronly Aer Lingus stew-ardess eyes Nell with concern. She hasn't released her grip on the armrests since take-off from Heathrow for the connecting flight to Cork. The woman assumes it's fear of flying, Nell doesn't know if there is such a thing as fear of arriving, and if this paralysis is the manifestation. She tries a reassuring smile but her face is frozen like the locked hands.

'Fine,' she manages to utter.

The stewardess takes in Nell's gelid face, the crisp black suit and makes another assumption.

'I'm sorry dear. Is it a—' a slight incline of the head, 'funeral?'

'No. My daughter is alive. She's alive.' Nell responds quickly. The stewardess looks confused then she squeezes Nell's shoulder and moves on.

The passenger beside her in Premier Class gives Nell a cursory glance, then shoves his head into his newspaper again. She's aware that her behaviour must appear strange, to say the least, but it's out of her control for now, like so much else.

'Hello?' she'd said.

'Is that you, Nell Hennessy?'

'Yes, Paudie. I knew it would be you. Tell me. Tell me the worst.'

'I don't like to phone up at this ungodly hour—'

'It's Ali. Tell me, Paudie. Please.'

'You said call any hour of the day or night if things didn't—'

'Is she dead, Paudie, please?'

'Dead? God no. Oh I'm sorry. I told Julia we'd no business phoning until the morning. I'll put the heart crossways on her, I said.'

Nell could barely hear anything after 'no'. She held the receiver to her cheek to cool the flush.

'Nell, are you there?'

'Yes, Paudie, I am. Yes, I did think the worst but I'm fine now. I know you wouldn't call at this hour unless something was greatly troubling you.'

'Well, it's this. Julia and myself have been keeping an eye out for you, like we promised and . . . Did you know about the fellow who's staying in the caravan?'

'What fellow? On Ali's land?'

'So you don't know of him. That's what I thought. He's I suppose what you'd call a class of a hippy. Or New Age, they're called now. That kind of thing. Ali gave him a bit of scrub for the caravan and he's got a pony. He's supposed to be renting but I don't think he gives her any money. Anyway, we started out a small bit worried about him, like you do, you know. He's a queer look to him. Well, I think so, anyway.

'He'd have the few pints every night in the pub when he landed first. But he kept himself to himself, not that he wouldn't talk to you polite enough if you said anything to him. But it's like he's been moving in on them, Ali and Nick and the small one. I couldn't be hugely specific now if you asked me. Only little things. He'd be serving behind the bar one night, not paying for his drinks the next night. Another day you'd see him getting the messages for them in the shop. Nick's been poorly this while now, and I think Ali sort of started relying on this fellow — Adam's his name — only I think it went sour on her.'

'Sour?'

A pause. Nell could imagine Julia in the background signalling furiously, itching to take the phone off her husband. Now that he'd worked himself up to calling at this hour of the morning, he would be determined to give the most level-headed account possible, for fear of being considered over-dramatic or impetuous. He would underplay his misapprehensions so that Nell could judge for herself.

'Julia is saying I should tell you everything,' he continued, confirming her suspicions. 'A few days back, Julia was in the kitchen over there and Ali said she was thinking of giving him some land, for him to build on. Giving? Julia repeated. You can't do that, she said, and next thing Ali started crying her eyes out, just bawling her eyes out in the kitchen. Julia thought there was more to this than met the eye. Is he threatening you? Julia said, because if he is, you've a right to get the Gardaí onto him straight away.

'Next thing, this Adam fellow walked in and Julia said a look of terror, was what you could only call it, came into Ali's eyes. She was shaking from head to toe at the thought he might have heard her. I said to Julia, when she came home and told me all this, we'll hold tough for a few days and see how things look and if we don't like what we see, we'll call Nell or we'll call the Gardaí or we'll call someone,

so forth and so on. I kept on going up for my few pints
every night and your man was serving behind the bar.
Perfectly friendly and what have you. So I thought maybe,
with Nick not too good, maybe Ali . . . Well, she's inclined
to be high strung sometimes, isn't she? Not saying a bad
word about the girl, you understand.' He paused again, fearful he might have caused offence.

'I understand. Go on, Paudie.'

'Well it's this – tonight or this morning I should say,
about an hour or so ago, Julia was here in the kitchen
making herself a camomile tea 'cause she couldn't sleep,
and she opened the back door to let out the cat, and she
heard a fierce commotion going on above in the house.
Loud enough to carry all the way down to us here. She
came up the stairs to get me, fast as she could. We stepped
out and first I heard nothing at all and we were about to go
back inside when I heard the first one. Ali's scream. Then
another one. It was a frightening sound, Nell. There was
real fear in that sound. Go on up, Julia says to me, and see
what's going on. So I put on my coat and we were standing
at the bottom of the lane outside, just about to go up, when
Ali herself runs down in her nightie and no shoes on. She
was screaming at the top of her voice. Nothing you could
make any sense of, but I'm sure I heard the word "shotgun"
in the middle of it all. Julia can't swear she heard that word,
she wants me to point out.'

'I don't doubt you heard what you heard, Paudie. What
happened?'

'We managed to calm her down a small bit until she
agreed to come in here for a cup of tea at least. We didn't try
to force anything out of her till she was ready. Then we
both started asking questions. I said, what's going on up

there? Is that fellow threatening you? What's this about a shotgun?'

'Go on.'

'Well, she was crying but quieter, calmer in herself. Then she started trying to make a joke of it all, laughing, stopping us asking any more questions. But Julia wasn't having that and she caught a hold of Ali by the shoulders and gave her a good shake. Stop it now, Julia said, you're hysterical. No, I'm fine now, says Ali. I have to say at this point, Nell, she didn't look any way fine to me. Her eyes looked funny.'

'Funny? Glazed you mean? The pupils dilated?'

'Hold on.' Paudie paused for a quick consultation with Julia, grunting his confirmation when he came back to Nell. 'Yes, you have it. That's how we'd describe her eyes all right.'

'Did you walk her back up, Paudie? Hold on a second, let me call you right back. It's not fair using your phone like this.'

'Will you stop. What's the phone for? Now, where was I? Oh yes. Indeed I did start to walk back up with her. Julia stayed below at the bottom of the lane, in case I had to call out to her for help or what have you – that's what we agreed on the cusp of the moment. Ali was a whole lot calmer and very embarrassed, too, as we headed up. I'm calling the Gardaí, I said to her. She stopped in her tracks, her two hands gripping mine. You can't do that, Paudie, she says. We argued round and round for a while until she finally says that there's stuff all over the house – she couldn't even remember where exactly – and she couldn't risk the Gardaí coming inside. I have to tell you now, Nell, I didn't immediately understand what it was she was talking about but I understood clear enough when she said marijuana. It's illegal here, you know.'

'Yes, I know. Here, too.'

'Anyway, I thought to myself, maybe she's right. I didn't want to be held accountable for herself and Nick ending up in court. So I thought, I'll check the situation out and see what story Nick might have for me. As you know, he's the level sort, not inclined to hysterics or what have you.'

Not inclined to anything, Nell thought, but held her tongue.

Paudie continued, 'But he hasn't been well, like I said. Anyway, we go in, round by the back door, into the kitchen. There's a funny smell everywhere and I suppose what you'd call evidence in an ashtray on the table. Ali's totally calm by now and I'm thinking to myself, she's been affected by the drugs and that's what all this is about. It's nothing to do with that Adam fellow.

'Nick came downstairs – he's like a pull-through for a rifle, Nell, as thin as that. His face the colour of cigarette ash. I explained to him how come I was there and he thanked me for looking after Ali and for not calling the Gardaí. He made her a cup of tea and sat her down. It was just a bad trip, he said. How's that? I said. What she was smoking, he said. Well, to be honest, I was much relieved to hear that. The screams and talk of shotguns and what have you, had rightly put the wind up me. I'll be off so, I said. They both thanked me again and that would have been that – only, as I was heading out, I caught sight of it, propped up against the back porch.'

'Of what?'

'A shotgun. Clear as I can see my own hand now. And I know enough to know it was cocked and ready for use. I looked back at the pair of them and they were hugging each other so I thought I'd hold my own counsel till I'd a word with yourself. Don't leave it till the morning, Julia said, 'cause she knows what I'm like and I'd be inclined to sit on my thoughts on the subject for longer than might be good. So here I am calling you, for fear I'd see the situation different in the light of morning. Though maybe that would be no bad thing, either. I hope you're not cross with me now.'

'Not at all, Paudie. I can't thank you enough. Whatever is going on there, it doesn't sound right.'

Another brief pause.

'I just said what you said to Julia here, and we're both a bit relieved you don't think we're only two old fools passing time before the grave.'

'If anything, you're more worried than you're letting on, aren't you?'

'There would be truth in that.'

'And I'm sorry, truly sorry, that I've put you in this position of having to make calls with bad news.'

'Your mother, you mean? That's a while ago now. Nell, why you couldn't come home for the funeral is your own business. We never made any judgements on you, we'd both like you to know that. We remember you fondly always as a young girl.'

'I've changed a lot since then.' A metallic laugh.

'Ah now, who hasn't?

'What you're saying, I take it, is that it's time to come home?'

'I think that's what I'm saying.'

'I'll book a flight this morning. I mightn't make it until tomorrow.'

'We can pick you up if you like. Where will you come into?'

'Cork, probably. And no need for a pick-up, thank you anyway. I'll hire a car.'

'All right. We'll be looking forward to seeing you whenever you get here. Sorry again for the lateness of the hour.
G'dluck to you now.'

'Good luck, Paudie. And thank you a million times over.'

The pilot tells them that they are flying at thirty thousand
feet and will shortly be commencing their descent into
Cork. The temperature there is a very agreeable seventeen
degrees centigrade and the west of Ireland is experiencing a
pleasant late summer spell, unlike most of the rest of Europe,
which is suffering early cold conditions. The rest of Europe.
The casualness of it lingers in Nell's mind. She left in 1970
when Ireland was geographically part of Europe but in reality was a small figure three flung out into the Atlantic, next
stop America.

She knows it will be different. What she wonders is what
will be the same. Celtic Tiger, Riverdance, Bailey's Irish
Cream, Guinness sexified, advertisements in French newspapers urging graduates *home* to work – these have not
escaped her consciousness. Flicking through the inflight *Cara*
magazine compounds the image Ali has tried to conjure for
her. Of this new Ireland. Glossy pages with relaxed, affluent-
looking young people. Computer companies seeking
support technicians, property developments in Dublin satellite towns. As far away as Leitrim is satellite now, Nell
observes with astonishment. Celtic clothes, Celtic jewellery,
Celtic glass, Celtic bars. An article on stress management.
Beautiful tinted photographs of islands off the west coast.
Second homes in Portugal. Offshore investment companies.
A country proudly selling itself. A country for sale.

Executives all around her in Premier Class. Their faces

incongruously young and purposeful. Laptops whizzing through spreadsheets. No one particularly excited about landing on Irish soil. Just another business trip. Perhaps a fleeting visit home if time permits. Nell has the strange feeling that she is a refugee.

After Paudie's call she had paced the bedroom for several minutes, trying to extrapolate from his words what might really be going on. She hadn't voiced her worst fear, that Ali might be back on heroin. But what of the shotgun? Maybe Ali and Nick had been fooling around, it had turned nasty, fuelled by drugs, Ali had threatened Nick, or Nick had threatened Ali. And what of this stranger – this Adam man? What was she to make of his infiltration? Clearly Paudie and Julia felt far more strongly against him than they had let on.

There was no prospect of sleep so she settled in the kitchen with a pot of coffee, waiting until a decent hour to call Henri. As a spear of morning light reamed the living-room shutters, she dialled his mobile. He answered groggily on the fourth ring. He listened, murmuring gravely as Nell told him the contents of Paudie's phone call. When she asked if he thought she should go, he said most definitely yes. He would of course go immediately if it was his child. That was unsaid, but understood. The unsaid reminded Nell of Marie-Louise. Good God, was Henri a grandfather? No, he laughed. Just phantom contractions but she was much calmer now. The boyfriend and father-to-be had called and a reconciliation was on the cards. Unsaid again between them: until the next time.

There was the question of Lulu. The old dog wasn't able for the flight, even if she had been allowed into Ireland from France. Nell did not express her parallel concern regarding herself. Henri was on his way.

By the time he arrived, Nell had booked flights for the following day. Her nerves were jangling with caffeine. Drops of coffee splattered the front of her peach silk kimono where her cup had taken a wobble on its way to her mouth. Lulu was freely rubbing her behind along one edge of the Persian rug.

Henri got straight to the point. 'Now you think it's heroin, or something new, don't you?'

'If it looks like a duck and quacks like a duck . . . I leave first thing tomorrow.'

'Maybe this Adam person is the supplier,' Henri said, lighting an untipped and inhaling to his toes. 'Any coffee left?'

'No. I drank the pot. I'll make some more.'

'I'll do it. Nell, you're shaking,' he added, moving ahead. She followed, wrapping her arms round his waist. He was right: she was shaking, quite violently now.

'Afraid?' he asked, grinding fresh beans. The cigarette dangled from the corner of his mouth, making his eyes squinch. His morning scent — torpid sweat, old garlic, tobacco, night whiskies, soap — drifted into her nostrils, into her mouth; she could lay it along her tongue for a moment, a soothing taste like warm milk. Familiar as her own spit.

'Terrified.'

Henri inhaled and smiled. Ash dangled perilously, a quick, practised flick of his head and it formed a perfect tube on the worksurface, a scoop of his hand and gone. 'You'll be fine. This is long overdue. You know that.'

'Thirty-two years. Bit of an understatement, I'd say.' Quickly, she pressed closer, tightening her grip from behind, one cheek against the cooling cloth of his shirt. For a moment, she had an idea that she could really burrow into him, past blood and liver and lungs, rest somewhere by his heart, in the groove of his heart, concave like the man curled into the curve of a sickle moon. She wanted to apologize for yesterday, for not throwing her arms round him instantly when he told her he was leaving his wife. But she was fully aware that, no matter how it turned out between them in the future, she could never have that moment back. She could never obliterate it from both their memories.

'I thought she was dead, Henri. Ali. Don't ask me. But I was certain, I mean really *certain*, when I picked up that phone. I thought, this is it, the call I've been waiting for, the call I've been dreading.'

'Do you want me to come with you?'

'Yes. But no. I'm not sure.'

'About anything it seems.' He pulled a wry grin. 'Now, you don't need any more coffee, do you? No, I didn't think so. Eat something instead.'

'I'm too nervous.'

He put the cup down and widened his arms. Nell stepped into the waiting circle and placed her cheek on his shoulder.

'About yesterday—'

'We'll talk properly when you get back,' he cut across softly. 'Things haven't been right for a while, have they? Between us, I mean. Not since Meredith died – before that really, since she first got sick. It's been a gradual thing.'

'What has?'

'I don't know what to call it.' He thought for a while. 'Withdrawal. The only word I can think of.'

'Withdrawal,' she repeated, turning the word over in her head, looking for holes, but it felt about right. 'Is that what I'm doing, withdrawing? Sounds like a tortoise retreating into its shell.'

He lifted his hands, fingers spread, taking in the gleaming kitchen, the white living room beyond. The room he's tried to make more user friendly with coffee cups, sedimenty wine glasses, an overflowing ashtray, newspapers strewn on the floor − only to find it immaculate again, on his return from the bathroom. Nell, he shouted once in exasperation, these little things are just signs of someone living here. It's like a pristine salon in an upmarket funeral home. What's wrong with a little clutter? She'd spent the rest of the day trying to ignore a forgotten mug of coffee on the overmantel. Tried, but failed miserably.

She could feel his chuckle before she heard it. A deep gurgling at the base of his throat.

'What?'

'Nothing. Nothing.' But something inexplicable felt lighter between them.

Later, Nell made breakfast, humming as she scrambled eggs. They ate in silence, squeezing hands under the table like young lovers. She felt ready to take on whatever disasters awaited her in Ireland. She made a thousand mental promises to herself about how she would behave with Ali. How this time, it would be different. How this time—

'I want you to be sure.' Henri cut across her thoughts. 'When you come back. Where we go from here. Is that understood?'

'You think I'll be gone for a long time, don't you? There's no reason for you to think that.'

His lips twitched in a little enigmatic smile. 'Nell, you don't pay a flying visit after thirty-two years. The things you left behind will still be there, where you left them.'

Nell experienced a flutter of surprise that he should put so succinctly what she had spent her adult life almost realizing, but never quite.

'But come back to me. Do come back,' he continued, moving away before she could respond.

'Right, I'm going to leave before I get impossibly sentimental. I'll take Lulu, of course. She can remind me of you.'

'A mangy bitch with cataracts? I'll get her basket and little bits together. You know the routine.'

'Milk last thing at night, feed in the morning, kick up the ass to make her walk. I think I know the routine. And yes, I will take good care of the old bitch.'

Nell traced her lips lightly along his cheek and went to gather Lulu's things. The dog eyed her soulfully, scenting betrayal everywhere.

The wheels touch down with a bump. She's forgotten to glance out the window at the countryside below, to monitor her own reaction to rolling green fields and home. There is only airport to her right now. Lots of airport, all black-tinted windows and gleaming metal. A sign saying Cork Airport, a sign saying Welcome Home. It makes a lump rise in her throat.

Inside, after a strange Immigration check, where the officers clearly scan by colour and Irishness appearance, the Arrivals Hall is a many-splendoured receptacle. Everything looks new, sparkly clean – expensive modern, Nell thinks the generic might be. A first-time visitor would think: small, intimate, pots of corporate money.

She waits for her bags and considers that her feet stand on Irish soil for the first time in so many years. There should be big feelings, huge even, but really there is nothing. Simply a sense of arrival. Another journey completed. No sense of the journey ahead.

As a bank of expectant faces wait in the main hall, briefly checking her out, eyes quickly moving on to scan the passengers behind, she has that curious, irrational response she gets on arrival anywhere. That somehow, for some unknown, inexplicable reason, there will be someone waiting for her after all. Then that equally inexplicable little stab of disappointment.

There's an indoor pond with orange and silver koi in the main hall beyond. See-through lifts whish silently between floors. A bronze Jack Charlton sits in the fish enclosure. A Please Do Not Throw Coins sign is partially obscured by thrown coins of varying currencies. Nell makes her way to the car rental outlet. Please Do Not Smoke signs, ignored everywhere by people smoking. She has to smile. Perhaps things haven't changed so entirely. Something makes her stop in mid-stride across the concourse. What it is she can't quite figure for a few moments. Her head moves this way and that, sensing, or is it listening? Suddenly it hits her: of course, the voices — all the accents are Irish. For years it has been a singular thing, a man in a bar, a young woman shouting on a boulevard, an interview with a musician on television. At such times, her own feeling of belonging to a tribe. Now that all the voices blend and sound the same, there is no longer a feeling of belonging, merely a sketched idea that she has arrived in this particular country with people who speak like this. Anywhere, in fact.

The young man behind the counter offers a range of extra services, all of which she refuses. Just the car, thank you, for now. A map? No. I know where I'm going. (That, she thinks might just be tempting the fates a little too brazenly.) Well, enjoy your holiday. Thank you, I'm sure I will.

Over then. Arrival. Not much of a deal, after all. Nell steps out into sunlight.

She finds the car with little difficulty and pulls out into the airport drive, bearing right at the roundabout on the main road, heading west. Five minutes along she realizes she has chosen the longest route possible. Everything in her body pulled her west immediately when there was probably a good, fast road between Cork and Kerry now. No matter, she would head towards the sea and hug the coast road through West Cork and up over the hills to Kerry. All the prettier, all the longer, before she has to face Ali's wrath. She has not forewarned them, thinking that a surprise raid may reveal more than if they have time to prepare. But Ali will look at her mother the spy with rage in her eyes.

The road widens ahead to a smooth dual carriageway. A sign acknowledges funds assistance from the European Community. Ali has already told Nell about this and much else. In fact, as Nell glances from side to side, Ali has done a pretty slick job all told, in keeping her up to date. The gargantuan size of some of the modern two-storey houses doesn't surprise her. Sleek, almost new, top-of-the-range cars speeding towards her, don't surprise. So far, the one thing Ali hasn't mentioned is neatness. This does surprise. Then again, Ali would not have had any other experience. The neatness of homes, gardens, window-boxes, pubs bedecked in flowers, these do appear strange at first. Otherwise, she is waiting for something to hit that remains in abeyance. She slides down the window, sniffing air, still in pursuit of strangeness or familiarity, one or the other she is prepared to deal with. But there is nothing. Just a woman driving a car – anywhere. The fields are uncannily green. That's it.

An hour along, she stops at a roadside pub for soup and a sandwich. The interior is immaculate. The odour of pub she was expecting is not present. A plump, friendly woman brings lunch to the table. Fresh homemade vegetable soup, unlike the powdered Royco Nell's mother used to serve, a lean honey-roast ham sandwich with thick crusts. She drinks a glass of Murphy's, fiddles with a crossword to avoid conversation and feels her jagged nerves begin to ease a little. Perhaps Ali won't be enraged. She will have some idea of what it has taken for Nell to make this trip. She will have every idea – and she will still be enraged. Nell sighs, finishes the food, pays and leaves.

The closest she has come to making this journey was after the first early-morning call made by Paudie about Agnes's stroke. It's your mother, Nell, I'm sorry to tell you but she's had a turn. A turn? Yes, a stroke. It's bad, Nell. You said to call if anything happened. Thank you, Paudie. I'll come tomorrow.

That was ten years ago. Nell did book a flight. Packed a bag, made it to Charles de Gaulle, vomited violently in a toilet by the departure gate, stumbled to a payphone, called Paudie – Agnes had improved in the night. She was at home in her own bed being nursed by her younger sister Hannah, who had arrived from Galway. It looked as if the worst was over. Nell gasped her thanks, fled past the departure gate and headed for her apartment. The apartment that Agnes had visited on a number of occasions, calling it very fancy indeed and was she to take it that Nell was never going to come home now, or what? Soon, Nell responded each time. And Agnes would change the position of the pin in her hat with her lips pursed and her head nodding acknowledgement of the lie. She would not step onto a street in Paris without her hat.

It was Hannah who phoned at four in the morning. Agnes had died in her sleep half an hour past. Another massive stroke. It was as peaceful a death as one could wish for if Nell wanted to look at it that way. Would Nell let Ali know? And when might they expect them for the funeral?

A numbness that shocked Nell took her over. She sat bolt upright on the bed for the next few hours. Not a tear, not a memory, not a vestige of grief, not even a precognition of grief. She sat, unmoving, waiting for remembrances, the last time she'd seen Agnes, childhood images, anything. But the only thing her mind would present was a vision of Agnes — dead. Nell could see the tall, burly frame stretched out beneath a white sheet. Dyed auburn permed hair, faded ginger halfway up, white at the roots. Waxy, rusted pallor, folds and creases of her wide face hanging limply from her skull. She saw her mother's glazed blue eyes staring ahead into nothingness. Brown, shiny patches around the sockets, twin spots of blue-black on either side where eye met bulbous nose. Pearl earrings. A gold crucifix nestled in the bands of her throat. Pink flannel nightjacket round her ample shoulders. Knobbled hands covered in age spots clutched together over her breast. Holding something. Something Hannah would have no doubt slipped under the fingers. Rosary beads? Nell closed her eyes to focus harder on the image. No, not beads, a small photograph. Agnes, youthful and tall and arrogant, in a striking hat with a feather and a pin, flanked on either side by her young daughters. Nell and Bridget. Two girls in white, puffed-out dresses with satin bows. Gazing up in awe and wonder at a woman who kept her eyes fixed firmly ahead. The woman they called Mammy.

It was Ali who called Nell further on in the morning. She was back in Oxford in those days and had called Hannah herself to get an update on her grandmother. Nell could hear the thrum of shock in Ali's voice. A voice which grew bell-like shrill as she screamed at Nell for not calling and letting her know. I can see her dead, Nell said, when Ali had to pause for breath. I can see her dead. But I can't believe it. I can't. Well, she is, Ali said after a while, her voice softening. Nell? Nell? Are you there?

Please Ali. She *can't* be gone.

It took her a while to register that Ali was still hollering down the line. Nell? You're in shock, can you see that? Call Henri or Meredith. Get them to come around and pack a bag for you. Arrange a ticket. All right? Keep moving. Keep busy. I'm going to Heathrow now. I'll call you from there. All right?

All right.

She knew Henri was away for a couple of days so she pressed Meredith's number. Then replaced the receiver after the first ring. She looked around the room, thinking: bag, ticket, ticket, bag. Ticket, ticket, ticket. She made several futile attempts to call Meredith but balked each time at the last second. She would have to voice it. She would have to say the words that would effectively end her mother.

Her mind was stuck. It was the most peculiar sensation she'd ever experienced, though not wholly unpleasant. As though she had imploded, fallen in upon herself like a black hole from which neither light nor matter nor thought could escape. When at last she fell into a deep sleep, she dreamt not of Agnes but of Bridget, her sister.

A series of strange, pungent dreams, brightly lit, too much
so, like technicolour. Strangest of all, she was her adult self
while Bridget was still a young girl. They were clambering
up Eagle Rock, with Agnes a shadowy figure at some distance behind. Bridget wore a red scarf round her neck. In
the garish technicolour it wrapped round her neck like a
vibrant, scarlet snake. The adult Nell had time to remark
how breathlessly pretty her sister looked, clambering over
rocks, eager for the top. Calling down to Nell, *C'mon, c'mon.*
The scarf uncoiled into the air behind her, weaving a sensu-
ous dance for moments on a current of wind. Bridget no
longer visible over the crest of hill. Nell bent down to pluck
the scarf from a clump of reedy grass where it landed, form-
ing a curled S. She held it high, calling to her negligent
older sister. But Bridget was gone. Nell wrapped the scarf
round her own neck and broke into a run. Following. Each
time the dream ended just before she reached the top. Each
time, she was spared what happened next.

She would wake to urinate, drink a glass of water and collapse onto the bed again. The light on her answering
machine winked a furious red. She hadn't heard the phone
ringing. Every time she pulled herself upright on the bed,
swung her legs over the side, ready to move, she would sit
there immobilized with her hands clutching the mattress.

When Henri and Meredith arrived together, finally
tracked down by Ali, Nell had lost all sense of time. Over
two days had passed. When she saw them, she started crying
and that released her from her catatonic state. Rolling sobs
that racked and left a throb in their wake. They took it in
turns, holding her, feeding her mouthfuls of soup, stroking
her head. Henri spoke with a distraught Ali on the phone.
He tried to explain the state they'd found Nell in, that she

was in no fit condition to travel anywhere. But Ali was shouting for her mother. She was past listening to reason. Granny would be buried tomorrow. Nell had to be there. Ali needed her to stand beside her. She couldn't do this on her own. When Henri patiently tried to explain for the umpteenth time, Ali just kept repeating, I want my mum. I want my mum.

Never before nor since had Ali referred to Nell as her mum. And never before had Nell not been able to run to her daughter's side when she was needed. Often when she was needed but not wanted, Ali was so fragile. This time it was Nell who was fragile, her face stretched over her cheekbones like crisp, newly starched linen pulled taut across a bed. Nothing like the confident, self-contained woman familiar to Henri and Meredith. She could hear them discussing her when they thought they were out of earshot.

I never went home, she said. After they'd dealt with Ali in as much as they could, and forced some nourishment into Nell. All she wanted. And I couldn't do it. Why? Why couldn't I do that for her? I can't even do it for her now. It's the most terrible thing. Never to have another chance. Never.

Henri must have slipped something into her coffee because she slept. It was turning dark again when she awoke, peering into the gloom at his slumped frame on the bedside chair. Almost in silhouette, a cheek listing sideways into the raised cup of his hand. He too had fallen asleep. For a long time, Nell stared at him, watching shallow breaths rise and fall along his chest. Occasionally, he twitched, the eyes would cinch tighter, forcing the spider lashes to curl higher at the tips. One dark lock of hair swooped forward across his brow. Sleep makes children of us all, she thought. How long he had sat there, simply being, watching, caring for her, she couldn't tell. Probably since morning. She thought she would never again love him so much as that moment. It was the moment when love moves up that notch that is recalled in bad times. When you remember that someone got you through this, or that, or something they didn't fully understand. That even you didn't fully understand. They'd been together, in a fashion, for five years.

His eyes flickered awake, confused for an instant, unsure where he was, then he saw that she was awake and calmer and he smiled. It's over. Nell said. I'm better now. It's over.

A hazy September late-afternoon light settles on hedgerows and throws distant hills into blurred hummocks. The hedgerows are storybooks, teeming with characters vying for life, for space. Nell is glad to find familiarity in this. Wild fuschia dropping red bells with purple petticoats over blackthorn, whitethorn, hedge parsley, rowans wrapped in brambles dripping with shiny blackberries. Ferns, wild thyme, dandelions and blazing orange montbretia thrust out from the undergrowth, threatening to eclipse the narrow, winding road ahead. She has passed through a series of inland towns with prettily painted houses and shops in the central streets. Objectionable, garish bungalows with pillars and conservatories on the outskirts. She has left the yawning Atlantic Ocean, sailboats frittering like white butterflies along the surface. Past elongated islands with circular fields injected into wide harbours. The car rising into a range of hills. Woods fall abruptly away and there is rock.

Granite-grey, lichen-covered, draped folds of glaciated crust. High, burnt hay breaks through in patches, keeling in the direction of wind. The surface of rock, heavily scored with deep, curled scratches as though a giant or some great bear ran twisting claws over every plane. Fading sunlight slips in and out of grooves and crevices, gleaming on raised ridges, drowning in dark troughs, throwing the whorls and scars into etched relief. Even in what pass for fields, there are great outcrops of granite as though thrust out of peeled-back earth. Bursting through like gnarled knuckles from a grave. Though the landscape has become more like her own now, where she is headed, it simply glides by the video-screen windows of the car, beautiful, grey, green – stark. There was a time when she would hardly have believed that there was anywhere beyond. This was everything and everywhere.

Then, the moment her uncle in Oxford presented her with that first mouthful of St-Emilion, she remembers it well, the world introduced itself to her palate. A sip of wine can invoke a blazing summer's day, texture of fine milled dust beneath her feet, the slant of afternoon sun over rows of vines sagging with full, globular, mature grapes. The pale straw hat of the vineyard owner's daughter. Time and location, features of the surrounding countryside, even the shadows cast along the landscape by passing clouds, minutest of details recalled in an instant by a taste or a scent. She can remember whole pockets of geography in this way, whole sections of an atlas, but the rocks outside bring nothing to mind. Then she realizes she has been looking at everything through narrowed eyes. Letting the past in like an envelope, seal slitted, but not fully opened.

She is at the highest point, the road levelling before a gradual descent. A ludicrously bottle-green valley to her left, dotted with houses – everywhere is dotted with houses –

curving up to more rockface sealing the glen off in the distance. Slick of water visible from a mountain lake. A narrow tunnel ahead, chunky and rough-edged as if hewn by hand, which is not far from the truth. Halfway along, a brief split in the tunnel's roof signals that she has left County Cork and is now in Kerry.

The sky is turning a light shade of violet. Nell is becoming increasingly worried about Ali's reaction. Her thoughts turn to Grace instead. Nell hasn't seen her granddaughter for nearly six months. She will have changed. Changes are huge, vast, in seven-year-olds. Every time she visits Paris, Nell is prepared for one grandchild and accommodates another. There is shy, almost surly Grace. Madcap, deliciously wild and endlessly curious Grace. The pensive, wistful child who comes out with the strangest, skewed logic. One of the bags in the boot is full of presents, clothes, dolls, 'making things' – anything Nell could get her hands on before the trip to the airport. These things will disappear into the same vacuum all other presents fell into. Where things go Nell has no idea, and Ali just shrugs in her irritated, distracted way.

She is on the home stretch. Hours after her plane touched down, with a tender, gentle-looking sky dissolving above the car. At last, she allows herself to think of Henri. The way his eyes avoided hers as he left. The pulsing muscle in his left cheek speaking the volumes his voice could not. She can think of him now because of the pang of loneliness that crept up when she first contemplated the narrow, isolated road ahead. His lips just brushed her cheek and didn't linger. Lulu, too, was strangely uncommunicative, draped over the crook of his arm, fully aware that there was some sort of movement going on and she was one of the things being moved. Usually there were protests. The janitor's family have taken care of Lulu in the past when Nell has to travel. Lulu has been perfectly content with them but that hasn't stopped her enacting a little leavetaking drama each time Nell has handed her over. Accusing mewls, sullen glances, a disdainful turn of her head when Nell has tried to whisper in her ear that she will be back soon. But this time it was as if Lulu sensed a difference, as if she knew this wasn't just any departure. Nell could have sworn there was a sadness in the cloudy eyes as they cast her a last lingering glance over the rim of Henri's arm.

The recollection brings with it a needle-sharp stab of guilt, because Nell is also aware that for the last few hours she has been glad to be on her own, a woman in a car, free of dogs and men and untidy emotions. Knowing a thought to be base and ignoble doesn't stop you thinking it. She wonders if everyone carries within them, a hidden world, a place where they constantly betray themselves and others, the existence of which they never reveal in words. Not a place entirely, more a gap, a yawning stretch between what they will admit and what conceal. In all her life, she has never encountered another being as compulsively honest as Henri. Barely a thought flits across his brain that he does not utter. She has tried to match that candour on many occasions but knows that there resides within her gulfs of muddy darkness she elects to glide across, without looking down.

She passes through a small, winding village, two rows of parallel houses, couple of small shops, two pubs and a white church set back from the road. Apart from window-boxes and neater frontages, smoother road and pavements, nothing seems to have changed very much. Nell's eyes sweep from side to side, in case Ali is around. Half a mile along, she can smell the sea ahead in the distance. She indicates right and turns up a lane just wide enough for one car. There are pull-in spots carved from the hedges all the way up, in case two cars meet.

There is Paudie and Julia's house on the right. Two-storey, whitewashed over bumpy stone with orange geraniums at every window. Absolutely picture-pretty with a red tongue-and-groove front door. Nell smiles; she's becoming a tourist. There is a sense of movement within but she decides to leave them until tomorrow.

Not much further along, the road widens slightly to accommodate a crossroads. Two tributary lanes feeding off this main artery such as it is. At the centre of the crossroads, starkly alone, stands Hennessy's Public House. Nell stops the car and stares for a while. When she left the house was dingy white. Now it is yellow. The windows have been replaced, four sash upstairs, two wide picture windows downstairs for lounge and public bar, either side of the main entrance door – half blue wood, half opaque glass – not replaced. Gay blue and yellow check curtains in the lounge window. Clean nets upstairs, which Nell takes as a good sign. Window-boxes however, would have thrilled.

A stand-up sign offers soup and sandwiches – to whom? Nell wonders. There can be little passing trade. Nell's mother did food for regulars, but the fact that Ali was choosing to advertise must mean another source of clientele has opened up. The place looks smart and neat enough. Nell feels hugely relieved. It is only now she realizes that she was half anticipating a scene from a cheap B Western. Tumbleweed, skeletal roofs, a creaky sign swinging in the wind. If she is really honest, the odd shotgun going off in the distance.

She puts the car in gear and is about to glide closer when

Grace comes out. Nell's jaw drops. The child's grown quite tall and is ferociously skinny. Red marks are dotted all over her twiglet legs under a pair of last year's shorts. Bony shoulders protrude from a flimsy singlet and it is evening, not warm enough for no sleeves. A thought which is immediately confirmed by Grace's shiver and arm-hold of her own body. Her hair hangs lank and featureless; it was always so shiny. Nell waits to see what her granddaughter intends to do – play, skip, walk somewhere? But no, she just stands there, head slightly downcast, though her scowl is apparent. Her feet scuff at a worn mat outside the pub front door, worrying it with the sole of her sandal. No socks, either, Nell notes, in this temperature. The top of Grace's body rocks from side to side, she keeps her hands on her shoulders in crossed-over fashion. There is something so deeply, intrinsically unhappy about the child's posture that Nell has to wait a while longer to compose herself. Net curtains and fresh yellow paint notwithstanding, something has gone terribly wrong in this house.

An elderly man steps out, leaning heavily on a stick. He stops to say something to Grace who does not look up at him. He pats the top of her head and he moves creakily along towards one of the narrow tracks leading down and to the left of the building. Nell remembers who he is: he lives in a small cottage by a crescent-shaped pebbled cove at the bottom of the lane. When she left, he was a tall, upright man who played the melodion in the bar on weekend nights. For a moment she feels that she has fast-forwarded into someone else's life.

Grace peers across the increasing gloom of evening. She is wondering about the static car but does not yet recognize her grandmother. Nell rolls down the window about to holler when Ali comes out. She, too, is painfully thin; even at some distance the gaunt, high ridges of her cheekbones are prominent and disturbing. She is dressed in paint-splattered denim dungarees, material falling sack-like from her slender frame. Her hair is shorn into a tight, bristly crop which accentuates the lines on her forehead. She seems angry, legs jiggling as she remonstrates with Grace over something. Grace ignores her and moves slightly away, turning her back. Ali reaches out and spins her daughter round to face her. She is shouting now. Nell feels that she must make her presence known. Ali will be furious if she thinks she's been secretly watched. Nell revs the accelerator slightly and shunts forward. Ali and Grace turn to face the approaching car, Ali squinting to make out the driver. Her mouth forms a silent O as she realizes who it is.

Grace comes charging forward. 'Nan? Nan, it *is* you!'

Nell brings the car to an abrupt halt and leaps out, lifting Grace high into the air, swinging her round. She covers Grace's face in kisses. 'My pet.' In her arms, the child feels angular, ill put together, light as marrowless, bleached bone.

'But you never come here, Nan.'

'Well, I'm here now, Gracie.'

'For how long? For a long time?' Grace wraps her arms round Nell's neck so tightly that Nell can't tell whether it's the lump in her throat or the stranglehold which almost makes her choke. She coughs. Dares to look in Ali's direction over the top of Grace's head.

'Hello, Ali, sweetheart. I hope this little surprise isn't going to backfire on me.'

Ali has remained at a distance, hesitating, now she takes long strides and covers the gap. She looks as if she is about to burst into tears. Her grey eyes are hollowed, triangular, a

dark ridge bisects her forehead. Nell has never seen anyone
look so close to their own skull. Ali flings out an arm to
embrace her mother round Grace's back; it pauses feather-
like in midair, then lightly touches Nell's shoulder instead.

'Hiya, Nell.'

'I made it. I finally made it.' Nell beams. 'You look well,
sweetheart,' she lies.

'Thanks. So do you.'

A shy silence, which is broken by Grace's whoop. She
wriggles free to her feet. 'I bet you've brought presents.'
Already vetting the car.

'Maybe I have. But first there'll have to be lots of kisses.
Oceans of kissing before presents.'

Both Nell and Ali smile indulgently and pretend to be
absorbed by Grace's little impatient dance round the car.
Their bodies have listed slightly towards each other, plants
towards sunlight, but there is an awkward pocket of air, of
turbulence, in the gap between them. Nell takes a deep
breath and grabs Ali's shoulders, pressing her closer. Ali resists
momentarily, then rests her shaved head in the crook of
Nell's neck. She begins to sob and Nell runs her hand up
and down her daughter's back.

'It's all right, Ali. Whatever it is, we'll fix it. Please, don't
be angry with me for coming like this.'

'Paudie called you, didn't he?'

'Yes. Yes, he did. He's worried about you. But you're
fine. I can see that. Whatever . . . well . . . if something
hasn't been quite right, I can see that you're coping perfectly
fine.' Nell daren't open her mouth any wider for fear the
black streak of lying will show on her tongue.

'Nick is ill,' Ali says, moving back again, pinching the tip
of her nose.

'That's worrying, of course,' Nell says, keeping her voice even, sympathetic, while her eyes move constantly back and forth from granddaughter to daughter.

What in Christ's name has happened to make you both look like this?

'Doctor Bennet gave up, couldn't find anything concrete to tell us. So Nick went to Cork for tests. They couldn't find anything either. But they said it might be ME. He hasn't any energy. I mean, none at all. Barely eats, just wants to sleep all day, then he can't sleep a wink at nights. You're going to get a bit of a shock when you see him.'

If it's anything like the shock of seeing you, my darling girl, Nell thinks, but she fixes a reassuring smile. 'Maybe while I'm here we could arrange for some sort of specialist to see—'

'There aren't any specialists in ME,' Ali cuts in, flintily. 'There isn't anything you can do that we haven't tried already.'

'I'm sure you're doing everything you can,' Nell responds evenly and mentally ticks off minefield one. She will have to be more vigilant than ever with Ali's high-frequency sensitivities.

'Okay, I give up,' Grace howls. 'Where're the bloody presents?'

'Kisses first.'

'How many exactly?' Grace sidles over.

'I don't know. What do you think, Ali?'

'Ten seems a fair figure.'

'Ten it is, then.' Nell hunkers down on her haunches, closes her eyes and purses her lips. Grace dutifully pays out her kisses, squeals after the tenth and burrows into Nell's cheek with a further passionate ten. They keel over sideways and Nell tickles Grace until she screams for her to stop. All the while Nell's probing fingers check her granddaughter out. Hollow indents between ribs, raised, angry fleabites, crusty scabs all over her scalp.

'Right.' Nell stands. 'Presents time. Will you help me with the bags, Ali?'

'I'll have to put you in Granny's old room.'

'That's fine.' Nell's heart plunges. 'Look, I know this is all so sudden for you, I never considered the mechanics. Would it be easier if I found a guesthouse, even for a few nights – give you time to prepare?'

'Prepare what, exactly?' Ali says a touch testily. 'A bed's a bed. How long does it take to prepare one? Just voomp turn the mattress, throw a couple of sheets and blankets. No big deal. You'll have to take us as you find us, you know.'

That's what I'm afraid of.

'Of course,' Nell responds with a smile, not unaware that she is adopting the same emollient tone Henri uses from time to time with herself.

She lugs one of the bags toward the pub door.

'No, around the back,' Ali commands. 'You don't want to have to talk to people just yet. I imagine.'

Nell nods and follows Grace's excited canter round the side of the building. She was dreading the first step into the pub in any case.

'It must seem very strange, after all these years,' Ali says from behind.

'Oh, I don't know. You've done a good job keeping me up to date.'

'Up to date?'

'On what to expect. The changes.'

'In the country, you mean? Yeah, well. The pub hasn't changed all that much, has it?'

'The place looks neat, cared for.'

'That's on the outside,' Ali chuckles, a touch grimly to Nell's mind.

Three things converge at once. One: Granny is Granny and she is still Nell and not Mum. Two: even if she hasn't admitted it to herself, Ali's been expecting her mother's arrival if not actively willing it and now she's not so sure. And three: Ali's Irish accent is deliciously rolling and soft, draped over her Oxford undertones.

A hand lightly grazes Nell's shoulder, falls away like a dusting of brushed snow. 'I'm glad you're here, Nell. Don't make me not glad.'

Circuit overload as a million responses trip through Nell's brain on their way to the cyber jam at the back of her throat. She is annoyed by the implication but pleased that she is welcome even if it will be short-lived.

'Of course,' she says, stepping into a pat of catshit already squashed by Grace's sandal.

CHAPTER THREE

Everything about Grace turns up. The corners of her conker-coloured eyes slant just at the edges. Her nose is slightly snubbed over a perfect cupid mouth with an upward crease at either side. When she looks mischievous, the pixie-like effect is heightened. The only thing that does not turn up is her hair, which is shoulder-length, multi-shades of brown and spaghetti straight.

Nell re-observes the child's upward quality, because anything is preferable to taking in the state of the kitchen. She just about managed to suppress a gasp when they entered through the small porch at the back of the house. The porch was bad enough, half collapsed and with stagnant pools of old rain, mounds of rotting dishcloths and clothes heaped high in corners, presumably thrown there with some vague, unrealistic notion of drying, then left to fester. Ali skipped through to the kitchen ahead of her, muttering something about the mess and how busy it had been lately and not to pay it much attention, clean-up day was tomorrow. Clean-up day was always tomorrow, that much was evident from Nell's first cursory look around.

'I lo-o-ove this,' Grace says, holding up a Jewel Girl Barbie. 'It's got things you can put on, diamonds and stuff.'

Rooting through this new formidable stash, there have been things she has lo-o-oved and things she has liked. Her eyes are dancing.

'I didn't want to get just another Barbie you put clothes on,' Nell says. 'You prefer them to do something, I remember.'

'I don't see the point of just putting clothes on,' Grace says in the adult voice she adopts at times which clutches at Nell's heart. 'You can put clothes on any old doll.'

'Precisely.' Nell agrees, daring to look around the kitchen.

The walls reek of damp, and white clusters of mould cling to peeling plaster. In one corner, the plaster has crumbled so entirely that wood slats show through. Paint is so faded that only an idea of yellow remains. Terracotta tiles on the floor are chipped and cracked everywhere, shiny with layers of grease. The Belfast sink is streaked with old tea stains, piled high with days of dishes, chipped cups, rimey glasses. More piles of crumpled clothes on chairs, floor, spread atop the black Aga. For washing, it would be safe to assume, hardly ironing. Fine dust from the ceiling, which has cracked like a dry riverbed, powders the Formica topped table.

There is an overpowering stench of old cabbage, soiled linen and drying clothes that have not been washed. Good God Almighty, a wooden chopping board on a dresser, with bread crusts, a tub of cheap margarine, spools of yellowing ham fat – this is the food station, no doubt. Sliced pan botulism for the gullible punters in the bar. What can only be called a cauldron on the Aga must contain the soup. Nell promises herself never to look.

A picture of Jesus pointing to His sacred heart in His rent-open chest hangs askew from a drooping nail. In another corner, a little shrine to the Virgin Mary, coated in dust with a bulbous red lamp in front. Stacked on a three-legged chair, books on the lives of saints, a bible, an old catechism Nell remembers from her schooldays. She notes that a tumbler of whiskey she'd spotted over by the sink has been removed.

While she makes her observations, Nell is careful to keep her eyes hooded and refrains from turning her head this way and that. But Grace, who misses precious little, is already darting her own eyes, trying to picture the scene as if for the first time. She is well aware that this is not normal. Visits to other houses could tell her that in an instant. Nell swears to herself that she will take it easy. If she is to survive longer than a week in this hovel, she will have to keep her mouth shut, voice only mild opinions – and only when asked. She will work on Grace with stealth and subtlety because Grace is nobody's fool and can smell an interrogation a mile off and Ali can smell an interrogation of her daughter a further hundred miles off.

Grace can divert a line of questioning with the velocity of an exocet. She never knows what she is supposed to be hiding, usually on her mother's behalf, but she knows that she should be hiding something. To be on the safe side and to ensure she makes no mistakes, she hides everything. There have been times in Paris when Nell has seen a dart of pain flicker across the child's face when she has asked something directly. Grace has had to resort to almost supernatural powers of reticence when Nell has turned on all her powers of persuasion. Bribes, cuddles, long night-time chats notwithstanding, Grace has managed to keep her cupid lips zipped and Nell has felt cheap and exploitative for hours afterwards.

The last visit, six months ago, Nell vowed she wouldn't ask Grace a solitary leading question. Just normal stuff, school, friends and so on. She determined that the poor child shouldn't feel diminished in her eyes for not coming up with the revelatory goods. She wanted her own relationship with Grace, not merely as a conduit to Ali. Once Grace felt she could let her guard down and trust Nell entirely, it was the happiest time they had yet spent together.

Nell is conscious of Grace's glance taking in her own unchipped red nail polish, the emerald ring and amber bracelet. A quick flutter of lids up then down again but Nell's gleaming ash-blond hair has been considered. The pink lip gloss she slides across her lips from time to time. Her black, razor-cut suit has been absorbed. Nell determines more than ever to keep her mouth shut for the longest time. She reaches across and plucks up the old catechism.

'I can't believe they're still using this, after all these years.'

Grace winces, recovers quickly, holds the Barbie up to show the jewels stuck on. Her brown eyes have that haunted, I-will-say-nothing quality. Nell can't believe she's already stumbled and she wasn't even taking a calculated jump.

A curtain swishes and the sound of brass rings shunting along a metal pole has a childhood redolence that makes Nell sit up straight. The heavy brocade shields the bar from the kitchen. Ali steps through and swishes the curtain closed behind her. For an instant there was the low hum of voices from beyond.

'Sorry,' Ali says to Nell, though she is eyeing Grace. 'Your first evening, but I can't shut the bar down. No one to help tonight.'

'This Adam fellow?'

'Sometimes he turns up, sometimes he doesn't.' Ali doesn't ask what Paudie has said. She can make her own assumptions.

'Maybe you should make a more formal arrangement,' Nell begins, then bites her lip. Second stumble.

Ali gathers bundles of clothes, sweeps them into one stinking pile in a corner as if that is what she has come in to do. She shrugs without turning round. 'We like it this way. Easy, you know, *nothing* formal.' She glances over her shoulder, adding, 'That'll be hard for you, of course.'

'Oh, I'll get used to it,' Nell counters lightly. 'I'm home now, I'd better get used to it.'

Ali's teeth catch her bottom lip. She looks ashamed. 'I'll just run up and see if Nick is awake. He won't believe his eyes when he sees you.' She lunges towards the stairs that lead down to the kitchen. Her movements have always had that sense of desperate motion, Nell thinks. As though she expects to be thwarted at every turn and therefore must do everything in a hurry before she loses focus, before she loses linear intent, which is what happens time and time again in mid-lunge. As if confirming Nell's thoughts, halfway up the stairs Ali stops and leans over the bannister rail.

'Food,' she says, struggling to gather up the loose ends of a thousand straying thoughts. 'You must be hungry. I'll fix something nice for us in a little while, okay?'

The prospect of eating anything prepared in this kitchen causes a swell of nausea in Nell's stomach. But Ali's eyes are glistening with remorse for her earlier sharpness and her longing to cook for her mother is making her breathless. Her legs jiggle on the stair tread. Nell is overcome with pity for this confliction of thoughts, this mesh of jangled nerve-endings, that is her daughter.

'I could eat something.' Nell smiles. She's about to offer to cook – Ali can hardly boil an egg – but she bites back the words in time. Ali's a thirty-two-year-old woman. This is her turf. Nell signed it over to her, lock, stock and beer barrel a couple of years back. 'Whenever you're ready,' she says instead. 'No rush.'

From the corner of her eyes, she sees Grace's shoulders subside with the breath she has expelled.

Ali runs up, then calls down from the landing, 'Grace? Stand in for me, darling. Just for a second.'

Grace puts Barbie to the side and quietly slinks out through the brocade curtain.

She's seven. Seven, serving in the bar.

Those days should be long gone. Kids serving pints. It feels as though she's stepped into a warped, pastiche version of her own past. All it needs now is some spooky merry-go-round music in the background while the kitchen morphs into wavery flashback. Nell allows her head to wilt into her waiting palms. It will take Herculean powers to keep her mouth shut, even past tonight. She tiptoes to the curtain and peers through a chink. The light is dim and she can barely make out two figures resting their elbows along the counter top. Grace stands on top of an upended plastic crate, pulling a pint of Guinness with the stroke of an expert. The tip of her tongue sticks out to the side, she's concentrating so hard. Nell cinches the curtain and sits again when she hears Ali's returning steps.

'He's awake,' Ali says; for a second she looks flushed with pleasure. 'Just give him a minute to shave, he wants to look his best for you.' She pulls a chair up to the table, sits, keeping Formica between them. 'So, Nell, tell me, how are *you*, anyway?'

The oldest trick in the book. Question the questioner.

'I'm well enough apart from this menopause business, which is a bit of a pain.'

'You're early, aren't you? Shouldn't you be turning fifty?'

'It can start earlier. Besides . . .' The sentence trails away. It goes unrecognized by Ali that her mother *is* turning fifty. She tends to treat Nell as an older, disapproving sister. The swot, the good one to Ali's wayward rebel.

Ali scrapes her chair closer.

'What're the symptoms – I mean for you, in particular.'

So I'm to be the patient, Nell thinks.

'For me?' She blows out a long breath. 'Flushes, especially at night. Sometimes I think I'll spontaneously combust.'

'Lots of kinetic energy there,' Ali nods. 'You could use that. You know, put it in to something. Go on.'

'Umm. Mood swings, I suppose. I find myself getting quite emotional about things that never used to bother me. A bit tearful sometimes. And tired. I'm slowing down, Ali. It's easier to get into my bed at night and harder to get out of it in the morning.'

She doesn't add, because Ali has it all ahead, that sometimes she feels the life force is being systematically sucked out of her.

'Does this change – do these changes, frighten you?'

'A little.'

'It must be strange for you, being out of control.'

'I didn't say that.'

Nell has the sinking feeling that Ali is storing up this exchange. If she senses criticism or censure in the future, a quick inversion and her defence will be Nell's take on things. In this, her new volatile state.

Ali catches the involuntary dart of Nell's eyes towards the bar curtain. 'We don't make a habit of using Grace in the bar, if that's what you're thinking. She loves it. Just the odd time, though. It's no place for a child. As you know.'

'I never enjoyed it,' Nell says. 'Maybe Grace is different.'

'She is different. She chooses to go in there, whereas you had to, didn't you?'

'Well, I had to help my mother, if that's what you mean. There was only us. No choice in the matter, really.'

'That's what Grace does. She helps me.' Ali reaches for a box of cigarettes, shuffles one out and lights it. She expels a ream of smoke up towards the cracked ceiling. Nell catches the slight tremble in her daughter's fingers.

'Sex?' Ali enquires. Nell raises her eyebrows. 'The change – does it affect your sex life?'

'In some respects.' Nell smiles tightly.

'How is Henri?'

Nell studies her scarlet fingernails. 'He's just told me he's leaving his wife, actually.'

'Well, that's wonderful news.' Ali clumsily reaches across the table. She squeezes Nell's hand then awkwardly pats. 'Isn't it?'

'I thought we were fine the way we were.'

'You thought,' Ali says, emphasising the you. A sketch of a smile at the corners of her mouth.

'Ali, why haven't you fixed the phone?'

Ali's hand snakes back. Her shoulders go up and down like fluttering wings as she considers. Eventually she dares to look her mother straight in the eye for the first time since Nell's arrival.

'I don't know.' Ali sighs. 'There are lots of things I don't know. Is that why you're here? To find out all the things I don't know?'

'I'm here because I love you. I want us to enjoy our time

together. Let's both of us try not to make judgements. I'm not a spy. I'm not the enemy.'

'This was all supposed to be . . .' Ali blinks rapidly, gazes around the decrepit kitchen. 'I thought it would be paradise. I'm making a terrible mess of things. I can see it in your eyes.'

'If I can help, will you let me?' Nell almost whispers, introducing the H word with caution.

'Maybe,' Ali says after some consideration. Her mouth twists into a bitter smile. 'But you know what I'm like.' She hops up quickly in that way she has, as if a dog has nipped her. A couple of head-forward strides towards the bar, then she retraces her steps, clamps a hand either side of Nell's head and lunges down to kiss her mother's forehead.

'Thank you for coming,' Ali mutters hoarsely. 'We'll get on, won't we? You'll stay for a while.'

It's a start, Nell thinks. Her brow tingles where Ali's lips smacked against it. No fanfare of trumpets, no trailing clouds of glory, then. Rather a sense that their genuine pleasure in being together, coupled with a concerted effort on both their parts, might just get them over past visits, to other places, when things didn't work out so well. It will be fine, she tells herself. I'm going to trust Ali. Above all, Ali hates the constant suspicion. Yes, there was cause enough for suspicion before with the drugs. And yes, what has brought her here after all – a three a.m. phone call telling you that your daughter is screaming around the place in the middle of the night, in her nightie with no shoes on: who wouldn't be inclined toward a little curiosity, to say the very least? A little concern? Still, that moist *mwah* of her daughter's lips on her forehead, lingers on.

With a lighter heart, she climbs the stairs. The awful kitchen does not seem quite so terrible. She has seen Ali in

Grace and Grace in Ali and herself in both of them. Slowly, slowly, one day at a time. Hour to hour. She will make this house relinquish its secrets.

Nick lies in candlelight. Nell's eyes quickly sweep over peeling rosebud wallpaper, the brass bed with one leg propped on a pile of books, the drawn, fusty curtains. His head is shrunken, propped up against soiled pillows, almost lost in the creases. Although she's been warned, it is hard not to exclaim aloud at his atrophied state. Thick, dark wiry hair is now sparse and frosted with white. Deep furrows lay tracks across his forehead. Long grooves along his cheeks as well, raised conspicuously by the smile he's attempting. His teeth look too big for his mouth. Two pinpoints of light emanate where his eyes should be, so far back in his head that she has to move closer just to see them.

'Hello Nell.' He shuffles up along the pillows. 'Gosh, this is a turn-up for the books.'

He has not adopted Ali's Irish burr. For some reason his modulated, Oxford graduate English, sounds quaint, stagey here.

'Nick.' Nell moves closer, easing her buttocks onto the bed beside him. She has to crane round to speak, but there is an advantage: she can turn away from time to time on the pretext of rubbing her neck or settling her spine.

'I look shocking, don't I?' Nick smiles. 'You needn't pretend.'

'I can't lie,' Nell responds. 'How long is this going on?'

'Me? Ill, you mean?' He coughs and spits into a basin. 'Feels like for ever, to tell you the truth. But to answer your question, a few months now, I'd say.'

Nell swivels, daring a proper examination. Nick has always been a bit of a mystery. In the years he's been with Ali, she's neither cared for him overmuch nor greatly disliked him. He's always been a sort of adjunct to her daughter, just . . . there. For the longest time. For his part, he's never made much of an effort to get to know Nell, either. The rare occasion he's visited with Ali and Grace, he's always been perfectly friendly, genial, easy-going. He's never forced his opinion on anything down anyone's throat. That is, if he's ever had a firm opinion on anything. Meredith liked him well enough. Henri likes him. There has been nothing not to like.

Ali's always maintained that Nick was a star turn at Oxford. Physics. She fell in love with his mind, she said. Nell could only take her word for that. His idle, meandering conversations offered little to support Ali's claim. And that ceaseless, vacant smile. Nothing seemed to get to him. He smiled through Nell's attempts at polite conversation when she first met him. Through her tentative questions, smiled but did not respond. Through her occasional and, yes, she admits now, perfunctory rants about how they were leading their lives, the waste of talents, the aimlessness. Until, years later, she came to realize that it was a heroin glaze and not a smile that had been so impenetrable.

In her heart of hearts, Nell knows that she's probably apportioned too much blame to Nick for Ali's heroin habit, for her wild, abandoned embrace of all things New Agey. She knows she has blamed Nick for Ali's dropping out of Oxford. Shiny English Lit career – splat – replaced by striped, rough wool jumpers, mange-ridden dogs and a cavalcade of caravans travelling the length of Britain. Years of sporadic contact. Of written requests for money with return addresses in obscure little hamlets in Scotland or Wales – an island in the Hebrides once. What were they looking for? What did they hope to find in those bleak outposts?

Finally, the phone call Nell had been waiting for. Ali was preparing to settle down. She was clean, drug-free after a period of methadone, was going to return to Oxford, the city not the college, with Nick. The travelling days were over, although she was quick to point out that those days might be resumed if they didn't take to a settled down sort of life. Jobs? Nell asked. The word threaded every conversation with Ali. Quick intake of irritated breath. Oh yes. Jobs, too. There would be jobs. A light giggle and Nell could see the cast of her daughter's eyebrows up towards Nick, signalling that yet again *that* word had been mentioned.

A period of relative normality followed. Nell was able to keep tabs on Ali and Nick through her aunt and uncle in Oxford. In general the bulletins were hopeful. Indeed there were jobs. A plethora of them. Ali seemed to pick them up as other people pick up their clothes in the morning. There was always some boss giving her grief, insisting she conform to some silly set of rules. Conforming was not Ali's strongest suit. Then the call to say that she was pregnant. The real surprise was how long that call took in coming.

Nell went to Oxford for the birth. It was a long home labour, Ali refusing painkillers because of the fear of instant addiction again. Nell paced the floorboards with her; there was little else she could do. Ali refused to be touched, she didn't even want a back rub. She was very frightened. Her eyes round as plates with pain and astonishment when contractions racked her body. *Why didn't you tell me?* It looked to Nell as if she were silently accusing her. If you really told your daughter, Nell thought, the human race would die out.

Ali's suffering brought back vividly the long night in Oxford when she herself was born. Nell was sure her own eyes must have shown the same outraged astonishment. How could it be that you could survive this? She thought she was being cut in two. Her aunt and uncle did all they could to make her comfortable but, like Ali, she couldn't bear the thought of anyone touching her. No more bloody water, no. I *am* breathing. I *am* pushing. There was only one thing she wanted. Her mother.

'You should be in a hospital,' Nell says.

'They can't find anything wrong with me. Besides, I'd rather be here with my girls.'

Nell can hardly bear to look at him. She turns aside and rubs the back of her neck. The room is gloomy and oppressive. She wonders about asking if he'd like the window opened, let in some badly needed fresh air, but decides against. She must be conscious at all times of not stepping on Ali's toes. Nick sees her sideways glance at the stuttering candle.

'My eyes get watery toward the end of the day,' he explains. 'I find candles help.'

'When were you last outside?'

'Oh, this morning. My energy level is highest then. I usually take a walk in the mornings.'

'That's good. Fresh air can't hurt.'

'Nell,' he says, placing splayed hands to lever his body more upright, 'sometimes everything hurts. I can't explain. There isn't one specific pain. More an all-over feeling of — of, well, hurt, I suppose. And with it comes the tiredness. I could sleep for days. I have to force myself to wake, for Ali and Grace's sake.'

'Is there any relief?'

'Oh yes. Sometimes I'm fine for weeks at a time. Ironic, isn't it? Me, with what they used to call the yuppie disease. Of all things.'

Nell inhales a deep breath, blows out her cheeks. Expels.

'Look, Nick, please tell me, I'd rather know up front, are you on something? Is Ali?'

'I knew that's what you'd think. The minute Ali said you were here.'

'And?'

He cranks his torso more upright. Shakes his head. 'No. Well, nothing serious, anyway. Bit of weed. We grow our own in the garden.' This with a hint of pride.

'What else?' Nell is thinking of Ali's jiggling legs, the discursive speech and disjointed movements. Could be speed induced or simply Ali. She was never a still person. Never composed. Always in search of some heightened or, conversely, deadened, reality.

Lying in her bed in Paris, Nell has often thought about her daughter's simultaneous waking up in whichever caravan in whatever town. Ali's eyes blinking in the light of a new day, widening with horror. *Reality!* Reaching for something – anything. *Get me out of here fast!*

Nick has glanced away. Nell waits.

'From time to time,' he falters, 'other stuff. Nothing too heavy. Please don't worry. We're not living some kind of druggy life here, if that's what you think.'

Already Nell is tired of being told what she thinks and what she doesn't think. It's too convenient, the way they use her as a sealant to plug the gaps between themselves. He's looking at her again, with pleading eyes. He's asking that she does not judge him or Ali, yet neither of them would ever consider extending her the same courtesy. Nick has never cared about her opinion before. Something rankles that she can't quite put her finger on. He's being too direct.

But she also sees that he is battle-weary, ground down. Perhaps his new candour is his own cry for help. He looks old and withered. She feels a spur of something she would never have uttered in the same breath as his name before: compassion. He is not the kind of man to inspire compassion; there has been too little of him on show to warrant it.

'What kind of stuff?' Nell presses, before he decides to dry up again.

'She mixes things a bit. I take it you've heard about the other night. Paudie's?'

'Yes. That's why I'm here.'

'It was a silly . . . We tried this mushroom. Ali had a bad trip.'

'I see. And what about a shotgun?'

'A what?' He gazes past her shoulder, puzzled frown furrowing his brow, as if trying to recall some minor forgotten detail. 'Can't help you there,' he says eventually. 'Nell, I'm not proud telling you all this.'

All *what* exactly? Nell thinks. He's just confirming what he knows she knows already. Putting a spin on it so that it looks as if he's being co-operative. Compassion quickly dissipates and she could strike him. Her fist curls around dusty, sateen material of the ancient eiderdown on the bed.

'I shouldn't think you'd be proud,' she says, hating the prim ripple in her voice. She resents the way they seem to enjoy forcing this role on her. Indignant elder, outraged of Paris. For pity's sake, Nick is a thirty-five-year-old man. She makes a decision not to buy into the old familiar song-and-dance act. What of their health, what of their futures, what about responsibilities – Grace? She senses he is waiting, allows the silence to drift around the room.

'Have you met Adam yet?' Nick asks, his face brightening at the name.

'Nope.' This is hard.

'You'll like him. He's been – well, he's been a godsend to Ali and me.'

'Is that right?' Too hard.

'You might meet him later. He usually drops in to say goodnight, see if we need anything.'

Like magic mushrooms, Nell thinks. And yet he did look genuinely glad, if not relieved, to see her. She wipes his slate clean again. She's come into this room carrying too much baggage, bags she knows she wants to drop at anyone's feet but Ali's.

'Don't be too hard on us, Nell. You've always struck me as a very reasonable person.'

'Yes?' She pulls her mouth down. 'Though for a reasonably intentioned person I can behave quite unreasonably at times.'

'The not coming home?'

She nods. His silent inquiry hangs in the air.

'I don't know, Nick. Many reasons. None. You know I've tried to explain to Ali in the past. But there's nothing *reasonable* about how you feel about home, is there? I just let it go on too long, let it become this huge journey I couldn't make. I think we all have to invent a version of ourselves we can live with. Mine happened to be elsewhere.'

'Mine too,' he says quietly.

'Nick—' But her words are eaten up by a scratching at the door.

'It's one of the cats.'

'One of? How many are there?'

'No one knows, really. Except Grace. She hoards the litters. We find kittens all over the place. In the attic, the men's toilet in the bar. For weeks she insisted on cleaning that toilet every morning before she went to school. None of the men had the heart to tell us there was a whole tribe of cats living in there.'

Nell adopts a fond smile, to match his, a slight, enchanted shake of her head. A litter of cats. In the men's toilet. How sweet. And Grace, slopping out every morning. Nell knows what those toilets are like in the mornings. Not pretty. Not wholesome. Not Weetabix.

'I'd better let you rest,' she says abruptly, getting to her feet.

'Nell, we're fine really. Please try not to worry too much.'

'I don't think Ali looks all that fine, Nick.'

'She's tired. What with me like this – and she's desperate to make a go of the bar. I mean, make it something really special. A place people will travel to. It's her dream, you know.'

'I can't see why myself, Nick. But each to his own.' Nell opens the door, and a scabby, mottled cat slithers through. Over her shoulder, she adds: 'If it was up to me, I'd tear this place down, brick by brick.'

'Adam's doing the bar for me. He pitched up,' Ali says happily. She's scurrying around the Aga with her sleeves rolled up. Nell does a quick, hasty check. No tracks. A huge relief.

'Can I hel— do anything?' she asks.

Ali dumps margarine into a pot of boiled potatoes, followed by a stream of milk. She mashes furiously.

'Everything's under control. I'll put the cabbage in with the bacon towards the end. What d'you think? Bacon and cabbage for your first night?' Ali turns, masher aloft, a beam on her gaunt face.

'Lovely.'

'Just sit. Relax.'

Nell sits. Grace sidles over, wiggles her bottom left and right like a duck, settles onto Nell's lap. They play with the Barbie for a while. Grace pretends to be absorbed but her sideways, upended glance is constantly trained on Ali. Her eyes are hungry for her mother.

'Grace, go and ask Adam to give you a bottle of wine for Nan. Tell him one of those nice miniature bottles – whichever costs the most. And a Power's for me while you're at it.'

'Actually, I wouldn't mind a coffee right now,' Nell says.

'Coffee is bad for you,' Grace admonishes, sliding off. 'And so are amphetamines.'

Nell wonders how bad hell can be, if this is purgatory.

The meal is unspeakable. Slices of watery bacon glistening with fat, cabbage drained of colour and taste, potatoes reeking of job-lot margarine. But Ali contentedly watches Nell's every mouthful, which she can ingest only by swilling out her mouth with the cheap Cabernet Sauvignon, which grows less cheap and insipid by the second. Ali sips her whiskey in between bites.

A number of times the curtain has moved a little, with Nell expecting to meet the godsend Adam any minute. But so far he hasn't shown his face. A low, deep voice, muffled by brocade, may have been his.

When they are finished, Nell with mounds of fat stacked neatly on the side of her plate, Ali leaps up, scrapes plates into tin bowls — for the cats she explains. The plates are then heaped high on the existing pile in the sink.

'Let me do those,' Nell says.

'No need,' Ali beams. 'I'll do them all together. In the morning. Talk to us. Tell us what you're up to. Where've you been this year already? No, wait! We'll go into the parlour. Grace, bucket of coal would you, pet?'

It's a long time since Nell heard the word parlour. What her mother used to call the small, one-windowed room off the kitchen. She follows Ali and is very relieved to find this place at least appears habitable. The walls have been painted white, quite recently, too. The old Axminster has been lifted to reveal a sanded and polished wood floor. Pictures and photographs hang on the chimney breast over the original black iron range. Candles and incense line the window-sill. Ali lights them all and sets a match to kindling in preparation for Grace's coal. Patchwork quilts and multi-coloured crochet squares drape a sofa and two armchairs. Low, squat chest of drawers serves as a coffee table.

'This is nice,' Nell says.

Ali looks around proudly. Her face is suffused by lambent candleglow. It adds a rosiness to the waxy pallor, animating her bony face. Nell doesn't confess to it lightly, but she has wished that her daughter were more attractive, at least made the best of her features. She has never known the adult Ali to wear the slightest trace of make-up. It was always the pretty friends at school who accentuated their eyes or shaped their already shapely lips. Ali eschewed embellishments, as if she could see eyebrows raised in disdain, hear a silent chorus: *and when she wears make-up* . . . Still, as though in response to some inner code of her own, she always presented glossy, well-conditioned hair, gleaming teeth. The natural things.

Plain girl's rebuke to the pretty girl's trivial pursuits. Or perhaps plain daughter's nosethumb to pretty mother. With the
travelling, however, came the end of shiny hair, and teeth
that were none too white.

'See? We're not so bad, after all. Eventually we'll get the
whole house done. But it has to be one room at a time for
now.' Ali's voice cuts across Nell's thoughts. 'Sometimes I get
impatient with myself. We're only here two years, and that
first year was a bit, well, confusing for us. I didn't really
mean it earlier when I said I was making a mess of things. I
do have a business to run on top of everything else.'

Business. The proud inflection in Ali's voice catches at
Nell's throat. This is it, big-time stuff for Ali. Instead of
what do you do? – Oh heroin, speed, pretty much anything
I can get my hands on – now it's, Do? I'm in business, a
businesswoman, actually.

Nell feels much of her misgiving, the second-guessing
and suspicions, begin to melt away. She arrived armed with
scepticism. Since she walked through the back porch, she
hasn't been able to stop herself doubting anything Ali or
Nick might say. In her anxious state, she's allowed for every
possibility other than the possibility that they might be quite
all right really, just encountering the quotidian struggles of
life. So Ali still messes with illegal substances from time to
time, but it's not heroin and it's not every day. Nick is
unwell, but he said himself he has weeks of feeling fine.
They're all too thin, but Ali's awful cooking might account
for that. The kitchen is a quagmire but in truth dirt has
never bothered them. And there's a business to run.

She promises herself that she will make no more assumptions. She will accept what they say or choose to tell her,
unless or until their words prove false. She promises to continue

making that promise even as she breaks it. That is the most she can offer for now.

'Tomorrow, you must take me round the bar,' she says, 'show me any changes you've made.'

'Not a lot, really,' Ali says proudly. 'That's the idea, you see. Keep it the way it was when Granny was here.'

'But Hannah—'

'Oh yes, she ran things her way when Granny died. I don't care for a lot of what she did. But to be fair to Hannah, she never wanted to take this place on in the first place. She always felt she was known around here as Agnes's sister. You know, a poor second.'

'She didn't have to take over. She could have gone back to Galway after the funeral.'

'She knew you'd just sell the place.'

'She'd have been right.'

'Anyway, she was happy enough to hold on until I felt ready to take over.'

'You mean you discussed this? When?'

'After Granny's funeral. Here in this room, actually. We had people back for drinks and sandwiches. Everybody was on about what would happen to the place now. It was pretty clear that you weren't interested.'

'When Hannah called to say she'd stay on for a while, she never mentioned anything about it being a stopgap until you took over. She said she didn't have a whole lot to go back to in Galway anyway and it would pass the time.'

'I told her to say that.'

'Why? Why, Ali?'

Ali smiles dreamily into the flaming sticks of wood. 'Because I didn't think you'd take me seriously. It wasn't just a whim, you know. There, I've surprised you.'

'You have surprised me. You're right, I wouldn't have realized how serious this whole thing was with you. Nick's just tried to get that across to me.'

'Nell . . .' Ali pauses. She's hunkered down, closing the glass doors of the small range. Her back is poker stiff. 'If you remember, we weren't exactly on chummy terms after Granny died.'

Silence for a while. Nell studies her daughter's profile. In the warm, rufescent light of the room, there is an intimacy between them which she is loath to fracture by reference to that time. For years they have managed to skirt round it, with the odd barb from Ali being quickly deflected by Nell. Both cognizant of the fact that one day they would have to get to it. Pluck that whole damn episode out to slap the slimy evisceration on the table between them. But they have both been afraid where that might leave them.

'Hannah tried to modernize – too many gadgets, one of those slot-machine thingies, for God's sake,' Ali is saying, signalling the silent truce will weather, for a while yet. 'Well, I threw that out, first day. And she wouldn't do soup or sandwiches, which was a big mistake, so now I have to build that side of the business up again. But we're getting there.'

'I'm impressed. Where does . . . I mean, you know, who . . .?'

'My customer base?'

Customer base. Oh joy!

'Yes. That's exactly what I mean. It was only the odd regular for food in Mammy's day.'

'Aha! This is the thing, you see. This is where I've spotted the potential. People have started using the strand at the bottom of the lane. Yes, instead of the sandy beach further along. It's more private. More sheltered from the wind with the two headlands on either side. They drive down there, practically park in the ditch and then around midday they stroll up for a drink. Then they decide they might as well eat something. Feed the kids while they're at it. I'm thinking of doing chips. Fish and chips, maybe.'

'You'll have to get new equipment,' Nell ventures.

'I *know* that.'

'Where d'you suppose Grace has gone for those coals?'

'Oh, she'll have stopped off at the bar to pester Adam, no doubt. She's crazy about him.' Ali smiles, stretches languidly into a yoga posture. 'I think it's her first crush, you know. She goes all limp and watery when he's around. Don't say anything, though, or she'll bite your head off. She's very sensitive where he's concerned.' She looks guiltily toward the door. Grace stands there with the heaped coals, scowling at her mother. She deposits the bucket with a resounding clang just inside the room and stomps off. Ali pulls a face to Nell and shovels the coal into the range.

'C'mon, we'll do your room.'

They climb upstairs, Ali stops to murmur something to Nick. Nell slips ahead to an offshoot of stairs which leads to a small landing with two doors. One leads to the attic via vertical open-tread wooden steps, the other leads to her mother's old room. She stands for a moment, her hand encircling the original black doorknob. She wants to be inside, placed, before Ali joins her. A quick inhalation and the door springs open.

The overhead light is on, throwing a pink, surreal cast round the room from the fringed satin shade. Ali has already deposited her bags and thankfully opened the sash window, but the air is stuffy and dustridden nonetheless. Sheets and blankets lie folded in a neat pile on the horsehair mattress.

Over by the window stands a fifties dark oak dressing table with triptych mirrors, central with two smaller wings. A velveteen, tasselled stoolbox. Nell knows the lid pulls up for storage. There is a matching tallboy chest in another corner, blocked-up cast-iron fireplace facing the bed and a fifties wardrobe with one scrolled doorknob missing. The old flowery carpet has been lifted, but the wood floor underneath is in poor condition. Otherwise, the room is as she remembers. As it was, when she saw it for the last time.

She eyes the bed with trepidation.

Ali has slipped in. 'She didn't ask for you in the end, according to Hannah,' Ali says quietly, her own eyes focused on the bed. 'I'm not saying that to be hurtful, if that's what you think.'

'Ali, please stop trying to think what I'm thinking.'

'Why? You do it to me all the time.' But there is a mischievous glint in her eye.

Nell nods, wryly conceding the point. They try to lift the mattress but a handhold rips away.

'Look, we'll slide it up against the wall and I'll flip it from there,' Ali says; there is a film of sweat over her top lip. She heaves from the bottom end while Nell hauls from the top. Grunting and whistling through their teeth, they somehow manage to stand the thing almost erect against the back wall. Ali climbs up on the wooden frame, facing her mother.

'Right,' she pants, 'when I say three, we flip it down. One, two, three . . .'

They make one final lift, then push down with all their might, sending the mattress into collapse amidst a cloud of billowing dust and Nell down onto the floor in a sprawling heap along with it. She moves to ease the pain in her buttocks and hears the rip of her black trousers on the blunted top of a nail sticking out of a floorboard. She opens her mouth to cry aloud in surprise, in pain, but finds herself laughing instead. For a while she holds her ankles, rocking back and forth in uncontrollable sobs of mirth.

'For God's sake, Nell,' Ali wheezes, trying desperately to swallow her own laugh. 'Are you all right?' She helps her mother up.

'Fine. Fine.' A rueful glance over her shoulder. 'I've torn my pants. And a cracked fingernail. Otherwise, I'll live.'

'We'll have you looking just like us before you leave,' Ali chuckles.

'Maybe you could fish out a spare pair of dungarees for me.'

'Are you serious?'

'No.'

'Well, they don't come in black, anyway.'

They make the bed in happy silence. The linen feels crisp, the blankets are soft and reasonably new. Ali has covered the mattress with a clean, quilted cover. Nell looks up and catches Ali's appraisal.

'You look nice,' Ali says, shyly.

'Do I? Thank you, darling.'

'I like the hair colour. It's more subtle, I think.'

'That'll be the extra grey. I don't need to add so many highlights any more.'

Their fingers lightly brush as they pull the counterpane up from the middle. A tingle of electricity shoots up Nell's spine.

'There.' Ali straightens. Gazes around to check what might be missing. 'I'll get you some flowers from the garden tomorrow. I planted when we came first and you wouldn't believe what we've had all year.'

'Is it all you thought it would be? You're happy here, Ali?'

'Oh this is it. I'm home.'

Nell looks at her. There's no doubting her daughter's sincerity: the grey eyes gleam with conviction.

'Funny that,' Nell says, making and breaking steeples with her fingers. 'I always felt a stranger here.'

'Yes. I know.'

'How? Did I say? I don't remember thinking that before.'

'You didn't say. Granny did. She knew how you felt.'

Before she can ask any more, Ali casts Nell a blistering smile before she leaves to let her mother gather herself, as she puts it. The smile lingers aroma-like in the room for a while, reminding Nell of the child her daughter once was. The little girl who flung herself into her mother's arms in the playground after school. Ali had curls then and sparkling, animated eyes, a smattering of freckles across the bridge of her nose. Nell would watch her for minutes before showing herself. Even then, she seemed somehow set apart from the other girls. A serious child, with a distracted air, worried little frown creasing her brow. She always looked like someone who'd forgotten something and couldn't for the life of them remember what that thing was. Taut frame alive with repressed energy which seeped out through twisting of curls over and over again round a nail-bitten finger, bony legs which jittered constantly.

Then the smile. Her whole face alight as she ran to Nell. A flashing beacon descending upon her. A sense of completion, of a part of her own body returning as she scooped the anxious frame into her outstretched arms, feeling it melt, subside into a rare stillness which evaporated as soon as the feet were on the ground again. They would walk in silence for a while, just swinging hands. For all the world like fond sisters. And Nell would absorb the other mothers' faces, knowing that they must feel the same for their children, yet wondering how that could be possible. How could there be bad things in the world if there was so much goodness, so much joy, each day, unfailingly, in one playground? Gazing down at Ali's pale, upturned face, there were times when Nell could have sworn that she was reinventing love.

She sighs and sits on the side of the bed. It's not something she's looking forward to, sleeping between these sheets. A bed which last contained her mother. She pulls up Henri's number on her mobile, then cancels. There's too much going on in her head to talk to him now. In the morning, after a walk, after her initial onslaught on that ghastly kitchen, once she is in motion, following a clear line, she will be able to feign chirpiness. She will be able to feign a degree of contentment that she is glad to be home. Finally.

Already she is planning the days. She will start with the kitchen. That should keep her busy for the longest time. She can feel her hands scrubbing; the prospect fills her mouth with saliva. Then she'll tackle Grace. Those fleabites, the poor little thing. As for the hair, doubtless that is its own nature reserve. She's always spent the first few days of any visit from Grace delousing her granddaughter, to Ali's amused irritation. Fleas, dirt, lice, these are natural phenomena to Ali. There are such huge things wrong with the world. While she cannot but agree, privately Nell feels equally certain that the huge things could be tackled with a greater measure of efficacy with a clean scalp and rash-free skin.

The bar can remain their own business. Nell has no notion of touching that. But the back porch – No, she stops herself. She won't do any of these things. She will remember that she is a guest in her daughter's house. If asked to do something, that's another matter. The head lice? Yes, she'll have to tackle them. God yes. But not immediately. She must glide sideways into things, so that Ali may only notice out of the corner of her eye.

The door is slightly ajar and a sweet, high, woody scent drifts into the room. Nick smoking a spliff in his and Ali's bedroom. Nell closes her eyes. No, not even the head lice. She will not not not interfere. Not in any way, shape, form or manner. All she will do is unpack her own things.

Her hands are on the drawer knobs when it occurs to her that Agnes's clothes may very well be still inside. She'd rather not, at least not yet, but she's got to put her own things somewhere. But the top drawer is empty. Not alone empty, but lined with floral-scented paper. Again, she has the peculiar feeling that Ali has been expecting her. Expecting someone, at any rate. The other four drawers prove empty and lined, too.

She starts to put her folded clothes away. The lining paper in the bottom drawer is slightly puckered; it's been laid out over a small tube of some description. Nell peels it back and extracts a blue lipstick case. Almond Frost – Agnes's colour. Nell holds it for a moment, remembering the familiar navy-blue tubes in convenient spots all over the bar, kitchen, upstairs bathroom. Even with a hairnet and curlers, Pond's cold cream slathered all over her face, there was always pink lipstick on her mother's mouth, Afton Major dangling from a corner. Nell pulls the cover free, unrolls the stick and immediately puts a hand to her own mouth in a shock of recognition.

Just as a mother knows all the secrets her grown-up child cannot remember, a mother's lipstick confirms her own replication. Here in her hand, though she has travelled miles, lived apart, thinks she has evolved into an entirely different person, lies proof that she has not, in fact, travelled very far. The pink stick has precisely the same curved indentation as a dozen lipsticks lying around her own apartment in Paris. Untouched towards the bottom, a carved-out smooth centre where it glided across the lower lip, fuller at the top again, with a pointed edge where the tip picked out a bow shape. Exactly as Nell applies her own.

She reaches into her handbag and pulls out a ridged, gold-coloured tube. Unrolls the stick, holds both lipsticks up to confirm. The same. Precisely. She hesitates for a second, then pops her mother's into a side panel in the handbag.

Outside, the sky is the colour of fading bruises. It stays light here much later than in Paris. Thoughts of her mother have set off a melancholia in the pit of her stomach. She aches for her apartment, for Henri, for Lulu. For a disconcerting moment, it feels as though she has come to the end of a film, to find herself alone in the theatre, watching the credits.

Daddy-long-legs fling themselves against the window-panes. The outside ledge is crispy with their fallout. She watches their ghoulish entwinings as they weave back and forth across glass. Queuing up to die.

A movement down below in the backyard catches her attention. A tall, lean man rolls a beer barrel. He stops, as though suddenly conscious of her eyes, turns, looks up. For a few seconds he stands there, his face in shadows. Nell gleans an idea of him. Dark, perhaps curly hair, a pointed jaw. She thinks his lips may be peeled back in a smile, thinks she sees gleaming teeth. A hand lifts into the air, casually, drops again. Her presence has been marked. Then he turns and rolls the barrel into the house.

There is no rational explanation for it – he was neither threatening nor provocative – but the moment he turned and fixed her with eyes she could not see, a searing flush erupted over Nell's body and face, and the back of her neck felt prickly with unease. Though he has long vacated the space, she continues to stare at where he stood. Adam. Willing her mind to construct the parts of him that remained in shadow. So that when she does meet him, in light, she will be ready for him.

A loud cry from Grace, downstairs, catapults that moment forward. Nell stands, rigid. Her head cocks to the side, ears straining. Maybe it was a fall. Silence for moments again. Then 'No, no, no!' Grace's cry carries up, water-clear. 'I don't want to!'

Nell's legs cover the room in a few strides. The door swings shut behind her.

CHAPTER FOUR

'The Lord is my shepherd; I shall not want. He maketh me to lie down in green pastures: he leadeth me beside the still—' Ali's voice stops abruptly. 'C'mon, Gracie, stop fidgeting. What's next? He restoreth my what?'

'I don't know and I don't care.' Grace shifts in her chair. Her voice is sullen. But it lacks the stridency that impelled Nell from her bedroom.

She stands at the top of the stairs, holding her breath, glad she didn't tumble head over heels into what is clearly a simple psalm lesson. But psalms at Grace's age? Since it's soon to be her holy communion year – Nell makes a quick reckoning – wouldn't Hail Marys and Glory be to the Fathers be more appropriate? And that old-fashioned language – maybe there is a post-modern twist, some sort of anachronistic joke, retro-religion, Nell can't access for the moment. Certainly, hard-core Bible was the last thing she'd anticipated. Nell sits quietly on the top step, careful not to make a creak, no easy feat on these stairs. She tucks her down-turned hands under her bottom. This is a wind-up, she decides. Ali's idea of a Welcome Home joke.

'He restoreth my soul: he leadeth me in the paths of righteousness for his name's sake. Yea, though I walk through the valley of the shadow of . . .?'

'Mama, Nan is here. Can't we take a night off?'

Despite her best efforts, an unmistakable groan of wood gives Nell's presence away. She quickly takes a few steps down, smiling lightly over the bannister rail.

'This brings me back,' she says. 'Is it a song?'

'No.' Ali glances up. 'It's a psalm.'

'I know. But I thought Grace might be learning it as a song. You know, *The Lord's my Shep-herd* . . .' Nell's attempt at the hymn fades away.

'She's learning it as a psalm.' Ali frowns.

'Oh.'

'I will fear no evil: for thou art with me; thy rod and thy staff they comfort me.' Ali intones by rote, her eyes off the text, gazing upwards to the cracked ceiling. Nell notices the Irish books lined up for the next lesson. A page open in an exercise book, shows Ali's spidery scrawl.

'I thought I might as well learn, alongside Grace,' Ali says, closing the pages.

'Rather you than me. It's a hard language, Irish.'

'Can you speak it, Nan?'

'Pog mo theoin,' Nell laughs. 'Years of learning and that's all that comes to mind.'

'Kiss my ass,' Grace translates with a giggle. 'Even Mama knows that.'

Nell steps past them and pours a glass of water from the Belfast sink's single faucet, conscious of Grace's plaintive gaze lasering two holes at the base of her skull in an attempt to be rescued. Nell stares out the window, a smile twitching the corners of her lips.

'Thou preparest a table before me in the presence of mine enemies,' Ali continues, a salty tang to her voice.

'Thou and thine,' Nell chuckles. 'God, I thought they'd be done with all that.'

'Yes, well.' Ali shrugs.

'Holy communion next year, Grace.' Nell settles on a sideways approach to this religious tutorial business. 'Shouldn't it have been this May? Seeing as you were seven?'

'I wasn't ready. App-arr-ently,' Grace mutters, throwing her mother a filthy look.

'Will you wear white?'

'I won't make much money if I don't.'

'If you stand in the bar with a hee-uuge holy face on you, you'll make a fortune.'

'Nell! Don't encourage her,' Ali laughs.

'Is that what you did, Nan?' Suddenly Grace is all ears.

'Indeed. And Bridget before me.'

'Who made the most money?'

'I did, 'cause of a little trick I made up. Which I'll pass on to you, if you like.'

'I like.'

'Well' – Nell pulls up a chair – 'at the start of the day, the dress is all white and perfect while you're standing there, hopping from one foot to the other.'

'Yeah. Go on.'

'And you can't look as if you're out there for money. Though everyone will know that you are anyway. You've got to look as if you've been sent out there, by your mother, to be admired. And you're tired. As the day goes on, God, you're so tired. And this is the trick: you've got to spill something on the dress. A mouthful of Coke should do it, down the front of the perfect dress. And you keep rubbing away at it. Your beautiful dress, ruined. You're heartbroken. Oh devastated.' Nell pulls a mournful face. 'You'll look to your mother. Mama, will this stain ever come out?'

'I like it,' Grace says. 'What you're saying is, they'll feel so sorry for me that they'll give me extra money.'

'Worked for me.'

'Didn't Bridget have any tricks?'

'Bridget didn't need tricks, Gracie.' Nell tickles a finger under her granddaughter's pointed chin.

'Right. If this lesson in extortion is over?' Ali interjects before an enthusiastic Grace can root about for any more lessons in manipulation.

'Back to Art and Fart.' Grace erupts into a fat cackle.

'Grace!' Ali smothers a grin, taps her daughter's knee. 'Cop on.'

'Thereoff and Smirnoff.' Grace explodes.

'All right all right. Joke over. You're just being silly now.'

'Thee and pee. Ver-ily, I say unto ye,' Nell offers, delighting in Grace's lavatorial guffaw.

'Nell! Don't do this!'

'What? What am I doing?' Nell is disturbed by Ali's agitation. Suddenly the easy banter is over and the air is charged with distressed molecules. Her daughter is standing, trembling violently.

'You're mocking me.'

'You? Oh, Ali, I'm not. I just thought—'

'You just thought you'd make me look a fool, didn't you? Well I—'

'Fool, cool, rule, tool, school,' Grace chants.

'Stop it, Grace!'

'Light, right, shite,' Grace bawls. She pulls away from Ali's restraining hand.

The molecules bounce back and forth across the room so rapidly that Nell's head spins. Grace's forehead has contorted into a fixed knot, her knobbly legs stepping back in half-hearted retreat. Her eyes send out hot pulses of silent accusation. Whatever this is about, it's not psalms. Ali pursues. Nell tries to place herself between them but Ali sweeps her to the side, reaching once more for Grace.

'Grace! Carry on like this and—'

'Bright, tight, fight—' Grace hollers, her face engorged with blood, angry veins standing out on the side of her out-thrust neck. This has erupted out of nowhere. Like an electrical storm. Molecules whizz over their heads, crackling, colliding, too densely packed for a simple pulling of the plug.

Before Nell can make another attempt at distancing them, Ali cries out, lunges, and makes a grab for Grace's shoulder. She loses her footing, stumbles and the hold turns into a shove instead. Grace staggers back, falling into her chair, which collapses sideways under the pressure, toppling her to the floor with an ugly crack as her elbow hits the terracotta tiles.

'Oh, Grace, darling.' Ali runs to pick her baby up but baby rises, spitting fury, angrily beating back her mother's caresses.

'Keep away from me!' Grace howls. Tears glint in her eyes but she is too enraged to unleash them just yet. 'I hate you. I hate you!'

With the velocity of a bullet, Grace is up and launches herself head-first at Ali. It's all happening so fast that Nell's eyes can barely make out who owns which limbs in the tangled frenzy. Until an extra pair of hands suddenly enters the fray, cleaving them apart with the cool precision of a machete.

'Enough!' A male voice resonates, then calmer, more soothingly, he repeats the word until a stunned silence descends on the kitchen, broken only by gasps for air.

Ali and Grace maintain a distance as Adam stands between them, a hand raised in both directions. It is clear from his stance that he is familiar with this routine. Moreover, it is clear that the last word rests with him. And, now that she has time to draw a ragged breath, it is clear to Nell where his power comes from. He is quite simply the most beautiful creature she has ever encountered.

He looks in her direction, a patient, enigmatic smile drawing his lips back to reveal a row of perfectly even, ivory teeth. The effect against sandalwood skin is startling. He is no stranger to this effect. Eyes, pinned on her now, are a fretwork of colour, browns and greens merge like tweed weftage, a nimbus of tawny ochre round the dark pupils. Tanned skin is smooth, a hint of oil over high cheekbones. Two long grooves from the tip of the protuberant bones to the corners of his mouth accentuate a smile which is at once candid yet intimate. A touch too broad for someone she's just met. His mouth closes but the smile lingers on curved lips. It looks as if he's suddenly found his way back into a daydream they disturbed momentarily. The look of a man two places at once.

He wears his hair longish, fingers of fringe swept casually across his forehead, curling up at the nape of his neck. Women would pay a fortune for the natural sun highlighted effect of burnt red streaks lifting an otherwise darkly auburn mane. He is what any man would wish to see of his own reflection. For that matter, with the slightest of tweaking, a softening here, rounding there, any woman too. If prototype Adam looked half so good, Nell could see why Eve turned her back on Paradise.

Livid molecules subside, slide down peeling walls, settle once more into a restive silence somewhere around their ankles. Ali and Grace stand a touch shame-faced, avoiding each other's eyes. Adam takes a step back, lowering his arms.

Peace reigns.

'Nell,' he says, extending a hand. 'Adam.' English accent, unplaceable, could be anywhere south, though nothing like as public-school as Nick's.

She takes his hand, a quick perfunctory pump, making sure that she releases first. The hand feels calloused and nicked. Warily, Nell elects to nod instead of speaking. Where to place herself with him? A difficulty compounded by the squall that has just taken place and her own impotence throughout.

'Gracie.' Ali's voice is still unsteady. 'Bed now, darling. Please, no more arguing for tonight.'

'But, Mama . . .'

'C'mon. I'll take you.' Adam hoists a squealing Grace onto his shoulders. Under his long, baggy sweater, Nell forms an impression not so much of bones moving in synchronicity, rather of mercury undulating, pulsating beneath skin.

'I'll take her,' Nell says, a touch more sharply than intended. 'My first night after all,' she adds, reaching up for Grace.

'Whatever.' Adam shrugs, winding Grace snake-like around his body until her feet land on the floor.

'Can you do the bar for another while, Adam?' Ali asks. Nell thinks she looks ashen and unwell.

'Sure.' He moves out as though separating squalling cats is all in a night's work. Nell takes pains not to watch in case he turns suddenly and catches her gaze.

Grace heads for the stairs. In an access of remorse, she turns and runs back to Ali, throwing repentant arms round her mother. Ali snorts back a sob and returns her embrace. Nell can only wonder at all this emotion both displayed and repressed. Already she is past exhaustion. Is this their nightly routine? It's hardly surprising they're both so inordinately thin.

Upstairs, Grace goes in to see her father. The knot has disappeared from her forehead and she appears lightened, as though relieved of a burden of conflicting feelings. Out the other side now; purged. Nick whispers, a pretence at a scold. He's heard the row. The room is muzzy and sweet-scented. Cool blue drifts of cannabis smoke spread out in layers from wall to wall, shifting shapes, blurring fixed edges. A foggy glow around the candle flame melts his face into shadow. Nell searches for definition, for something concrete but, like so much else since her arrival, there is only that continuing sense of circuitous mutation, things morphing even as she looks at them. Perhaps the secret lies in glancing slightly to the side to make the object of attention come into focus, like a faint star emerging on the periphery of vision. Nell tries this with Nick, her eyes resting to the left of his head, on the crumpled pillow. The cloudy features resolve and she is seized by a spasm of pity for him. What she sees is a helpless love for his daughter. And an unmistakable sadness.

He smiles with the too-big teeth, as if to say: they've been at it again. Nell smiles back, taking in his pre-rolled spliffs for the night ahead. She's almost too tired for sleep, so determines to come for one later, to make sure she does.

Grace is clinging to her father, her head nestled into the side of his neck. He draws her hands down and kisses her knuckles. There's a little murmur between them which Nell can't catch. Then Grace leaps to her feet, grabs one of the three cats in the room, and swishes out, beckoning Nell to follow.

Grace's bedroom lies at the top of another little offshoot of stairs, above Nell's offshoot. When Nell opens the door, a scrawny cat flies out by her legs; she swallows a scream.

'A lot of cats, Grace.'

'Too many,' Grace concedes but not with any conviction. She often readily repeats the words of adults, even when she disagrees with their content. In fact, Nell has often considered that one of the problems between Ali and Grace is that they both want to be mother.

The room is thankfully a little girl's room, complete with cuddly toys, pink wallpaper, a couple of dolls in one corner. Barbie duvet looks none too clean and a kitten poking its head out from under the single bed doesn't augur too fantastically. However, it's pretty much an average seven-year-old's den. Nell isn't sure exactly what she was expecting, or for what she was bracing herself. Something out of Dickens, maybe.

'Sorry about earlier, Nan,' Grace says, taking care her back is turned as she slides into jimjams. Her voice light as sifted flour.

'Can't be easy learning psalms.' Nell silently heels a couple of kittens out through the door, keeping her voice just as aerated.

'Mmm. You get used to it.'

'Funny. I thought by now things would be different. In school, I mean. I didn't mean to interfere, Grace. I'm sure Mama is only trying to follow the curriculum.'

'The what?'

'It's what they set out, for you to learn. At school.'

'Oh yeah.' Grace turns, her face blank and devoid of expression. Then a hint of panic. 'Will you stay a long time, Nan? Will you?'

'As long as you want me to, darling.' Nell takes the scrawny sack of bones in her arms. Grace squeezes hard for a moment, then hauls the covers back and jumps into bed.

'How much do I love you?' Nell bends over for a kiss.

'Up past the big bang and back again.'

'Beyond all . . .?'

'Beyond all time and space and everything.'

'Night night, sweetheart.' Nell makes a cross of kisses: forehead, cheeks and finally chin. Thrilled that, every time, Grace remembers their nocturnal mantra.

'Nan? D'you believe in God?' The question shoots out in Grace's manner, the big things slipped out in a sideways dart. Nell hesitates a moment, strokes her granddaughter's conker fringe to the side.

'We'll talk about that over the next few days, okay?'

''Kay.' A pregnant pause. 'Because Mama says you don't, and that could be a problem.' The knot is back on her forehead. Nell smooths it loose with her fingers.

'I'll be careful what I say. Thanks for the warning.'

Nell opens the door to leave and a kitten slips back in. Outside, she stands with her hand on the doorknob for a while, listening to Grace's murmurings to the cats. When there is silence, she goes back downstairs.

Ali is busy, fussing around, tidying up, as if she spends every evening clearing the decks. Her embarrassment about earlier is palpable. 'I'm going to have to leave you for a spell,' she says in a cheerful way. 'I have to take over from Adam.'

'I was thinking of going to my room for the night,

anyway,' Nell says. 'I've brought my laptop. I'll be able to work while I'm here.'

'Good, good.' Silence, then, 'Gracie okay? Asleep d'you think?'

'She talked to the cats for a while, but she was quiet when I left.'

'It's difficult. I want her to fit in, Nell.'

That is as much as Ali elects to offer for now and Nell doesn't push.

'I thought I might ask Nick for one of those joints he's rolled,' Nell says. 'Would he mind?'

'Why would he mind?' The first genuine grin from Ali since Nell came downstairs. 'It's not as if we're short. It's our own stuff, you know. Top quality. We could sell it and make a small fortune.'

'Is that right?' Nell murmurs. There's nothing else to say so, she smiles and heads upstairs once more. Never in all her life has the prospect of her white-walled apartment – linear chrome-gleaming kitchen, big, wide, sumptuous bed with its cream, squashy duvet and broderie anglais, feather-stuffed pillows – seemed so outstandingly attractive, as right now.

The joint does make her sleepy, but not sleepy enough to feel confident she will have safe dreams. Nell lies in bed, head resting back on the upraised wings of her arms. She's listened to muffled voices head out into the night air from the pub below, the chinking of glasses being stacked, light switches flicking off. The tread of Ali's footsteps upstairs and into the room below, low murmur of exchange with Nick. Then silence.

A silence broken by bubbles of air spluttering through pipes. Ticking as the house winds down for the night. Some erupting louder than others. Hot water, restless and seething in the cistern. Floorboards creaking in the attic above her head. Tick, tick, tii–iick, go the pipes. The house is whispering. A little, ineffective breeze tries to rattle window-panes, gives up, goes away, returns and manages to tremble glass, just a touch. She is here, in her mother's room, listening to sounds so familiar she has forgotten them. So familiar, they have integrated into a tapestry of memory so that their sudden recollection is almost brutal in its poignancy, in the way the peal of a church bell can evoke a wedding or a birth; individual moments spliced into vivid compression, so that the moments relived, how-ever fleetingly, are more potent by far than the originals. Or the suddenly happened-upon handwriting of someone long dead can make the finality of their departure seem absurd, if not debatable. How much of us is of the moment, she wonders, how much tinted by all the moments past?

Around three, when she has almost slipped into a hazy, smoke-induced sleep, Grace creeps into the room. Nell isn't sure at first if the child is fully awake. She peels back the bedcovers and the little ghost wafts in. She curls into Nell, bony rump resting against Nell's abdomen. There is a constant clicking which signals that Grace is sucking her thumb. Nell hates herself for doing it but the thought of head lice makes her sweep her own hair high onto the pillow. She leans across and sketches a kiss on her grand-daughter's cheek. The face is spectral, ethereal in the room's dim light.

'Grace?'

'Yeah. And everythink,' Grace manages without removing her thumb.

They sleep. Breaths calibrating into unconscious rhythm.

Grace is gone in the morning, when Nell wakes. She checks the time on her mobile and calls Henri. He is outside with the vineyard manager. Across time difference and distance, his voice is silkily calm. Nell stretches back, wiggles her toes. She tells him briefly about yesterday, concentrating mainly on mechanics – the journey, arrival, Ali and Grace's reaction. She keeps it light and airy.

'So it's okay,' he says, knowing full well from her voice that it is very much not okay.

'Yes. And you?'

'I'm fine. Lulu sends her love.'

They talk for a while about inconsequential things. Lulu's diet: Henri maintains the little dog is not half so fussy as Nell makes out. Nell asks about the plans he's drawing up with the manager. When there is nothing left to say on safe subjects, Nell presses the phone to her ear.

'Nell? Have I lost you – are you there?'

'I'm here. Just listening to you breathe,' she smiles.

'How strange is it all? Really?' he asks.

'Very.' She pauses. 'But then I always knew it would be.'

She wants to ask if he's spoken any further to Lucienne, wants him to bring the subject up of his own accord; but there's a lengthy silence. Was that an impatient sigh from him?

'Well,' she says.

'Look, I have to go now,' he says, a sudden note of irritation in his voice. 'I'll call you later.'

He's severed the connection, cutting across her ''Bye, then.'

She dresses, black jeans and a charcoal cotton sweater. Throws her head forward to brush her hair from the roots, already imagining her scalp as unwelcome host to the mother of all lice parties. She wants to scrub her body from head to toe, but decides to take a walk first. Why should she bring up the subject of his wife? She never asked him to leave her. If he's having second thoughts, that's his problem. She feels unreasonably, irrationally angry at him, yet knows that on the face of it he's done nothing wrong. He's entitled to feel a little impatient, a little disappointed.

Beads of condensation cling to the window-panes. Outside, green fields look as if they've been mainlining chlorophyll. High, white, endless sky spills technicolour light over everything. The technicolour of her dreams. She half closes her eyes to mute the onslaught of colour.

There are no signs of life from Ali and Nick's room as she passes. In the kitchen, an emptied bowl of cereal on the table. It rests there like an accusation. So Grace gets herself up and out to school each morning. She adds the bowl to the mounting pile in the sink. Another thing to tackle later. The brocade curtain separating the bar from the kitchen is drawn back, letting in stale fumes. She takes a step toward the opening, decides against, heads out through the back porch instead.

Clean, crisp air is a welcome relief. Above, the sky is a nacreous white, tinged in palest blue. The good weather is set to hold a while longer. A shaft of warm yellow leans over the roof from the east. Though her shoes are not up to it, she elects to walk down the fields in the way she used to access the sea as a child. She can smell salt on a cool, gentle breeze.

It ruffles Ali's autumnal flowers, weaves in and out through the small vegetable patch that lies to the right. Tucked in a corner, shielded by a rush screen, the tops of a tall marijuana crop lean sideways. The flower borders are neat and well cared for, almost suburban. Clearly, Ali loves her garden and lavishes attention on it. It's almost as if the pretty marguerites are smiling a welcome at Nell. She smiles back. Good good. Garden. Good.

Further along, the land becomes tufted and unkempt. Patches of rock jut up through grass – once the ships or hospitals or shops she made of them with Bridget. Were they always so low to the ground? She used to think the clumps of granite towered above them like cliffs. Even the fields look small. They used to be prairies. How big can she have grown, to make her past so small?

She lifts a leg over a dry-stone wall at the end of the first field. At the bottom of the next field, which falls at a steeper gradient, lies Adam's caravan. It is small and rounded and was once white. A battered, rusty car stands at some distance, as though disavowing any knowledge of the caravan. Behind, tethered to a stunted, wild apple tree, is a piebald pony. Its head turns to watch her approach with little curiosity.

Nell bears right, reckoning on the old break in the ditch still being there to give her access to the lane running down to the sea, parallel to these fields. A movement in the caravan catches her eye. Adam stands washing from a bucket of water with his back to her. He is naked, the top of his buttocks just visible above the window line. A lean body, sinewy with ripples of movement beneath smooth skin. Again she gains an impression of liquidity rather than solid bone informing his movements. This mercurial fluidity lends a careless, casual grace to the way one arm extends above the

tousled head, while the other hand slides a sponge or a
bunched-up cloth down from raised wrist to the scooped-
out pit beneath his shoulder. Just above the swell of buttocks,
there is an old shiny circular scar in the hollow of his back.

Flat morning sunlight strains through the mud-splattered
window, throwing one side of his torso into warm, glyptic
relief, while the other is an impressionist canvas, leaving the
eye to fill in what it knows to be there. He is barely over
thirty, in such prime that Nell wonders if she has captured a
moment, a moment he will never know to be recorded,
when he stands poised on the meridian of youth and beauty
before the inevitable, slipping decline into age and mortification. She wonders at that weal on his back, if it isn't where
his tail was removed, for surely only the devil himself could
appear so entirely perfect at this hour of the morning.

No, not a demon, she thinks, her eyes transfixed, as are
her feet, which will not move on despite her best efforts.
There is something intrinsically and magically innocent
about his pose. Perhaps it is the tossed hair, that childlike
just-awake quality. Or perhaps it is simply the unselfcon-
scious movements of a person unaware that he is being
watched, the concomitant vulnerability it lends them. While
she is a thief stealing glances. She has to remind herself of
Paudie's words on the phone, the warning he was trying to
convey. There's a danger of falling into that most human of
traps: imbuing physical beauty with inherent moral goodness.

Adam bends sideways for a towel and the spell breaks.
Nell quickly moves on, fearful that he may have realized
her presence and may call to her. She clambers over the
crossed long limbs of two alders, into the lane beyond. The
road used to be just a rutted track but it is gravelled now. Still

narrow and winding but wide enough for single traffic. A desultory bark from a dog as she passes a gate leading to a single storey white cottage at the bottom of the lane.

It seems like a dead end at a line of wind-torn trees, but there is a curved path through a tangle of brambles, worn and hacked over centuries by human feet and hands. A canopy of flat conifer branches momentarily blocks out the sky overhead. Then the path opens out, there is sky again and a crescent-shaped cove flanked on either side by two pockmarked headlands.

Her feet make the full crunching of horses' hooves over cobbles as she makes her way to the water's edge. On first appearance the smooth, rounded stones are uniformly grey; on closer inspection, they are anything but. It is the muted, pastel effect of infinite tides. Within the water, the true colours show through. Lilacs, yellows, grey marled with veins of white, small ebony stones glistening with silica. Chalky copper pebbles which leave a dust on her fingers. She selects a number of flat, shale-like circles and sends them skimming across the water's surface. They leap obligingly – one, two, three. Where they land, the stones end and there is soft yellow sand as far as the eye can see into ocean.

The air is uncannily still. All the way out to where two black rocks erupt before the unbroken line of horizon, the sea rolls out in a placid, barely rippling rink. So clear and composed, it resembles a lake rather than the great Atlantic. Above, the sky drifts down to meet it, more solid-looking than the sea, spongy, albescent: she is reminded of candyfloss, half expecting to hear a sizzle where licked by glassy water. Seagulls catch an invisible upwind, doling out their mournful cries. Where the slanting eastern sunlight catches their wings, they are transformed into circling silver-foil *M*s.

She breathes in deeply, filling her lungs with the oxygen of childhood itself. Even her blood seems to have thinned, rushing through veins as if in a quickening response to something primal and beyond words. Once, she loved this place, this spot where her feet are planted now, with a girlish ardour. Her entire body is like a sensory board, responding. How could she have forgotten? But you don't really forget, she thinks, you merely submerge.

By her feet, tiny lapping waves make the sound of Lulu's tongue slaking in and out of her water bowl. Nell pulls off her shoes and socks, rolls up the bottoms of her jeans and steps in. The shock of cold makes her scalp tingle. But it is exhilarating. The only thing fresh and discriminate in the past twenty-four hours. Here is sea. She can touch it, wade into it should she so desire. Tomorrow, it may have changed appearance, it may be rough and the colour of smoke, but it will still be sea. Something she can connect with. In a similar fashion, she wonders if by some strange design, with both feet in the water, she isn't connected to all things in the Atlantic. From humpbacked whales, to dark, blind, grey creatures dredging ocean's depths, to another person – somewhere – standing by another country's edge, feet immersed, eyes fixed unknowingly in her direction.

From the corner of her eye, she sees a tall, powerfully built man run over the crest of headland to her left. Nell steps back out of the water, wriggling her toes, watching his approach as she waits for her feet to dry. She squints as he looms nearer. Thinks she can't be right, squints again. Yes. He is black. As he draws closer she surmises he must be over six and a half feet tall. The ends of his loose jogging pants lie closer to his knees than his ankles. Against the soft, pearly sky, which accentuates his darkness, he cuts a powerful if not intimidating figure. She can hear the steady crunch crunch of his trainers over stones. It can't be easy keeping up such an unwavering pace across such a surface.

It occurs to Nell who he must be. Ali has told her of a small nearby hotel having been given over to the state for refugee housing. Croatians and Nigerians, in the main. If he has come from there, and there is little doubt in her mind, he has already run or jogged over ten miles this morning. There isn't a lick of sweat on his brow.

He keeps his eyes fixed firmly on the next headland, as though she is not standing there at all. Nell figures he may be aware that his big-shouldered approach may be somewhat daunting to a lone female on an isolated strand. She feels obliged to let him know that she is isn't worried. Then she wonders why she should feel such obligation. The fact is, he is large and prepossessing. And yes, he does cut a strange and unfamiliar sight in the grey and green landscape. Precisely because he is so unfamiliar. Nevertheless, she makes a grunting, guttural noise as he passes. A hello and goodbye and I'm not afraid, all rolled into one. If he hears, he does not acknowledge. Runs on swiftly until the huge frame appears to glide effortlessly over the next headland. Her eyes train on empty space for a while.

Nell looks into the water again. An oval, smooth stone catches her eye. Pinkish with concentric swirls of cream. For some reason she can't put her finger on, it brings to mind her mother. To do with the day Nell learned to swim, that was it. Her eyes sweep the line of horizon, back and forth.

It was a morning like this, grainy, relaxed sky, the sea shimmering beneath an early-morning August sun. Nell was eight. She sat, not far from where Nell, forty-eight, stands now. Arms tucked around the crook of her knees. Watching as Agnes's powerful forearms cut swiftly across the crescent harbour. She swam every morning before the bar opened for business, throughout Nell's summer holidays. It was as though she took over the entire ocean, cleaving from headland to headland, far out in full tide.

That morning, Agnes came out of the water, shaking spray as usual so that it flung off her black, oily costume like drops from a seal's pelt. Auburn perm tucked solidly under a rubber cap that clung to her scalp and tied under the chin. The rubber compressed her forehead, folding it into concertina layers, practically obscuring the pale blue eyes. She was a formidable figure rising from the sea. Nearly six feet tall, with shoulders like a man's, firm trunk-like thighs beneath the low-cut swimsuit. Usually she emerged and wrapped herself in a towel and a contemplative silence for long periods, mindful of Nell's scrutiny but ignoring her at the same time. But that day her big arms flapped Nell to her as she stood knee-deep, beckoning.

'C'mon,' she said. 'You'll have to learn sooner or later.'

'Not today,' Nell responded.

'No, Nell. I'm not going to indulge you in this any more. You're nearly nine years old. I can't have you not swimming.'

'Mammy, I'm fine. You know I won't go near the water, so there's no need to worry that anything'll happen to me.'

Her mother seemed to wrestle with an internal debate for a second. Her tongue was visible between firmly clenched lips. Telltale fingers tapped against one thigh. Nell knew the signs and began to scramble to her feet.

'Nell,' Agnes commanded. With a few long strides, she covered the distance between them and carried Nell, wriggling and hissing to the water's edge.

'I don't even have on a swimming togs.'

'You've shorts and a tee-shirt on, that'll do fine. Who'll be looking at you, anyway?'

'I'm not going in.' Nell continued to struggle but she was no match for her mother's strength and determination. Agnes waded out, carrying her wriggling daughter in the cradle of her arms. By screaming as loud as she could, Nell hoped in vain that someone from the cottage at the foot of the lane might hear and come running to rescue her.

'Will you whisht,' Agnes said. 'Whisht now.' Her tone softened and she deposited Nell on her feet. The water closed round her waist, so cold it made her gasp.

Agnes settled her hands on Nell's shoulders, bending down to look into her face. 'Trust me, Nell, won't you?'

The plaintive quality in her voice, usually so commanding, so self-assured, caught Nell unawares. She held her mother's eye, then let her own gaze slide out to sea. It was huge and terrifying.

'Nell?' Agnes had turned from her, hunkered down with her hands coming back over her shoulders. Nell looked at the summoning hands, looked at the vast sprawl of ocean again. Her fingers coiled up until Agnes was able to take a firm grip.

'C'mon, pet. C'mon. I've got you.' Agnes murmured soothingly, taking a step further out with every word, Nell splaying out like a wedding train in her wake, until, with a quick hoist, Nell's arms wrapped tightly round her mother's neck and the thick legs kicked back in one powerful surge. They glided forward on the strength of Agnes's backward thrusts, Nell with her eyes squeezed tightly shut.

'Don't let go of me,' she whispered, fearful her mother intended shock therapy for her fear of water.

'I won't. I promise.' Agnes spluttered between mouthfuls of water.

From the shore they must have looked like some strange two-headed beast. Or a mother seal carrying injured calf on the length of her back. Heads bobbing up and down, hardly causing a ripple on the expansive tide.

'Kick your legs hard as you can, between my own,' Agnes gritted.

Nell obliged and their pace increased. Her eyes were open then, little triangular crests of glistening water all around. She swallowed a mouthful of brine and had to concede it wasn't so bad, really. Agnes was trying to laugh in between her own mouthfuls. It must have taken every ounce of her not inconsiderable strength to keep them both afloat. Nell laughed with her and for the first time in what seemed an age but was in reality just under two years, since the day Bridget drowned, she experienced a lightness of spirit, a feeling of pure, prismal joy and she let out a loud, protracted whoop.

When she was certain Nell was fully at ease, Agnes negotiated a turn and slowly, with tiring leg strokes, brought them back to shore. They rested by the water's edge for some time. Content with silence. For both were aware that something big had happened between them. They sipped hot, warming tea from the flask Agnes always brought down, passing the plastic mug back and forth between them.

'Ready now?' Agnes asked, screwing the emptied mug back onto the flask.

Nell nodded. And for the next few hours, regardless of the pub and its opening time, they circled round and round, Nell with her legs kicking back, arms pawing water furiously in front, her mother's arm keeping balance halfway across

Nell's belly. Nell was swimming on her own before she realized the arm had been withdrawn.

'There,' Agnes said. 'It won't be water that takes you from me now.'

Nell slips the pink stone into her jeans pocket, still not entirely certain why it made her recall that day. She gazes around, half expecting to see Agnes's broad rump emerge from behind a towel. Half expecting to see that crooked, equivocal smile on her mother's lips, the one that neither bestowed approval nor denied it; but was always ambivalent to Nell and likewise, or so it seemed at any rate, was always reserved expressly for her.

Halfway along the winding track carved through brambles, she meets Adam. He stands aside but still the path is so narrow that she glides against him momentarily, feeling an ebb and flow of viscous movement as muscles contract then relax beneath baggy jeans and oversized jumper. His smile is perfectly open and affable, as though they meet in this spot every morning. In daylight the tweed eyes are startling, the halo round the pupils distinctly star-shaped. His skin is glossy as though buffed, or exfoliated. A crooked line of stubble along his chin, missed by his razor.

Nell knows she should say something, offer a greeting – they've already met, after all. But she's flummoxed as to what tone to adopt with him. If he poses a threat to her family, she wants him to know that she is aware and she will be a force to be reckoned with. If Paudie has misunderstood things, Adam is just a helpful stranger who has happened to fall into the bosom of a family at a time when they have sore need of him.

'Hello,' she says. That was surely neutral enough.

'Hello,' he responds, lifting his shoulders, dropping them

again. A shy gesture, she thinks; surely he's not that? Yet, the crooked almost pained smile on his lips and the way his eyes are hooded would confirm an impression of shyness, certainly of discomfiture. This does not fit in with her immediate construct of last night.

'Swim?' he asks. She is sure now that he is as desperate for words as she is.

'No, no.' Nell waves a hand; it connects with his arm briefly. 'Just a morning walk. You?'

'I've washed already. But it's such a nice day, I thought . . .' His words trail away.

Nell quickly scans his face. If he does know that she watched him, there's no evidence in sight. She notes he's carrying neither swimming trunks nor towel.

It's as though he's waiting to be dismissed. Nell isn't sure how to move on, either. She wants to touch him, she realizes. It manifests in a tingling at her fingertips. She stares at her shoes and flexes the fingers which itch to reach out toward him. A peculiar, incomprehensible sensation.

Adam makes the first move to break the impasse, and his long sweater catches on a spray of brambles. Mindless of the thorns, Nell grabs the longest spine with one hand, while with the other she pulls his sweater free. She is conscious of pain, but at some distance. Her hand uncoils and there is blood and several thorns still embedded in soft flesh. He reaches for the wounded hand immediately.

Before she can pull her arm back, he bends his head and niftily picks out the thorns with his teeth, spitting to the side each time one is prised free. His grip is surprisingly assured for one so diffident moments ago. They've barely met, yet with one movement she has connected with his teeth, saliva, lips. The moment feels absurdly intimate. Nell watches the silky movement of his hair as it glides forward, then back again. Her free hand lightly touches the top of his head in what seems like a caress, so she turns it into an abrupt push. He steps back quickly, releasing her.

'I'm sorry. Did that hurt?'

'I'm fine.' Her tone is sharp. She tries for something lighter. 'Can't have you eating out of the palm of my hand.'

It falls flat. As though registering an elliptical insult, his eyes flicker with hurt. The look of a small boy who has just had his handmade gift rejected. He takes another step back while simultaneously Nell feels her own body list a touch closer, as if there is some invisible, elastic substance between them, pulling then releasing, then pulling again. Suddenly, almost brutally, he severs the cord, turns his back on her and walks quickly on. Nell watches the swaying of branches and brambles where his movement has disturbed them, until all is still and silent again. Her punctured hand slips into her jeans pocket and curls around the smooth, pink stone. It has a cooling effect. She moves on.

Clambering over the stone wall above his caravan, she notices something she missed on the way down. A notice, coated in plastic, nailed to the trunk of a twisted rowan tree. It's a request for planning permission, signed by Ali, for erection of a single-storey dwelling. Nell glances over her shoulder, gauging. It would be situated roughly where the caravan stands now.

Back at the house, a bleary-eyed Ali moves between the bar and the kitchen, setting up for the day's business. Nick hovers around the Formica table as though uncertain where to place himself. Uncertain, the word that best sums him up,

Nell realizes. Even out of the foggy bedroom, there is a blurred triangularity to his spare frame, like indistinct, distant sails, as though in the blink of an eye he might vanish over the horizon. Along the ashen cords of his neck, an exaggerated Adam's apple rolls up and down; the motion looks painful. He seems taller than she remembers, perhaps because his body looks so scooped out and hollowed. He offers her a quick, watery smile, then concentrates on the contents of his muesli bowl. Each chew has the slow, deliberate appearance of a cow ruminatively chewing cud.

She walks to the sink, trailing her eyes along the terracotta floor. It occurs to her what she's actually doing, what she's been doing since she arrived yesterday. Looking at everything with a vaguely detached air. Fending, blocking, so that every time a familiar item reaches her retinas, she's already prepared for it. She doesn't want to be jolted or startled by any sight or sensation which will inevitably shout *thirty-two years* to her.

But little things strike out of nowhere. The bar of carbolic soap by the sink, the dry surface scored with black gashes. Always carbolic in the kitchen, Knight's Castille in the bathroom. One of the tiles on the floor has a triangular chip missing. She used to worry the remaining tile with the tip of her shoe. The brass rings holding up the curtain, screening off the bar – thirty-one rings, she knows without counting – two more than the corresponding metal-rimmed eyelets. The door of the black Aga: it would still hitch and jiggle a touch in her hand, if she opened it. A spider's web weaving up from the right-hand corner of the tall dresser, clinging to the ceiling. She looks. Yes, of course, there's a new one.

Suddenly, it's like a punch into the solar plexus, the spot

under the chestbone that leaves you winded and gasping for air. She saw how her defence screen had been up yesterday, how she had managed to keep everything at surface level. This was her home. She grew up in this kitchen. Now, when she isn't prepared, it's managed to slice through the suit she's made of her top layer of skin. It's underneath, has always been underneath, buried deep where second skin grows, where second skin deflects whatever the first layer has let in.

'Are you all right, Nell?'

'What? Fine. Fine, thanks, Nick. It's just . . .' She stops, unable to go on. How to explain she feels as though she's just fallen into her own grave? Ali's stopped bustling for a second and is looking curiously at her, too. Then she heads into the bar. Nell follows.

'Oh, while I think of it,' Ali says airily over her shoulder, 'Paudie dropped by to see if you'd arrived safe and sound and if you wanted supper with them tonight. Unless he hears from you, they'll expect you about seven.'

'Fine.' Nell waits to see if Ali's going to get round to asking what Paudie's told her exactly, but she's humming, spraying from a can.

The front door is wide open, letting air circulate round the fumid interior. No punters yet: the first few stragglers won't show until about eleven. Air is draped in the heavy, pungent odour of hops, stale Guinness, cigarette smoke. It is the odour of her childhood, and for a second she wants to cry. There was never a morning she left for school without that granular sourness filling her nostrils. She wonders if it is the same for Grace.

Another scent cuts across: lemon polish from the round table tops which Ali has just polished. Nell stands gazing around in wonder. Ali was right,. Nothing much has been altered from her mother's time, aside perhaps from a couple of new glass refrigeration units behind the counter. At elbow-thrust level, the optics still hang in the same place and in the same order, whiskies all together, vodka, gin at the furthest end. The Formica counter top is studded with black cigarette grooves, brown circles of beer stains, fused now into the surface, a disparate, bedraggled Olympic logo. Panelling facing out to the public remains just a corrugated veneer of shoe-scuffed hardboard. Tall wooden stools rack up alongside the counter, tops grooved into the shapes of bottoms. The floor is grey and concrete. Walls the same peeled yellow as the kitchen. Faded posters advertising dances in nearby halls from Nell's teenage years, retro chic now, no doubt. A few more recent, telling of local amateur dramatic performances. A square of cork with notices pinned all over, offering fishing trips, sightseeing tours, bed and breakfast. A blackboard is new, offering homemade sandwiches and soup. It should come with a health warning, like a packet of fags.

The bar opens through to the small lounge beyond. Just an extension, really, with one enclosed nook where the women used to sit when Nell was very little. Clearly this section has not been used for a long time. The chairs are covered in grimy sheets. In spite of this, Nell can see the loving care with which Ali tends the bar area. However dreadful the kitchen, in here tables gleam, glasses shine, there isn't a trace of dust on any of the knick-knacks lined up above the optics. In here, she keeps house. A couple of signs of progress, though: matchboxes showing the exterior of the pub on the back, matching beermats, a display of chunky candles in fancy black Celtic-style holders.

Nell grows aware of Ali's eager scrutiny. She has to clear

her throat because truly she is feeling more than a little choked.

'What did I tell you?' Ali says with pride. 'Perfectly preserved.'

Nell manages a watery smile. Behind her daughter, tucked into the frame of a mirror speckled with mould, are photographs of Nell's mother at every age. Bridget and Nell, too, from babies upwards until just before Bridget's accident. A couple of faded black-and-whites of her father. Nell moves closer, extracts a photograph of Bridget smiling over her shoulder as she sits at the piano. Judging by the age, it could have been days before she drowned. Nell has not seen this one before. Her eyes scan the empty space over by the gents' toilet where the piano used to stand.

'I'm afraid it fell apart one day.' Ali gestures to the space. 'Hannah tried to move it into the lounge and the whole thing sort of sighed, she said, then the back fell out and the rest just followed. She said it was quite funny at the time because it looked as if it was happening in slow motion. D'you know, I couldn't remember if you played or not. Can you? Did you?'

'No. Bridget was the musical one.'

If who we are to become is already there in childhood images, the Bridget who never became is here in Nell's hand. The jaunty angle of her head, white ribbon slipping halfway down messy golden hair, eyes squinting against the sun but burning with mischief. A face electric with possibilities.

There is her father, Samuel, a tall, lean man with folded arms, standing outside the pub, smiling sheepishly for the camera. Braces holding up trousers that look too baggy. Stark grooves and deep hollows from the emphysema that raddled his still youthful face. He died when Nell was three and sometimes she thinks she can remember his cough behind the counter and around the house. But it must be her imagination. He spent practically the last year of his life confined to his room. When they were both older, Bridget used to taunt Nell with her memories of him, asking her mother, Da really loved tapioca, didn't he, Mammy? Da used to say I could run faster than a seagull can fly, usen't he, Mammy? Of course, Bridget never had any recollections of what Da used to say about his youngest daughter, Nell. So Nell pretended that he used to come to her in dreams, driving Bridget crazy by not passing on whatever deep secrets he'd divulged about heaven. She'd just smile enigmatically: sorry, can't tell, Da made me promise.

Here is her mother behind the bar, sleeves rolled up to her elbows, feigning a smile for the camera. She hated having her photograph taken without her hat on. Whoever was the hapless perpetrator, he didn't know his subject. A tourist, perhaps. Certainly, Agnes's regulars knew her better than many of them might have liked. Nell had often seen grown men go flying out through the front door from the force of Agnes's kick up the arse. A little bit of messing, the odd vomit in the toilets, slobbery proposals, of which there were many – a near-six-foot widow with her own pub *was* a woman to be sniffed at – all these things Agnes would resignedly if not happily endure in order to sell her quota of nightly pints. Tone it down, tone it down now, was all she'd say to the kind of language she would skin a man alive for using in the kitchen. She wouldn't, however, under any circumstances, tolerate fighting or gambling. The first hint of either and she was out, round the bar counter like a streak of lightning, hand out to grab the collar of a culprit who wouldn't get to so much as blink before he found himself in a sprawling heap at some distance from the front door. Belgian tourists, too, who had the temerity to take out a pack of cards. Out they went, a line of Flemish disconsulates. Agnes was unrepentant: feckers only ever bought one glass of coke with four straws, anyway.

Nell smiles, continues to shuffle through. Funny, the collection confirms an image she had of her mother when she was a child: the top half of Agnes, big breasts, white blouses with cardigans, pearl earrings, perms always in mid-fade, a small bald patch showing piglet-pink scalp at the back of her head; bottom half, a counter lined with lacy half-drunk glasses. A sort of barroom centaur.

'Look at these.' Ali makes a spread arc of black-and-whites on the counter.

'Oh, I remember that evening.' Her mother, hat on, posing for photos with the Dubliners. 'They just came in for a few pints. She was so excited, she got it back to front and told them that they were great fans of hers. Kept them posing all night. She was a dreadful snob, you know.'

'Funny with it, though.' Ali's smile lingers as she looks over Nell's shoulder. For an instant Nell has a spasm of pain, wondering if Ali ever looks at images of her with such intense fondness. Still, to prolong this moment of closeness Nell speaks of Agnes.

'Shopping with her was an absolute nightmare. I'd do anything to get out of it. Especially shoes – God, shoes. Or sandals I suppose they were, really, with elastic across the toes for her bunions. She made everyone in the shop look at the bunions, said she'd lose ten pounds in weight if they ever fell off. Always the same shoe shop in Kenmare because the man served her tea while she tried on everything in her size. I'd wait for it with my eyes closed, holding my breath, then she'd say the same line every time: I'll take these. How much are they? He'd tell her and then she'd say, and how much are they to *me*? He'd take ten per cent off, she'd say make it twenty and he'd just say, right you are then. His son tried arguing with her once. I don't know if they ever found the body. Fool of a boy.'

'She really thought she was somebody, didn't she?' Ali smiles. Nell feels her daughter's breath damp and moist along her own cheek. It scents of muesli and orange juice. 'And those bloody hats. All that, and then there was the bucket for her pee in the back porch – she couldn't be arsed going upstairs. Her bed always smelled of pee too.'

'Uh-huh,' Nell grunts. She could have done without that reminder.

Ali steps back and the echo of her breath on Nell's cheek grows cold and clammy.

'English accent which could cut glass when the odd English tourist wandered in. She used to act like the Queen Mother. I'm sure she based the hats on that woman. And the stiff little wave she gave from the Morris Minor.' Nell motions. 'You'd think royalty was passing. A rabid republican behind it all. Did you ever hear her sing "The West Awake"?'

Ali looks rapt, shakes her head.

'You'd swear she'd fought and died for Ireland. Not a dry eye in the house.' Nell sighs, replacing the photographs round the mirror. 'I hated all that. All that snivelly national-ism in the bar.'

'I miss not knowing you both here. Together *here*, I mean.'

'Well, you saw us together in Oxford and in Paris, Ali.'

'I think it would've been different. I think—' She stops,

her mouth opening and closing, trying to find the right way to articulate what she's trying to say. 'I think I'd have asked the same questions – but the answers would have been different.'

'What questions, what answers?'

'You know. About you. All that time after Bridget. I'm not connecting – just don't get a *feel* for it.'

'Feel for what, exactly?' Nell can't contain a note of flinty impatience. God, she loathes this New Agey shit. Ali would have her wear her emotional underwear like a badge of honour. She's been trying to stretch her mother out for dissection since she was a small child herself. Clearly, Nell hasn't surrendered the requisite quotas of emotion, angst, grief. Nothing would do Ali anyway but total, blitz-out incontinence. What then? In a role reversal, Ali becomes consoling, stoical mother? It's not her own inner child she's been ranting on about finding all these years, it's Nell's.

'Forget it.' Ali shrugs, concentrates on polishing a glass.

'Look, Ali . . .'

'Yes?'

'What is this? Don't you think I missed my sister?'

'I never said that. It's just, well . . .'

'What? Just what?'

'It's part of my history too.'

'In what way? Yes, she would have been your aunt. But you never got to meet her. You didn't even know she existed until Mammy told you when she started coming to Oxford.'

Ali haws on a glass and rubs furiously. 'Don't you think that's odd? You must have told Uncle Albie and Mary Kate not to mention her to me. Why did you do that?'

Not even twenty-four hours landed and already Nell is feeling the old frustration stick in her throat like a fishbone that never really goes away, just dislodges to give her peace sometimes. Always the same old ding-dong repetitive refrain between them. Ali banging on about her history again, trying to look into someone else's luggage, to sort herself out. Nell shuts her eyes briefly and wills her voice into a calm monotone.

'Look, Ali, let's not go down this road again. Maybe I just wanted to enjoy the new life I was living away from home. I missed my sister, of course I did. When she died, I thought I'd never stop crying. The same when Mammy died. That's what you do. You cry. What else is there? Then I took it in. I took it all inside, and I dealt with it. If you live long enough, you lose people. It comes to us all.'

'To you more than most,' Ali says in a quiet, probing tone.

Nell concentrates on the photographs for a while. She knows where this is leading, the simple $x + y$ equation, Ali has always wanted to formulate her mother. Always focusing on the tragedies in her life, rarely the achievements, or the moments of pure, unadulterated happiness. Always trying to see Nell as a heroic victim, her stoicism born of quiet endurance and unarticulated suffering. When Nell punctures that construct of her, Ali grows impatient.

'Look, Ali, I've dealt with things in my own way. Please, allow me that. Maybe I'm not as complex as you seem to think.'

'Sometimes I still cry for Granny,' Ali says. Her eyes have welled up but she tries for a smile and it ends up a washed-out affair, plastered across her face.

Nell touches her cheek. 'Course you do.' After a while she adds, almost to herself, in wonder, 'She was a complicated woman.'

A genuine twitch to Ali's lips now. She doesn't respond to Nell's enquiring glance. Nell hesitates a moment, then, 'Ali, was I a bad mother?'

Too late. The words lick back and forth between them in a pause which sees Ali's shoulders quiver up in line with her ears. She's wounded. Nell wants to claw the words back into her throat. Wants to say she was in fact thinking of her own mother when she uttered them. That it was not meant at all subjectively, nor even personally, for that matter, rather, an idle musing, meant objectively, universally – one mother as opposed to another, say. But the question, and Ali's take on it, is too visceral for either of them to shrug off.

'You do realize . . .' Ali clears her throat. 'You do realize the full implication of that question, don't you?'

'Oh, Ali—'

'No. Let's deal with this. Nell, I don't want you assuming responsibility for me. If I don't measure up to whatever your notion of good mothering is, I can only say I'm sorry. But those are your expectations, not mine. Nothing has been deliberate. I didn't set out to be an opposite of you.'

'How, an opposite of me?' Nell is stung.

'Come on. That's pretty obvious.'

'The way I dress, career, the *clean* apartment is what you mean.' A voice tells Nell to stop. It's old ground. If they get stuck now, so early on in the visit, they'll go round and around until they're both dizzy. Won't even mean anything after a while. It will just be words. A prelude to a leavetaking by one of them. Never for very long though, just long enough to draw breath.

Nell has often wanted to say, let's make it a good while this time. No contact, no breathless, panicky, late-night calls, no long, protracted silences to whet my worry, sharpen my apprehensiveness. No me coming after you, having to come after you. No you sinking deeper into some new quagmire of your own making, one arm reaching for help while the other thrashes me back. Setting yourself up for failure, insisting I watch, then furious because I do. Better yet, if Ali would say it. Let's take a break. I'll be in touch in a few months or so – meantime, I'll be fine and you can put me out of your head. But Ali clings on by her teeth. She'll never be the one to call for time out, despite the accusations she flings at her mother for spying or meddling in her life. It's not enough that she falls down time after time. She must be *seen* to fall down. She must grind her mother's nose in it.

Nell takes a deep breath and pulls back from the precipice. 'It was a crass thing to ask. And I know I've made other mistakes in the past, but try to remember, I was only sixteen years older than you myself.'

Ali's wounded shoulders flutter back down. A loud exhalation of pent breath. 'Believe me,' she says, retreating back to the kitchen, 'I've always held that in your account.'

A leathery exhaustion takes hold of her body. It started at the top of her head and worked its way down. She doesn't want any of this. Doesn't want to be here. Doesn't want to have to deal with any of this . . . this stuff. Other people's stuff. Other people's clutter.

'Oh fuck you all!' Nell's foot lashes out at the corrugated sheath under the counter top. This already, and she hasn't even come close to mentioning shotguns. 'Sorry,' she adds mindlessly to the counter.

She performs what she can only describe as a skulk into

the kitchen. But Ali is outside in the garden, her lean back rigid as she stoops over and over again, ripping at weeds with bare hands. Nick sips tea from a mug, still standing over the table. He gives Nell a quick empathetic grimace.

'I've said the wrong thing again, Nick.'

'She's tired. Double the workload with me so useless.'

'Useless? That's not a nice word. You're unwell, that's all. Are you happy to be here? Or was it all Ali's idea?'

'At first I wasn't sure. But now, in spite of being sick, I'm happy to be here.'

Nell believes him. An uncertain man, certain of something. For some reason she finds comfort in that. She sighs and looks around the chaotic kitchen. What does she want for her daughter? What is the thing she assumes her daughter does not have? Is it her own sense of order, of measured time and space?

As though reading her thoughts, Nick sets the mug down and rubs his hands together.

'She wants you to be happy here too,' he says, discounting his own words with a little self-deprecating moue, as if nothing he says should be taken all that seriously. Still, he continues and she is grateful. 'Don't ask me why. We just lock into things, I s'pose and there's no rational explanation. Along with the dream of one day running this pub, Ali's had this idea of you coming here, seeing her do it.'

'And she thinks that will make me happy?'

'No, she thinks that will make her happy.'

'She wants me to be proud of her. Is that it? But I am. In so many ways. But this . . .' Nell frowns, waves a hand expansively, taking in the bar, the kitchen. 'I don't understand why she's so anxious to take up where I left off. This is *my* – I mean it's me. Not her.'

He considers for a while, egregious Adam's apple oscillating along windpipe. 'I don't know, Nell. I don't get on very well with either of my parents. My father would give anything for me to take over the ghastly family pile in Gloucestershire. Even he calls it that – the ghastly pile. *Ghaa-astly*.' He mimics an older man's orotund derogation. Dry amusement and a vestigial flicker of something else, fear maybe, in the hollow eyes as they show more animation being someone else than he's shown being himself for as long as Nell can remember. He pulls a face, catching her scrutiny, before continuing: 'He's a tough old stick. Can't see why I wouldn't want to be just like him. Far as he's concerned, failures as eldest sons don't come much bigger than me.'

'Oh I'm sure—'

'No. Really. That was the family joke, the sort of humour we had. To be honest, I thought it was funny myself, he'd introduce us, starting with the youngest, working his way up to me, and he'd say, and this is Nick, the Failure. We'd all fall about laughing and the poor guest didn't know which way to look. My sister was, the Bike, and she did put it about. Mind you, she had the title before she started putting it about. So in a way, you never really knew in our house if it was all made up for you beforehand or if you were playing along. There was always that little kernel of truth in the nicknames, that's what made them so cruel. The old man thought his tag was the Führer, that's what we said in front of him. He liked that. But what we really called him was the Fuckhead, as in: watch out, Fuckhead's gunning for you. Even my mother – 'Go see what's taking Fuckhead so long, will you, darling?' Of course she didn't know that she was really the Page – as in blank.'

'I didn't realize your family was so charming.'

Nick chortles and takes a sip of tea. Its progress down his gullet is that of a snake weaving beneath stretched cotton.

'You know, I think people did think we were quite charming in some respects. Over the top eccentrics. What you'd expect really from ghastly pilers. We laid it on a bit too, fishing, hunting, ho ho hoing. Bit self-consciously Brideshead Revisitedy and all that. A merry bunch indeed. Everything had to be funny, made fun of. But I think . . . I think we were lost, you know, in our own joke.' This last he brings out with a cough rattle which sends him to the sink. A hand pressed to his chest, he spits out several gobs, while the other hand flaps feebly behind his back. In a gesture of embarrassment or apology, Nell assumes, studying her feet so as not to mortify him further.

When the fit is over, he wipes his mouth and takes another swig of tea, allowing it to roll round his mouth first in preparation. Then a series of trickling spurts down the back of his throat in stops and starts, elixir-like.

'Sorry about that,' he manages eventually. 'I bring up all sorts of goo in the mornings. It's disgusting, I know.'

'Your lungs have been checked?'

'Yes. All's well in that respect. Unbelievably.'

'Your family. You were saying . . .?'

'Ah yes. What I was getting to? Look, it's pathetic, but I couldn't breathe in the same room as Fuckhead. It's like he took up all the air. He sort of swelled, filled up all the space around, with himself. He took, well, everything, I suppose.' He looks away, mouth fixed in a bitter clamp, levelling his voice before he continues, 'I remember that choking feeling, even if I haven't seen him for years. My sister tells me he hasn't got long more, gone a bit doolally. He's smaller, she says, shrivelled up a bit, not half so commanding. She says I'd feel sorry for him if I saw him now, all broken and full of regrets. But I don't want to feel sorry for him. I'd rather go on hating him the way he was, thank you very much. Where's it written that you have to make your peace, anyway? Unless you need to for yourself, what's the point? It's only bullshit. So maybe Ali wanting to step into shoes you stepped out of is a kind of a compliment really. That's all I wanted to say.'

Nell reappraises this pallid creature with her head cocked to the side. She returns his self-effacing grin. Nick voicing an opinion, a conjecture – and one that lies gently with her and rekindles hope. For the first time since she's known him, she feels a warmth begin to spread, a swelling fondness.

'Thank you,' she says.

A shabby grey cat materializes out of nowhere and springs up onto the table. Nick gently nudges it off again. From the ground the cat gives him an aggrieved look through red-rimmed, slightly protruberant eyes, not a healthy specimen. Either of them.

'Oh, don't mind me,' Nick says, turning away, but not before she's caught a flush of pleasure on the sunken cheeks.

Nell goes to her room. Best to put distance between herself and Ali for a while. Usually it works this way; after a little spat, the subsequent truce will hold for longer because of the spat. Mothers and daughters are not entirely different from lovers, she thinks. Both have the capacity to destroy and to reconstruct once more. But with each reconstruction a little strip of skin, a transparent graft, must be lifted from somewhere to seal up somewhere else.

She aches to be with Ali when she is not. Then, when she is, she sometimes experiences her daughter as an oppressive weight draped across her shoulders. And it is true, she has to confess, there have been times when she has looked at Ali and shocked herself with the thought: I could live my life without you. And the thought is terrible, all the more terrible because she knows Ali has read it in her eyes, so that she ends up overcompensating to the point of insincerity.

If I fail, Ali once said – with, to Nell's mind, inflated grandeur – I fail on my own terms. I have the right to be wrong. Fine words indeed, if an individual were capable of admitting when they were wrong. Two overdoses would be sufficient to indicate to most people that something was wrong. Each time Ali's life gets back on track after a steep and perilous slide, Nell is encouraging to the point of mania. Of course it's false. Of course she doesn't really feel such optimism. Of course Ali knows this and hates both of them for the façade, the heightened feeling of unreal, unwarranted hope. And when Nell drenches Ali with approbation, with surgent praise, it isn't a child's open-faced delight she encounters, it's a look of silent accusation and glowing contempt.

Do not assume responsibility for me.

How can you not be responsible for that which you've made? For what they've made of what was given? And yes, the not given, too. Sometimes it seems as if the not given is the only precinct a child wilfully chooses to remember. Not give so much – in fact, give nothing, and their subconscious might kick in to compensate. So that the least good thing will be remembered to gloss over the cracks, and a reasonably happy childhood is conjured from the miserable.

Why can't Ali ever give her credit for all the times she *has* turned up to bail them out? The deposits on flats she's unstintingly coughed up, the clinic in Hertfordshire – she should have checked if they offered Air Miles or Green Shield stamps at the very least.

Look – she mentally addresses an effigy of Ali plastered across the ceiling – I could have burned you with cigarettes. I could have been out every night, instead of studying like a lunatic. I could have forgotten to wake up for the four o'clock feeds. I could have brought men home every night and made you call them Uncle. The things I could have done, to make you realize the good mother you've actually had.

Nell has to smile and stretches along the bed. The stone in her pocket digs into her thigh. She draws it out, holding it up to the light. New colours emerge from behind the over-layer of predominant salmon. Molecules of fizzing gas, here, in the arc of her hand between thumb and forefinger. Solidified now, silenced, until time's continuum will blaze them out into infinite space once more. Then it suddenly comes to her what this stone represents. She sits up, eyes scanning the room.

She tries under the bed, on top of the wardrobe. Surely Ali hasn't got rid of them? Not items so intrinsically bound up with a woman she idolized. The large chest contains only Nell's clothes. She checks the bedside cabinets, the drawers of the fifties dressing table, catches the almost fever-ish expression on her face in the triptych mirrors. Her cheeks gleam with a sheen of sweat; she is at the highest point of a scalding flush. She puts the backs of her curled fingers on either side of her face in an attempt to cool down, but even her knuckles feel hot. Nothing, nothing – the room has been swept clean. Prepared in readiness for Nell's own arrival, she realizes.

Turning about, her knees bump against the velveteen

stool. It doesn't move. She tries another little nudge, some thing or things pin the stool to the ground. Her hand snakes down to lift the lid but it is fastened. She kneels to get a closer look and sees the top has been sealed with a line of nails. More a line of tacks in reality, removeable if she can find something to prise them loose. She pulls out various steel implements from her manicure case and begins to wrestle the tacks free. One by one they ping up and out until the lid yawns open with one final push of her hand. And there they are. Filling the box to the brim. If she upended the stool and dashed them to the floor, she thinks they would slowly, magnetically, unstoppably, glide one to the other to take on the large, broad form of Agnes.

Nell picks up one stone and turns it over. There is her mother's familiar script, the careless dash of writing with big loops, slanting to the right. Felt-tip almost faded now, dissolved into lime. She lifts out another stone, and another. Some are legible, some just a blur. But all will show a date and a place. So that she would remember, she explained. Exact moments of time.

There is a slight tremble in Nell's hands, plucking and dropping stones at random, as though her body, too, is remembering.

CHAPTER FIVE

It is late afternoon when Nell goes downstairs. She is ready to face Ali now that she's managed a few hours' solid work. One essay completed on harvesting and picking options, a couple of e-mails, and she's succeeded in simplifying her wine-tasting itinerary to a reasonably satisfying degree. Work gives her focus, straight lines to follow. Tapping lightly on the keyboard of her laptop, she has been able to forget where she is and remember where she is going.

Ali is tackling the pyramid of dirty crockery in the sink. She hums lightly with her back to Nell, who takes this as a hopeful sign, an emollient gesture.

'Can I do anything?'

'What? Oh yeah. Here.' Ali flings a dishcloth. 'I'll wash. You dry.'

They work without speaking for a while. Nell also hums. She regards Ali from the corner of her eye. Her daughter seems composed again, that is, as composed as Ali gets. Though there was a time when the fretful, gyratory limbs and wincing facial muscles appeared to lie utterly still under a pall of deathly composure, body mirroring the slack, heroin-laden gaze. So much so that Nell had longed for uneasy limbs again, for twitches and nervous tics signalling life.

Then, it had seemed as though Ali lived in perpetual twilight, a place not of this world. *Darling girl, why so far away?* Had she not loved her daughter well enough or long enough or just enough, enough, enough? How much was that? Was there some sort of measuring scale?

In the beginning Ali tried to hide the using, pretending to be ill with some virus or other when Nell made an unscheduled visit. Or a spy swoop, as Ali called it. She would stay in bed, sheets pulled up to her chin, her distant gaze settling somewhere in the air above her mother's head, her face meringue white, almost translucent, angry spots pitted across her forehead. Everything about her droopy, languid, as though she had turned to oozing ectoplasm. Nell used to want to plough her two hands in physically to wrench whatever was left of humanity from the lifeless mannequin. But it would have been like trying to draw a spine from a jellyfish.

After the first accidental overdose, Nell came to realize that it wasn't that Ali wanted to die. She wanted her mother to save her.

'Who's doing the bar?' she ventures.

'Nick. He's feeling pretty good today. Said he had a nice chat with you. Want a cuppa?'

'I'll do it . . . Ali? Truly I'm—'

But Ali flicks her apology away with a scouring pad. They are back on track once more, for how long Nell can only wonder. They sip tea and hum together, laughing with girlish embarrassment from time to time when they collide.

Nell remembers long baking afternoons in her aunt's kitchen in Oxford, Ali creaming butter and sugar together, her lips finely crenulated with the effort. They would dance to the radio, grinding hips though Ali's reached just above her mother's knee. Invariably, Ali had to rush off in mid-dance for a poo. She always left it to the last minute and then ran with one hand pressed to her bony buttocks, which convulsed Nell every time. Then the call *Ready*, a signal for assistance and Ali would be sitting on the throne, grey eyes watery with daydream, flushed and dewy-faced, a little goddess. As though the purgation of what little impurities her tiny body could hold, gave an evanescent beauty in its wake.

Adam walks upfield, shunting into a jacket. He gives them an oblique wave and passes by the side of the house, protean phantoms of grey smoke from his roll-up trailing his footsteps.

'I hope he remembered to call the Guinness people last night,' Ali says with a frown.

'How call? The phone's not working.'

'There's something wrong with the lines,' Ali murmurs vaguely. 'They're working on it. Anyway, he uses my mobile.'

'The one you never turn on?' Managing to keep her voice the right side of dry.

'Yes, well. I turn it on to use it, don't I?'

'If you say so. Where is it now?'

'Adam has it.'

'And that makes sense, I suppose?'

Ali has the good grace to concede a wry smile. 'Suppliers mainly speak to him in any case. They've got used to dealing with him.'

'I see.' Deep breath. Nell plunges in. 'Ali, where does he come from? I mean, what's going on? He either works here or doesn't. If he's got your phone and you trust him to do

the ordering . . .' She lets her voice trail off. So far she's succeeded in asking as if her questions were an addendum to
some other imaginary conversation.

'You never know with Adam. He's thinking about staying
on, but that's not really his scene. You know how it is.'

No. Tell me how it is.

'Mm-mm.'

'I don't know what we'd have done without him the last
few months, what with Nick so ill and me trying to run this
place pretty much by myself. Paudie and Julia give a hand if
I ask them, but I don't like to ask too much. It's not like in
Granny's day when you could rely on them. They're getting
on, you know. Paudie's not as sharp as he was.' Ali turns
pointedly. 'In his head, I mean.'

Is this Ali discounting anything they may have said
already? Or perhaps attempting damage limitation before
Nell dines with them this evening? Nell licks her lips; sweet
crystals of her mother's almond frost settle on the tip of her
tongue. 'How did he find here?'

'Adam?' Ali considers, pulls her mouth down – her shrug
is exaggerated, Nell thinks. 'Dunno. How does he find anywhere? Far as I can make out, he's been just about
everywhere. All over Europe. Think he was in Scotland last.
Yeah that's right, I remember he told us he took the
Stranraer–Larne ferry. Worked his way down along the
country. Pitched up here one night for a pint, we started
talking about this and that, turned out he was looking for a
place for his caravan and we said—' Ali breaks off and gestures airily at the field below.

'You've applied for planning permission for that field, where
his caravan is parked. A valuable site these days, I'd imagine.
Sea views, if the line of trees were cut down at the end.'

'He has money,' Ali says pointedly. 'It's just an option we've discussed.'

'Why the pony?' Nell asks, though it is the question she is least interested in having answered.

Ali's back is poker stiff. 'He saw it at a fair, bought it on a whim, really. Grace adores the old thing, as you can imagine. Terence, she's called him. Don't ask.'

Nell doesn't ask. Neither does she point up the possibility of an animal grazing considerably enhancing a squatter's rights. She vaguely remembers some difficulty Agnes had in the mists of time with a local farmer who took grazing from her land for free.

'So he's just a sort of a . . . drifter, really. Is what you're saying? Until now.'

Ali throws her a sharp glance, Nell maintains a fixed smile. Interested but not too interested.

'S'pose. A bit like we were – me and Nick, I mean – except Adam moves around on his own. Says he doesn't even take the caravan sometimes, just ups and leaves, buys a new one wherever he pitches up. I don't think he cares for belongings much.'

'Well he must belong himself – to someone, to somewhere.'

'Look, where are we going with this?' Ali's suddenly tired of the hide-and-seek routine.

'I'm just a little curious.' Nell moves a pile of stacked plates. 'I mean, aren't you?'

'If his history isn't important to him, why should it be important to me? He goes where he wants to go. No reason. People live like that. Maybe it's no bad thing. The more you know about people sometimes, the less you like them. That could be just me though.'

Nell begins to gather dirty laundry from what seems like all corners of the globe. She makes a little seesaw up-and-down movement with her shoulders. You might be right. You might be wrong. 'Ali?' *Easy now. Slowly. Slowly.*

'Mm?'

'I was just wondering, has he offered to buy this plot? Actually offered money?'

'Not in so many words. But we chat. It's just left loose for now.' But the question has troubled her. Two livid spots colour her cheeks, she stretches across to hoist the window up as if for air.

To hell with it. 'Is he threatening you, darling? In any way? Please just—'

'Is who threatening?' Nick asks from just inside the brocade curtain. He holds the food order pad from the bar. His expression is light, easy – of someone who has stepped on the tail end of a gossipy conversation.

'*No more,*' Ali hisses under her breath to Nell. 'Oh, the bloody tax man,' she tosses over her shoulder at Nick.

'Vultures,' he says affably, tearing off a sheet from the pad and thrusting it towards Ali.

'Two cheese and ham toasted, one egg mayo, one bacon and one plain cheese – no butter.'

'Plain cheese toasted or—'

'I said plain. I'd have said toasted.'

'Fine. Nell, can you take over here?' Ali sweeps a hand across the remaining dishes in the sink, all business again, though Nell catches the warning in the grey gaze.

'Sure.'

Glad of movement, and with Ali's blessing now, Nell seeks out a pair of ragged rubber gloves and throws herself into a frenzy of activity around the kitchen, picking up everything that can be washed, scoured or, in most cases, both. She heaps the first pile of washing into the machine in the back porch. Sorts colours into mounds and stacks in a trail leading to the machine. When all the dishes and pots are washed, she dries and places them neatly in cupboards. Bleach — where? Yes, tucked into a corner under the sink, rust around the holes of the ancient tin. Not a grain will shake loose: it's all solidified. In a temper with it, Nell hacks at the top with a serrated knife, half peels it back and hacks further into the contents. Clumps of white chalk-like substance fall into the sink. She selects a few choice lumps and rubs them over the tea stains both inside and outside the filthy basin. The tobacco brown begins to dissolve.

With the plug in and, mercifully, hot water running, she tips under the tap anything she can find under the sink where the bleach came from — soap powders, salt crystals, washing-up liquid. The acrid smell of ammonia makes her eyes water. She thinks she can hear a chuckle from the food corner, but when she turns Ali's cutting crusts with the concentration of a surgeon.

Ali steps through to the bar with the sandwiches. Nell grabs the wooden chopping board she used and scrapes a wire brush back and forth across the surface until a germ would have to be gladatorial, if not numinous, to survive. She keeps an ear cocked for Ali's return but, judging by the rising swell of voices beyond the curtain, an extra pair of hands was needed.

Next the floor. She quickly sweeps, scooping up stuff which a few days earlier she would have been loath to look at, never mind cram with impatient hands into an already overflowing rubbish bin. Lightning dart to the backyard to empty bin. A mop. A mop? She looks around, on fire for a mop. There is something resembling one flung up against a wall in the porch, ashen cobwebs holding the strings together. No matter. It will do. The terracotta tiles are visible again by the time Ali returns, and Nell is leaning both fists on the Formica table, breathing heavily, willing the incandescence back down her cheeks, her neck, her chest, to wherever it surged from in the first place.

'God, that was quick.' Ali whistles, glancing around.

'Oh, I just,' pant pant, 'was in the mood. If it's okay, I'll tackle the walls tomorrow. You know, give them a rubdown. Then, if you don't mind, I could make a start on upsta—'

Ali's face contorts, as though she's wrestling with something, then her head flings back and she lets out a howling laugh.

'What? What?'

'Nothing,' Ali gasps. 'Only we had a bet on you, how long you'd last. I won. Nick said you'd hold out for a couple of days – the clean-up, I mean. But I knew. I *knew*.'

'I'm glad to be such a source of amusement. Tell me, is my face the colour I feel it is?'

'What d'you feel?'

'Scarlet. No, puce by now.'

'D'you really want the truth?'

'I wouldn't ask if I didn't want the truth, Ali.'

Their eyes lock. Just a brief second before Ali turns and makes a deal of clearing away the sandwich things.

'You only feel that. It's an illusion. You look fine. Normal. *Everything's* fine. That okay?'

'It'll have to be, I suppose. For now.'

Outside in the yard, Grace stands – or, rather, hops from foot to foot with her schoolbag on her back. She's engaged

in imaginary conversation, scowling, thrusting an accusa-
tory finger at her invisible interlocuter. Now a hand on her
hip, an open-mouthed look of disbelief before she launches
into the fray once more. Finger stabs, outrage, a long stream
of invective before she's apparently had all she's going to
take and a leg lashes out in a decisive and definitive kick.
Nell smiles to herself. Ah, where did that come from?

'Nan!' Grace exclaims when she comes through. As
though she'd forgotten her grandmother's arrival. It's not
like her. The putative argument must have been very intense.

'Hi, darling. How was school?' Nell embraces Grace and
helps with the straps of her bag, so they can squeeze together
harder.

'Grand.'

'Did you walk or take the bus?' Ali asks.

'I walked.'

'Anyone walk with you? A friend?'

'No.'

'Good day?'

'Fine.'

'Play any nice games?'

'Not really.'

'Was Miss Kelly in a good mood?'

'All right.'

As Grace fends questions, she saunters around, picking up
a crust of bread here, a lump of cheese from the fridge,
hoarding an apple under her grey school cardigan for later.
Her nonchalance is feigned, Nell can see by the way Grace
casts Ali sidelong, furtive glances as though gauging the
mood today. The child came in surly with that little knot on
her forehead, as if someone had taken a swatch of skin
between thumb and forefinger and twisted, but the brow has

loosened until pancake smooth as Ali's remained consistently cheerful and chatty.

Nell sits and listens to them for a while, allowing their easy mother–daughter exchange to wash over her, without the usual tidal undercurrents. Maybe this is how they are, how it is, most days. As Ali recounts an anecdote about her morning in the bar, Grace munches and nods. Her mother's fluctuating moods passing like weather across her daughter's cordate face. Long cloud scowls, mirroring Ali's, followed by radiant smiles.

'Oh, Ali,' Nell remembers, 'I meant to say: I found Mammy's stones in my room. I'm glad you kept them.'

Ali has to think for a while. A frown fritters, then disappears. 'Ah yeah. I wasn't sure what the hell they were, so I just sealed them in that stool box thing. What are they, anyway?'

'Didn't you notice the writing on them?'

'Writing?' She wrinkles her nose. 'If I did, I thought maybe they were for good luck or something.'

Strange that Ali never noticed her grandmother's habitual collecting of stones on their walks together.

'She used to call them her memory stones,' Nell explains. 'If she enjoyed a walk or a day out somewhere, she'd always bring a stone back and write the time and the place, sometimes who she was with, that sort of thing. When she was gathering her thoughts, as she put it, late at night, or saying her prayers after the bar, she'd look at the stones and all the walks would come back to her. All at once. That way she'd get the value of any good moment, a hundred times over, she said.'

'That's nice. Kind of what you do with labels, wine-bottle labels. In a way.'

'I hadn't thought of that, but yes.'

'Can we do that, Mama?' Grace asks.

'Start our own memory stones? Sure, Gracie. We'll go for a walk later and pick our first big juicy stone from the strand below.'

'I'll paint them.'

'I don't think we paint them,' Ali says.

'But I can if I want to, can't I?'

Sensing an argument looming, Nell interjects: 'What I was wondering Ali: while I'm here, it would be nice if we could do some of those walks. You know, together. Or with Grace when she comes home from school maybe.'

Ali's face slowly splits into a delighted smile. Her mother has always enjoyed solitary strolls.

'Yeah. Yeah, okay.'

She turns, to hide such obvious delight, Nell knows – it's a bit too raw, too embarrassing. But Grace makes no bones about her pleasure. She has fixed her grandmother with a meteoric dazzle. Ever the vigilant child mindful of her fragile parent, she is grateful for kindnesses shown her mother, even if she doesn't understand what is being offered.

'Nan?' The snub nose wrinkles when Nell gives her another little squeeze.

'Oh, I know. I must stink a bit. Sweat.' She can smell her own armpits.

There's a stifled snort from Ali by the sink.

'You could do with a wash,' Grace says in her grown-up voice. 'And did you brush your teeth at all today?'

In the tiny bathroom at the top of the house, complete with gurgling wall-mounted cistern and faux marble linoleum peeled into curls at every corner, Nell's first shower takes for ever. The shower head, which has to be held, offers a thin dribble and the water has turned cold by the time she rinses her hair. The towels look none too fluffy, but they're clean and dry. When she rubs steam from the mirror over the sink, the face looking back, clear of make-up, looks old and saggy. Some mirrors are more unkind than others. This borders on cruel. Perhaps more vindictive than most because she last looked into it when she was a fresh-faced teenager. It isn't that the years haven't been kind, it's just that they've been.

Bingo! Meredith shouted the day Nell couldn't read the tiny print on a menu in a restaurant and pulled her newish spectacles from her bag. Meredith brandished her own serious bi-focals. Why didn't you tell me? Why didn't you tell *me?* Under here – Meredith squeezed the loose skin under her top arm – tell the truth, does it wobble when you wave to someone? Like the jowls of a jowly dog running? And here – she pointed to her breasts – veins? Not so bad as yours, Nell laughed. Everything goes exactly when it should, Meredith said in a doleful voice, eyes, skin, the waistline – and I don't know about you, but I still can't believe that I've turned into such a walking cliché. What's the next bit? Incontinence, Nell said.

Poor darling Meredith, she never got to the next bit. A sharp pang makes Nell's eyes water. It comes in waves: missing someone. The same after Agnes. Dull background noise crackling on busy days when there isn't much time to think, sharp as a needle when you forget for one single moment and something makes you suddenly remember. The guilt of forgetting, even for a second, in the first place.

When Nell returns to her bedroom, Grace is there

clacking stones into neat towers. Of course, the little nosey parker had to check out for herself what the women had been talking about earlier. The stacks collapse when Nell shuts the door and Grace quickly flings them back into the stool box. Henri's gift of the winestopper lies on the floor beside her. She's been rooting about in Nell's bag as well. Nell scoops it up.

'Darling, it's very delicate. Please please don't play with that. Anything else. Henri gave it to me.'

'Why didn't he come with you? I don't cry if I go down the snake any more.'

There is a catch in Nell's throat imagining Henri's patient, resigned smile as he pored over the snakes and ladders board with Grace for the umpteenth time. They just sort of latched onto each other from first meeting. Nothing grand about it, nothing spectacular. A quiet, mutual ease, shrugged into like warm old winter coats.

'I rather you with make-up on,' Grace offers, scanning her grandmother's face on naked display, hair wrapped in a towel.

'Well, let's do it.'

'Will you do me, too? Mama never wears make-up. She should really.'

'She doesn't need it as much as me.'

'Oh she does.'

'Grace? You won't say that to Mama, now, will you?'

'Uhhh.' Grace mimics a simpleton.

'No.' Nell chuckles. 'Indeed I don't think you're thick. You're what my mother used to call as cute as a shithouse rat. My little darling.'

Grace gives her a coy smile. The pixie that's got the cream. They have one another's measure.

Little keeper of secrets.

'Let's do you do me and I do you.' Grace rummages in Nell's cavernous toilette bag, her skeletal frame tinselly with enthusiasm. Nell sits on the bed, offering her face. When her eyelids are shut awaiting shadow, she casts about looking for a suitably innocuous way to get the conversation onto Adam. But Grace pre-empts with her own oh-so-casually put question.

'Why did you never marry, Nan? Didn't my grandad ask you?'

Nell stretches her lips into an O for lipstick, but she can barely contain her smile at Grace's tangential technique. Years of being on the other side of interrogation have served the child well.

'Plenty of people asked me.' Nell buys into the familiar routine.

'Not my grandad, though.' Little glitch of emotion on the possessive; anyone listening would think the child bereft. Both of them are well aware this is Grace's way of batting out of the game, before it's even started, any questions which might come her way.

In truth, she has evinced as little interest in the identity of her grandfather as Ali has in her father. Nell considers it eternally to Ali's credit that she's chosen never to make a big issue of the subject – she might have done, when looking for accusations to fling at Nell in the past. She might have reasonably harboured or invented or conjured all manner of grievances about her mother's reticence, her lack of concrete information, but for whatever reason, known only to Ali, she's simply accepted the truth of Nell's few responses. Namely, that it was a one-off, a careless act born of ignorance and, yes, curiosity, and that the young man in question never knew he'd become a father.

Throughout Ali's childhood, Nell constantly steeled herself for the inevitable. What was my daddy like? Did you love him, did he love you? What does he look like? Do I look like him? Daddy daddy daddy. Why shouldn't a child become obsessed? But no, for one whose hurt barometer was always keenly monitored, on this, this huge subject, Ali has accepted minimum information with maximum sanguinity. By turn, Nell has been hugely relieved that she hasn't had to invent a fairy-tale romance. Moreover, there has sparked the hope, when hope was sorely needed, throughout the darkest days of Ali's drug abuse, that the apparent lack of her daughter's interest might simply lie in the fact that she was, despite everything, grateful still to be alive. To have been allowed life.

'No. Not your grandad.' She opens one eye. Grace is smacking her lips in automatic response to the lipstick she's slathering on Nell's mouth.

'Gracie . . .'

'Did you love him?' Mascara is being lavished from on high.

'No-oo,' Nell responds cautiously, wondering where this is leading.

Grace does a version of her adult, disparaging face.

'I was young and foolish. Not half so wise as you.' *And how*, she thinks. He was a local boy, several years older. She wonders if he's still around. Would she even recognize him? Would he know her? Quite likely they could pass one another on the street without so much as a spark of recognition.

Just the one time and the first time. In a graveyard,

standing up. The chapel yard was a good place to neck
because there were dim lights on throughout the night.
They'd had a couple of dates before, smoked a few cigarettes, rolled around the stones on the crescent cove below,
nothing more than a few slobbery kisses, a hand pawing
lonesomely around inside one cup of her bra. The night in
the church grounds, they shared some vodka she'd nicked
from the bar. She'd put it in a plastic Lourdes bottle of Our
Lady. Up and up she'd pressed Our Lady's neck, filling the
body until she screwed the head back on. A separate bottle
for undiluted orange squash.

They took alternate sips from the bottles, giggling, retching at the foul taste. Then in the graveyard he'd pressed her
up against a headstone, unzipped his flies, scuffled his pants
down to his knees and looked at her drunkenly with his
thing in his hand. She'd never seen an erect penis before but
she knew where it was supposed to go. She wriggled her
slacks down to her knees and, with a lot of grunting and
mutually curious glances downwards, they managed to prise
the tip into her vagina. There wasn't time to think about
pain, he came so quickly. Afterwards, they finished the
vodka, got sick in the bushes and went their separate ways.
She never went out with him again. He never knew she was
pregnant when she left. Thus was Ali's fine and noble prove-
nance, her entrance onto the world stage, executed. Her
place in history marked.

Grace stands back to survey her handiwork. She works in
eyeshadow with her thumbs then takes another look. The tip
of her tongue extrudes like a newborn mouse.

'Tell me about Adam,' Nell glibly inserts into the silence.

Grace shrugs. What's to tell? "Course you can't marry
Henri,' she says, daubing blusher, 'because he's already married,

isn't he? And if you kill his wife you'll be a murderer and you'll be a double sinner. And that'll be hell for ever. And I mean for ever.'

'What's to do?' Nell holds her hands up.

Grace considers for a while. 'Well, you *could* kill his wife. Something quick so there wouldn't have to be too much blood – no blood at all if you sort of . . . choked her.' She mimes garrotting her own scrawny neck, followed by a ruminative pause. 'Then you could be really really sorry for it and go to confession, tell of your big sin and God'd forgive you. He *has* to, you know, even if he doesn't want to.'

'I'd rather not kill anyone if I can help it.'

'I'm only saying. Don't take this the wrong way, Nan, but you're a bit old not to be married.'

There's something here, Nell is sure of it. But what? Her mind performs somersaults trying to access what Grace is trying to convey in her own inimitable fashion. A false move now, a wrong word, and the mollusc lips will seal, perhaps for the rest of her stay. Nell hums, waiting. Aeons pass.

'It'd be good if Mama would marry Daddy.'

'You think?' A million qualifying questions but Nell manages to hold tough.

'Mmm.'

Truly the child is made of impermeable granite. Another aeon. But, feeling safe in Nell's enduring silence, Grace takes her first wobble. 'It'd just be them then.'

'No Adam, you mean.' Nell responds too quickly, immediately seeing she's blown it. The only way round Grace is by the back of the house and she's just stormed through the front door.

'Whatever,' Grace says airily. 'My turn! My turn!' She

feigns a babyish excitement at having her face done, signalling end of probe for now.

Holding a perfect pout, gazing up at the ceiling, Grace
manages to keep her face deathly still as Nell applies first eyeshadow, then mascara. A pose she must have seen on
television or already in the genes of girls so young. Under
Nell's lightly dusting fingers, the upturned eyelids are peach-
soft, delicate as gossamer with the faintest of ribbony veins
running down to the edges. Grace's mouth is already slackly
open, spoiling for lipstick, her tongue snakes back and forth
over the slightly ribbed surface of protruberant lower lip,
keeping it moist. Every gesture an exact replica of how Ali
used to sit through this same ritual. That is, before she
rejected all such frippery as demeaning to herself and her
womanhood.

Nell brushes powder onto the tip of the snub nose, cannot
resist a moment longer, leans down to kiss, powders again,
kisses again.

Grace's eyes are slitty with pleasure. 'Stop,' she admonishes. 'You're smudging me. Do my lips.' The mouth opens
wider, commandingly.

'What colour?'

'Red.'

Nell dabs a fine sable brush on her reddest lipstick. Traces
a Cupid's bow outline, before filling in. She's about to seal
with gloss when she observes a slight swelling in the right
corner of Grace's lower lip. Probes it with a finger, gently,
but the child winces. There's a tiny fresh cut just inside
where the flesh grows slick and dimpled. Possibly pierced by
a tooth.

'Did you have an accident, a fall today, darling?'

'It's nothing. I bumped into a . . .' Perplexed frown.

'A what?'

'A wall at school.'

'Strange nothing else got bumped. What were you doing? Walking around like this?' Nell stomps up and down with her lower lip thrust out as far as it will go. Grace watches seriously for a second then erupts into giggles, which she tries to cover with a glance of corrosive disdain. The attempt at sarcasm on the lurid features makes her look like a twisted Lolita, a little hungover gipsy queen.

'Am I done?' She slides off the bed to stand in front of the three-way mirror. With her chin raised and lips in full pout, she examines her face from every angle. 'I am gorgeous, amn't I?'

'You're the last word.' Nell echoes her own mother, allowing Grace to feast on her reflection, before continuing: 'You know, I was thinking, now you're so gorgeous and all maybe we should get a lotion for those old fleabites.'

'Okay.' Grace shrugs.

'The thing is' – Nell licks her lips – 'there wouldn't be much point if you're going to allow all those cats into your bedroom at night, would there? We could make up a nice bed for them in the kitchen. They'd love the stove. You'd be doing them a favour.'

'I like the cats with me.'

'It's not very hygienic, sweetheart.'

'They're my *friends*.' That coiled torsion on her forehead reappears.

'Well, you have friends at school, don't you, and you don't sleep with them,' Nell persists, but Grace has skipped to the window to bring the subject to a close.

'Look, there's Adam.' She pounds on the glass with both fists. Her eyes have taken on the sheen of polished marbles.

Skittish, excited stance entirely at odds with what Nell assumed was the child's wish for him to leave.

It seems that Grace is in two minds about Adam. Perhaps Ali, too: that was a flush of anguish, earlier in the kitchen, at the prospect of his leaving. Their responses to him, so transitional, reactive as guttering candle flames whipped from side to side by capricious winds. Maybe this is the trick she must master, learning to flux with a confliction of emotions, as do Grace and Ali, learning to let the flame right itself.

Nell stands behind Grace, looking down to where Adam stubs out a roll-up with his shoe, hands thrust deep into jeans pockets while his eyes take in Grace at the window. When he registers her flamenco face his mouth curves into a slow, relaxed smile. Grace makes an exaggerated pointing motion, signalling he should wait there, she's on her way down. She runs without a backward glance at Nell, who is obliged to keep up the long-distance stare. He shuffles uneasily from foot to foot. Though ostensibly she knows no more about him, as her eyes eat into the angled planes of his upturned face, the dips and pockets of firm, sunned skin, it isn't the rumble of suspicion she recognizes in the deepest recess of her stomach, it is, no point in denying, yes, yes it is, an unmistakable lurch of desire.

Then a glimpse of her own face in the triptych mirror. A clown stares back. Twin red circles on either side of her nose, spider eyelashes fanning above and below the eyeline with black liner pencil, a scarlet gash of mouth carrying on long beyond the line of lips, halfway across her cheeks. A creeping flush from her neck up past jawline to meld the lot into one awful, garish visage. No, not a clown, something else there . . . the round, wide-eyed effect, stretched, elongated lips – by design or accidentally, it's a scream Grace has painted on her face.

She reaches for tissues and begins to rub furiously just as Grace runs outside and flings herself at Adam. Flea-pitted leg stalks circling his waist as he swings her round. Her pleated uniform skirt billows, revealing dingy white knickers and the lower reaches of milky, concave abdomen. Her vulnerability is at once shocking and exquisite, like a single drop of ruby blood on an alabaster throat. They move as one into the house and Nell continues to stare at empty space for moments, finding their easy solidarity disturbing in a way she can't quite cohere. It's not difficult to see why even she, with all the weight of her suspicions pressing upon her shoulders, should find him so compelling. A child of nearly eight can see his beauty. It's more than that, more than his elusiveness, his silence, the weightlessness behind his glance. It's the nowness of him. That's what separates him from anyone she's ever met. His absolute carnality.

That's just being fanciful, she chides herself. Buying into Ali's notion of a man in flux, mindless of his own history. Everyone has form, she thinks, watching as a few strands of late afternoon light refract against the caravan windows in the distance. It's human nature to find a way to manifest your experiences, collect your memories. Books, photographs, letters – for her own part, she still has Ali's first booties, a lock of hair from Ali's first haircut. Around her feet lie her mother's memory stones. There must be *something* in that caravan to reveal him in a fuller light. She'll just have to wait for the right opportunity to take a look.

Her mobile trills. It's Henri, sounding more cheerful than earlier that morning. He asks what she's doing.

'As it happens, I'm here, looking like a screaming clown, surrounded by stones, standing by a window, looking at a caravan, wondering what's inside.'

He laughs so hard, she has to hold the phone away.

'What did I say?'

'I think you're my caravan, Nell.'

CHAPTER SIX

Out to the west, the sky is on fire. Bands of scarlet leak and drip onto a sublayer of deliquescent gold stretched across the length of horizon. The line is pierced by twin black molars pushing up from the sea, jagged rocks called the Bull and Calf. Where a desultory wind skims across flat, glittering surface of Atlantic, it carves a complex series of spools and eddies which coil and re-coil so that the entire ocean looks like one giant fingerprint.

Nell has stopped a little way down the narrow road to Paudie and Julia's cottage. She is on the opposite side, peering through a tangled hedge of blackthorn and wild rowan. From here, she can see a stretch of sandy beach all the way along to the next jutting headland. The tide is still going out, pulling back from shoreline in slow, deliberate sucks. A tall man silhouetted against the backdrop of a swollen, dying sun runs along the edge, water closing over his shoes. The same man, Nigerian, she presumes, taking his evening run this time. Or maybe that's all he does, spends day in day out running. Does he think if he keeps on going he won't notice where he is? It won't matter that this is not his home? Maybe he thinks he's just passing through and it might be anywhere. She imagines him as a small boy, winded and panting after the day's exertions, two ponds for eyes, gazing at a speck on his father's atlas. His father telling him that this speck, this tiny, far-flung island, will one day become his place of exile. No, the boy exclaims. He laughs, surely. That's nowhere. Not here. Not Africa.

Maybe he labours to lay claim to foreign soil with every footfall, pounding the earth until she submits, becomes his own, as though his feet can subdue what his heart can not. Most likely it's the converse in that when he leaps clear for infinitesimal fractions of time, feet splayed in mid-air, he truly does belong to nowhere. It could be, she thinks, he's just looking for connections. Seeking out points of similarity to his own country, familiar axes to pivot unfamiliar terrain. He runs because that is what he's always done. The only thing left to him in an alien place. Whatever compels him, he cuts a lonely, isolated figure shadowing an ebbing sea.

She is reminded of her early days in Oxford. Back then, as strange to her as this part of Kerry may be to the Nigerian. Sixteen, with everything foreign, including the strange-feeling incubus growing in her womb. The enormous, red-brick houses of Summertown suburb, where her uncle and aunt had lived for twenty or so years, had a witchy, over-powering quality that frightened her at first. The trees lining wide boulevards looked weird, so straight and tall, so many leaves – nothing like the windswept, tormented specimens at home. Her nostrils constantly tingled with the acrid scent of petrol. Everybody sounded posh. Her clothes looked dull and provincial. The miniskirt, it seemed, was over, girls were wearing neither here nor there things called midis. Her hair was all wrong, pulled back in a tight ponytail with no parting. The first thing she did in her room at the top of Uncle Albie's tall, rambling house was to let her hair down to sluice a central parting with a comb.

She was plump, getting plumper, not just from pregnancy but from constant almost methodical overeating. As if she were attempting some kind of evenness of form, trying to let the rest of her body catch up with the growing mound in front. She arrived looking like any teenage girl swathed in puppyfat. Two months on and the fat was clearly a baby. When she opened her mouth and people heard the accent, saw her state, the sidelong knowing glances made Nell feel the caricature Irish girl forced to come over on the boat. It was only beginning to sink in what had happened in her life. That it was now out of her hands. She was a problem to be discussed in hushed terse phone calls. A child waiting for letters from her own mother. A mother-to-be waiting for her own child. Unlike the long, sloping figure down on the strand, she didn't run. She got fatter and fatter until her eyes seemed to dissolve into her face until, in the end, she was hidden from herself.

She looks until he disappears behind a large outcrop of black rocks. The dying sun burns up the western sky. It feels as though her entire body is opening to the scene below, letting her homeland in, pore by pore. It's useless to resist. Even the air feels sweet in her lungs. All these years she's managed to live without this place. But it was only a physical absence, she sees that now; the place continued to live within her; it's as if she stood right here on this spot, yesterday evening and all the evenings before that. You never really leave home – it comes with you, Meredith said about Yorkshire once. Why don't you ever go home, Nell? I don't know. *I don't know.*

'Nell, is it you?'

She starts at the sound so close behind. A hand briefly grazes her shoulder.

'Paudie?' Nell frowns, then remembers to clear her face. He knows how old he is; her expression doesn't have to tell him. But he's chuckling softly.

'I'm on the last shirt,' he says. 'But you, now, you're only an older version of yourself. Welcome home, Nell girl.'

Nell takes his extended hand for a formal shake. The ring and small fingers are curled into his palm with arthritis or rheumatism, the hand knobbly with explicit, twisted veins like burrowed worms. His white head juts forward at a slight angle and looks as if it hasn't sat straight on his neck for some considerable time. Bulbous eyes with deep hoods above and below the eyeball, a long beaky nose and narrow lips give the impression of a tortoise sneaking a quick peek from under its shell.

'I'm eighty-two, to answer your question.'

'It's good to see you, Paudie. You look great.'

'I look wrecked,' he smiles. 'C'mon. You'll find Julia's weathered better than me.'

Nell follows him to the cottage. His gait is spritely enough and he makes a point of keeping in front of her. They step through the front door straight into the living room. There is a fire in the grate but it's gas over mock coals. The room is so stringently clean a solitary mote of dust would fling itself under a broom. In the furthest corner, by a large flat-screened television, there is a stand with a computer, printer and a phone with incorporated answering machine. Sweet peas from the garden give off a high almost sickly perfume.

Julia steps out from the kitchen, twisting her hands dry

on folds of apron. She is as beautiful as Nell remembers
even if the cloud of yellow hair is now pearl white shot
through with silver. At least ten years younger than her
husband, with her chalky, unlined skin dusted with fine
hairs she could get away with twenty years younger. There
is a fierce intelligence in the cobalt gaze, which takes in
Nell so swiftly and comprehensively that it feels like endo-
scopic surgery. Her broad smile is direct and guileless; it sits
on her pale, moon-shaped face independent of silent questions.

'Nell Hennessy.' She pumps Nell's hand with vigour. 'I
was beginning to think I'd never see this day.'

'Hello, Julia.' Nell hangs back, a touch embarrassed, but
Julia has clasped her in a tight embrace. Three firm claps
between her shoulder-blades and she is released again.

'Let me look at you.' Julia's eyes sweep up and down. 'We
were just saying if we'd know you without knowing you
were coming. If we met you, say, in Killarney or somewhere.' She turns to her husband. 'I would for sure, anyway.'

'Ah, she has her mother's eyes. You'd know them anywhere.'

'C'min to the kitchen.' Julia grabs Nell's hand. 'You can
talk to me while I'm finishing off.'

A delicious smell of pot roast permeates the kitchen. Nell
realizes she hasn't eaten a bite all day apart from a crust of
buttered bread in the morning. Julia busies herself checking
the vegetables, setting plates inside the oven to warm.

Nell looks around in astonishment. It used to be a hap-
hazard collection of separate units, a damp, airless room
where she used to cadge jelly. Now it's like something out of
a brochure – light, airy, with streamlined built-in units of
limed wood with black granite worktops. In the centre, a

pine table is set for three, a candle glowing at either end, reflecting warmly on the crystal wine glasses. A bottle of red wine in the middle, open and breathing. Nell recognizes the label. It's a good, reliable claret, if to her mind generally overpriced. Nevertheless her throat aches for anything halfway decent.

'Tell us what you think.' Paudie pours half a glass, handing it to Nell. She sips and it is better than she'd expected. It will have set them back a good ten pounds or thereabouts outside France. She pulls an approving face. Paudie grunts his pleasure and fills the glass up to the rim.

Nell moves to the back window. A long, narrow garden inclines to an abrupt end by a cluster of stunted yews. Beyond them, bald, striated rock on a gentle gradient until one huge cone which dominates the darkening skyline. Eagle Rock, though there were no eagles as far back as Nell's childhood and it is more a large hill than a rock. A smattering of crusty sheep weave across its surface helter-skelter-fashion, all the way up. She senses Julia's eyes on her back but can't trust herself to speak yet.

'A long time, Nell,' Julia says softly.

Nell clears her throat. She can feel Julia's breath at the nape of her neck.

'There's a road up there now, if you could call it that, but the odd tourist attempts the drive every now and then.'

'Is that right?'

'Yes. And you'll be glad to know they've put a sign by the lake, with a warning.'

'That's good.'

Julia is level with her, eyes trained on the peak of the hill. She reaches for Nell's hand and draws it across her own body, under her breasts.

'D'you know, there isn't a day when we don't think of your mother, poor Agnes, the walk back down with the one child. What must it have been like in her head? We can't even imagine.'

'No, we can't,' Nell says, giving Julia's fingers a quick squeeze before turning back to the room.

'We took advice,' Paudie is saying, filling half-glasses for himself and Julia. 'There's a shop in Killarney with a woman who'll go to any length to help you out. Normally we get a nice German white from her – there's one in the fridge if you'd rather to this?' Nell shakes her head: this will be fine. Paudie continues: 'We told her you were something big in wine – like your mother used to say, God rest – and she said we wouldn't be disappointed by what you're holding now. So she didn't leave us down, Julia? I said, she didn't leave us down?'

Julia nods in a distracted way. She hums lightly under her breath, hands flying in several directions, skewering meat, draining water from a pot of chopped turnip. Paudie sidles up and his wife issues a series of orders from the corner of her mouth. For moments it's as though they've forgotten Nell is standing there. So entrenched in their own routine. She is struck by their kindness, heading off to Killarney on a wine-buying expedition like that; the cost of petrol will have equalled the wine.

'So, Nell,' Paudie says over his shoulder, 'what d'you make of our friend above?'

'Let her get her legs under the table,' Julia remonstrates.

'Plausible, d'you think?' Paudie ignores his wife.

'Plausible?' Nell considers for a while. 'Yes, I suppose you could say that. It's difficult to know what to make of him, to tell the truth.'

'I s'pose the little girl was beside herself to see you,' Julia interjects, sending Paudie a quick but unmistakable frown.

'What did Ali have to say for herself when you brought up the shotgun business?' Paudie sets down a bowl of steaming potatoes on a woven mat to protect the table. The spuds are floury and burst from their dark jackets like fresh-fallen snow on grey slush.

There's a little silence. Julia's shoulders go up and remain poised in mid-air. Paudie has lifted his eyes to gaze directly into Nell's; she sees that the pale irises are frayed and tatty-looking, tiny lumps of red and yellow cluster in deep by the gaunt bridge of his nose. He seems to be squinting.

'I haven't got round to it,' Nell says reluctantly.

Julia's shoulders come down in one swift decline. Paudie looks to his wife's back with pursed lips, then returns his attention to their visitor. She can tell he's disappointed but doesn't wish to appear rude.

'Why so, Nell?'

'I did ask Nick but he didn't seem to know anything about a shotgun . . . Paudie, it's a little more awkward with Ali. If I say it straight out and she denies it, we haven't any place left to go, if you follow me. Then she's just waiting for me to leave. I mean, we've already come close to a serious falling-out and I've hardly been here a minute. I will get around to it but—'

'But you have to take her slow,' Julia interjects. 'I told you, Paudie, didn't I?'

Paudie fiddles with the table, keeping his eyes averted while he takes this on board. His eventual clear-faced smile suggests that he's decided his own integrity is not being called into question.

'I s'pose you know your own know,' he says, signalling with a bony forefinger for her to sit.

'Not to mention,' Julia seals it for him, 'she won't want to be landing the pair of us in boiling oil.' She sits and carves the roast onto the warmed plates.

They clink glasses and toast Nell's homecoming and, if there were awards for prudent reticence, Nell figures they should receive an admirable first. As they chew and idly chat about the surprising late summer, the new building going on everywhere, the hand Ali is making of the pub and the ridiculous prices houses are fetching all around, their unvoiced questions about her own past thread the air.

'So, Nell, to get back to that fella.' Paudie ignores his wife's warning glance. 'Nothing much has struck you between the two eyes yet?'

'She's only just landed, man.'

'I was talking to Nell, Julia. Have I a right to talk? Thank you. Go on, Nell.'

'There's nothing much to say. I barely saw him last night, then I bumped into him down on the cove this morning. He seemed friendly enough. Quiet. Ali and Nick do seem to rely on him quite a bit. But that's all for now, really.'

'Well, now, I'll tell you what's all. I went up the day before yesterday to see what was going on, just in case you didn't come, like.'

'Not that that's our business,' Julia adds quickly.

'Of course not that that's our business,' Paudie says with a hint of irritation. He has to settle himself in his chair again before continuing. 'Anyway. I had my couple of pints and your man was serving behind the bar. No sign of Nick or Ali. Are they all right? I ask him. Fine, he says, Ali's just taking a rest. She's worn out, I say, she's been having a tough old time of it. I say this like it's a question, you know, for him to pick up on if he's of a mind. But not a word. So – in case you don't come, and I'm only saying in case – I think I'll push him on a bit, see where we go with that. Maybe she should see a doctor, I say. Maybe a doctor should be called. By this, I'm wanting him to think that there's a whole slew of people that could be called at any time.'

'Paudie.'

'I'm getting to it, Julia. Anyway, I start talking to John Joe Twomey on the stool beside me. About how Ali's not looking one bit well or happy in herself these last few weeks. How she's thin as a greyhound. John Joe knows well what I'm up to and sets up a loud response by way of much the same thing. Of course, we're marking your man's card. In the middle of it all, in walks Ali with two eyes out on her like cauliflowers – a fool could tell there was crying involved. She gets herself a drink and whispers something to himself, then she goes back inside the curtain again. There's silence now, 'cause we can see she's in a bad way. Maybe we've started to look, I don't know, accusing or something at your man. Maybe we're overdoing it a bit. Anyway, he's pulling a pint for John Joe and I s'pose our eyes are boring holes in his skull, when he gives a little up of his shoulders—'

'Paudie.'

'Will you stop?' He sucks his bottom teeth and turns a shoulder from Julia. 'And then he asks John Joe if he'd know anyone would buy the caravan off of him.'

'You think he might be leaving?'

'Or staying Nell, girl. You know Ali's the planning permission applied for? You do? Well, that's only since your man arrived. Whatever way it is, I'd keep a close eye on the till.'

Julia looks a little embarrassed as she ladles mounds of

sherry trifle into glass bowls. 'Sure you're home now, anyway. Will you stop long?' The question is lightly put, but Nell can't help but detect the weight of other questions behind it. What brought you away in the first place? Not that it's any of our business.

Nell opens her mouth to say something, closes it again. Funny how with some people you remain a child for ever. Parents, aunts, uncles, old neighbours. The people who in last will and testament fashion are the executors of your experience, the repositories of your information. 'That was a beautiful meal. Thank you.'

'You're more than welcome.' Julia's blue eyes gleam irresistably. She leans across and gives Nell's hand a quick squeeze. 'Now that we have you, why don't you take us back a bit? First, I should tell you that there wasn't a sinner around knew about the child until about two years down the line. Your mother kept that quiet about it. I s'pose we all put two and two together when you left so sudden, but then, when we hear nothing and there's no sign of you, we think maybe it was the way the pair of you had a row or something. Then Agnes goes over to see her brother-in-law in Oxford and comes back with photos of a toddler. And still she says nothing. And, as you're well aware, you took whatever crumbs of information Agnes chose to give and woe betide if you asked for more.'

'Well, I was pregnant leaving,' Nell says.

'Ah.' Paudie fills her wine glass. His eyes dart across to Julia.

Nell immediately understands what's troubling them. 'Don't worry.' She glances from one to the other so they can read the truth in her eyes. 'It wasn't either of your lads.'

'Relieved to hear it.' Julia stretches back in her chair.

'Because they did a fair share of ramming before America. I wonder they didn't leave an orphanage-full behind them.'

Paudie snorts with pride. 'Finian's a welder now, Nell, in Boston. Earning a fortune,' he says. 'Declan's in Florida, not doing quite so good.'

Enough said on that subject for Julia's liking, she squeezes Nell's hand again.

'So you went to Uncle Albie in Oxford. Doubtless himself and Mary Kate were only thrilled to have his late brother's girl, seeing as they'd none of their own.'

'They couldn't have been kinder to me,' Nell responds.

'He was a bit of a dandy, if my memory serves,' Julia says.

'The cravat, you mean? The cigar?' Nell chuckles. 'Oh, he liked the finer things in life all right. He practised at it – read the right books, went to the right plays – by "right", I mean whatever a critic he admired had recommended. Always the correct grammar – God, he was a stickler for words, even correcting his own customers in the off licence sometimes. That could be embarrassing. And table manners? I never heard him raise his voice except to roar: did someone leave the sty gate open? Are we pigs we have to eat and grunt at the same time? He took me in hand and I didn't mind a bit: there were plenty rough edges to smoothen out. Corny, I suppose, but he did sort of become a replacement – an accidental father. I couldn't even remember my own. Then again, we always think, whenever things turn out the way they do, that fate played a hand, when really everything is accidental and whatever happens happens merely because something else didn't. We just like to make it fit into a scheme. Anyway, he was a gent in every way. A lovely man.'

'I s'pose you got to that funeral?' Paudie interjects in a dry voice.

'I did. I did, Paudie.' She smiles to show no offence taken. They're entitled to be curious, for all their equanimity. 'I owe my career to him. It was mostly wine he sold in the off licence. He'd got quite a local reputation by the time I landed myself on them. He started giving me little tastes, telling me estate histories and so on. Mary Kate was put out at first – she's only a child, she said – but he said if I was old enough to have a baby I was old enough to appreciate good wine.'

'Paudie, open up that white in the fridge. We're only settling in.' Julia shifts her rump into a more comfortable position. 'Go on, Nell.'

'Ali was born. She was a beautiful baby, good and quiet as you could hope for, not that I had anything to compare her with. I started helping Uncle Albie out in the shop more and more.'

'And of course Mary Kate took the baby over.' Julia cuts in perceptively.

'Yes, pretty much. It was difficult for her, being childless, having this new little person in her house from day one. She worshipped Ali.'

'You'd a right to be jealous.'

'I was and I wasn't. I was ruthless enough, the way you are when you're young. It suited me to let all the day-to-day minding to Mary Kate. Ali even slept in their room until she was about two. Then Mammy started visiting regularly and she fell head over heels in love with Ali, too. I never saw her so . . . Well, the upshot was, after four years in their house, I wanted my freedom. It wasn't my proudest hour, to tell the truth. Don't ask me now but – oh, it was selfish, yes, ungrateful too, but I thought I was becoming part of them, that this was going to be it for the rest of my life, part of this accidental family. And because I couldn't face Mary Kate's grief, which is the only word for it, I wrenched us both out of there far too brutally. I got a job working my way up from scratch in a wine merchant's, studying every night in a tiny two-roomed flat. And I started spacing out our visits to Uncle Albie and Mary Kate. They didn't say all that much but they were very hurt. Ali missed Mary Kate, too, I wasn't around a lot of the time what with work and exams. Then, about seven years later, I was offered a position in Paris, so much money we could live on my expenses alone. I grabbed the chance, although Ali didn't want to leave Oxford or her aunt and uncle.'

'She'd have been what . . . eleven or so then?'

'Yeah. A thin little thing, not very sure of herself. She was miserable in France. I sent her to an English-speaking school but nothing helped. That was the start of a bad time between us. We used to be so close. But as much as I was thriving, loving every minute in Paris, she was fading away before my eyes. I remember one night, just before I sent her back to Oxford, she was crying in her room, I mean the kind of crying that makes you think that hearts really do break. She kept asking why she had to be there. This wasn't her home. She'd always be a stranger here. That got to me, I have to say, because for me it was as though I'd found the place in life I hadn't even known I was looking for, and I wanted Ali to be part of that. But she kept asking what had she done wrong. Well, a week later, I sent her back to Uncle Albie and Mary Kate. She stayed there until college.'

Julia takes a sip of wine; she strokes each of her fingers in turn. 'That must have been hard on the pair of you, apart for such long gaps?'

'You'd think so, but it wasn't really. We seemed to get on better at a distance.' Nell pauses to let them take that in. Fearful that flat, unmitigated candour may estrange them, but she feels she owes them no-frills honesty.

'Of course,' Julia remarks, 'like yourself and your own mother.'

It's Nell's turn to consider. 'Maybe. But I don't think it's that simple. There were layers between Ali and me, things we couldn't get through, and even if we'd known what those things were I doubt we'd have found a way. I haven't had another child to see how it can be different. Sometimes I thought the only way I could reach her was through Mammy or Mary Kate. In some respects Ali was like a – a channel for Mammy and me. We communicated through her. Mammy was very disappointed in me, as you can imagine, falling pregnant like that, so young.'

'Agnes never spoke of you only in the highest terms,' Paudie says in a quiet voice. His white head has listed even further forward, he's been concentrating so hard. 'There was nothing she wanted more than for you to come home, even for a short visit. That's not by way of accusing you now, you understand?'

Julia shifts uneasily in her chair. 'Nell, just tell me this – and God knows we all do strange things – but was it, d'you think, a sort of punishment you were dealing her? Not coming home because she sent you away?'

'She didn't send me away. Don't think that. I left. It was what I wanted.'

'But—' Paudie is checked by a quick tap to his hand by Julia.

Nell has turned from them, her eyes trained on the hump of black hill in the distance. 'I don't know. You get used to things in dreams. It's hard to believe they're really there, or at least *still* there when you see them. Of course, it's always been Mount Everest in my mind's eye. Not much of a hill, really.'

'Talk away, Nell. We've no pressing engagements. It was your own decision to leave, you say?'

Nell nods. She exhales heavily in response to their silent question: but why did she never come back?

'If I could give you a simple answer, I would. All sorts of reasons. Look, Uncle Albie used to tell me about Paddies on the constructions sites in London, how they never stopped talking about home, on and on, always living in the past as if the present was just a penance to be got through. Of course, what they were really doing was reinventing childhoods which can never have been as idyllic as they liked to make out.'

Julia pulls up closer. She darts a quick glance at Paudie.

'Go on, Nell. Finian and Declan are talking about coming back for good next year, so we've what you might call a first-class interest in this subject.'

'Well, Uncle Albie worked on the sites when he first went over. The pub went to my father and there wasn't much left for the younger brother to do but leave. There was plenty of building work in London in the postwar years.'

'Faith, then, I put my own time in yonder. No dogs, no Irish, I recall when I was looking for a room,' Paudie says.

'Yes, Uncle Albie told me about those signs pinned to the lodging-house doors. Then he started telling me about the Paddies when it was becoming clear that I wasn't going home for a visit. Not that it was a huge deal, you have to understand, it wasn't. I'm never going home and that's that. It wasn't shame about the baby or fear of disapproval, it wasn't that I didn't want to face the father — he meant nothing to me, there was no broken heart and it wasn't as if he'd attacked me, as Mary Kate once asked. I simply . . . kept putting it off. Uncle Albie told me about some of the Paddies he worked with. When their holidays were coming up, they'd buy grand new suits, get haircuts, shiny shoes, the lot. They'd talk and talk about going back, what they were going to do, who they were going to see. For weeks they'd be out of their heads from excitement and whiskey. Buying presents for brothers and sisters, half of John Lewis for their mothers. And then they'd get to Paddington to catch the boat train, wave their mates goodbye, slip into the nearest pub, get slaughtered and take a bus back to their lodgings to spend the next two weeks in a drunken stupor. Uncle Albie said he knew several of them who did the same thing year after year. They never once made it home.'

'Why so, d'you think?'

'Who knows? You can only guess.' Nell shrugs. 'For my own part, I let it get too big. If I went back . . . it wouldn't be how I made myself remember, how I drew the picture. You called that night, Paudie, to say Mammy was gone, and I thought I'd be struck dumb by all the things I wanted to say, all the things I'd never get to say or even do for her. I didn't want to see her as anything but tall and broad and full of life. I couldn't even come for the funeral, and, believe me, I will always be sorry for that.'

Julia gives her a keen-eyed look, sensing perhaps that Nell is holding back, but she decides not to press.

Nell takes a deep breath. 'You asked me, Julia, if I was

punishing Mammy by not coming home.' Her voice is so low they have to strain to hear her. 'No, I suppose, is the only truthful answer. I think it would be more true to say I was punishing myself.'

Nell stirs a cluster of sugar grains into her espresso, just the wet tip of her spoon dipped in the sugarbowl. She tastes: the liquid is a degree below scalding, black, sour, caffeine-ridden – perfect, in fact.

Julia, satisfied that her guest is content, settles back into her armchair, swollen ankles resting on a small footstool. 'Finian bought me that machine last time he was home. I like a good strong coffee in the morning, but I take it with milk. 'Course, I'll be up all night with the jitters after this lot. Still, we don't have company that often. We rather tea in the afternoon, don't we, Paudie?'

'What's that? Oh, tea.' He has been gradually sliding his long frame lower in his chair, until he is almost horizontal, anchored at the top by one arm clutching a seat-rest in clearly a seasoned fashion. The women have been talking for hours, having moved out to the living room for brandy and coffee. From time to time, Paudie has interjected a guttural affirmation, to signal that he's still listening, but for the most part he's been quietly snoring in the corner.

A number of times, throughout the remainder of the meal and since, Nell has noticed that his long-distance vision is not the greatest. She's tested him, pointing to things in the garden, and he's had to screw up his eyes tightly to focus, and once actually stepped out to ask her to direct him to the spot she meant. She felt sneaky and ill at ease testing him like that, all the more so because she's sensed that Julia is onto

her. There isn't much passes between this couple that one or
the other isn't onto within seconds.

It was a relief when Paudie slipped from the conversation
to allow the women to get on with it. She could sense his
hankering to get back onto the subject of Adam for a while.

'You must be looking forward to the idea of Finian and
Declan coming home after all these years.'

Julia wiggles her head this way and that: it's debatable.
'The *idea*, yes. We've always fancied the idea.'

'And now?'

'I don't know.' Julia sips her milky coffee, replaces the
cup on its saucer and pushes it away from reach, as though
the contents are suddenly repellent. 'Whatever I say, it'll
sound terrible.'

'You're speaking to the woman who couldn't make her
mother's funeral, remember?'

'Well, we're on the phone once a week. We've the e-mail
now, sure. I send them both a message every morning of the
week. It's the best thing ever. It's an awful thing to say, but
I'm going to say it. We all get on fine with a bit of a gap. I
know when there's trouble in the camps or when things are
brewing, but I can stop out of it and wait for things to
blow over. The grandchildren only see the best of us and we
only see the best of them. And I'm afraid that'll all change
to the bad. I just couldn't be listening now to one or the
other of them telling me that Dad should have his hip or his
eyes seen to. You'll have noticed that, Nell? He's a bit of
trouble with the long sight? That's not to say he doesn't see
what he sees.'

'No. I'm sure.'

'Anyway. They want to build two enormous houses. And
no, I can't say as that prospect fills me with sheer delight. Ah,

you get selfish with age, but more than that, too, you get a taste of freedom and you don't want to give it up. All their youth your children want to be free of you. It never occurs to them a time might come when you want to be free of them, too.' She stops and peers across at Nell. 'Listen to me, and you burning into that chair.'

Nell puts her hands to her cheeks, they're on fire.

'It used to be the back of my neck would get me,' Julia says. 'The heat!'

'Yes. There, too.' Nell rubs a hand along her nape. She checks her fingers: they glisten with sweat.

Julia quickly fetches a glass of iced water, which Nell swallows in deep gulps.

'And sometimes, I'd get a funny sort of a tingling feeling beforehand, especially in bed at night. D'you get the night sweats, you do?'

Nell rolls her eyes. There is a cap of perspiration circling her scalp.

'I couldn't explain that tingling to a sinner.' Julia sits again. 'It was like a – a presentiment or some such.'

'I do know what you mean. It feels like a warning or something,' Nell says.

'No, I don't envy you. I'm glad to be done with all that. Though you'll be a bit sad in yourself, too, I can see that. It's a strange time for a woman, knowing that side of her life is coming to an end.'

'Yes.'

Julia pours two more tinctures of brandy. They sip in silence for a while, contemplating their own thoughts. Paudie hisses and crackles, for all the world like a transmitter, receiving, analysing, regurgitating the contents of the women's conversation.

'The darkie faces will be strange to you, too, Nell,' he says eventually, through a long yawn.

'Sorry? Oh, you mean the refugees. I've seen a man running along the beach, night and day, or so it—'

'That'll be Bola.' Paudie creaks into a more upright position, the clicking of bones almost audible. 'Nigerian. He's here with us a year now. Has the odd pint of Guinness up at your place. Lost his wife. We don't know the story, but there's a daughter that he's trying to bring over.'

'He's a lonely sight down on the strand.'

'Crucified with the loneliness. All of them. Not that he'd say more than a word or two to you. He's not very friendly – no business here, the poor man. He should be above in Dublin where there'd be more of his own kind. But it's the policy now to send them out to rural areas till they've got papers and can work and so on. Only it takes for ever, and there's hostels full of them with nothing to do.'

'They'd have shops in Dublin with their food. And we've no religious facilities for them down here,' Julia says a touch shamefacedly, plucking at stray threads along the hem of her skirt.

'I s'pose beggars can't be choosers.' Paudie darts a glance at Nell, to see how that might lie with her.

'And we were glad enough of a helping hand ourselves, once upon a time,' Julia adds, but her sentence ends on a rise, as though she's reasoning aloud, or asking a question.

'Ah, that was different entirely.' Paudie dismissively waves an arm.

They're both staring intently at Nell, weighing up her possible reactions. All the black babies they adopted on paper, finally come home to roost.

'Of our generation, Nell' – Julia licks her lips, choosing

her words with great care — 'the only *exotic* face we ever saw was on the telly or maybe the odd doctor in the hospital.'

'Ah, that's not it.' Paudie bunches his fists in frustration.

'You'd a fair few drinks tonight, Paudie,' Julia warns with a glance that is a mixture of reproach and indulgent affection. 'You'd want to take it easy.'

'I suppose it takes some getting used to,' Nell offers cautiously, 'people coming into the country, instead of . . .' Her voice trails away.

Paudie's frustration is increasing. His jaw is out, lower lip clamped stubbornly over the top. 'Plenty hoodwinkers as well.' He ignores a cautionary glance from Julia and wags a bony finger at Nell. 'You've to vet strangers through and through, I'm telling you. You're setting store for the future. D'you follow, Nell? D'you follow?'

It could be Adam or the Nigerian he's talking about.

'I follow,' Nell says in a calm voice because he's getting agitated again.

'I won't be called something I haven't decided yet to be.' Paudie's voice rises indignantly, his hands scrabble at the bulbous armrests, trying in vain to lever himself more upright.

'Easy, easy, Paudie. There's no one in this room calling you a racist,' Julia remonstrates.

'One minute I'm a racist and the next I'm not seeing what I clearly saw, up against the wall of the back porch in the house above. *Clearly* saw. After direct reference was made to it in this very room. Dir-ect reference.'

'He's a bit — and still half asleep,' Julia whispers apologetically to Nell. Louder, still to Nell, she says: 'Did he put the heart crossways on you, down on the strand?'

'Adam?' Nell's head is starting to spin.

'No, Bola, the Nigerian. I was down there myself one

morning, picking periwinkles, when I looked up and saw this, what I could only call a giant, coming over the cusp of the hill. I all but flung myself in the tide.'

'He is big,' Nell murmurs, fearful that anything she says will set Paudie off again.

'Very aloof.' Paudie sucks his lower teeth. 'No business here with friendly people.'

'Still . . .' Julia shrugs.

'A big man like that, running night and day. Very aloof. And a face on him . . .' Paudie's voice trails off, his shoulders heave up and down.

'Not to mention' — Julia stacks cups, casting a quick wink in Nell's direction — 'a face on him black as the ace of spades.'

Nell has to smother a grin. She's not the only one going through the change of life.

Inky clouds chase across a swelling but diffident moon as Paudie walks Nell home. A beam of torchlight picks out the road in front of them. Otherwise the night is velvety black and strangely still. Nell glances up just as the moon is gobbled by a large expanse of vapour.

'Rain, I'd say, Paudie.'

He looks up. 'It'll hold a while yet. There's no malice in that.' He stops in his tracks, mulling something over, the torchbeam sweeping back and forth across the sky. 'Nell, I'd like to say sorry if I seemed rude to you back in the house there, if I was a bit cranky.'

'It didn't cross my mind.' She gives him a reassuring smile. 'But I do understand that you're worried about Ali and I'm glad you called me.' Best not to mention anything else.

She takes a step forward, thinking he may be ready to move on, but he's still standing with the torch pointed up at the sky. Nell waits.

'I wish we could've done more for yourself and your mother all that time after Bridget.' He lowers the beam to gauge Nell's reaction. 'There, I've wanted to say that for many a year, and now I have.'

'What could you have done?' Nell steps toward him.

He exhales a long sigh. 'I don't know. We could see you were in trouble, the pair of you . . . Hard times, Nell. Hard times.' Despite his willingness to leave the subject there, she can see he is still very troubled. That he has been so genuinely troubled for all these years touches her greatly. What few thoughts she has had of him and Julia have been simple, childish memories in the main. Now she can see that she has never been very far from their thoughts. Perhaps they viewed her abrupt departure as some kind of failure on their part. She left, and they didn't know the story; they got the beginning and were denied the middle in the customary manner in which lifetimes are eked out and explicated for good neighbours.

First they were denied Bridget, then Nell. Their sense of order, of equilibrium, of lives following coherent and predictable wave lines, was sundered. Their sense of closeknit community, of every man not for himself, of troubles shared, thrown back in their faces in the light of sudden absences and doubtless, the permanent, grim line of Agnes's clamped lips.

'It was like a flame went out for all of us, Paudie. No denying that . . . I was the serious, I suppose you could say *good* child, while she . . . Well, Bridget was the golden girl, simple as that, with a very special place in Mammy's heart. But I didn't mind that because she was special,' Nell says in a low, soothing voice. 'She was blonde and pretty and could dance backwards. Who wouldn't adore her? No, you couldn't make her alive again, Paudie, any more than I could, or poor Mammy. It was a hard time for us and, yes, it was always between Mammy and me but we couldn't help that. There was nothing you could have done.'

'I'll take your word for that. Thank you.' He moves on, light picking out the road again, though she senses the continuing disquiet of his thoughts.

At the top of the road, he turns again, expression less troubled. His tongue pokes out, circling his thin lips tentatively. 'I remember something from those first few days, when the shock was still on us all, no one knew what to do for yourself or poor Agnes. She couldn't hardly speak for grief.'

'Yes.'

'Myself and Julia were trying to see to the funeral arrangements and what have you – we didn't think you'd be able for anything, you were so small – but you insisted on helping us pick flowers and choose the readings for the church. And then you opened up the pub, all by yourself, three days after. I came in behind the bar to give you a hand, and I kept asking if you were ready for this. If it wasn't too soon. And to this day, I've never forgotten the look on your little face, with your hair swept back into the tightest ponytail by your own hand that morning. It has to be done, you said to me, clear and see-through as running water. It has to be done. For God's sake, you were what – seven? No, I'll never forget that.' He gives her a shy smile and turns away.

The pub door is open to the night air. There's a hum of conversation. Nell decides to walk through the front of the house.

'Won't you come in for a last drink?'

'Ah no, I've had my share,' Paudie says softly over his shoulder. He raises the torch in salute. 'Let you enjoy your time with your daughter now.'

Nell stands, looking inside for a while, surprised to find the place fairly packed for a weeknight. Mostly young men and women, chatting animatedly, rubbing bodies with little thought for intimate space. A number of Dublin accents, late holidaymakers. Pastel cotton sweaters draped casually across shoulders, in a way she used to think only tourists did. There are peals of laughter, a trilling mobile phone, a youth answers, chuckling into it, one finger in an ear to hear the better. The place is buzzy, no doubt about it.

Behind the counter, Ali works at a furious rate, pulling pints up like a magician to let them rest and settle on the countertop. She is flushed, her eyes shine. All the time she keeps up a series of running conversations with customers. A wink as she hands someone change, a little out of the corner of her mouth aside to a group of girls to the far right. They explode into giggles. She moves along, and a quick word to an elderly man sitting on a stool at the centre, her face deferential, interested in his response, giving him time before she scurries to serve someone further along, throwing the end of her sentence back at the elderly man to let him know they haven't finished, she'll be back. Her fingers move like a nimble typist's over a cluster of empty pint glasses, magicking them out of sight. An impatient toss of a dishcloth over one shoulder, ready for action. She glances up, hungry for the next business. Head nodding the long order through to the end. And a bag of cheese and onion? Sorry, we're out of crisps. Bacon fries, though? A packet of bacon fries duly slung along the length of counter.

A tiny concentrated frown as Ali's hands dip in and out, filling glasses, tonging ice cubes. Toward the end of the order, she stands for a moment, mentally recapping, mouthing various instructions to herself. She turns slightly from the crowd, one finger tapping her lips, and in that gesture Nell might be gazing at her own mother. It's uncanny. Ali looks nothing like Agnes, yet there it is, the tilt of her head, eyes scanning optics for a reminder, the gentle press of finger to mouth. Ali remembers the last of the order and bustles into action again.

Nell steps in, stands there, unsure where to put herself. She looks around like a wallflower at the school dance. Layers of cigarette smoke bank up to the ceiling. Someone brushes against her, says sorry, moves on. Behind the counter, Ali hoots at something one of the girls in the corner has said. She looks in Nell's direction, a hand shielding her eyes to focus the better. A little start, then a pink flush swells on her bony cheeks. Her eyes widen. She beckons Nell across the crush of bodies, points to an empty barstool in front of the counter. Nell sits. Her own cheeks burn.

Ali mouths something to the gaggle of girls in the corner, a thumb jerked back in Nell's direction. They nod, pull their mouths down, raise their eyebrows. She looks as though she will burst with pride. 'What can I get you?' she shouts across to Nell.

'I don't know,' Nell hollers back. 'I could have another brandy, I s'pose.'

Ali uncaps a bottle of rare cognac from a shelf high above the optics. She polishes a balloon glass and pours. The amber liquid sloshes round the bottom of the glass when Nell swirls. She sips, the liquid trickles down in a series of satisfying burns, an afterglow lies like woodsmoke on her tongue. Ali's head is cocked to the side expectantly. Nell breaks into a broad grin. She could vault over the counter and kiss her daughter on the bare lips. It's a taste she hasn't enjoyed for the longest time. She sips again and it as if she is holding in her mouth nothing but good, as if the years of estrangement had never happened. A surge of joy lodges in her throat.

She is tasting her daughter's heart.

'My mother,' Ali beams to the elderly man in the centre. 'She's come home.'

CHAPTER SEVEN

Home. Nell stops in her tracks for a moment, looking around. Nearly two weeks and she still can't believe how easy it's been, how fluid. As if she's stepped into a parallel life: the Nell who never went away, the Nell who stayed with her mother in her motherland. Perhaps it's the fine weather, but she feels unusually content, sated each evening on pleasant memories. Pleasant walks with Ali and, sometimes, Grace. Aside from the glitches at the very beginning, it's been a gentle and unspectacular return. And everywhere she senses Agnes's presence. Perhaps it's just wishful thinking but she senses it's a forgiving presence.

Whisht. You're here now. Walk on a bit.

Each morning she phones Henri, delighting in telling him little silly tales about Grace, or her thoughts at Agnes's grave yesterday. She tries to paint a composite picture for him, so that the sights and smells and places revisited can strike him with a similar sense of wonder and immediacy. Of course they can't, and he doesn't pretend; it was her childhood, after all. Still, for these spells of time, she feels closer to him than she has in years, in the way that's only possible once you peel back years and reveal the child before the adult. She describes the landscape folding around her like arms welcoming her back. He laughs when she gets too fanciful – it's so unlike her – but he doesn't say much when she tentatively asks about Lucienne, his decision to leave her, as if he wishes to demarcate two separate journeys, one perhaps contingent upon the other.

If there's time, she heads out for a walk before getting Grace ready for school. No matter which track she takes, she has the strong, no less strange, presentiment that motherland and mother have somehow fused identity. There's nothing fatherland about here, nothing masculine in the soft, matronly contours of these hills, the low rolls of mountain peaking into gradual, gentle cones. Nothing Alpine in the green, leaky folds of green. Nothing soars, except the birds. Even the stark and windswept shorelines affect the knobbly, arthritic joints of an old incontinent woman.

A glance up at the sullen, constipated sky. Where is the rain? Where is the idea of water constantly seeking you out? This flinty dryness is not what she remembers.

Sodden, irregular fields holding rain in mirrors stepped across their surface. That was how it was from her bedroom window. Further along, the notion of sea nibbling every shoreline, trying to get in, while on land water dripped and seeped and skulked, finding a way through everything, bubbling up through knife cracks in granite. Mercury beads on the broad leaves of hazels and alders. Twists of white barley-sugar frothing down every rockface. Even the water was breached by water in treacherous underground streams jetting up into lakes. Low skies coming down as rain, as mist, pressing on your shoulders, coating your tongue when you spoke, getting in your eyes, clinging to eyelashes, so that faces too, became blurred and indistinct.

The rains of her childhood, each with its own personality. There was the powdery spray you didn't even know was there until it dog-licked your face in an instant and frizzed hair on contact. The slanted, stinging, persistent night rain, coming down as if it would never end, gleaming through the pub's window like shoals of tiny silvery fish. Summer rain, after thunder, solitary fat drops crackling against the ground: you could dance between them at the start, until an impatient growl and the sky would open to belch out barrelfuls. Rain mixed with ice into a slushy paste which left white rime round the top of your shoes, once dry. Winter rain, teased by wind, catching you from every angle, needling your face while it beat through your coat from behind, soaking hoods, darting in under impotent umbrellas, driving in over the tops of wellington boots. It poured, pelted, bucketed, teemed, drizzled, flooded — was called hard, soft, gentle, pitiless, reflecting the mood of whoever was commenting on it that day. Was called a curse. Was called simply *weather*. What weather hardly ever did was stop.

But when it did stop, the sky peeled back like a dingy bandage and everything underneath looked glittery and washed. Everything looked new. The green so fresh and tingly, it was almost more than her eyes could bear. Air tasted of vanilla ice-cream. Distant hills came into focus again, the ocean stretched wider than she'd remembered, trees stood out individually from hedges, arms spread out, sunbathing. It had all been there, all the time, under the rain. As it has been, under exile.

Still, there are changes, impossible to overlook. This motherland is wearing lipstick. She's varnished her fingernails. A light golden tan spreads across her body from a warm and sunny summer. She drives a sleek silver car with last year's registration plates. She drapes expensive cotton sweaters across her shoulders. Her local shop bakes its own baguettes, offers fresh croissants each morning, has a wine licence. Her perfume gives off a high, heady scent which drifts round corners. The scent of affluence.

Several times a day, whenever Nick takes over in the pub, Nell and Ali have walked for miles and miles. Sometimes ambling wherever their feet take them, sometimes following a route prescribed by one of Agnes's memory stones. For the most part, they've walked in companionable silence, neither wanting to rile the other by a careless or dismissive comment. Nell has had time to reflect on the real changes that have taken place. Beyond the obvious signs of a new affluence, quite at odds with her childhood years, beyond the large houses, the cars, the Timberland boots and Gap sweatshirts – which may all be ephemeral or superficial – she's sensed something else, something she couldn't quite put her finger on the first couple of days. It came from within, from inside people themselves. It hummed in the air in the pub at night. An undercurrent, a quiet acceptance of their lot. No more than was deserved. She's watched the young girls' smiling, confident faces, barely twenty years old, the measured directness of their gaze. None of the shifty-eyed insecurity of her generation, the squirming uncertainty. She's looked at the assured, youthful faces, unburdened by their parents' history, or their grandparents', and thought with growing astonishment, *This is all you've known.*

Sometimes, in the bar, she's felt that Ali wanted to communicate something. Other times, halfway up a hill, or dodging waves along the shoreline, Ali has suddenly straightened, turned with purpose as if to confide, her mouth slightly open in advance of the unformed thought. Nell has waited but then Ali has evidently thought better, offered a light grin instead and walked on.

Adam has eaten supper with them most evenings before his stint in the bar. She's been extra careful not to interrogate him in front of Ali but on occasion she's glanced his way to find that he's been quietly studying *her*, as though he's trying to make up his mind about something. She's held his gaze for seconds until he's looked away again, but there's been the unsettling impression that they've been circling each other, sniffing, trying to figure out. He's cracked silly knock knock jokes to Grace, sending her into peals of girlish, gratingly forced laughter. When Nick's sat with them too, the men have called one another 'mate'. They've clapped hands on shoulders in awkward, manly gestures, yet Nell has sensed something in Adam's demeanour towards Nick, something at odds with his boyish grin. Yesterday, for a brief moment, as Adam ladled stew onto Nick's plate and leaned across the table to pass it to him, she thought she'd captured that elusive thing: a tiny shadow of contempt flickering in the cinnamon-flecked eyes. But then he asked after Nick's health with such apparent concern and interest that she thought she must have been imagining it. In truth, while she keeps an eye on him when he's around, he barely costs her a thought when he's not.

What you don't know about someone, you make up. In the way that a quiet stillness, a reflectiveness like a canvas, is the star quality some actors possess. The propensity to be anyone, to reflect whatever moods and feelings of the day. Adam, she's come to think, is like *weather*.

She's about to heave a leg over the drystone wall on her way back up the fields when his voice behind gives her such a fright that she nearly stumbles. She swings round.

'Sorry,' he says. 'I thought you knew I was here. I didn't mean to creep up on you.'

It's the only opportunity since the first morning she's had to speak with him alone. She sits on the wall, hoping he'll join her. When he does, she gets the impression he's been waiting for this chance, too. His hands fold contemplatively over a rustling carrier bag on his lap. They're both breathing deeply, looking up at the white duvet of sky, as if this is a ritual they share each morning. She'll be late for Grace, but no matter. The child is used to getting herself ready for school; seeing her off has been for Nell's own pleasure. She studies his profile from the corner of her eye. He's gazing down at Terence the pony when he swivels of a sudden, his wide smile disarmingly brilliant.

'You look happy,' he says.

'Do I?'

'Happier. Than when you first got here, I mean.'

'I suppose I am.'

'Must be strange, though, after so long, being home.'

'Well, yes. Strange but good. So far,' she adds as an after-thought.

'How long will you stay, d'you think?'

It seems an oddly abrupt if not proprietorial thing to ask, as if she's intruding on his turf and not the other way round. A couple of days back, she overheard something which rankled slightly in a similar way. Ali was talking about a harvest festi-val coming up, how she'd like to take Nell. Adam responded that her mother would be gone by then. She didn't hear his words exactly, as she was just coming down into the kitchen, but he didn't say 'probably' or 'might', he said 'gone'.

'What about you?' she asks, keeping her voice friendly, conversational. 'How long will you stay?'

He pulls his mouth down, an exaggerated shrug. Who's to say how long? Who's to say anything about anything with any conviction? She gets the distinct impression he's mocking her. At the very least, playing a game to his own set of rules. He can't know that she's such a solitary being herself that she knows well the difference between casual chat and a probe. He's not sitting on this wall for the good of his health.

'Where's home for you?' She idly knocks two loose stones together.

'Originally? Kent, you could say. But we moved around a lot.'

'We? Your family?'

'My father and me. There was just us. Mostly we lived in trailers. He got itchy feet if we stayed any place for too long.'

'Must have been unsettling for a young boy.'

'Whatever you're used to, I s'pose.'

'Do you ever go back?'

'To Kent? Nah. Nothing to go back to. Old man croaked years ago. Booze,' he adds, before she can ask. 'Amazing he lasted as long as he did.'

He pulls a roll-up from a pocket, lights it and inhales deeply. The tweed eyes glitter with amusement. Full pink lips peel back, his head turns slightly and he lays another dazzling smile on her. No doubt about it, he's quite breathtaking and no doubt about it, he's testing her, offering a little so that he can glean whatever knowledge he's after in return. She smiles back, perfectly friendly but it doesn't quite reach her eyes. He's waiting for her to ask the dozen questions he's anticipating, and when she lets the silence ride there's a little spurt of satisfaction in sensing his confusion.

'D'you think you could ever stay?' he asks after a while.

Nell takes her time. Moves her head this way and that.

'Maybe.' Her eyes deliberately wander past his chest to the planning-permission notice on the rowan tree. Who knows? She might take a notion to build herself. 'Now that I've found my way back . . .' She lets her voice trail off with a shrug. 'What about you?'

'I don't know.' Suddenly he looks serious as the beautiful eyes sweep across the fields, up to the house, back down to the caravan, as if he's torn by conflicting emotions, the wandering minstrel battling with a side of him that yearns to settle, to call somewhere his own. She gives him a sympathetic, encouraging smile, making sure it reaches her eyes this time.

'This could be home, I s'pose,' he adds in a quiet voice.

'This?' Nell's smile doesn't drop, but he's made his first mistake – and he knows it.

'Around here, I mean. This area.' A tiny frown pleats his brow, but he recovers quickly, sliding from the wall in a graceful, liquid movement. 'Who knows?' He moves downfield.

'Adam?'

He turns.

She points to the plastic carrier bag in his hand. 'Something for the house?'

'Just a bunch of herbs. Here, give them to Ali for me.'

'I don't think I recognize half that lot. What on earth can she be cooking?'

'Oh, they're not for cooking.' He blows a stream of smoke sideways. 'They're for Nick. She knows what to do with them.'

'No! You can't make me!' Grace bawls at the top of her voice. Angry veins stand out on her neck. Her eyes are puffed out like sweetbreads. She looks ragged with tiredness but something else as well, her every gesture conveying a taut, almost painful rage. Nell has walked in on a blazing row between Grace and Ali. She checks her watch. Grace is already late for school. Her uniform is only half on. A tight-lipped Ali pulls the child's arms through the sleeves of her cardigan, kneels and slams Grace's feet into her shoes.

'You're going to school and that's *it*.'

The peace of the last week was too good to last. Nell looks from one to the other with a sinking heart. Maybe there was another argument about the bloody psalms last night, which Nell thankfully missed. Did Nell hear footsteps creak on the stairs in the middle of the night? She thought it was part of a dream, but it might have been Grace, searching for a favourite cat. Little wonder the child looks so sleep-deprived.

'You talk to her, Nell. She won't listen to me.'

'What's up, Gracie? Why don't you want to go to school, pet? Is it homework?'

'I'm just not going.'

'Eat your cereal. You're late already.' Ali breathes heavily, trying to calm down. She pours milk onto the mound of Frosties and slides the bowl towards Grace.

The quiet moments in the morning with Grace Nell has loved. The normality of it, Grace munching cereal, eyes still glazed with sleep, a flush on one cheek where it had rested on the pillow, hair hardly shown the brush. The way she gave a distracted smile from time to time before returning to the profound depths of her daydream. The way a drop of milk dribbled down her pointy chin, dangling on the tip until Nell flicked it away with a finger. The rucksack carelessly flung against the door portal. Every morning a big new day beginning.

Not so this day. The honeymoon period is definitely over.

'Eat!' Ali lifts the bowl and bangs it down. Half the contents slosh over the rim.

In a lightning strike, Grace sweeps one arm, sending the bowl crashing to the floor. The knot on her forehead stands out like a fist, her face is scarlet. 'You don't listen to me! You never listen to me!'

Ali collapses into a chair, holding her head in her hands. 'Grace, you're going to make me cry.'

'Good!'

'Maybe she's not feeling well, Ali. Maybe one day off school wouldn't—'

'Nell, you don't understand. This would make it the third day this month alone. Last term it was twelve days. *Twelve.* I'm on a warning from the school already.'

'Grace.' Nick stands at the bottom of the stairs. He's dressed but looks drawn and spectral in the grey morning light.

Grace's breath comes in short rasps. Her mouth works constantly, fighting back tears. The battle is lost and she knows it. The heavy artillery has arrived. How can she resist a father so ill and one who looks at her in such a sad and loving way? She crumples visibly, but not before she pins her mother with smouldering, accusing eyes until Ali is forced to drop her own.

Nick moves quietly toward his daughter and tips her chin up. She looks at him and one loud pent-up sob escapes. Tears glitter on her cheeks. Nell has the distinct feeling that whatever is going on between them all, it's only partly about school.

'C'mon, sweetheart,' Nick says in a soothing voice. 'C'mon, now. I'll drive you.'

Grace wavers for a moment, gulping back further sobs. She angrily jerks her head away when Ali tries to flatten cowlicks in her hair. Without a word, she turns, slings the rucksack on one shoulder and follows Nick through the back porch.

Nell stares expectantly at Ali for some moments. She places the bag with Adam's herbs on the table. Ali just nods in acknowledgement, draws her hands down along her cheeks and lets them rest splayed across her lower jaw. She looks ready to burst into tears herself. Nell makes to move to her but stops when Ali quickly raises a hand. Nell can only hover indecisively.

'She's probably just tired,' she says. 'I'm sure I heard her rambling about last night.'

Ali looks at her, looks away. She puts her knuckles on the table and wearily hoists herself upright. A deep breath, summoning energy, and she heads to the bar to start the morning routine. 'I'll pick the pieces up later,' she says of the bowl.

The village hasn't changed all that much. Although she's passed dozens of new houses stepped along the hills on the outskirts, the centre is still one winding street with brightly painted three-up, two-down cottages, a couple of grocery shops with striped awnings, two pubs, the more imposing of which is rendered back to the original stone, with wooden benches outside, facing out to passing traffic. The church is still painted white and stands alone, incongruously large compared to the cottages on either side. There's a craft shop further along and a coffee house tucked into an alleyway leading nowhere.

Nell stops halfway up the village. Passing cars have to veer in and out to skirt the parked cars which mount the narrow pavement. There is a sleepy almost siesta air at this hour of the day, compounded by the overcast, sagging sky. A couple of young girls pass in slashed jeans and tee-shirts; they link arms and laugh. Their language is foreign. At first Nell assumes they're late tourists but, when one of them steps into the bar and immediately begins serving drinks, she realizes they belong most likely to the Kosovan contingent at the hostel. Ali has mentioned the possibility of hiring casual staff from the hostel. No one local wants to work for the low wage that is all she can offer.

When a dog sniffs her ankles, Nell is suddenly aware that she's been standing rooted to one spot for possibly half an hour. It is as though the street represents an intransigent Stop sign in the carriageway of her life and she is stuck in the middle, unable to move forward, unwilling to move back. Here, under the soles of her feet, a pavement she pounded each day on her way to school, footsteps retraced almost to the toetip after last bell on her way home. She knew everyone in these houses. Said Hello, 'lo, hiya, twice daily, back and forth. Thought then that she would stay here for ever. How could you leave? Why would you? What more could there be?

The sweetshop where she used to spend her weekly pocket money is now a residential house with the large picture window festooned in lobelias and geraniums. She's glad to see that small, self-important dogs still swagger around the place, though, arguing it appears, chatting, delivering news. Moving from door to door, if they could sidle up with paws folded across their chests, mouths crooked for gossip, they would. Busy, inquisitive snouts, stiff stubs for tails, they dart around, effortlessly dodging oncoming traffic as if the cars don't exist. Lulu would be splatted in seconds.

Lulu. Right this moment, Nell wouldn't mind being tucked up in her apartment with the cantankerous little bitch. Waiting for the familiar sound of the lift door closing in the corridor outside, Henri's footsteps stopping at her door. Strange to find that, after years of continuous travelling, it's here she misses him in a way that's deep in her gut. A missing which resembled a subdued wave of grief earlier this morning when he had to cut off abruptly in the middle of telling her about a crisis on the Estate.

She walks on, half expecting to come across herself swinging around a corner, straps of her school bag crossed over her chest in front, white knee socks, worried, distracted frown. 'Lo, 'lo, 'lo.

At the top of the street, she goes into the chemist's shop. Inside, an elderly man with black-rimmed spectacles held together by tape serves her a new supply of tea-tree oil, calomine and lice lotion. She couldn't hold back a minute longer and started dosing Grace last week. She takes a sneaky glance at the herbal shelves to see if there's anything on the market here for flushes that she hasn't tried in Paris. Need any help? the man asks. No, no, she says, just looking. He says they wouldn't mind a drop of rain now after the last couple of dry months. Strange to be saying that, he adds. It's been niggling him since she came in the other day, but her face looks very familiar. Nell tells him who she is. Oh, for God's sake, he says. He used to be at school with her, a few years ahead, of course, but he remembers. And Nell thought he was elderly.

Wasn't there a sister, too? A terrible accident, if he remembers right? Yes, Bridget. Drowned up at the lake in Eagle Rock. He nods soberly. There's a sign up there now, he tells her, warning of that underground stream under the lake. There haven't been any more accidents, thank God.

They chitchat a little while longer, what happened to whom, who went where, who came back. How come he's never seen her around for the holidays before? Nell shrugs, pulls her mouth down – beats her. She pays for the purchases and leaves. He holds the door open for her.

The village comes to an abrupt end a little further along. The road climbs and she can look back and see the ocean in the distance, the village descending but ending long before the line of sea. Tall, manic hedgerows are interspersed with neat privet rows where bungalows and new stone houses cut into the wilderness. Clouds bulge with suppressed light and rain. The hedges give off a sweaty, mineral scent, an almost self-aware ripeness. Their job is done for another year. They want some peace, some rest.

She walks for another ten minutes until there are mostly low walls and little hedgerow remaining. A series of neat white bungalows, with clipped front lawns and fading roses trailed over arches, leads to Nell's old primary school, set apart and back from the main road. A white rectangle with tall, narrow casement windows and a black slate roof, picture-pretty with an engraved plaque on the front-facing wall. That was it in her day, but it appears to be empty or maybe it serves as a hall for occasional use because the main school, a modern prefabricated building, stretches out at the rear. It's as though the original building has been preserved for purely decorative purposes. The front playground is deserted, though she can hear the noise and shouts of children at play from the back. There is a narrow passageway running alongside the buildings. Nell steps through, hoping to catch a glimpse of Grace. She peers through a criss-cross mesh of steel wire. Tall plants and shrubs block a clear view but she can see legs pounding concrete, a football hurled back and forth among a group of boys. Girls of varying ages squeal with pleasure playing catch.

She slipped out earlier without telling Ali where she intended to walk. All morning, Grace's impotent, glittery tears kept haunting her. She thought maybe she might catch a glimpse of Grace in the schoolyard, playing, being happy. Maybe they might walk home together. Her eyes scan wall to wall of playground, her heart giving an excited little blip each time she thinks that laughing girl is Grace, or that one.

But when her eyes at last light on her granddaughter, Grace is not laughing. She mooches against a far wall, not moving except for the constant kick back of her heels, a bored drubbing, against brick. It's as though there's a halo of exclusion surrounding her. Occasionally, she moves her head this way and that, following the line of another girl's run, a stiffening in her slight frame as she represses the almost irrepressible urge of small children wanting to run, one after the other. Further along the wall, two older girls with black skin and braided hair hold swinging hands and refrain from joining in also. But their seclusion looks more deliberate, more self-elected, than Grace's. A teacher comes out, ringing an old handbell. The sound is disturbingly familiar. The children fall lightly into long, loose lines and begin the march back inside. Grace hangs back and then does something which forces an involuntary cry from Nell's lips. She knows this movement so well, knows exactly what Grace wishes to convey by that bend forward to re-tie the strap on her shoe. She is saying, I would have played if my shoe wasn't so loose. This she tells herself every day to alleviate her suffering because no one will play with her.

Nell covers her mouth with her hands. Tears prick the inside of her eyelids. Grace has half hobbled, half hopped to the very back of the queue, still looking vexedly down at the troublesome shoes which, in truth, would transport her round the schoolyard at warp speed if another pair of shoes deigned to chase them. Three girls of Grace's age, sporting sleek ponytails of various lengths, giggle and stamp their feet just in front of her. She's the last child in the line. She's hanging back, but when she takes a step too close, one of the girls swivels, gives her an excoriating look and elbows further distance between them. The ponytails swing excitedly into class. Grace gives that tiresome buckle one last irritated glance, raising her ankle slightly to the side. The knot on her forehead stands out like an engraving. And then Nell's heart is pierced: just at the entrance, she attempts one devil-may-care skip, the limp, lukewarm hop of a dog grazed by a car's bumper. The door closes and Grace is swallowed up. The last child in. No doubt, the last child out. Nell slides away.

The first few months back at school after Bridget's death were very strange. Aside from the jumble of emotions she couldn't even begin to sort through, there were simple, physical things which threw her day after day. One prepared school lunch on the kitchen table, instead of two. Baubles in the bathroom for one set of pigtails. The sound of her footsteps on the walk to school, singular and distinct in their own rhythm, no longer stepping up the pace to fall into line, or hanging back so that her sister could catch up. There was the business of limitless chips for dinner and two slices of Battenburg cake, if she wanted, because it would still last the three-day span between herself and her mother. Her sweets lasted for ever without the threat of filching fingers. And in the evenings, one set of homework strewn across the floor of the parlour, no accompanying piano from the bar as Bridget practised her scales over and over again, under the watchful eye of Agnes.

In the beginning, there were dramatically sympathetic glances, teary-eyed looks, hushed tones breaking off into silences as Nell approached clusters of children in the schoolyard. Bridget had been by far the more popular sister, a flamboyant gang leader, a maker-up of games, the girl you had to ask if you could join her gang for release hunting. *Join our gang for releeease hunting.* The girl to whom you relinquished your skipping rope if she expressed an interest in it. The girl who wore her long red scarf, picking her out as captain, as if there could be any doubt. The scarf-bound legs together for three-legged races, cordoned dens, flew in the wind like the red badge of courage when rival gangs made a sortie, looped round backs for chain hunting. *Join our gang for chaaain hunting.* In the classroom, she was the girl who back-answered teachers but never to a degree that got her into serious trouble, only sufficient to keep the flames of her leadership constantly fanned.

If challenged, Bridget could be ruthless: you were excised from her company, the ambits of her sovereignty, with one cutting look, a cutting word and a push. Equally, when she wished to bestow favour it was like the first day of the summer holidays. She cleaved you to her side, asked your opinion in front of everyone, loudly stood up for you if there was even the hint of an insult from a party currently out of favour. It was intoxicating. No less to Nell, her younger sister, who by and large received the same treatment as everyone else. And suffered like everyone else when Bridget's favour was revoked in an instant, with no explanation, no sign of a warning. Just as when you were in with the queen, you were in with every small, fickle body in the playground – when you were out, you were on your own.

Still, there was a certain cachet to be had from being Bridget's sister. While Bridget could be quite merciless in her dealings with her sister, all the while reinforcing her own tribal rule, there was nevertheless, an understanding, never quite put to the test, that, should you attempt to treat Nell as harshly as her sister on occasion, you wouldn't be in the better for it. Thus Nell was protected to an extent, safe in the spectral rings orbiting her sibling's planet. She knew better than to try to outshine, or exercise any gravitational pull on the other jetsam orbiting with her. She was quiet and studious, preferring books to yard games, a neat lined-up pencil case to skipping ropes with flashing handles. On the sports field Bridget outran, outjumped, outfoxed even the sixth-class students. Nell watched. And cheered when Bridget sent her a sidelong glance to check that she was cheering.

For a while, after Bridget's death, it was as though her very absence still exercised a pull. As though the children in her class, in the schoolyard in general, still circled the empty space she had once so compellingly occupied. She was spoken of in awed, reverent tones; in effect she had performed the ultimate transendence, she was a deity. Until a testing trickle of dissent – without apparent repercussions – swelled slowly but inexorably into a flood of half-remembered slights, long-nursed grievances, grudges, and Bridget was plucked from the sky.

Within months she was the nasty little bitch who gave

everyone such a hard time. There was joy and release in being part of the turning tide. She was dead and there was nothing you couldn't say about her, nothing for which she couldn't be ascribed the blame. She was the tyrant and now they were free. Her former best friend, a girl called Avril O'Mahoney, led the revolution. Henchwoman number one saw her chance to wear the golden crown, and the first manifestation of her reign was the realization that there had to be a bloodletting, a sacrifice.

There followed years of relentless and exquisitely executed persecution of the dead queen's sister. Nell didn't have a prayer. On the one hand, the fun of Bridget, the mad, shiny-eyed fulguration of her presence, was a terrible loss. No one, not even Avril O'Mahoney in her best attempts, could come close to thinking up the wild, crazy games that Bridget tossed out with the ease of spit from her mouth. On the other hand, here was a chance to pay her back for all the cruel jibes, the fat jokes, the loss of face. Cruelty swelled on its own momentum. While privately many of the girls Nell's age and older considered her an innocent victim and felt sorry for her, publicly there was something irresistible, something entirely seductive, about watching someone else get it. And get it good. Moreover, every day, so you didn't get a chance to get it.

Nell was isolated. No one dared walk to or from school with her. Far too risky. Her pencil case was ransacked incessantly. Notes were pinned to the back of her uniform cardigan. Her flask was smashed so many times that Agnes made her take a plastic bottle of milk each morning. Her head was rammed down the yard's filthy toilets too many times to count. The nuns could see what was happening and made obligatory and ineffective little spiels from time to time about the heinous crime of bullying. If anything, things only got worse after such a spiel. How could anyone take the hypocritical admonishments of the nuns seriously? The women were masters of the art of bullying themselves. They had degrees in it.

The children were drugged on their own cruelty, revolted yet fascinated by the lengths to which they were apparently prepared to go. She was the perfect victim, rarely complaining, bowed-head enduring, accepting their excesses as if it were only her due. She learned just the right moment to cry, when their thirst was slaked enough to desist for a while. She learned how to melt into walls at playtime so that she didn't stand out and invite humiliation. She learned games she could play in her head while keeping her face impassive and inanimate at all times. She learned a skulk suitable for the runt in the pack, a slipping in and out of shadows, a way to eke out the interminable hours of play in long silent steps spent behind the rusty, corrugated rain shelter. If a gang came around and found her, their eyes lit up with the avarice of children happening on a hidden treat long forgotten.

Throughout the years the bullying continued, Nell never once told her mother. Agnes had her suspicions, of course. How could she not, when her daughter came home from school each day bruised, yet never with any companions or friends around to do the bruising. Though she came close a couple of times, Nell could not bring herself to let her mother know. It was like a dark, throbbing layer of skin she wore beneath her outer skin. She felt that she would be physically sick if she even tried to speak about it. How could she say, to a mother immersed in grief for her golden child, that everybody hated the dull brown sparrow left behind?

No, that thought was too close to her heart, too close for voicing, or even, for tears.

She turned the hate in on herself — it was impossible not to, though in the beginning she had tried finding ways not to let them in, not to let them past that top protective stratum. And then there was Agnes herself; the curious, ambivalent smile did not invite confidence. At home, too, the loss of Bridget was an immovable boulder with a surface they could only skim with their eyes, from opposite sides.

Things began to improve around fourth class. By sixth class the memory of Bridget was all but expunged from the school, for everyone bar Nell. A young French girl, Aimée, joined Nell's class. She was quiet and studious, too; her English wasn't perfect and Nell helped her out. Best of all, she had no knowledge of Nell's spell in purgatory. The two of them in turn were adopted into another circle of quiet girls, swots, and Aimée taught them how to say I love you in French, in a corner of the yard at playtime. I love you and you are so beautiful it breaks my heart. They swooned around clutching their hearts, heady with their own feeling of sophistication. I love you and you are so beautiful it breaks my heart. That was the business.

Nell didn't get pushed out of the queue for the water tap any longer. She remembered to pass her bag of sweets round the whole class and never complained when it came back empty. She was good at sums and let anyone who wanted to cog from her copy book first thing in the morning. She came in extra early each morning for that reason. On the way home from school, she tagged along behind the quiet girls, increasing her pace day by day until her footsteps fell into line alongside theirs. It was a gradual incline. Nothing spectacular, nothing like the luminous, outrageous returns to favour that occupied her dreams. Nevertheless, anywhere was higher than rock bottom. From the whole tormenting process, however, Nell extracted a singular and useful lesson. She had learned how to be alone. She had learned the two primary benefits of being alone. One, you can't hurt your own feelings. Two, you can't hurt anyone else's, either.

By secondary school, when hormones and puberty were laying waste to all the girls around, Nell was quietly and convincingly protected by a coat of steel armour plate. She brushed past the older Avril O'Mahoney on the school bus one day and heard herself say, in a very soft voice, Fuck you. What did you say? Did any of you hear her? What did she say to me? Nell stopped halfway down the aisle of the bus, turned with slow deliberation. Louder. I said, Fuck you.

That was the day Bridget stopped inhabiting her dreams and Nell stopped haunting her own house. The day she knew she would leave, first chance she got.

She leaves the graveyard, moving round the chapel to the entrance. The steps leading to the front door make her catch her breath of a sudden. It's as if she's just stumbled into an old photograph, the kind that shocks you, that there was ever such a time, that there was ever such a you. Headstones are too calculated, too clinical, a start, an end date, a name, a line or two to span a life. These steps are the real memorial. Her eyes carry over every indent, mossy crack, the shiny smooth edges. She sits at the top for a moment with her hands tucked round her knees. She could close her eyes, slide her fingers along and read them like braille. All these years, they have been preserved, every crack and fissure in place, filed away in a corner of her consciousness – likewise every mass, holy communion, confession, funeral, that went with them. Huge events shape us – the births, sicknesses, deaths cut swathes from our lives, set things off in new directions, leave indelible marks. But it is the tiny things – a set of steps, a glance of disappointment, a shiny shoe buckle, tiny betrayals, the odd well-appointed fuck you, the hours spent behind a dripping, rusted rain shelter, the endless accretion of memory stones, one piled on top of another – that really stack us into the shape we become.

She goes inside, filled with a longing to bundle Grace into her arms. The interior is cool, vanilla walls with dark stained-glass windows. Oak pews with cushioned knee rests in front. She sits at the back and watches flickering candles up by the entrance to the altar. An idea of prayer flits across her mind, more an instinct, a response to some faint echo. For years she has disbelieved with far greater conviction than she ever believed unquestioningly as a child. Still, her hands automatically clasp together, she moves forward onto her knees. Almost as if Agnes is behind her, quietly insisting.

She can hear the soft intonation of her mother's prayers, the pp-pp sound of her lips pressing together, a rich, oval Amen before the next Hail Mary. There was a day when she watched Agnes cross the street from the grocery shop to the church, her hands weighted down with bags. Nell was nine or so, at the height of her persecution at school. Her heart gave a little flip when she spied Agnes. They could walk home together. One day's reprieve from the constant baiting and name-calling all the way home.

On her way into the chapel, Nell had reached down and picked up a smooth, shiny lump of shale. With it curled in her paw, she'd tiptoed down the central aisle to where Agnes was bent forward across the pew nearest to the altar. Her shoulders were rising and lowering slightly with the intensity of prayer. Three fresh candles winked from the stand by the altar's brass rail. Nell slid into the pew behind her mother, savouring the passing seconds: just the two of them in the dimly lit chapel, together.

She leaned across, lightly tapping Agnes's shoulder with the shale, then extended it on the outstretched palm of her hand. But Agnes froze. For the briefest of seconds she flinched as though she'd been touched by fire. Soundless tears were coursing down her face and, too late, Nell realized that her mother had been crying, not praying. She saw her own horrified face reflected in Agnes's twin black pupils. Her hand curled round the piece of shale again, prepared to withdraw, but Agnes recovered herself in time and reached for it. She slipped it into her coat pocket and leaned back to stroke Nell's cheek. But Nell was already out of her pew and running, still on tiptoe, up the aisle and out onto the street. Later that evening, Nell burrowed in her mother's coat pocket, found the stone, ran downfield to the small cove below and flung it into the waiting ocean as far as her hand could throw. She did not offer another.

Nell's right hand makes the sign of the cross, impossible to resist. She decides to wait for Grace. She positions herself outside on the top step again until the first trickle of small bodies begins to pass. The three ponytails swish by, arms linked, black patent shoes slickly eating up pavement. Nell steps out onto the street, and there is Grace trailing them at a distance, very much alone. Nell makes a point of shouting her greeting loudly, with a hint of excitement. Grace's face lights up and she runs into her arms. Out of the corner of her eye, Nell sees the surprised ponytails swivel, they check her out from head to toe. One of them sucks a lollypop, eyes as round as the pop.

Right, ladies. Bell's gone. Round one. Off we go.

'We're going into that shop over there,' Nell says in the over-loud voice, 'and you can have whatever is your heart's desire, Gracie.'

'Anything?'

'Anything.'

Grace beams. She casts the girls a sly glance under her lashes, pleased to see they are every bit as attentive as she hoped. Nell and Grace swing arms, crossing the street. The girls are huddled now, whispering. In the shop, Grace whirls dervishly, throwing anything she can put her hands on into a basket before her grandmother changes her mind. Boxes of chocolates, a pencil case, comics, long chew bars, bottles of Lucozade – which Nell happens to know she hates – one orange, one apple, three packs of after-dinner mints, bubble gum, gobstoppers, several cans of catfood, a sliced loaf. Nell lifts the sliced loaf, shrugs – whatever – dumps it back in the basket. They stagger out with the loaded bags, mindful of the keen surveillance from across the road. As they walk along, Grace lifts various items out for a look, holding them aloft to keep her audience's attention. Ooh! Aah! Megachew bar, the longest chew bar in the world. She's always wanted one of those.

Nell has to turn away to hide her grin. *No need to teach you the game, girlie.*

Louder, maniacal slurping as they walk along. No trace left of this morning's furies. The pink slimy thing about a foot long disappears entirely inside her mouth. Pulls back out on a slick of spit, making a smacking sound at the end. The level of concentration is nothing short of phenomenal.

She'll make some man very happy one day, Nell has the ungrandmotherly thought.

'All right now, Grace?' Nell bends to kiss the conker head gently.

The head gives a quick tilt. 'Yeah.'

An old banger coughs and splutters on the road as it passes. Nell swivels, realizing the driver was Adam. His hand extends through the driver's window, waves a backward greeting to them. Her own hand curls in a too-late response.

Grace watches the car until it disappears around a corner. The bluish skin under her eyes is stretched and taut-looking. She hurls the megachew bar into the ditch and walks on.

'A fly got on it,' she says over one hunched shoulder.

CHAPTER EIGHT

A li is baking apple and blackberry pies. A sight to be seen indeed; Nell has to cover her smile. Flour everywhere, on the table, on the floor, the makeshift matting of old newspapers spread across the floor. In the tufts of Ali's spiky hair, streaked along her cheek. A dusting across the bowl of wet, juicy blackberries she's picked. She gives Nell and Grace a quick smile, holds up a circle of clumpy, brownish pastry for them to admire.

'Yum,' Grace offers in a doubtful voice. She swigs a glass of milk down, wiping a white moustache with the back of her hand. Her eyes widen a little, looking at Nell, who desperately wants to say to Ali, Don't you know you're supposed to grease the dish before you lay the pastry on? But she doesn't because this is Ali's peace offering to her daughter. She doesn't say anything when Ali chucks in the chunks of fraying apple, chucks in the floury blackberries and lays the second layer of pastry on top, forgetting to sugar the fruit.

'That's just the first,' Ali says. 'I'm making two.'

'I was wondering about that. If one would be enough.'

Over by the sink, a slimy grassy concoction lies at the

bottom of a perspex jug. She's seen it a couple of times before and didn't want to ask. There is information she can live without. Some formula, no doubt, to make them all greener, gooder. She's probably had some and didn't know it.

'We passed Adam on the way. Where was he off to?'

'I think he was meeting one of the Kearney brothers. The builders.'

'Oh? To look at a house?'

'Plans for a house. For the site below. That's if he decides to build.' Ali gives a quick cursory check over her shoulder. Nell manages to keep her expression bland, but only just. All very well this talk of building; where's the talk of actually buying?

'How was school, Grace? All right in the end?' Ali's voice is so cheery bright, she could light up amphitheatres.

Grace shrugs, pulls a face. She's trying to blow a bubble from a wad of pink gum. A black and white cat weaves in and out round her ankles. She bends to pick it up, nuzzling her nose into its neck.

'You could ask somebody, for supper, if you like.'

Grace pretends not to hear; she murmurs to the cat. The public phone rings in the bar outside. Someone picks it up. Ali checks to see if Nell has registered that it's been fixed.

'It serves as the house phone, too,' she says. 'We don't get many calls.' She hums 'Amazing Grace', giving her daughter's cheek a quick tweak on her way to the Aga.

The first pie is slammed in and the door closed with relish. Ali checks her watch, pats her chest breathlessly. 'There. What, about two hours d'you think? Less?'

Nell takes a deep breath, jiggles her head. 'I'd give it a check in, oh, say, under an hour?'

'You think?'

'No harm in checking. The Aga, you know.'

'Yes, there is that. I could get into this baking, you know. It's kind of relaxing.' In spite of this, a wormy vein stands out on her temple, signalling one of her migraines. Baking not one but two tarts is a lot of concentrated effort on Ali's part. Nell feels a little throb of pride.

'You used to love it when you were a little girl.'

'Did I? Where?'

'In Uncle Albie's house. We used to bake up a storm.'

Ali frowns, trying to remember, rubs a floury hand along the unmarked cheek so that, with a chevron on either side now, she resembles a Mohican squaw.

'Funny. Now you say it, I do remember something, fairy cakes, or butterfly with cream in the middle.'

'That's it. We'd scoop out the top and make two wings.'

'But that was with Mary Kate, wasn't it?'

'No, Ali, that was with me.'

'I know, let's have a baking party.' Ali claps her hands, turns glowing eyes on her less than enthusiastic daughter. 'Would you like that, Gracie? Bet your friends would love that. What d'you think?'

Grace watches the cat slide over her arm in one long continuous movement; it unrolls like a swathe of ermine. 'Okay, yeah.'

'Tomorrow maybe?'

'Soon,' Grace says.

'Right. I'd better get on with this second pie then. I wish I'd told you get some cream, Nell. I think there's some ice-cream, though.' Ali flies unsifted flour into a mixing bowl. 'What's in the bags, Gracie?'

Nell groans inwardly, moves to spirit them away, but

Grace is already eagerly showing off her booty. She tips out bag after bag on top of the flour-covered table. Ali folds her arms, nodding, as golden boxes of chocolates follow dark green mints. Nodding, as stripey, rustling packages heap up in mounds. Tubes of mints and Refreshers roll onto the floor. Lollipop heads gleam like rubies. The table is buried.

'Hey,' Ali says with a fixed, glassy little smile, 'it's like a party.'

'And I wasn't even good,' Grace says in astonishment.

If she could stand behind herself and take a running kick at her own backside, she would. Of course it wasn't intentional, raining on Ali's blackberry and apple pie parade; nonetheless, the damage was done. Nell walks downfield, inhaling deep breaths. She'd love to close her eyes and wake up in her apartment, surrounded by her own life, her own things. In a day, her visit has turned on its head. She can feel it all going horribly wrong. The rosy-tinged nostalgia of the past week is slipping through her fingers, memories seem unpleasant, with dark, broody edges, too pungent and far too raw. Things she had long forgotten, lying in ambush, waiting to jump out at her. There's that itchy, scratchy feeling in her second skin to get away, be by herself. It's years since she's been surrounded by other bodies for such a duration.

Visits to Oxford were often missions to find out the lie of the land, to see if Ali was back on heroin or not. She stayed in nearby hotels, eschewing Ali's chaotic shambles of a flat. There wasn't room for her, she said, though Nick bought a second-hand sofa-bed. Not in your living room, I can't do that to you, she said. She wouldn't stay with Uncle Albie and

Mary Kate, because that would have been unfair to Ali, seeing as she wouldn't stay with her. She said.

When Ali and Grace came to Paris, it was usually for a long weekend. There were a thousand trips to pack into such a short time. Their feet hardly touched the ground. There were holidays, of course, paid for by Nell. Ali and Grace would join her at the appointed airport in the middle of a wine-tasting tour. Somewhere hot, so that they had a beach or a pool to occupy their days while she worked. Then there were Christmases when she whisked them to a chalet in the snow. Nick was a fine skier, the couple of times he came along. Ali never learned but she seemed happy to watch Nell take Grace onto the learner slopes, decked out in a quilted snowsuit with fur round the hood, Nell's Christmas present to her granddaughter. Look what Nan got me, and I wasn't even good.

When Agnes was alive, before Grace was born, they all congregated at Uncle Albie's and Mary Kate's for Christmas, occasionally Easter too. Then Nell would stay in her old room at the top of the house. But only ever for a few nights because there was always a trip to London to be combined, once she was in the country in the first place. You're a busy woman, Agnes said; mind you don't run yourself into an early grave. For years she hadn't added her usual coda: and next Christmas we'll all sit around a table in Kerry and there won't be half the running and racing, isn't that right?

There was only one occasion, a Christmas in Paris, when Agnes looked Nell in the eye and came straight out with it. You're not coming home. Never. Is that the way? Nell speared a slice of turkey, cutting it into tiny pieces. No, I wouldn't say that, she said, not never . . . just, not yet. I have tried, Mammy. I have. Agnes set her fork and knife side by side on her plate. Never, she repeated, her face darkly resigned. For the rest of the day, they didn't dare catch each other's eye. Nell left for Sydney two days later, leaving Agnes and Ali behind in the apartment for the rest of the holiday. You're a busy woman, Agnes said at the airport; mind you don't run yourself into an early grave.

But Nell didn't find the constant travelling in the least exhausting. If anything her sparking plugs were energized at the prospect of the next trip, packing for the next airport. Somehow, it was always she who was doing the leaving.

Although, she has to admit, she has been slowing down a lot lately. A couple of times she's cancelled at the last minute and gone to bed with honey and lemon drinks, in an effort at convincing herself she's nursing a cold. She lies under the bedcovers, listening to silence reverberate around the room, like a thing she can touch. Sometimes she snakes a hand into the air to let the silence coat her skin. Feeling it penetrate, creeping all the way through every layer, moving down past her armpit, over her breastbone, through the embroidery of twisting sinews and tissues until it spears right into her heart. At such moments, she knows the peace of the grave her mother had so often predicted.

Nell pulls her hands down the sides of her face. It's this, she thinks, the everyday commerce, the everyday transactions of human exchange, the unspoken shivery businesses, the unintentioned slights both exacted and received, that really exhausts. The endlessness of it.

Has she left it too late to endure this everyday commerce with Henri? she wonders. Answering questions when she wants to be quiet. Checking his mood when he is silent: has she done something wrong, said something wrong? A continuous presence, the apartment already filled with him, his things, when she returns from a tour. His face on a pillow beside her every morning, his snores throughout the night. The clattering in the kitchen as he prepares an evening meal, conversation throughout, when she usually eats to the accompanying breathy sound of pages turning on her book. Worst of all, as she prepares to leave, a voice asking, when will she be back?

The whinnying of the untethered pony cuts into her thoughts; he plucks at scrubby grass to the side of the caravan. Nell glances quickly over her shoulder. She can't be seen from the house, at least not downstairs. This might be her only chance to look inside the caravan. She moves closer. A swift look up the field: still clear. The decision is made before she has time to consider. She wrenches the door handle, expecting resistance, but it swings open freely. A gusty inhalation to the foundation of her lungs and she steps inside, closing the door behind.

Inside, she stands still for a moment, exhaling, before she takes a deep sniff in anticipation of must, smoke, body odours, sweat perhaps, soiled laundry, cooked food – what is this tin can, after all, but a capsule for smells? A sealed container for every human effusion imaginable. Strangely, the air is chaste, nothing to give her an olfactory sense of *him*.

She has always relied on her nose to crosshatch a fuller picture, making up her mind whether she likes or distrusts someone from the secrets their skin reveals. The telltale exudations as readable to her as body language to another. Henri laughed when she told him, thought it was a ludicrous idea that you could *nose* people like wine. What if they've just farted? he joked. What if— Oh shut up, I'm sorry I told you now.

Some months later he said he'd taken to practising her

little habit. Inhaling people. He was loath to concede but thought there might be something in it. But he couldn't keep a straight face when Nell wanted for instances. Instead, he mocked the pair of them for their fancifulness. *As if.* The soul in the sweat glands, seeping through.

Adam's soul resists disclosure. She breathes in again but aside from a faint, residual pepperiness – an echo of hash – it is as though the atmosphere has been bleached.

The interior, too, comes as a surprise, being considerably more spacious than she would have expected. Everything compact, doll's-house miniature, tucked-in neat and tidy. Not a book or a used ashtray or the dregs of coffee in a mug to make it seem used or lived in. If anything, she is reminded of her own apartment.

Along one wall, there is a small steel sink with wood veneer built-in cupboards aligned above and below. One opens to reveal a fridge with nothing inside bar milk, some eggs, a bag of tomatoes. A bottom tray pulls out containing clear plastic bags with what appear to be more of the herbs he gave her for Ali. A cubicle toilet behind another door. Beside that, single wardrobe with shelves along the bottom, one pair of trainers, couple of sweaters, an extra pair of jeans, boxers and tee-shirts rolled into a ball at the back of one of the shelves.

She moves up to the other side of the caravan. A bank of cushions along either wall, with a table which folds down in between. The cushions lift and pull out to form beds, one either side, though when both pull out they must form a double across the width of the room. Back at the phalanx of cupboards, she opens them all. Nothing but a couple of pots, mugs, mismatched plates, saucers with no cups, three bowls. A stack of drawers offer no more than the same mismatched array of cooking utensils, frying pan, odd knives and forks, spoons of varying shapes and sizes. Dishcloths.

She opens each drawer with a growing urgency. There must be something. An envelope, a passport, a driving licence, medical card — for God's sake something, anything, to indicate he comes from somewhere. To show that he exists, is on some computer file for something. How can there be so little of a person? Just where he sleeps, what he wears, what he eats from, where he craps. Her eyes sweep back and forth, looking for a shelf or a cupboard or a concealed door she hasn't yet tried. But the inventory appears to be complete. There isn't anything more. She stands in the middle of the room with her shoulders up around her ears, hands raised, palms turned upwards in defeat. It's just not feasible. Everyone holds onto *something*.

One of the cushions on his bed is still slightly raised where she lifted it. She pats it back into place but it doesn't align perfectly with the next cushion. There is a slight gap and beneath, on the ground, under the mesh of metal bedsprings, there is something. Quickly, feeling a telltale flush of panic and anxiety creep up her cheeks, she pulls all the cushions off and reaches down. She still can't see in the shadowy corner. There's a small gap in the springs and she plunges an arm through, fingers inching across dusty surface until they connect with a small sheaf of papers. She manages to draw a few towards her and quickly tucks them into the waistband of her jeans, pulling her sweater down. There's still something solid under there. The tip of her middle finger rubs against cold metal, something cylindrical. She strains her arm further inside, just as the rattling of a broken exhaust sounds right outside the door. There's barely time to straighten, pat the cushions into place, before Adam stands at the door, one foot poised on the step, one still in the field.

Nell just looks at him. Really, there's nothing to say.

Aside from a rapid contraction and dilation of his pupils, nothing in his face shows what he feels about this incursion. His eyes flick from side to side, taking in where she might have been, what she might have seen. As she's standing by the pull-out bed, he will assume that she's rooted about under there. He steps up in a lithe movement that makes her jump, pulls the door closed behind him.

'What are you doing?'

'I just wanted to see what it looks like inside. Caravans . . . fascinate me.' *Caravans what? Christ.* 'The way they're laid out,' she blunders on. 'You know, things having various functions. Like sofas turning into beds,' she adds wanly. 'I'm sorry. I should have asked. You weren't here so I just . . .'

A concentrated, meditative frown splits his forehead, a man in solitary, oblivious of walls, deep within himself. Although his thumbs are tucked into loops on his jeans and he hasn't moved any closer, his presence fills the caravan. The way his pupils continue to swell then contract, as he pins her with the tawny eyes, is quite disturbing. A trickle of sweat runs from her scalp down the length of her neck. She puts both hands to the middle of her waist, to keep the loose pieces of paper in place. Already she can feel one about to furl over her waistband. If it slides down her crotch she thinks she will herself curl over and die.

'I'm sorry,' she says again, to break the disconcerting silence. 'Look, I'll go.' A tiny step, but he doesn't move. She's only succeeded in getting closer to him. The last thing she wanted, because now she can see there's a tight ridge of white over his top lip. His breaths come in shallow rasps. He is more than angry, he is incandescent.

'Tell me something.' He manages to keep his voice even. 'Why do people think they can do this? As if a caravan isn't your home, doesn't rate the same rules. You wouldn't just walk in a house, would you? Anybody's house?'

But this isn't anybody's field. It's my daughter's field.

But she doesn't say any of that, because then he would know for sure that she entered with an ulterior motive. Better if they can both pretend, at least, that she's just been a bit rude, a little thoughtless.

'You're quite right,' she says airily, determined that he won't see she's intimidated.

'Am I? Quite right? Thank you.'

Nell blinks back her surprise. Of course he's right, she did just patronize him. He's perfectly aware that it's not much of a home to be defending, that it's not even situated on land he owns. They both know she has the upper hand. He can hardly call the police. Something about the way his raised, hackled shoulders lower helplessly, the expelled, frustrated breath, makes her see beyond this moment. She can see the endless series of these moments he must have endured as a child, an adolescent, now an adult, still going through the same humiliation. Still relying on the kindness of strangers at thirty years of age. She knows what it's like to be the outcast, to be *other.* She is also aware how addictive that otherness can become. To the point of obsession.

'Adam, I can see I've upset you. Forgive me. I won't intrude again.'

His eyes flicker up. Sceptical at first, he scans her face for traces of insincerity and, finding none, his anger and frustration seem to dissolve. The dark clouds roll away from his face

and the sun comes out – that dazzling smile. Impossible not
to reciprocate with a curl of her own lips. He moves closer,
blocking light and air so that there is nothing but him. That
restive energy, coursing silently through his body. Grains of
sand contained in a smooth glass shell.

'It's only intruding if you're not invited.'

'So I'm invited now? Thanks,' she says in a light, jokey
way, growing ever more aware of the awkward stance they've
somehow managed to set up. Like two amateur actors, facing
off, unable to use their hands naturally. Her own feel like
two heavy stumps, pinned solidly to her sides.

'I'm here by invitation too,' he says.

'Yes. I know. Ali explained.'

'She says you're worried about me being here. That's why
you came.'

'Maybe.' Her head falls forward, loose locks of hair screening her face. 'But it was time to come home in any case.'

It's impossible not to be over-conscious of his close prox-
imity. She should use this moment to ask him straight out
what his intentions are. If he has money to buy land as Ali
maintains, she's seen precious little sign of it in here, not so
much as a cheque book. Yet she feels strangely tongue-tied.

'What's Ali told you about me, anyway?' he asks.

'Not a lot.'

'She talks about you all the time.'

'Does she?'

'Mostly in a nice way. Yeah.' His thumbs unhook from the
jeans, arms fold out behind in a langorous stretch, fingers
lock together tightly. The motion makes an arc of his body,
so that it looks as if he's restrained while attempting to press
closer. 'So what d'you want to know, Nell? What's the burning question?'

The direct approach catches her off guard for a moment.

'I think you can figure that out for yourself.'

'Am I going to rip Ali off? Take advantage of her kindness and generosity?' Though he's smiling, Nell detects a bitter ring to his tone, a metallic edge. 'She's a grown woman, you know. I think she can handle herself.'

'Do you indeed? Well, I'm not so sure.'

'So you intend sticking around until you are sure. Is that it?'

'Have you got a problem with that?'

They're both smiling now, it's perfectly conversational, they might be discussing the weather. To a degree, she thinks, they are. But he's much more complicated than rain, she's certain of that. And he hasn't answered any questions, merely asked his own.

He considers for a while, the silence heavy and laden between them. She blinks when the hands behind his back suddenly unlock and the taut body acquires a languid, fluid grace again. A slow, easy grin breaks on his face, inviting trust, inviting confidence.

'Why should I have a problem with you being here? You're family. I'm only the guest, after all.'

'A very welcome guest. You've been a great help to Ali and Nick. Thank you for that.'

There. That should have patronized him sufficiently, hammered in the boundary pegs. But he doesn't appear to be annoyed, if anything, he seems amused.

'You don't trust people very easily, do you?'

'No, I don't.'

'I s'pose that's why you, me — we're on our own.'

She starts when he reaches out to brush stray wisps of hair from her face, gently tucking them behind her ear, fingertips whispering against skin as his hand withdraws again. Her cheek is on fire where he touched. She could cover the distance between them with one step and the temptation is almost irresistible. His smile is so tender, as if he is waiting for her to confide her entire history. What a relief to put all suspicion aside, lay her head on his shoulder and wait for his arms to press her close. Feel his youth running through her, making her wet and alive and somehow, new again. Somehow *present* again.

His head is cocked to the side, wondering how she'll react to what was, in effect, his intrusion on her person. The smile on his lips, shyer now, questioning: has he overstepped the mark? And in an instant she realizes she's been played like a ukelele.

She waits for the flush to subside. When she meets his gaze full on, her eyes tell him he's made a big mistake. It's satisfying to see a cloudy film of doubt drift across the tawny irises, the quick swell of pupil, a tiny frown creasing his forehead. Slowly, her hand reaches out, pressing lightly against his chest. He bends a touch closer, about to say something but she increases the pressure against his chest until he must either resist or take a step back. A slight hesitation, still not entirely clear about what message she's sending. Then he steps abruptly to the side, clearing her path to the door. For a brief second, the beautiful features appear marred with roiling clouds again. The ugly, complex expression of a spurned adolescent. She takes her time, making sure she doesn't bother to turn and close the door behind. Aware that he's watching her all the way up the field.

At the stone wall, she lets out the breath she's been holding and inhales deeply. The air is busy again; from a distance a pungent odour of split pine cones, desiccated berries, October rot, sea spray.

The back of the house looms closer, chipped plaster showing brick, black metal pipes making no attempt at concealment, bulging down from roof to ground drains, a creeping mesh of dark scars. She sees herself a girl behind those walls, flitting from room to room in shadowy silence. No sound to posit her existence save an occasional creak on a tread of stair as she moves up, then down again. Dim light filtering in rain-beaded windows. Creeping through empty passages, empty rooms, looking for someone. Haunting her own house. Perhaps she's still there. Perhaps she's never really been anywhere else.

It was a shotgun under the bank of cushions. She's sure of it.

'Maybe he likes to shoot birds. I don't know. If he didn't say anything. Didn't actually threaten you—'

'I don't trust him, Henri. It was very, very subtle. Practised, almost. You could miss it so easily. The way he seems to invite your questions but really it's you who's being questioned. And then he brushed my hair back from my face.'

'Ah. The true sign of a serial killer.'

'Will you please stop laughing at me? Henri, is somebody there with you?'

'I'll explain later.'

'Explain what?'

'Nell, I can't stay on much longer. Listen, just think about this: maybe it's you.'

'What do you mean?'

'I think you know.'

'You think I'm fixating on him so I don't have to think about other things. Us.'

'Let's not go into that. Not right now . . . So there was nothing at all in those papers you took from the caravan?'

Nell flips through the sheaf again. 'Just crap. Exactly what you'd expect from someone who drifts around. Map. Brochures of a few inns or hostels, an empty envelope, for God's sake.'

'Well I don't think Agatha Christie need turn in her grave just yet.'

'Where are you? What's all that noise in the background?'

'Traffic. I'm in Paris.' There's a pause. 'No, I haven't moved in, if that's what you're thinking.'

'That's not what I was thinking. Actually . . .' *What I was hoping. Is it?*

'Nell, I have to go.'

'Henri . . .'

'I'll call you tomorrow. Try to relax, okay?'

'No, wait.'

But the line is dead. The answering service comes on the instant she tries his number again. For some reason it feels like a punch in the gut. She opens her mouth to say something, aware that, for seconds, she's been breathing into the phone. The tip of one shoe rolls one of Agnes's memory stones back and forth across a plank of floorboard. She feels foolish, a girlie, someone who's forgotten grown-up responses, the complications and intrigues of grown-up relations.

'Henri, it's me. Look, I just want to say — what I'd like to say — God, I hate leaving messages on these bloody things. I miss you. Okay, I'll talk to you tomorrow, or if you get a chance you could try me later tonight. Okay, that's it. I miss you. Sorry, this is a stupid message. I love you. 'Bye.'

She sits perfectly still, as evening slips across the walls of the room. The house is unusually quiet.

Grace is in the bath, hollering and splashing about like a half-beached shark. Nell has treated her hair again with lice shampoo and sponged every inch of her slender, pitted body with disinfectant. The bathroom smells like a medicine cabinet. There are a couple of old, yellowed bruises up by the child's clavicle, as if someone has caught her roughly by the neck. Of course, there is a non-response when Nell questions her, but Nell is certain in her own mind that the ponytails have something to do with them. Grace's back is a perfect violin shape, tapering in at the waist with carved precision. Tiny whorls of silky hairs form along her lower arms and just above the tops of her buttocks. Rinsed conker hair glides down between her shoulder-blades, sleek and shiny as an otter. She loves the water, all the more for being so unaccustomed to it, Nell thinks, while pleading for the tenth time for her granddaughter to step out into the waiting towel in her arms.

'No no no,' Grace sings. 'Just an-udder minute.'

'Grace, you've been in there over an hour already. Look, the water's cold.'

'Well, I won't be in it again for a while, will I?'

'You're a brat. That's blackmail. Right. Five more minutes while I shoo some of those cats out of your room. And I'm not taking no for an answer this time.'

'Nan? Pass me in the Jewel Girl Barbie, will you?'

Nell finds the doll thrown in a corner, with two kittens curled around it. She picks them up by their necks and deposits them at the top of the stairs. They immediately turn for Grace's room again but she nudges them with her shoe, none too gingerly. They mewl a reedy protest but descend all the same. She plops the doll into the water with Grace and returns to the room. Glad to be busy, to be on the move again.

Another kitten under the bed and a quite ferocious-looking tom tucked up in a toy box. Nell sends them packing. The smell is stifling; she flings the window open. She rips the bed linen off, turns the mattress, tucks in crisp, Aga-dried sheets and puts on a new duvet cover. She is scooping piles of dirty laundry into her arms when the first grunts sound from the bathroom. Uh uh uh. Grace? Drowning? She drops the laundry and runs.

Grace is propped up in the bath, holding the Barbie with its legs spreadeagled.

'Uh uh,' Grace grunts, her face contorted.

'What're you doing?' Nell demands.

Grace bursts into a smile. She giggles. 'She's making a baby,' she beams. She emits one long moan and makes the doll thrash about.

'I get it. *Having* a baby.' Nell proffers the open towel again, her expression brooking no further argument. 'C'mon. You and I have a date with a fine-toothed comb, young lady.'

For the next hour, back in Nell's room, Grace hollers the house down. She wiggles incessantly, launching her bony elbows in backward thrusts into the pit of Nell's abdomen. It's a battle to the death and Nell is determined to win.

'You're bloody hurting me!' Grace howls.

'You want to be eaten alive, do you?'

'At least there'd be something to eat. You're taking my head off.'

'Don't be such a—'

'When're you going back anyway?'

Nell stands with the comb in mid-air. 'D'you want me to go?'

'No-oo,' Grace draws out with a touch of remorse. 'It's just normally you go before a long time is up.'

'Yes,' Nell concedes. 'Normally I go before a long time is up. But not this time, Grace, if that's all right with you.'

Grace pulls a whatever face, but Nell can see that secretly she's pleased. They continue fine-combing for a few minutes in silence. Nell whips the towel from Grace's shoulders with a flourish. The child doesn't wait for a second signal, almost tripping as she runs from the torture chamber.

The scent of Ali's apple and blackberry pies drifts upstairs as Nell makes her way down. They smell surprisingly good, if a little cremated. She knuckle-taps Nick's door.

'Can I get you anything, Nick?'

He shakes his head. His eyes are red-rimmed and water courses from both corners – not tears, she is relieved to note. A guttering candle throws giant shadows along the far wall. He signals the streaming eyes and pulls a face. 'I try reading and end up incontinent.'

Nell plucks a wad of tissues from a box. He wipes his cheeks and blows his nose hard. It must be lonely for him cooped up in this dreary room for so much of the day. Equally, it must be galling to find himself so debilitated just when his life was about to follow lines, take on a shape, a business to run. After the peregrine years, the pointless, aimless wanderings, his mind was ready for mainstream but his body scuppered him in the end. Now there is only stasis, some days less bad than others, the most to be hoped from any hour that someone will walk through the door and grant him a moment's company. Nothing will surprise him when he grows elderly. He already knows what it feels like.

On the bedside table there are numerous bottles of pills, silver foil packages, an untouched cup of tea with a congealed skin of milk and behind that, at the bottom of a glass, a residue of that green, slimy liquid she's seen in the kitchen a number of times. She lifts it and holds it to the candlelight. Brown flecks swirl in the otherwise viscous concoction.

'Adam's herbs,' Nick grins, then sticks out his tongue to show how ghastly the taste is. He shudders. 'I can never bring myself to finish the end bit.'

'The herbs were for you?'

'I think he fancies himself as a bit of a witchdoctor, to tell the truth. But what odds – I've tried everything else.'

'He makes this mixture every day?'

'Most every day. Or Ali does. Let me tell you, it's every bit as awful as it looks.'

Nell dips her nose into the glass, wincing at the foul stench, which is vegetal and sewery, not in the least herby. She takes a tiny sip and rolls the liquid round her mouth. Thousands of minute nodules lining her tongue, so accustomed to analysis, to decoding the syntax of taste, find little familiar in this substance. Lemon balm, perhaps, a touch of mint, but these serve to mask rather than delineate the overall sour, stringent bass notes.

'I can honestly say' – Nell peers over the rim once more, closing her nostrils to further assault – 'it's the most disgusting thing I've ever smelled or tasted in my life.'

'Bound to do me some good, then.' Nick grins. He takes the glass and drains the dregs. 'Bah.' Another shuddering grimace.

'Nick,' Nell begins cautiously, 'I was wondering if you've

noticed anything strange with Grace lately. I don't think she's very happy.'

A quick flash of his eyes, then he concentrates on a space above her head. 'No, she isn't,' he says after a time.

'Can we do anything?' she persists in a quiet voice.

He inhales deeply. For a second she thinks he's going to cry, but then he exhales with a shrug. A little shake to his head. Clearly he's thought about this. Maybe he thinks of little else. His concern for his daughter may be the reason he won't endure a stay in hospital for a proper series of tests.

'Maybe you can do something,' he says eventually. 'I can't. What can I do?' he adds with a hint of self-disgust.

'You won't always be sick. Try not to think that way.'

'Sick? That's nothing to do with it. I wish it were that simple.'

'What was that simple?'

'Nothing. Nothing,' he repeats with a shrug. 'I'm just feeling sorry for myself.'

'Nick—'

He stops her with a raised hand. 'I just stay. That's all. That's all I know how to do.'

She looks at him with surprise. He has been unremarkable, irritating even in his disconnectedness, a willowy space cadet with an ability to glide through company, gone before you knew he was there, but he has been constant. And the reason he has been so constant is that he loves her daughter, in his simple, unquestioning fashion. She's never taken this on board before, perhaps because he is not a man to speak of love, never expecting it to slope in his direction. If forced, she thinks he might have spoken with a degree of irony, an agnostic as to love's existence, until her daughter's neediness shook him by the throat and forced him to the side of the fence he had previously only observed from a great distance. He may have introduced Ali to heroin, while she introduced him to the drug that was Ali. What could be more potent to a man with no self-respect than a woman with less? She recalls his family, the cruel, baiting humour they used for both persecution and self-protection. He has not given Ali a nickname, not even a pet name. This, Nell thinks, must be a good omen.

'We'll see what we can do,' she says, patting his clammy hand, keeping things in the plural – he feels superfluous enough.

When she turns at the door, his eyelids are already drooping heavily, a ragged sigh for breath and he is asleep. Below, in the kitchen, Ali's laugh tinkles with girlish affectation. She glances up as Nell descends.

'Look,' she says breathlessly, pointing to the pies on top of the Aga. 'Success! A bit of black round the crusts but I cut that off. I've had a slice and it was good. On the sourish side, but I like it that way.'

At the table, Grace and Adam mop up gravy with crusts of bread. Grace's hair is still wet but her face is milky, with a warm flush along her cheekbones. A kitten lies curled up in her lap.

'You'll have some stew, Nell?' Ali ladles into a bowl. 'Adam? Seconds?'

'No. I've had plenty, thanks.'

He hasn't met her eyes. Now that he has concluded the business of eating, he is anxious to be out of there. Nell can see the twitch in his shoulders, the telltale jiggling of his knees under the table. He wants up, out, away – how well she understands. It surprises her, how well she understands. When he does look in her direction, she is startled by the frank surliness in his gaze. For all the world what her mother used to call a dose of petted lip. As if earlier he'd offered her something particularly prized, particularly cherished, and she'd thrown it back in his face. Himself, of course, that's what he was offering, she's certain now as she draws a chair, making sure to keep up a light, neutral smile. A bell sounds in the bar and he scrapes his chair back.

Ali puts a hand out. 'I'll get that.' She scurries past the brocade curtain.

Nell ladles stew. Beef, she thinks, though it's difficult to tell, the lumps of meat are so macerated. Pulped carrot hopelessly drowns in almost black gravy.

'It's lovely,' Grace says, reaching into the pot to dunk another wad of bread. A ribbon of sedimenty liquid dribbles down her chin.

Adam toys with the last drops in his bowl, drawing a crust across the surface into a mesh of criss-cross lines. He chews with almost comical concentration. His jiggling legs make all the chairs judder slightly but he doesn't seem to be aware. Nell holds a mouthful in an effort at trickling it back into her throat without actually tasting. The effort fails miserably. She suppresses a gag.

Another mouthful. This time she has to chew. Although the meat has fallen apart from hours of cooking, it's still sinewy and goes on for ever, like chewing gum. Her jaw aches. Really, she should get some sort of lifetime achievement award for the meals she's managed to ingest since her arrival. She takes a deep breath, tries spooning some of the mixture onto bread, see if that is any improvement. A lump of gelatinous carrot glides down the wrong way and she chokes, eyes stinging, reaching for a glass of water. When her eyes clear, she sees that Adam is focused intently on her every move. Waves of dark, earthy animosity emanate from the tense frame. Even when she looks at him directly, he doesn't drop his sour stare. It's a wonder that Grace hasn't remarked.

'Apple and blackberry pie next,' Grace says with glee.

Ali comes in from the bar, rubbing her hands on a dish-cloth.

'Wait, Adam.' She puts a hand on his shoulder. Digs out almost half of one pie onto a plate and slides across to him. 'Don't go without pudding.'

'No. Not for me.'

He's still making to rise but Ali presses down harder. A tight grin looks more like a grimace.

''Course you will. It's homemade!'

Adam shakes his head, pushes the plate to the centre of the table.

Still Ali's hand grips his shoulder. ''Course you will,' she repeats limply.

Nell feels her own legs begin to jiggle spasmodically. She wants to scream at Ali to drop it. Enough with the home-made pie already. But Ali is like a woman obsessed. Grace begins to murmur furiously to the kitten. Ali draws the plate back to its spot in front of Adam. Little shards of light refract off her retinas. She cuts the slice into two. 'You can manage half, can't you?'

'Ali . . .' Nell begins.

Adam is murmuring under his breath. The lean frame stretched on a leash. His head is turned to the side, eyes trained in a fixed glare on Ali's fingers curled around his shoulder bone. He is simmering.

'Just a taste won't kill you,' Ali persists in a strangled attempt at joviality. 'C'mon, a bite, even.'

With a sudden backward lash, Adam draws his hand back and swipes away her restraining arm. His chair scrapes a retreat with an angry squeal. Though his eyes are hooded, his cheeks burn with a high flush, nostrils frill from rapid inhalations. A white, bloodless circle around the lips.

'What d'you think I am? A fucking pet?'

Grace raises the pitch of her murmuring to the cat. Ali retreats a little, a hand pressed against her chest as she tries to compose a jokey expression but fails miserably. There's a telltale tremble to her lower lip.

'I'm sorry Adam. It's just—'

'I don't like pie. I never did,' he adds in a softer tone.

'Well, now we know.' Ali attempts a feeble smile. Her shoulders flutter like twin, scrawny sparrows. She darts Nell a look to see if her humiliation has been duly absorbed. Nell concentrates on her stew, humming under her breath.

'I'll go and—' Adam breaks off, jerking his head toward the bar. 'Yeah.' He turns on his heel and leaves.

For a while there is silence, broken only by Grace's incessant muttering to the kitten and Nell's equally incessant low hum. Ali's face is stretched taut; she tries to pluck something from the corner of one eye. Eventually, she draws the offending plate away and chucks the pie in the rubbish bin. By the sink, she stands with her back to them, head down, arms stretched out carrying her weight. Her knuckles are white.

'Can I have my pudding, Mama?' Grace asks.

''Course you can, sweetheart.' Ali turns with a broad, forced smile. She stands with a knife hovering over pastry. 'How much do you want?'

'I'll have the same much Adam didn't want.'

'Good girl. Good girl.'

She brings the huge slab to Grace. The bluish worm on her temple clearly throbs. She presses her fingers to it.

'Migraine?' Nell gurgles through a mouthful of gristle that just won't go down.

'What? Oh yeah. Not so bad, though. I'll live.'

Nell briefly encircles her daughter's wrist. 'Have a lie down. Wait for it to pass.'

Ali looks at her. Her eyes have welled up. She nods rapidly. 'Maybe an hour or so. It's been a busy day.'

As Ali trudges upstairs with heavy footfalls, so unlike her usual jittery pace, Grace wolfs her pudding until she hears the click of the door upstairs. She pushes the plate away. A flick of her eyes at Nell, warning her not to say anything about anything right this minute. Nell gives up on the glutinous wad in her mouth and extracts it with a sigh of relief.

Wait for it to pass.

Will it ever though? She's been so busy watching Adam, she forgot to keep one eye on her own daughter. How could she not have seen from the beginning? What Grace instinctively understands. Perhaps Nick, too. Ali has found her home at last – but lost her heart.

Grace has gone down to the caravan to feed Terence the pony. Before that, she lined up shallow tins with leftover stew for at least a dozen cats outside, another half a dozen in the kitchen. She put milk in bowls for the kittens, with a little spot of the shop catfood for each, in the centre. The mounds swelled from each tin like mini-volcanoes out of snowy meadows. She summoned her charges with her usual low cat cries and they came downstairs at once, practically tumbling over one another on the stairs in the crush. Nell got on with the washing up but watched out of the corner of her eye as Grace knelt to murmur a word or two to each animal as they devoured supper. The kittens each got a stroking as well. She divided her attention fairly and quite methodically among them all. When they'd finished, she stacked up the tins and took them out to rinse at the outside tap. Lined them up in the back kitchen for tomorrow. Clicked her fingers rapidly with a tiny frown: what next? Oh yes, Terence. Off she went. All this effort so that the cats, the kittens, the pony, might live another day. There were no preconditions, no accountabilities, no credits expected in return. Nell watched the wraith-like figure glide down the first field until she disappeared over the stone wall.

The sky is a murky indigo as Grace clambers back across the wall. Twenty minutes at least. Doubtless Terence had to have his share of stroking and murmuring, too. If only people could be so easily satisfied, Nell thinks. If only a gentle touch and a soothing murmur could take the ordinary pain of living away. Yet there are times when there is nothing else. When someone dies, for instance, what is there to do in the face of grief, but stroke and murmur, all knowledge and certainty reduced to primal, instinctive gestures? Grunts of sympathy when words are too affected, too *much*.

Sorry for your troubles, sorry for your loss, a few neighbours muttered, so sorry, so so sorry. They lined up to shake Agnes's hand as they flooded into the kitchen. She stood at the door, mechanically nodding. Nell helped Paudie and Julia make endless pots of tea, bring in whiskeys from the bar for the men, sherries or red lemonades for the women. Bridget wasn't even out of the lake yet; it was another two days before the divers managed to pull her body out. Yet everybody, Nell included, kept looking around as though expecting to see a small body stretched out on the kitchen table, or tucked in a corner on a stretcher. A focus for all this grief. If there was a death, there should be a corpse, shouldn't there? And without it, as Nell poured cup after cup, she still harboured a ridiculous germ of hope, that any minute now Bridget would skip through the door, hair gleaming in a halo of gold, to look curiously at the massed throng – what's this game? I don't know this game. Okay, then, what're the rules? She knew, from the strange way her mother's head kept listing toward the door, that she was harbouring the same redundant hope. Until they saw Bridget dead, they could still see Bridget alive.

She starts when Grace comes crashing through the door.

'All done,' Grace says.

'Homework, I s'pose, Grace. D'you want to take a cup of tea up to Mama first?'

She rinses and dries a mug, almost knocking the perspex jug of green slime, Adam's herbal tonic, with her elbow. She places it in the fridge, not sure if the mixture is supposed to keep. Grace takes the tea and goes upstairs, slowly, carefully, holding the mug with both hands.

When they did bring Bridget home, only Agnes was allowed to see. The decomposing body, fished from its watery lair, was considered too traumatic a sight for a young girl. She saw one blackened fingertip, though, poking out beneath the shroud. Agnes caught her looking and hastily realigned the loose drapes. She spent the whole night in the kitchen so Nell didn't get a chance to look under the covers. In the morning, the hearse arrived to take Bridget to the church. There wouldn't be a morgue.

In the churchyard, there was more shaking hands, more sorry for your troubles, men with caps to their breasts, women gripping Agnes's forearm in little squeezes; it might so easily be one of their own children. Rain pelted down on their heads by the graveside. Nell watched the first clumps of gravel shovelled on top of the coffin turn to sweaty clay. It dribbled in grey streaks across the surface. The priest made the sign of the cross over the open maw in the earth. Paudie and Julia knelt down to place holy medals and scapulas in the grave. Bridget's teacher placed a folded school tie. Avril O'Mahoney dropped her rolled-up best skipping rope. Nell felt a clutch of panic. What would she put in? Why hadn't anybody said?

Agnes was delving around in her deep coat pockets. She pulled out several stones. Large, smooth pebbles laced with her own distinctive handwriting. They fell from her fingers one after another, making dull thuds as they knocked against wood.

Nell was wrestling with the top button of her overcoat. At last it pinged free and she reached inside to unwind Bridget's red scarf, wrapped tightly around her neck by Julia earlier that morning. She began to draw it out, battling as the innermost coil tightened across her windpipe. The men were taking up their shovels again. Nell shook from side to side, holding what she'd managed to unravel high in the air above her head. Julia and Paudie paused in their prayers to look at her. Just as the last skein slithered free of her neck, Agnes turned, a light flared in her eyes, but she said nothing. She took the scarf from Nell, pinned it against her chest with her chin while she gently folded it into a tight rectangle. She stuffed the rectangle in through a gap in her coat buttons, it lay across both breasts, making

her look like an over-stuffed chicken. Nell's empty hands
fell limply to her sides.

Now that scarf will always be between us Mammy.

Nell waits for Grace to come back. When there is no sign of
her return, she carries another mug of tea upstairs, for Nick.

They lie in candlelight. Nick is half asleep, with Grace
burrowed between him and Ali, her arms stretched round
her father's neck. Nell catches the tender, feathery strokes of
the child's fingers, tracing Nick's brow, along the plane of his
nose, brushing lightly across his lower lip, delicate, investiga-
tive touches – it's as if she's according him the same
inarticulate comfort she gives to her cats. He smiles sleepily
and Grace tightens her protective embrace.

Ali looks pale and unwell, stretched fully clothed along
the counterpane. With one hand she holds her Bible up,
straining to read the tiny print in the gloomy light. Unaware
that Nell is watching by the door. Ali intones something that
sounds like a psalm. She breaks off in mid-line, nudging
Grace's back gently with her elbow. Grace is to finish the
passage. It's a strange tableau, a not-normal scene in a not-
normal family. And yet there is something vulnerable and,
yes, pathetic about them in this strikingly conjunctive pose –
Nell has to swallow a small rock in her throat. This is it. Her
family. Here they are, in circumstances she could never have
foreseen. Yet here they are. Her life's work, not so good, not
so bad. Getting by, in their fashion. If she could close the
door and preserve them for ever in this moment of stillness,
she would do so gladly.

She decides to leave them to their privacy and goes back
downstairs with the mugs of tea. She sits by the table, sipping

from one of the mugs herself. Could this religion business be the root of Grace's problems at school? Until Ali came to Ireland and suddenly took to all things holy with the zeal of Saul on the road to Damascus, Grace didn't have any religious instruction. Ali and Nick were, if anything, militantly aetheist. Or maybe it's her accent, not fully local yet; it lies about midway across the Irish Sea. She decides to pay a call on Grace's teacher, get to the bottom of this once and for all.

A light wind rattles the kitchen window. After a grey, torpid day, night has pulled in quickly. The sky, the little four-square patch she can see, is streaked with dusky charcoal. A couple of widely spaced fat drops of rain splat against glass. Then silence.

She waits for torrents, for pelting. For what was called *weather*. It can't be far away.

CHAPTER NINE

It was Aunt Hannah who first realized that Nell was pregnant. She was down from Galway for one of her twice-yearly visits and burst in on Nell spewing her guts one morning, in the bathroom. She'd been watching with her head cocked to the side for a number of days in any case. The swelling breasts hadn't escaped her attention.

'How far are you gone child?' she asked that morning.

Nell knew better than to dissemble. 'Around four months.'

'I see.' Hannah rubbed Nell's back to ease the retching. 'I'm surprised you let yourself get caught, I'd be lying if I said otherwise. You know the facts of life, don't you?'

'We were drunk.'

As Hannah held Nell's hair back to stop it falling into the sink, Nell briefly, and with precious little detail, told her about that night. She omitted the Our Lady of Lourdes bottle for the vodka. It could hardly be classed as proper sex – she was highly unlucky.

'Unlucky?' Hannah repeated. 'Anyone would think you set out to get pregnant, child.'

'Please don't tell Mammy.'

'She'll see for herself soon enough. You can't just plop a baby into her lap. Things will have to be decided, so we'll tell her now. When you're done vomiting.'

Typical Aunt Hannah pragmatism. Even Nell had to smile.

'She's going to eat me alive.'

'She'll be cross. You can bank on that. But sure, you're not the first, you'll hardly be the last. What possessed you? You were always such a steady girl. I didn't even know you were doing a line.'

'I wasn't. I mean, I'm not.'

'It's not a married man, is it?' Aunt Hannah frowned.

'No.' Nell spat a last mouthful of drool into the sink. Aunt Hannah patted her mouth with a towel. 'He's just a lad – it was only that one time, like I said. He doesn't have to know.'

'Well, he'll know when he sees you pushing a pram, now, won't he? You've no business marrying him, anyway. Right. C'mon then. Let's get this business over with.' She grabbed Nell's hand, then stopped in her tracks. 'And for God's sake child, don't tell her it was in the fecking graveyard.'

Agnes was in the bar, setting up for the day. The doors were still closed. Aunt Hannah gave Nell's back a little prod ahead of her. Agnes immediately stopped polishing glasses when she saw their serious faces. Hannah jerked her head to Nell: out with it. Nell stood there, shuffling her feet, she kept her head down.

'Nell?' Agnes broke into the silence.

'Oh, Nell,' she said after a long time, her voice shaky with disappointment.

Not anger. Not accusation. Nell would have rathered shouts, recriminations – anything but that quiet, resigned disappointment. When she at last looked up to meet her mother's eyes, she saw there a look she'd only seen once before, and her chin dropped low on her neck again. At that moment, she knew with absolute certainty, not in a girlish, theatrical fashion, though this was the stuff of high family drama – but with a visceral clarity that she could never survive that look a third time in her life. She'd made the right decision.

'I'm sorry, Mammy, but I've already—'

'Whisht now. Let me think.'

For the next couple of hours, Agnes and Aunt Hannah calmly went through a variety of options. Agnes kept the pub door locked and ignored the occasional rattle of the handle, a few raps on the panes of glass. She went through three pots of tea with her sister. Between them, they filled two ashtrays with half-smoked cigarettes. Nell could have the baby in Cork, then they'd have to get somebody in to help out while she went back to school. The same for university, of course. Agnes could only do so much with the bar to run. Hannah could come down to see them through the first few weeks. That'd be the hardest time until they got a pattern going. Or Nell could take a year out of school – that might be an idea. Or maybe the best thing would be for her to go to Albie and Mary Kate in Oxford – Mary Kate would only love to have a baby to mind. Mary Kate could travel over on a plane with Nell, once they'd got a pattern going. Hannah favoured that notion, not that she wouldn't come down if that was the route they planned to take. At no point was the possibility of adoption brought up. At no point in that initial discussion did Agnes demand to know who the father was. As inconsequential to her as it was to Nell.

Nell listened through it all. The rest of her life was being

decided, here, at the kitchen table. Already the baby was
common property. There wouldn't be any university. There
would be a pub to mind and an infant, in that order. A girl
infant: it never crossed her mind that she might be carrying
a boy. In time, there would be a doting Agnes teaching her
granddaughter to play the piano. In time, three generations
of women, pulling pints. In time, three sets of memory
stones paving three roads to nowhere.

'It's all done already,' she told them.

'What's all done?'

'I've already told Uncle Albie on the phone. He's fine
with me going over there.'

The women folded their arms and looked at her.

'You were going to leave and not even tell me,' Agnes said
in a flat voice. 'I was going to hear about it on the telephone,
I suppose. That's nice. That's very nice, Nell.'

What Nell didn't add at that juncture was that she had no
notion of coming back.

In the bar, beyond the muffling curtain, the sound of
voices has picked up. It's quite busy – a cadence she's long
forgotten – low throaty laughs, clink of bottle against glass,
matches scraping a number of times unsuccessfully, then
bursting into flame, the *pshht pshht* of bottles opening, ching
of the old-fashioned till, tumbling of coins, finite ring of the
till drawer closed again. The hum of conversation rises in
volume, swells into the kitchen. She always did her homework in the parlour for that reason. It was difficult at times
not to see the bar outside as an extension of her own family,
her own house. It was like a ceaseless invasion. Even on
Christmas Day, Agnes served her regulars free drinks, as
thanks for their yearly custom, before setting about dealing
with the turkey and ham. More often than not, there was

some poor hapless bastard asked to join them, if he didn't have a better invitation. Agnes made sure her daughters were never churlish about that. It wasn't just about business, it was about simple decency, simple neighbourliness. There were times when Nell felt there were far too many neighbours in the world, and they were all eating in her kitchen.

Around the age of fourteen, she began to notice there was a change of atmosphere when she stepped behind the counter to give her mother a break. The dull brown sparrow, poor Nell, was growing up. She looked at the men, took their orders with the same reserved courtesy, but her navy blue eyes gazed back at them from behind layers of clumpy black mascara and her practised, often bored smile from lips coated in vaseline for shine. She still refused to allow herself to be drawn into the kind of wandering, idle conversations her mother could slip into at the drop of her hat, but she began to make her opinions known with a dart of an eye sideways, or a tuck of hair behind her ear. Not huge in the line of universal coquetry, but in that bar, at that time, it was monumental.

She could see some of the younger punters eyeing her. Wondering if she'd done it already, wondering if she might do it with them. The faces lined up at the bar every night, represented the world coming in to herself and her mother. There was rarely a time when they went out to the world. The pub ruled their lives, the pub's clock ticked like their own heartbeats. Even sleep was dictated by the toll of the last orders bell. The air they breathed reeked of stale beer, Afton Majors, wet hay at harvest times. Sour stout farts that lingered for hours. When a loud one rattled off at the counter, Agnes would say, Mr Guinness, doing his job. The air followed them to bed, slipped in under the sheets to lie with them all night. It stuck to their clothes, threading in and out through every fibre, clinging on even through a boil wash. In the morning, a pall of smoky, grainy cloud hovered above the kitchen table, waiting for them. It never seemed to bother Agnes but Nell felt close to choking by her fifteenth year.

The only relief was when Nell walked alone, or with her mother.

'There was a hurling match.' Adam's voice so near, makes her stiffen on the chair. He's bent down close to her ear. She gets the impression he set out to startle her. 'I'll have to get Ali. It's busy.' He moves away; she can still feel his breath damp on her skin.

'No, don't disturb her. I'll come and help.'

He turns, not bothering to hide his surprise. 'It's too busy for that. I haven't got time to show you the ropes.'

'This was my house. I worked in that bar every single day of the year. I think I know the ropes.'

He hesitates, one hand on the banister rail. Nell stands. An impatient bell ring from beyond the curtain. Adam puts one foot on the bottom stair, about to dismiss her, about to run up.

'Leave her alone,' Nell adds firmly. Her home. Her daughter. She steps toward the bar, turns at the entrance. 'Adam?'

The foot on the stair hovers in midair for a second. He glances up, looks back at Nell. Both feet are on the kitchen floor again. This time he's elected not to challenge the authority she's assumed. But from his glowering expression, she figures it's just a matter of time before he really puts her to the test.

It feels as though the rest of her life has never happened.

The last few steps from kitchen to pub, the pulling aside of this curtain, curious faces with glasses tilted in her direction, spectral fingers of smoke wrapping round her hair, over-flowing ashtrays on the counter demanding her attention — all here, all the time, waiting for her.

Before they left for the airport, Agnes made one last laconic attempt to make Nell change her mind. It was as if she knew that her daughter was leaving for good, though they continued to speak in terms of her return. But every stitch she owned was packed into a trunk on the back seat of the Morris Minor.

'I'm not so sure this is a good idea,' Agnes said, doing up the top button of her coat.

'We've been through all this, Mammy. It'll be easier for you if I'm not around with a belly getting bigger every day.'

'That's my look-out.'

Nell tapped a foot. 'Will we go so?'

'Mind you wrap up well. Albie says they get a fair share of snow.' She put her hat on.

They were hardly down the road when Agnes stepped on the brake, about to stop to give Paudie a lift into the village. Any trip with her was a series of stops and starts, veers off in opposite directions to drop someone or other to their door. It was a wonder they ever got anywhere. And when it rained, which it nearly always did, they really didn't get anywhere. The car turned into the local taxi service. The only people they didn't pick up were genuine hitch-hikers, youths in jeans with long, scruffy hair. The cheek, Agnes would say to their cocked thumbs by the roadside. Bleddy cheek.

'Not today,' Nell said of Paudie's tall figure striding ahead of them. She indicated the trunk in the back.

'You're right,' Agnes said, stepping on the accelerator so hard they almost knocked him down instead.

Both remained very quiet for the rest of the journey to the airport, Agnes cluck-clucking about another driver's carelessness from time to time. She maintained a dignified forty miles an hour the entire distance. There was so much to say, they couldn't say a thing.

At the departure gate, they hung back, watching other people say their goodbyes. Agnes thrust a *Woman* and *Woman's Own* into Nell's hand. 'You'll be glad of those. Up there.'

The final call for her flight was announced.

'That's me,' Nell said.

'That's you.'

They quickly embraced. Nell breathed in deeply at the side of her mother's neck. Agnes stiffened, taking an involuntary step back. She turned away and let out a stifled cry.

'Nell. If I wasn't . . . If you ever thought—'

'Don't say it.' Nell recoiled. 'Please, Mammy. Not now, please.'

Agnes took another step back, patting her chest. Two hot livid spots swelled along her cheekbones. The deep hoods of her eyelids undulated as her eyes scanned the floor from side to side. 'Can we take it as said?'

'We can take it as said.'

Nell quickly pressed her lips to her mother's cheek, clamped a hand to her mouth and shot through the departure gate like a scalded cat. She didn't look back until the top stair of the ramp into the plane. Among the sea of bodies pressed against the public viewing window, she thought she saw a hat with a feather. But she couldn't be sure.

Like riding a bike, Nell thinks, using the spatula to cream off the top of a pint of Guinness, plunging the glass under the spout to fill to the brim again. She lets it settle while she gets the rest of the round. A whiskey, half a lager, change for the cigarette machine. Mostly the prices are marked by the various drinks. She tots up the total in her head, takes the offered note, gives change, hands the perfectly proportioned black-and-white pint over. She's motoring now, hardly having to ask Adam where anything is, or how much it costs.

When she first faced the sea of faces, her heart plunged. Her hands shook, holding the first glass. Before she had time to think, though, she was serving and it all seemed quite natural. A few of the older men recognized her straight away, though she couldn't say the same for them. Nevertheless, even if she didn't know individual names, or recognize individual faces, she had a vague cognizance of which family they might belong to. Whole generations delineated by the arc of an eyebrow, the pattern of lines on a forehead.

She was greeted initially with restrained curiosity and genuine warmth. A couple of young girls took the trouble to enquire after Ali. They seemed disappointed she wasn't there as usual, as if she'd become part of the texture of their day. The elderly man on the stool in the centre gave her some news of a boat he'd been fixing and asked that she pass it on to Ali. He was sure she'd like to know, as she'd been keeping tabs on his progress. Someone else asked after Grace and her menagerie. Nell responded to each query with a flush of pleasure. Before she had time to realize what was happening, she was slipping in and out of conversations started by Ali on previous nights. Conversations which would neither have ends nor reach conclusions but simply roll around to be picked up by whoever was standing behind the bar the next night. The world coming in.

Adam worked the top end of the counter, while she stayed down by the curtain to the kitchen. She noticed wryly that he didn't have much to offer in the line of idle chitchat. Neither was any expected of him. But he was greeted affably enough. He seemed calm under pressure, as though internal restlessness was subdued by the constant motion of his limbs. If anything, in his quiet, measured way, he seemed quite at home. If anything, perhaps too much so.

Paudie's eyes widened when he first walked in, then squinted tightly as if trying to take in the sight of Nell plonked behind the bar. He opened his mouth to remark the occasion, then grinned instead and ordered the first of his nightly quota of pints. She took extra care pouring the drink, conscious of his eyes watching her every move. He nodded approval when she placed it on the counter, not a drop slopping over the side, just the way he used to like it. No bubbles on the yellowy cap, just a smooth mushroom brimming over the edge of the glass and no more. Solid, opaque black the rest of the way down; she would never hand it over until fully settled. He waited a while until the drink was exactly ready to his liking, working his mouth in readiness, a meshing of lips she instantly recalled. He swallowed the first mouthful, ran the back of his hand across cream on his top lip, nodded again. Grand.

He hadn't greeted Adam when he came in and he continued to keep one shoulder slightly at a turn from Adam's end of the bar. Though he said nothing, Nell stiffened under his silent scrutiny every time she had to ask Adam a question, and every time she had to brush past him in the tight space behind the counter she could see Paudie's eyes lower, just a little.

For her own part, she found the closeness more than a little disturbing. In a rush to get past her, Adam had to put his hands on her hips from time to time, to shunt her slightly out of his way, and she nearly jumped out of her skin. She felt his breath on the back of her neck and almost expected a subsequent kiss. And, yes, there was something thrillingly illicit about the inadvertent close-ups. It wasn't difficult to see how Ali could be affected night after night when the rain poured down outside, while in here there was the bottleneck closeness, a pair of lean hips gliding silently behind her, a whispery touch of fingers on her hips, to insinuate her to the left a little. Of course it would seem like their arcane mating dance, known only to them. Aside from his almost blatant physicality, she was beginning to understand Adam's attraction, the powerful magnet he possessed: the thing you can't have; entirely for and by himself, he could never be owned. Exactly the kind of man a woman seeks out, to break her heart.

To the side, in the furthest reaches of the bar, by the cigarette machine and the door to the toilets, Bola, the Nigerian, sat at a table by himself, still on his first pint of Guinness, though he'd been there for over an hour. Concentric rings of cream picked out the time in intervals of twenty minutes, all the way down his glass. There were two free chairs at his table. He didn't seem to know anyone. In the congregation of white and lightly tanned faces, with his head bent forward, prayer-like, he looked like the statue of St Martin de Porres her mother used to keep in the kitchen.

When he first came in, there was a brief lull in the evening's trade. Nell poured his pint and attempted a little chitchat. In truth, just a little test to herself, trying out her new bar skills. She'd seen him running on the beach several times. Where was he from? Lagos, he said. How was he finding it around here, after Lagos, after Dublin? she asked, reaching for his glass for the second fill. Peaceful, he responded with a twist of irony. He deftly changed the subject to her. She explained that she was Ali's mother and this was her first time home in over thirty years. She thought there was a hint of sadness as he wondered aloud if it would be as long for him. Nigeria, he meant of course.

He swallowed the first mouthful and she expected him to be gone from the counter when she returned to the spot, after getting a round. Paudie was right, he didn't seem like much of a talker, yet she sensed he wanted to communicate. Up close, he was much younger than Nell had figured. Deepest brown, shiny skin, stretched and taut over apple cheekbones. He wore his hair shorn to the scalp. His eyes were heavy-lidded, tapering to a slight tilt at the edges. They had a haunted quality which made him appear older until he spoke. Full, pink cushiony lips with clearly demarcated ridges. He towered above every man at the bar. And stooped his head a little, as though conscious of that fact.

He hung around the counter for a while, throwing what seemed like idle questions whenever she came near. To do with coming home, the changes, her daughter, until she realized what he was seeking: reassurance about his own daughter. He hadn't seen her for a very long time. She'd been sent to live with his sister for her own safety and wouldn't leave Nigeria now unless his sister could get papers, too. When his wife died, he had had to leave in the middle of the night, without saying goodbye. Probably the child has been feeling abandoned all this time. But he would make it up to her. When she came. If she came. But every week he waited for the paperwork. So difficult now with this new programme of repatriation to Nigeria.

Wouldn't he consider going back? Nell asked. He gave a slight shake of his head and swallowed another small mouthful, careful to eke the pint out. He didn't have to say about too many memories. She wondered about his wife. He said she was a journalist, he was an architect. How did she die? He put a finger to his breast making a stabbing motion. Five, he said, all in the heart. Bullets? No. No, he repeated after a while. A knife. She wanted to ask more, but it was as if his face had closed. The dark, almost black eyes settled in a fixed stare somewhere up by the optics. She knew that if she pushed he would give her polite but mechanical answers. And she instinctively understood that this was all he had, all he possessed: his story. How many times already had he been forced to use it — to barter it — in exchange for asylum, for sympathetic handouts so that with every recounting, he must have felt himself diminished, his wife's brutal end, prostituted for his own safety, the future safety of a daughter who, in all probability, would only just recognize him.

That's what you have when you leave, sometimes, she thought. The clothes on your back and your story. Compared to his, hers was such a simple, such an *obvious*, story. Sixteen-year-old Irish girl in Oxford, left home to have her baby. All her memory stones reduced to that. All of his, laid out like baubles at a street bazaar, on sale cheap, just the price of his survival. I'm sorry for your loss, she said, instinctively laying her hand on his. So very sorry. He shrugged. Of course you are, he said. Not in a sardonic way or even in deflection. People died, people were sorry, the people who had to live with the loss were simply and ineffably more sorry than others.

'Pint of Guinness, please.'

It's Bola again, for his second pint. From the rings in the first glass, it will get him to closing time. Nell half fills the glass, finishes off another round, takes the money.

'Tell me,' she says, tilting his glass under the spout again. 'D'you think you'll ever see here as home?'

'I don't know.' He sifts through coins with a thumb. 'But I hope my daughter will. Or her daughter,' he adds with a shrug. He looks at her. 'When you can't go back, home is where you are.'

Nell smiles, yes, she'd go along with that. She looks out at pitch night through the pub window. 'Will you run in that dark?'

'I have a torch,' he says.

'If you'd put out your thumb, someone'd give you a lift,' a man mumbles beside him.

'How'd they see him?' another man laughs.

'They would see me if I smiled.' Bola pulls back his lips, showing snowy teeth. It's more a grimace than a smile. But it's clear that neither he nor the men have taken offence. It's just barroom banter, and he's well able for it. He takes his pint back to his perch, weaving his way through the throng with the skill of a football player. Nell catches a glimpse of Paudie's face as the giant Nigerian passes him by. For a fleeting second a look of genuine fear flits across the elderly man's face. Then he gazes ruminatively into his pint again. He hitches up his shoulders, to rid himself of some unpleasant thought.

The crowd starts to thin around eleven, until there are only a handful of stragglers by half past. They send Adam silent, penetrating glances, doubtless wondering if he'll oblige with the afters or not. He ignores them and eventually they give up. Paudie inclines his head toward Nell and makes his way to the door. The few remaining follow not long after. There is only the sound of water running as Nell washes then rinses glass after glass. Adam empties ashtrays, wipes the counter top.

He goes into the kitchen and returns with a cashbox. 'The till,' he explains, catching her curious glance.

The notes are flattened and placed in individual piles in the box. He takes several large notes and shunts them into a jeans pocket. Again catching her look, 'An agreement I have with Ali.'

'What? You take when you need it?'

'Pretty much.'

Does he know Ali's in love with him? Of course he does.

Nell pours herself a brandy; he nods assent when she wiggles a glass. He stacks dripping ashtrays upside-down, whips cloths into a bundle for washing, checks the doors to the chiller units, remembers to turn out the pub lights behind them on their way into the kitchen. It's as if he is the host going through the nightly housekeeping routine and she, the guest, being guided to her chambers. Nell sits, expecting him to follow, but he stands, downing the drink in one gulp.

By the fridge he hunkers down. The shiny circular scar peeps over the rim of his jeans. He takes a carton of milk and is about to straighten again when he sees the herbal mixture at the back. He takes out the jug and pours it down the sink.

'I like to make it fresh every day.'

'What's in it?'

'Just this and that.'

'And here I was thinking it had to be some extra-precise old family recipe.'

'No,' he responds with a shrug. 'Nothing precise. I just make it up as I go along.'

Like your life. Your story. And you're not selling. 'Adam?'

He turns expectantly, one hand already on the back porch door.

Nell taps the base of her back. 'How did you get that scar?'

'This?' He swivels looking behind, one hand unconsciously rubbing the old wound. 'It's ancient. I fell on a glass.'

Subject closed, but she persists. 'How old were you?'

'I don't know. Eight – nine, maybe.'

'Funny, you'd think a glass would shatter' – she puts her wrists together, spreading her hands out – 'this way.'

He shrugs, deadpan, looking beyond her.

'It looks to me,' Nell continues, 'more the sort of wound you'd get if someone rammed a broken bottle into your skin.'

He looks at her then, restless tongue poking inside a cheek. Whatever torments he's endured at the hands of a drunken, peripatetic father, he'll keep them to himself. The strong, silent type, she thinks, with a sad inward laugh, broodily though utterly dependable in movies. In real life, their own walking prison cells.

''Night,' he casts over his shoulder.

'Goodnight, Adam.'

In the silence of the kitchen, her ears strain as though, beyond the silence, conversations still continue. Or the curved enclosure of the silence, harbours in its core a faint, distant afterglow still pulsating with countless spoken words, snatches she will hear if she listens hard enough. Her mother's nightly refrain: c'mon now, girls, up to your beds, no forgetting teeth and prayers. The slick acquiesence of bolts sliding into metal sheaths, rattle of keys, a click, rattle again, chairs reshuffling into fixed positions beneath the Formica table, a stampede of feet on the stairs, the race to get under the covers first. Muffled giggles. Rain tiptoeing across roof shales.

It isn't silence she's been hearing all those years in the Paris apartment. Rather, she's been straining for the memory of sound.

Nearly every surface in the kitchen still holds a frost of flour from Ali's baking earlier. She squeezes a damp cloth and begins to wipe. It doesn't seem right to leave her mother's kitchen in such a state before bedtime. Agnes liked everything in its proper place, surfaces wiped, floors swept. She gathers the loose newspaper pages strewn across the tiles. Something catches her eye. A photo in the local paper of Nick and Ali standing in front of the pub. Her eyes strain to read the editorial, which is yellowed and splatted with marks. It's just a warm, friendly piece about Ali's arrival, some time back, to take over her grandmother's pub. Her old-fashioned intentions, how she wants to run it. That the locals are glad to see the continuity. A piece commissioned in exchange for advertising, no doubt. She's about to scrunch it up when she is struck by the date at the top of the page. A week, no more than two, before Adam's arrival. A turn-up out of the blue, which might not have been quite so casual, so accidental, after all.

Nell rinses a last few items under the running tap. The perspex jug is almost empty but in the wide base there's still an ounce of residue. She looks around, empties one of Grace's Lucozade bottles and pours the gloopy mixture into the neck. It glides down slowly, green lava magnified against the glass. She screws the top back on and slips the bottle under her sweater, goes upstairs.

She imagines shadows dancing across the kitchen floor, supple-limbed, effortlessly fluid ghosts, long after she has gone.

The dream has returned. The one she hasn't had for, it seems, hundreds of years, the one where she's gasping for breath but there's only frothy water being sucked in through her nostrils. Another gulp for air and she's choking on a tidal wave plunging down her throat. She can see light, up there somewhere. If she could just – but there's something holding her beneath the surface, pulling her down. It's Bridget's hand, in a vice around her ankle. She tries not to breathe water again. But it's impossible. It flows into her head, into her ears, her eyes, bursts in a relentless torrent all the way down her windpipe. Her lungs gurgle. If she could just—

She wakes, rasping for breath. The sheets and her nightie are drenched in sweat. Her temperature must be at blazing point, nuclear. For a moment, she can't figure out where the hell she is. Slowly, the room comes into focus. Rain beats against the window in a rhythmic staccato. Weather at last. Long drops runnel in crooked channels down the panes.

The wind picks up, rattling the window-frame. Getting cross now, as Agnes used to say.

When the dreams got so bad that they made her cry aloud in the night, Agnes came up to the top room, pink bedjacket draped over her meaty shoulders. If it didn't look as though Nell would be able to fall back to sleep, Agnes scooped her up like a limp carpet roll and carried her to her own bedroom.

It was the old mattress then, with the hollow in the middle. It smelt of her mother, how she imagined her mother would smell from the inside if she were tucked up in the hollow of her womb. There was a small red nightlight over the headboard which cast a warm, rosy glow across that side of the room. Round balls at the head of every raindrop on the window-panes, reflected a thousand nightlights. If she half closed her eyes, it seemed to Nell that she was staring straight at the stars.

It always took a while for both of them to sleep again. Agnes's stomach rumbled as her breathing relaxed into wheezy sighs. With the dip in the centre of the bed, there was no choice but to press together, Nell flat on her back, her body curved at the waist, hip touching her mother's turned back. If she whimpered aloud in the middle of the dream again, Agnes did a little shimmy with her bottom, letting her know she was still there. Sometimes Nell made herself stay awake the night through, listening to the rise and fall of Agnes's breathing calibrate with the beat of rain against glass. One becoming indistinguishable from the other so that, after a while, it seemed to Nell as though her mother rained breath.

When the dreams began to fade, coming every couple of months or so, instead of almost nightly, she missed the wordless, muzzy closeness of those nights in bed with her mother. Daylight brought sharp edges again, clarity of vision – there was no avoiding the trajectory of Agnes's defeated gaze, fixed on an empty space which always lay directly to the side of Nell. No matter where she stood, that vacuum stood beside her. A space which, conversely, was occupied by absence.

A creak on the stairs beyond the bedroom door startles her. She pads to the door and opens a crack.

'Grace? Is that you?'

Grace freezes halfway up the top flight. Still fully clothed, she must have fallen asleep in her parents' bed. Nell had assumed she'd gone up to her own room hours ago. She doesn't turn round.

'D'you want to sleep in here with me, darling?'

In the dim light, Nell can just make out the quick shake of her granddaughter's head. Grace mumbles something, then trips up the final steps. Her bedroom door clicks shut. Nell stands there for a while, looking up the dark stairwell. It must be her imagination, she checks herself, and she creeps back under the covers.

Water hurls itself in wavery sheets against the glass. Nell lies on her back, unconsciously arching sideways so that one hip thrusts out into the far side of the bed, looking for someone. No, she thinks, looking at the blurred window, just a trick of the light pleaching hairs across Grace's scalp, making it look wet. She's never been out in *that*.

CHAPTER TEN

Bridget looked like the twirling ballerina in Agnes's jew-ellery box; the box contained mainly loose buttons and spare change. Round and round she pirouetted on top of the kitchen table, red scarf looping in the air, golden hair spark-ing like straw caught in the sun. Her cheeks were flushed and her eyes had a crazy, demented quality. She could have turned for ever. Stockinged feet swivelled all the easier on smooth, glassy Formica.

'Will you stop now, Bridget,' Agnes laughed, clapping her hands together. 'You'll make yourself dizzy.'

In the far corner of the kitchen, Nell neatly sliced the crusts off a ham sandwich for someone at the bar.

Bridget began to laugh breathlessly. 'I'm never stopping. Never!'

At that moment, Julia walked in with a crochet pattern for Nell to borrow. She was going to make a poncho with a fringe round the edges. For her age, she was the most tal-ented knitter and crocheter, Julia had ever encountered, she said.

'Oh my,' Julia exclaimed. 'Watch you don't get dizzy.'

'She's like a deer, that one,' Agnes said.

The women stood in the centre of the room, widening their eyes with every turn, making little gasps of astonishment. As ever, spurred by an audience, Bridget whirled even faster. She coiled the scarf high above her head lasso-like, so that in the blur of movement it was impossible to tell where girl ended and the long skein of wool began. Nell hummed. She cut the sandwich into four precise triangles. Out of the corner of her eye, she watched her mother's face. The eyes sparkled, her skin had a girlish bloom, she stood with one hand pressed to her chest. Bridget hardly stopped but managed to execute a perfect turn, to start spinning in the other direction.

'Would you look at that,' Agnes said.

'I'm never stopping. Never never never!'

'D'you see what your sister's up to, Nell?' Julia said over her shoulder.

'You're supposed to have pointy shoes, if you're going to do it right,' Nell said.

'Do what right?' Bridget asked.

'Do ballet right,' Nell responded. 'It's not proper ballet unless you've pointy shoes. Any eedjit can turn on a table.'

'You can't,' Bridget said, getting breathless. 'I saw you last night, trying to do this. You fell on your arse.'

'Bridget!' Agnes remonstrated. But a hand clamped over her mouth to hide a giggle. Julia gave a little snort, too.

Nell's cheeks burned. She hadn't known that Bridget was watching from the top of the stairs and hadn't said anything. If it was pity that stopped her, there was no worse humiliation than that.

'All right, girls,' Agnes said, though it was only one girl taking time out. 'C'mon now, customers won't serve themselves. And if they do, we're in trouble.' The usual feeble joke, recited at least once a day. 'Bridget? You'll be sick. Stop now.'

'Just this last one. Watch this.'

And truly with the agility of a deer, in such an exquisite crystal of a movement it made Nell's heart stop, Bridget paddled furiously with one foot until she'd gained enough momentum to raise the leg clear out behind her. Next she bent from the waist while still turning on the ball of the other foot. Straight and clear as an open compass pivoting on a single pin. She must have managed at least four free spins before she gradually came to a stop. Her eyes rested triumphantly on Nell.

'See? How much you know. It wasn't ballet at all.'

'Ice-skating!' Agnes clapped her hands again. She glowed with wonder. 'Bridget, what's the world going to make of you at all?'

'How can you ice-skate without skates?' Nell muttered sourly.

Bridget jumped from the table. She picked up an apple and chomped. 'In your head. Your head tells your feet you've skates on and—'

'Oh this is just stupid. Out of my way Bridget.' Nell barged past. 'There's a man half starved for this sandwich.'

Agnes chuckled. 'Thank God we've Nell – to keep our feet on the ground,' she said.

She's late down to the kitchen to put out Grace's breakfast. The child is already munching. She blankly stares out the window. Harsh rain of the early hours is reduced to spits now, more spray hissing from a frying pan. The sky is grey and leaden, holding back, plenty yet to come.

Twin dark circles under Grace's eyes are greyer than the clouds.

'Did you sleep okay, Grace? Once you went up to your own bed?'

'Yeah.'

'You look a bit tired to me. How was Mama's headache last night? Any better?'

Grace turns her head from the window. She doesn't respond. Nell fetches the child's navy raincoat from a peg in the back porch. It's filthy.

'This the one?'

She holds it out while Grace shunts her arms backwards. At least her hair looks clean and reasonably shiny.

'Your lunch,' Nell remembers.

'I did it already.'

'That won't do,' Nell says, sifting through Grace's idea of lunch. One triangle of processed cheese, two chocolate biscuits and a packet of crisps. Quickly, Nell starts to butter bread for a sandwich.

'I'll be late for the bus.'

'It doesn't matter. I'll drive you.'

When she turns round, there's no sign of her grand-daughter. The door to the yard from the porch is still open. Grace is outside, hunkered down, stroking a cat. It slithers under her hand until the last flick up of its tail, turning to start all over again from the head first. Seeing the attention, a couple more appear out of nowhere, sidling up to their benefactor. Grace keeps up a low constant stream of her own cat talk. It's okay, it's okay, she murmurs over and over, trance-like. As if something bad has happened to them and she's here now to make it all better.

'I always think dogs would tell you anything. Woof woof

and out with it. But cats, much more inclined to keep their secrets, what do you think?' Nell almost winces at this clumsy attempt.

'They're *cats*,' Grace says with disdain. A look that says: how could you demean us both with such a cackhanded effort. Pulease.

'Have you got a hat?' Nell asks.

'It doesn't matter if my hair gets wet.'

'Be a shame, now it's all clean and shiny.'

'It doesn't matter.'

By the wall, the last of Ali's climbing roses have taken a battering. Petals scatter about, veined and mulched like saturated butterfly wings. Nell snaps off a few remaining stalks with intact rose heads. The thorns are widely spaced but she misses one and it pierces her finger. She sucks, then draws it out with her teeth.

'C'mon, Grace. We'd better go.'

Reluctantly, Grace straightens. Nell presses a drop of blood with a thumbnail, sucks again.

'A thorn,' she responds to the silent query. 'I'll clip the rest off in the kitchen when I come back. I'm going to put these in my room. Put a vase in your room, too, if you like. D'you like roses? Except for the damn thorns, of course.' She realizes she's absolutely desperate for a smile, anything, a slight grin would do. *Just don't be so unhappy, Grace. Please darling.*

Grace gives the bouquet a dull look. Her mouth works, mumbling something Nell can't quite catch. She bends closer.

'Sometimes what?'

'It doesn't matter,' Grace says, hitching the rucksack onto her shoulders. She walks to the car, slings her bag on the back seat and gets in. Eyes fixed on some point in the distance, the raised cluster on her forehead curling tight as a cyclone.

I do not like you, one little bit, Nell thinks, keeping up a fixed smile. Grace's teacher, Miss Kelly entertains her in the staffroom. The room is a clinical shrine with modern furniture and shiny potted Swiss cheese plants. As soon as Nell said who she was and that she wanted a word, the young woman set the class a task and beckoned Nell summarily. Almost clicking her fingers all the way down the pasteurized corridor.

In her twenties, with wispy blond hair cut choppy and flyaway over a pointy face with a shiny, translucent nose. She's what Nell's mother used to call, a noody nawdy. All flickery efficiency and magazine compassion, masking a closed little nugget heart. She slides a cup of tea across a wide desk. Nell sips and murmurs her thanks.

'Well,' Miss Kelly begins, 'I was beginning to wonder if anyone from that house, was ever going to come and see me.'

That house.

'I've sent notes home with Grace, you know.' Miss Kelly idly flips through a batch of computer printouts by her cup and saucer. As though – while she's in here anyway – such a busy person, she couldn't possibly concentrate on just the one task at a time.

'Notes?' Nell enquires. 'What about?'

'About Grace's behaviour, of course. I've repeatedly asked her mother to come and see me.'

'What behaviour exactly?'

'She can be quite rude and surly, I have to say. Lately,

there's been a marked disimprovement. She doesn't seem to make any effort with the other children and when she does . . . it's, well . . .'

'Yes?'

'Inappropriate.'

'How so?'

'She's quite well up on the facts of life, isn't she?'

'No more than any young girl her age, I'd have said.'

'Hmm. Maybe. And then, of course, there's that mumbo-jumbo she goes around spouting. Old-style psalms and what have you. The children don't know what to make of it, I have to say.'

Mumbo jumbo? The Bible?

'It's not the days of the nuns now, you know,' she adds with a twitch of knowing smile. 'We concentrate on a wider, more secular approach. All part of socializing the children.'

'I see. Where are we going here, Miss Kelly?'

The translucent nose wrinkles. It doesn't care for a straightforward pinch. The computer sheaves fairly fly through nimble, galloping fingers.

'Then there's the business of the fleabites, and she's always scratching her head, you know.' A deep pained intake of breath. 'I'm sorry, but it has to be said. No one wants to sit beside her.'

It has to be said, does it? No one wants to sit beside her. You witch.

'Grace's mother – my daughter – tends towards, I s'pose you could call it, an alternative life style.'

'Oh, please don't think we have any problem with that.'

'I'm sure you don't.' Nell inclines her head graciously. 'However, I can see how it might cause problems for my little granddaughter.'

'You look so young.'

'Thank you. Now, I've already treated the bites and lice, so hopefully that small problem can be cleared up quite quickly. I'll speak to Ali about the Bible lessons. She can be evangelical about something that's new to her. But with the best of intentions. It has occurred to you, of course, that she may just have gone a bit overboard in her effort to help Grace fit in?'

'Indeed.' Glassy nose gives her cup a profound look. Occurred to her ass.

'And Grace's father has been very unwell.' Might as well throw the kitchen sink at it. 'That's bound to affect her behaviour.'

'Bound to.'

'And of course she's an only child – facing a lot of changes in her life, all by herself.'

'Its own set of problems, you're so right. I'm the youngest of four myself.' She rolls her eyes, twitches up the corners of her lips. 'The baby in the family, you could say. The dote.'

'What? Oh yes. Anyway, I suppose what I'm trying to say is that it takes a while to settle in anywhere. Only two years, after all, since Grace left her school in Oxford. What I wanted to ask *you* Miss Kelly is: is there anything, you think, the school might be able to do to help?' Nell daintily sips the last of her tea, chinks the cup back onto the saucer.

'We-ll,' Miss Kelly draws out doubtfully.

Nell pulls at the hem of her black skirt, presses her knees together. She puts a curled forefinger to her mouth in a polite clearing of the throat.

'Maybe you could explain about the cats and her sick father. You know, to a few of the girls in her class. Maybe you could give them the special job of looking out for Grace until she fits in a bit better. It's a difficult period for her. I know when I was a little girl and I had a difficult period myself, I'd have loved it if someone was looking out for me. Young children can be quite cruel, don't you think? But they can be very kind, too.'

Miss Kelly slides her fingers along a pen, turns it, slides down again. She is giving Nell's proposal her most sedulous consideration. Her lips purse with concentration.

'I think that's a grand idea. I'll set it in motion as soon as I get back in the classroom,' she decides eventually. The pen collapses, rolls away; all finished with that. 'A little chat works all the wonders in the world. I only wish that all the parents were as reasonable as yourself. Some people take the slightest bit of criticism as if it's directed at them personally.' She rises, with her hand extended. ''Course you'll have a word with her about the grunting and "making babies" nonsense as well, won't you?'

'Of course,' Nell smiles, a little taken aback.

'We like to stick with the Department of Education's sexual information programme. It works best with the small ones. No one wants to overload them.'

'I'll have a word.' Nell pumps the limp kipper hand a second time. At the door she turns, frowning. 'Just out of interest,' she says, 'you look vaguely familiar.'

'I do?'

'Might be I went to school with your mother.'

'Might be indeed.' Miss Kelly beams. 'Avril's her name. Avril O'Mahoney. Did you know her?'

Agnes has her own headstone. Ali must have insisted on that. A blueish granite rectangle with black lettering. It still looks new beside the weathered stone shared by her husband

and daughter. There's a plastic wreath, laid quite recently, and a jam jar of faded summer flowers. The centre is filled with white chips, possibly marble. Round the borders, a couple of weeds straggle through, but clearly they're not allowed to survive for long, Ali makes sure of that. In loving memory, the granite reads. Her stones should have been buried with her. Strange that Ali didn't think of it. Still, she had more than enough to keep her occupied, Nell thinks, with a stab of guilt.

A line of crows look down from a stretch of cable. They take little sideways steps towards one another, feathers riffle, before a hurried retreat, as though singed by the intimacy of touch. Seconds pass, of rigid composure, and off they sidle again, compelled. The cable quivers with crows bumping into one another. In profile they look like a row of sleek umbrellas shaking off rain.

Nell wonders what is left of her mother. Down there, under the earth, is there any liquified pulp still clinging to bone? Are there little tumbleweeds of steelwool hair up by her scalp? Has her wedding ring slid down one atrophied finger? Do her teeth show through peeled back lips? Is the memory of her . . . lonely?

She looks around. She should have brought flowers; something, at any rate. The human imperative to bring things to a plot of ground containing a dead person is beyond anyone's explanation, yet it's true, she thinks, she does feel mean and empty-handed, as though she's come home and brought no present for her mother. She rummages in the deep pocket of her raincoat, and something small rattles against the Lucozade bottle. The roll of Almond Frost lipstick. She places it by the headstone and covers with a handful of white chips.

*Sorry for your troubles. Sorry for your loss. So so sorry. But I am,
Mammy.*

Out on the street, a light mist of rain coats the pavements, leaving dry patches under the striped awnings of the
shops. She can hear her hair frizzing. The slow, burning
flush that started by her mother's grave begins to subside as
she steps into the chemist's. The man with the bandaged
glasses nods a greeting. He says she's brought the rain with
her but for once it's a blessing. Is she planning on staying
around much longer? She's not sure. A while longer, anyway.
Nell puts more tea tree oil on the counter, a box of tampax
for a period which may or may not come, high-strength oil
of evening primrose for the menopause. The arrivals and
departures hall that has become her body.

She gives him the money and puts the Lucozade bottle on
the counter, too. He pulls a face when she invites him to
sniff the malodorous contents. It's a herbal mixture her
daughter's partner takes to boost his immune system.
Presumably. He pulls another dubious face. Well exactly,
Nell says, would there be – is there any way he might be able
to analyse the contents for her? Just so's she can be certain
he's not taking something that might turn out to be harmful
to his health? He stabs the broken spectacles tighter on the
bridge of his nose. No facilities here for anything like that.
He'd help if he could, naturally. People seem to be labouring
under the delusion nowadays that anything, so long as it
grows in the garden, must be good for them. They could be
doing irreparable harm to themselves. He's lost in thought
for so long that Nell thinks he must be considering the various irreparable harms. She's about to slide the bottle back
into her pocket when he circles the neck. What he could
do – he's a nephew, a lab technician at a hospital in Killarney.

He'll give the stuff to him this evening. It might take a while, mind. Nell tells him how grateful she'd be. She gives him her mobile number, thanks him again. Not to mention it, he says. Not to mention it, he repeats holding his hands up when she offers to pay for the test.

Outside, the mist has let up for a little while. Patches of white sky break through the mantle of cloud. A spear of light settles on her face for a second, moves on. She turns, looks back down the winding village street. How many years has she left? Ten? Twenty? Thirty? Where will she lie, waiting for lipstick?

That question has been settled for Henri since the day he was born. Like most Burgundians he is an adamant exponent of the *terroir* concept, the intellectually appealing notion that a plot of soil plays the determining factor in a wine's character. Everything – the slant of sun across a particular slope, the minerals in a patch of soil, the porousness of that patch, whether it holds rain or immediately lets it trickle through, the general wind direction through the lines of vine, the wild yeasts, the proportion of rocks sprinkling the earth – everything counts. There isn't a factor that doesn't contribute to his *grand cru* and *premier cru* vintages. And in time, when he goes in the ground, he will become his own wine. Like his father before him, long buried on a southern slope, a mile from the house he was born in.

She checks her phone: several work-related messages; she nods them through impatiently. Two days now and still nothing from Henri, no response to her message. She got the answering service again when she tried to call, but so far hasn't left another. Perhaps he's having second thoughts, not as certain as he thought he was. About leaving Lucienne. About Nell.

The thought stabs her heart, all the sharper for being so unexpected. Maybe she's left it too late. What a small thing it would have been to offer him her company. To say, as she walked out the door with her suitcase, I'll be back on Tuesday, or Wednesday, or Thursday. To say: talk to me while I cook, tell me about your day. To accept the small claims he would make of her life. To make him . . . not in any way enduringly ecstatic but, rather, moderately content in a moderate everyday way, simply by ending the wanderings of his toothbrush. Why should this have felt such an onerous commitment?

They've been through the various stages of love, so like grief – denial, anger, acceptance – so why had she balked before these final stretches? What was so difficult about saying, yes, get your things, move in immediately? She's seen with Henri that love can go away, lie dormant for whole tracts of time, but come back again, a little sheepish perhaps, a little startled to be caught gatecrashing the same party. But it does come back. Or perhaps it did come back, time after time, for Henri. Just not this time.

She shivers, though the day is not cold. Never, in all her travels, has Henri seemed so estranged. In that place where the darkest thoughts reside, she understands, with absolute clarity, that she's been waiting for this, his change of heart. Waiting for him to fall away, leave, while she turns from him, not wanting to see.

'In all the universe, this is my favourite place,' Agnes said, standing on the last ridge of grass before it curved in a dip down to the long stretch of beach. She placed her hands on her hips, gazing left and right, taking in the sweep of sand, the spindly witch fingers of black rock creeping into the sea, the light blue wash of sky – as if she could lay claim to all that she saw. In her own mind, Nell thought, but sure, you haven't been anywhere else Mammy.

Behind them, partially screened by a line of trees, stood the house Daniel O'Connell was brought up in. His uncle's house, in fact, as Agnes pointed out so many times, inculcating both daughters, then one, with her own sense of place. How many times had Nell listened to the story of the 'Liberator'? How the great man had used his skills in the lawcourts to achieve the once unthinkable, Catholic emancipation for the Irish. The legendary orator, elegant tactician or scheming fox, filled with a fierce, burning love of his homeland. Oh, the Brits had to listen to him, all right. We'd be curtseying to the Queen, Nell, only for him. Sometimes it felt as if Agnes herself had played a part in his destiny.

'Imagine it, Nell,' she'd say, widening her arms to the beach. 'We're walking where the man himself walked. What thoughts did he have, d'you think, looking out at that great ocean? Hunting Cap is what the uncle was called. Did I tell you that?'

Nell would nod wearily. Yes, a thousand times.

'He brought up the oldest two lads of his brother. Daniel and Maurice. There were ten children in all. Just think how different things might be for all of us if those boys had stopped at home.'

Nell would peel burst bubble gum from the skin of her top lip. Even then, she knew her mother had a somewhat empirical view of the Irish constitution. With a slant that tended toward the global.

On and on Agnes could drone for hours, about how the course of history could turn on the head of a pin. About how what was written in stone today, was, in fact, shaped by some arbitrary, random event of yesterday. Hunting Cap funding the education of his oldest nephew, for instance.

''Course, take one look at the house, stuck out here all by itself, and it won't take you long to guess how he made his money.'

'Smuggling.' Nell would look out to sea and wonder what it would be like to be on a boat, gently bobbing toward the horizon, going on for ever. Never coming back.

There was always that faint note of mania to these recitals of her mother's. As long as they were talking about Daniel O'Connell, or Paudie's appendicitis, or the tax hike on spirits, or anything in the least tangential or inconsequential – they were relieved of the need to talk about anything else. Though Agnes's eyes would often flicker to the side of Nell when she spoke, forever addressing an absent child. She just couldn't say: it's sharp today, or I'm having a bad day, or I wonder how she would have turned out. For a woman who usually measured words with lapidarian precision, on their walks she spent them with the abandon of a gambler who'd just placed everything on the red and won.

'Smuggling. Among other things. Young Daniel was mad into the horses. Riding, hunting, you name it. He'd a wild youth, for a man that was going to go on and liberate his country. But look around you, Nell. Can you think what a childhood he had? Can you just imagine? All that beach to himself and his brother, the woods next to the house for exploring, that fine big house to rattle around. On a fine day, he might have stood where I'm standing now, and thought: just let me at it. Did I tell you what he wrote to his wife, Mary?'

'Yeah.'

'Next to you and my babes, he wrote, I love Iveragh. Uibh Ráthach, of course, was how he wrote it.' She turned, her eyes glowing. 'Isn't that something?' Her eyes skimmed the waves, willing herself to be happy. 'I know exactly what he meant.'

As Nell gazed at her mother's back, she wondered what she could do to prevent another O'Connell threnody. She really couldn't face it. There was a baby growing in her stomach and Aunt Hannah on the way from Galway. What Agnes missed, Hannah would detect in a matter of days. No doubt about that.

But Agnes didn't seem inclined to talk that day. All morning she'd been pensive, her eyes fixed on some distant place. She was quiet in the pub through the afternoon, too.

Nell took a deep breath; the pure air contained crystals of sea. 'Mammy?' she began tentatively.

'C'mon. We'll walk along the edge here. See how fast the tide's coming in below?'

From up there on the high grassy bank, it did look as if the ocean was hurling itself at the shore. Huge, rolling curtains of water, shattered into broken china pieces along the sand. The white pieces clung for seconds but were sucked back into water by the powerful swell. Agnes walked ahead of Nell, her feet carving a conduit in the long grasses, close to the edge. A pale amber wisp of light clung to the entire line of horizon. It had rained earlier and everything had that just-washed, glittery appearance Nell loved.

'I've something to tell you. This is going to make you very cross. I'm so sorry but . . .' Nell whispered a dozen possible starts to a conversation which was about to change her life. 'How can I tell you . . .'

She was almost up to Agnes by then, forced to pull up

abruptly when, of a sudden, Agnes stopped in her tracks. A guttural sound came from her lips, as though someone had just punched her. Her head plunged forward. She gave a huge shudder and wrapped her arms round her waist. Nell could see the white, bloodless tips of her fingers. She didn't even reach for her hat when a whip of wind blew it away. She stood still, for the longest time, containing herself with her own hands, until her head slowly stood erect again. Her profile turned to the sea, with such a look of profound longing, it almost frightened Nell to see it.

'What a beautiful day,' she said, hoarsely. 'Such a . . . What I wouldn't give for Bridget to see this day.'

And she walked on. Heedless of her hat flitting among the sand dunes. Nell ran back for it and when she turned, Agnes stood poised at the edge of the grass bank, before jack-knifing down in one clear swoop onto the soft sands below.

It seemed to Nell as though her mother had just fallen off the edge of the world.

Charcoal grey of the sea reflects the lowering early evening sky, just managing to hold the rain back. She can almost hear the battalions, drills, of rain stamp their feet with impatience behind the cover of cloud. Far out in the ocean, the waves make a booming which almost makes the shore vibrate. A constant snowy white frill surrounds the Bull and Calf rocks. The women stroll at a leisurely pace along the tawny sands of Derrynane beach. They've walked to the far end, left, where a wrecked trawler sits high on the grey boulders that hold it captive for ever. They turn and increase their pace for the long sandy stretches ahead, broken by fingers of black rock which they will have to skirt round or clamber over. To their right, the sand comes to an end in a scooped-out hollow, rising up to banks of grass fractured in golf-course fashion by puddles of sand. The dark grey gabled end of Derrynane House can be seen through a line of beech trees, leaf edges just on the turn. The gable is covered in rectangles of roof slates, faced to the wind. Daniel O'Connell's house.

'Did she go on and on about him?' Nell points to the house. 'When you walked along here? Mammy, I mean.'

Ali starts. They've been silent for so long, perhaps she thought she was alone. She doesn't look at all well. Skin so pale it's almost translucent. Everything about her looks brittle, as if she could be snapped in two with very little effort.

'What? No, not really. She mentioned him in the pub sometimes. We didn't walk all that much, you know. Hardly at all.'

'Even when you came on summer holidays?'

Ali pulls a face, trying to remember. She shakes her head. 'Not that I recall. Of course, with me, I just wanted to be in the pub all the time. It was my doll's-house.'

Instinctively, following the same urge, they move down to hug the shoreline. White sherbet fizzes round their shoes, draws back as clear water again. A couple of people pass and nod greetings. A lone fisherman, in silhouette against the bleak sky, casts a line from the end of a clump of dark rock, which carries a good distance into the sea. He must be drenched. Angry spray constantly rises high into the air on all sides of his perch.

Nell gives Ali a sideways glance. Though Ali hasn't said anything, it's clear that she's in two minds about Nell's approach to the school. Not that Nell didn't expect ambivalence. No matter what she does, it's going to be seen as interfering. It always is. She licks sea mist from her lips.

'Look, Ali.'

But Ali stops walking, places a hand on her mother's shoulder. Her smile is forced, but forced with genuine intent. 'Why shouldn't you speak with Grace's teacher.' It doesn't end on a question up-note. 'You're entitled to talk to anyone you like. You're concerned about your granddaughter, and you're right to be.'

'Why do you say that?'

'Even a fool can see she's troubled.'

'It's not just the school, is it?'

'No. Not just.' Ali shields her eyes, stares out to a white band of light along the horizon's rim. 'I wanted her to fit in. That's what all the psalms and stuff was about.'

'I figured.'

'But I got it wrong.'

'Well, you—'

'I got it wrong.'

Nell cups a hand to Ali's cheek. 'Talk to me. Tell me about Adam – the truth this time. Has he been threatening you in any way?'

Ali gives a little bitter laugh, moves her head away from Nell's hand. 'Yes, but not in the way you think. Not the way Paudie thinks.'

'What, then? You can tell me, darling.'

'So you can fix it?' Her eyes glitter with tears. 'That's what you do. You come and fix things, and then you go away. No, I don't mean that badly. It's the truth. You're quite delightful. It's me. I don't know why it makes me so angry – there's no sense to it. Oxford, Cardiff, the bloody Hebrides, for pity's sake. Always you turned up, watched and waited, watched and waited, poking at the problem, whatever the problem was, wherever, needling it until you got it to the surface. Presents for Grace, the best clinics for me when that was the problem that surfaced. We've had our rows, bitter enough sometimes, but on the whole you've been remarkably tolerant and patient – and yes, delightful too.'

Nell takes an involuntary step back. Surf surges round her ankles in an instant. 'And sometimes you hate me for it.'

'Sometimes. Yes, I do.'

Ali gives a little shrug, as if to say: go figure. She turns and walks on again. Nell remains rooted to the spot for a few moments, then steps up her pace, to catch up.

'What am I not getting to the surface this time? What can't I fix?'

She stops, hoping that Ali will turn round but she's already clambering over a cluster of rock, smooth and oily as seal's pelt from the constant hammering of the sea. Nell calls, louder. 'Your heart? Is that what's broken?'

Ali stiffens. She remains still for a moment, then quickly retraces her steps to her mother. Her fists clench and open repeatedly, as if, internally, she's trying to reason something out.

'You know what it is? The ridiculous thing that makes me so angry with you sometimes?' She's up to Nell, one hand circling her own throat as if to force the elusive words up. 'It's the way you uncomplicate things to your own satisfaction. There's the problem, you think, let's just take it out and have a look. Where's my scalpel? Just a tiny incision here and—'

'Ali! That is so—'

'Of course it's unfair! Don't you think I know that? The complication of things again. The contradictions! How could anyone not see the best of you? There's none of that nitty-gritty, rubbing shoulders, everyday kind of shit the rest of us muddle through. No one ever has to see you on your bad days, your bad, the whole world sucks and I wish everyone would drop dead – but slowly, miserably, in agony – days. You make sure you're gone, or we're gone, before the initial euphoria at all being together runs out. Before any shabby, scabby little things about yourself can show through. Dear Jesus! The only way I can stick myself sometimes is the shabby, scabby stuff of other people. And is that right? You bet your arse it's not. But who wants to play with the good girl in school? Who wants to be around someone who's always going to look and act and think better?

'You're in and out like a sort of benign surgeon, a stitch here, a bandage there. What's this? A broken heart? What've I got in my black bag for that? She's miserable in Paris? Send her back to Oxford, back to Uncle Albie and Mary Kate – she was happy with them, wasn't she? Until you decided that you weren't, of course. And why? Because they'd begun to see us as part of them. Everyday, rubbing shoulders, part of them. Don't think I didn't admire how you set about building your new life. The study, the dedication. The light on in your room into the early hours of the morning. The way you picked up French, just like that' – She clicks her fingers. 'I was young but I knew that you were making something of yourself. You weren't going to settle into anybody's set of preconceptions about unmarried mothers. You weren't going to be yet another girl who had to take the boat, to find herself lost in a strange place far away from home. And still you found time to take me to the park! My God, was there nothing you couldn't do? Nothing you can't do?'

'Apparently not.'

'Please don't think I'm trying to place any of my problems at your feet. That's the opposite of what I'm trying to say.

Please, at least let my mistakes be my own. I don't want you to say, what's the problem? let me fix it. And then if you don't say that, or imply it with just the way you sit on a chair, I do! See, I'm messy. All over the shop. I want to make you proud and then I'm furious with myself for wanting that. Mostly — and I say this with loads of equivocations — I don't want you to take responsibility for me.' Her face twists, holding back tears. 'I'm tired of failing, bone tired of it.'

'Who says you're failing? But your happiness, yes, I do feel responsible for that. I can't help it. Don't you feel responsible for Grace?'

'No — yes. Oh, I know I'm being ridiculous. If there's anything I'm cross about — all right, let's get to it: I just couldn't understand you not coming here with me those summers. Every year you promised, then you always found an excuse. What was it this time? Granny used to say. She'd say it with a smile, but it hurt her. I loved her so much and I couldn't believe that this wonderful, delightful mother of mine, could be so — callous is the only word. The same with Mary Kate, the day we moved into that awful flat. Couldn't you see how you were pulling the heart out of her? Couldn't you see it?'

'Yes, I suppose I could. But at the time I thought it was the right thing to do.'

'Uncle Albie, Mary Kate, Aunt Hannah — you should have seen them standing round Granny's grave. They kept looking at one another, doing these little confused shrugs. Hands out, like this. Fingers out, like this. No one could understand. The thing was, they were embarrassed — no, mortified — for Granny. Even the priest mentioned you, said you must be sick or something.'

Ali looks hesitant, her eyes flicker up and down, checking Nell's reaction. This subject they've managed to skirt around for so many years.

'Go on,' Nell says. They set up a rhythm, feet sinking into wet sand at the same time. Ali slips her arm through her mother's.

'They laid her out on the bar counter. Did you know that?'

Nell shakes her head. There's no scalpel for this one.

'You wouldn't have believed your eyes. The night they moved her from the pub to the church, she was stretched out on the counter, hands crossed on her chest, like so, and there was so much singing – you couldn't believe the people who stepped up to sing to her. Rebel songs, like it was their own mother racked out there, by the Black and Tans – oh yeah, she regularly gave me the condensed history. The queues were backed out the door, down the road as far as anyone could see, just waiting their chance to say a few words to this . . . this dead person – there's no other way to put it. Paudie and Julia were inconsolable. I thought the queue would never end. And still they came, murmuring words as they passed her body. When they placed her in the coffin, there was a frightful hush, broken only by the odd sob here and there. Paudie and five other men hitched her up on their shoulders and the crowds outside made a space for them. The coffin was draped in the Kerry colours and a small bit of Galway, Hannah saw to that. Right in the middle, someone had placed a photograph of you and Bridget.'

'Oh.'

'All the way, they shouldered her down to the village. When those six men grew tired, six more stepped in to take their place. Everyone held a candle. It looked as if they were coming out of the ditches. All you could see was this weaving line of flickering lights. And when we got to the village, there wasn't room to stand on the pavements. People were spilling onto the road. The church bell tolled her in, the lonesomest sound. The doors had to be closed on the crush of people – I only just made it in myself. There was genuine sadness, Nell. A real thing you could feel everywhere. They were losing somebody very special. Someone who'd figured in their lives – for some of them, since the day they were born. And it wasn't just locals. Tourists, people who came year after year, some of them had made the journey. There were Northern Ireland accents, English, Scottish – just about everywhere. I couldn't figure out such grief. I mean, my own I could understand well enough.'

'No more for a while, Ali, please.'

'Nell, I want you to be there. With me. Can you?'

'All right.'

'Usually they keep the coffin closed but Hannah got them to open it for the last time in the church – there were so many people who couldn't get inside the door of the pub. They filed past, hundreds of them. I looked at her face. It didn't look like her, to tell the truth. She had her lipstick on, you'll be glad to hear, but apart from that it was just a waxy-looking body lying there, with a nose far too big for the head. I thought about my own life, the messes, the mistakes, the non-stop wandering around, what was I looking for? Where was I going? I thought, who the hell will pitch up to pay their respects to me? Why would they? And I thought of all the pints she'd served; I swear I could see them, stacked up, scraping the sky. All those conversations night after night, when she was tired or depressed, but still could be bothered.

She talked to people when no one else would talk to them. When I say talk, I mean just a greeting sometimes, a g'dluck as they headed out the door. I looked at her and I thought, where's it all gone? All that talk, all those pints, what was the point? She'd never gone anywhere, never travelled except to visit you, events of the world passed her by, for the most part, so what was the point?

'I waited until what the church could hold had passed the coffin, then I stepped up with Hannah. Paudie and Julia stood beside us. Julia kept grabbing my hand. Then I leaned across and I kissed her on the lips. I breathed in, sucking all that past out of her. She gave it to me. She did. I looked back at the faces and I saw that that was the point. Of course, that was it. I made up my mind then and there: I was going to put down roots, stop still, like her, and that way . . . there might be some point to me as well.'

When she's finished, Ali takes a deep ragged breath and stares out to sea. They remain lost in their thoughts for a long time. The sky is the colour of smoke as evening draws in. They walk on, arms tightly linked, squeezing elbows every now and then, for reassurance. After a while, Ali stops still. She studies her feet, trying to find the right words.

'What is it? Tell me.'

When she looks up, Nell is forcibly struck by her haunted expression.

'The thing is . . . The thing is, I used to think, wonder . . .'

'What?'

'If you didn't love her, when would you stop loving me, too?'

'Oh, Ali.' Nell claps her hands to her face. 'How could you ever . . .? It wasn't that I didn't – good God, the very opposite. Look at me. Please.' Ali looks shy, pained, bright red spots glowing on her cheeks. Nell tips her chin higher with the crook of her finger. 'Nothing in this world would ever make me stop loving you. Nothing. Do you believe me?'

Ali nods furiously, mortified and elated in equal measure.

'And I wish I could say sorry to Mammy, not just about the funeral. For all the years.'

'You know, don't ask me why, but I think she understood. There was something between you, wasn't there?'

'Yes. Here. There was always something between us.'

The gentle shushing feet plunging into wet sand makes them turn round. Bola on his evening run. He gestures as he passes, just a slight incline of his head. Water closes over the tracks made by his huge feet, twin tracks which carry until the next outcrop of rock. He fades out of sight. Running over the phantom sandcastles of Daniel O'Connell and his brother Maurice.

CHAPTER ELEVEN

Sometimes people . . . people have . . . Sometimes, some-times . . .

'What was it she said?' Nell says aloud to the ceiling. She turns onto her left side, punches the pillow for the fifth time, trying to settle back to sleep. All night, Grace has been on her mind. Her pixie face scrunched up in a tight knot, the way she mumbled when Nell pricked her finger, then turned away – it doesn't matter. That dead look in her eyes. A look Nell remembers as if it were yesterday: brushing her teeth, glancing up to find, not herself in the mirror above the bathroom sink but a strange girl whose navy, opaque irises reflected no light at all. For years after Bridget's death, the stranger looked back at her. For years, even the mirrors were dead.

Since the walk on Derrynane with Ali, it hasn't stopped raining. The kind of rain that makes you think of Noah's ark, the kind that looks as though it will never cease. It drums against the bedroom window in a constant refrain, plashing up from the window-sill outside in arcs of silver beads. The ticking of the house winding down for the night, usually so loud, fades to an intermittent whisper, by comparison.

Much earlier, she'd gone to bed after helping out in the
bar for a while. When it looked as if Adam and Ali were
going to serve long past closing time, she took herself off,
hoping Henri might call. But not a whisper, not a word.
She's left three messages now.

Grace went to bed, relieved of several head lice and the
dreaded psalms. She told Nell that Ali said they wouldn't be
doing that any more. Grace wrinkled her nose. What God
wanted with all that praise, in any case, she'd never figure
out. Wasn't it enough to be God? Why'd he want to be
praised for it? Nell was damned if she knew. But she thought
that something lay a little lighter with the child. Or so she
hoped.

Outside, she hears a sound. A steel keg crashing on the
ground, then a raised voice. She keeps the lights off and
pads to the window. Down in the yard, through the distort-
ing screen of rain, she sees Adam and Ali. Arguing, it
appears. Ali wears a light blue towelling robe over white
pyjamas. The robe is saturated, dripping from the hem. Her
bare feet stand in a puddle which reaches her ankles. She's
furiously gesticulating, waving her arms about to make a
point. Adam leans over the keg, clutching handles on either
side as if he's just banged it down. Nell can't be sure, but Ali
looks close to tears. Or maybe she is crying already. A hand
constantly draws under her nostrils. An occasional word carries up to Nell, but nothing to give her a firm clue as to
what the disagreement is about. She wishes she could open
the window, but it's so creaky they would hear immediately.

Nell squints harder. As Ali makes her case, Adam keeps his
head bowed over the keg. He nods once or twice. It's a reasonable stance, the listener, but Nell can see, from the tight,
rigid way he keeps hold of the handles, that he is a coiled

spring. Rain hits his gleaming head at an angle, flies up in ricocheting drops. His sweater and jeans cling to his slender frame, snug as skin. The head jerks up suddenly when Ali says something. Nell can only see the white of his eye. She wants to shout a warning to Ali but it's too late. His arm snakes out, wraps round Ali's wrist. In a blur of movement, she's flung like a rag doll against the porch wall. He turns and strides downfield. Nell waits just long enough to make sure that Ali isn't seriously hurt. She's sliding down the wall with her face in her hands, shoulders heaving up and down, in a pitiful state.

Nell fumbles about in the dark for her clothes, practically keeling over sideways as she tries to shunt into her jeans with trembling hands. She bumps into the door and runs downstairs in pitch darkness. In the porch she steps into a puddle of leaked rain; she's forgotten shoes. Outside, there is no sign of Ali. Nell stares back into the darkness of the house for a moment – no, she would have heard her come in. The only sound she can hear is her own rasping breaths, scraping against her lungs.

Halfway down the fields, she thinks she should go back for boots. Ankles sink deep into liquid mud, as though the earth itself is melting. The door of the caravan is slightly ajar. A dim light shines within. Nell's heart pounds against her breastbone so hard she has to put a hand to her chest to contain it. The look of black rage on Adam's face just before he lashed out: at that moment he was capable of anything. Surely Ali hasn't been stupid enough to go after him? She must have seen the rage. Certainly she felt it when he swung her by the wrist. No, she'd never be that stupid. Yes, yes she would. She would. Nell stops still with her eyes closed for a second.

She can hear voices inside. A low male thrum followed by the higher, plaintive pitch of Ali. Then silence. Nell lets out a long, pent-up breath, creeps closer along the side of the caravan, painfully conscious of the sticky, squelching noise her feet make with every step. She drops to her haunches by the slit of open doorway. The light's too gloomy and the crack isn't wide enough to afford a view of anything. The silence continues within. Curtains are drawn in the windows. There's nothing for it. Nell takes another deep breath, grips the door and pulls slightly. She waits for the telltale creak, but the hinges are well oiled. It takes a moment for the shape of figures to materialize. At first it looks like one body, but lower down there's another set of bony shoulders. The spiky orb of Ali's head, her back to the door. She is on her knees. Adam lifts his chin suddenly, dreamlike at first, then he looks full square into Nell's eyes. His lips form a silent O, as if recognizing an old acquaintance, then slowly compress to curl up at the edges in enigmatic smile. He allows his head to fall forward again. Nell turns, an arm pressed across her midriff. She stumbles back up into darkness.

Sometimes people have thorns on the *inside*. Nell wakes with Grace's words ringing in her ears. At last, it's come to her. Yes, darling, sometimes they do. It's a vain hope, but she'll stick to it: that the child has only heard sound effects. *Uh uh uh*.

How was it possible for a thirty-two-year-old woman, no young girlie, of more than reasonable intelligence, with all the things she'd ever craved – no, pined for – coming together, falling into her lap, fixed home, fixed family, nothing temporary – how was it *possible* she could let herself fall instead into the thrall of this nomadic hustler? Oh, entirely possible. For all her brave talk, Ali has always been as vulnerable as newly fallen snow. Adam is the drug of the day, and it's written all over her daughter's crushed face that he's brought her to exquisite, heart-piercing highs of self-abasement which heroin merely kissed.

She has to force herself to remember that little grey-eyed girl, running toward her in the schoolyard, nervous and brittle even then, remember looking around at the other mothers, who looked like mothers and not someone's big sister, reaching down, scooping her up, dousing her for brief moments with brilliance. With dazzling smiles that fell on her upturned face like sunlight. Making her strain, stretch up, like leaves on a plant in a shady corner, hungry for light, leaning into the rays. It wasn't that Nell ignored her, far from it; more that her luminosity dimmed everything by comparison when she was there, leaving everything dim when she wasn't. Nell herself was barely out of her teens, dull brown hair newly golden, bands of tinkly silver bracelets around both wrists, rings on every finger, long skeins of cheesecloth scarf wrapped round her neck, edged with rows of tiny metallic globes. A tinny jazz riff when she strode along the pavement, a hand groping air behind, searching for Ali's fingers. So determined to keep moving forward that it simply didn't occur to her that the frenzied pace might be too fast for a child.

What does Ali think? That she can build a hutch for him in the garden, keep him like a rabbit? That she can keep him in her sights in a way she couldn't with her own mother, her gran, Mary Kate, endlessly ping-ponging between the houses, between the women?

Wearily, with a dull, throbbing head from lack of decent

sleep, she swings her legs over the side of the bed. A heel slides along one of the brochures she took from the caravan. A remote hamlet in Scotland, heathery hills, the usual backdrop. A plump, youngish couple on the last page stand before their premises, arms folded, welcoming smiles a touch too forced. Nell thumbs their number. A man responds with the name of the inn. How may he help? He sounds cheerful and friendly.

'Are you the owner, Mr Simms?'

'Last time I checked, yes. Can I help you, madam?'

'I'm sorry, this isn't a reservation. This may sound very strange but I want to find out if a particular person has stayed with you in the past. Or maybe worked there.'

'Police, are you?'

'No. I'm calling you from Ireland. My daughter runs her own pub here. It's just that . . . Well, there's a man working for her and he had your brochure. I wondered if you could tell me anything about him.'

There's a long silence before he responds in a distinctly chilled tone.

'Name of?'

'Adam. I'm sorry, I don't even know his surname, but I can describe—'

'You'd better speak to my wife,' he interrupts tersely. 'Hang on.'

'You should have seen Bridget skating on top of this kitchen table.' Nell spirals a finger on the Formica top. 'Round and round she went, just as if she had skates on. And when she ran, Ali, it really looked as if her feet weren't touching the ground. She was like a deer, a gazelle. You know the Yeats poem?'

'Two girls in silk kimonos, both Beautiful, one a gazelle.' Ali smiles. She gives her mother a shy, hesitant look. Nell smiles back. She could barely bring herself to look at Ali earlier in the morning, barely contain the impulse to catch her by the shoulders and shake until her teeth rattled. Look what you're doing to yourself, to your family. All the old familiar rants. But what was the point? No one knew better than Ali. It wasn't a matter of conscience or common sense. Obsession never is.

Ali made up the herbal slime for Nick, and when she wasn't looking Nell tipped it down the sink. When she turned, Nick was at the bottom of the stairs, but he didn't say anything. Though it was grey and gloomy in the kitchen, reflecting the heavy skies outside, it seemed that a small, faint smile brushed his lips.

Julia made one of her frequent morning visits, popping in for a pot of tea. She chatted about this and that but her eyes were rarely peeled off Ali, who looked so frail that both Julia and Nell were afraid she might not get the mug to her lips each sip. Constantly, she turned her head to the porch door. Waiting for Adam. Instead, Nick flitted in and out of their company, well enough himself to see that Ali was particularly fragile. Dark, bruised circles under puffy eyes. A wormy vein throbbing at the side of one temple; you could see her heartbeat. When she got an opportunity, Julia turned to Nell, her mouth agape, a little shake of her head: what's going on? Nell signalled she'd talk to her another time. Julia pressed her hand tightly before she left.

Fancy a walk? Nell asked, once the sky lifted. I don't think so. Not today, if you don't mind, Ali said. Of course I don't mind. But she wasn't going to let her daughter out of her sight. Let's just sit here and not do anything, Nell said.

Yeah, that sounds about right, Ali responded, looking over her shoulder to the porch.

'Yes, that was her. A gazelle,' Nell says. 'The day we went up Eagle Rock with Mammy, she skipped ahead of me just like a gazelle. My feet were much more solid on the ground and I couldn't keep up. Her red scarf unwound from her neck and I ran to pick it up. When I looked up again, there was no sign of her. She was already over the top of the hill. Mammy was still a good distance behind us. I wrapped the scarf round my neck and trudged up to the top. No sign of Bridget immediately. Have you been up there?'

Ali nods. Holds a fresh, hot mug of tea to one cheek. 'I never told Granny, though. Grace walked up there with me a couple of times. She likes it, thinks it's spooky.'

'It is, especially when cloud comes down. Everything gets shrouded in that dry-ice effect, with dark boulders scattered everywhere and the waist-high grasses, leading down to this black, still lake — I thought it looked like the Earth might have done, at the beginning of time. There was a white mist that day and I couldn't see another figure. I thought maybe she was hiding, behind a big outcrop of rock or something. No sign of Mammy behind. I walked down towards the lake, though I was quite afraid. And then I saw Bridget. She was wading in the water, up to her knees. I thought, Mammy will light off her. Shoes, trousers all soaked. She turned and saw me. I called to her, don't be stupid, come back, Bridget, look, I've got your scarf. It was still round my neck.

'But she laughed. She looked like a little ghost coming up out of the water, something out of Camelot. The water looked like ink, not a ripple on the surface. A dead thing. Her arms were waving at me to come and join her. C'mon, *c'mon.* I thought, no way am I going in that. Mammy will shoot the pair of us. But Bridget's wild laugh, it was so infectious. It made you want to stand right beside her. Anywhere. Would you believe, I took off my shoes? Such a *good* girl. The water was freezing. I took one step – God, it was cold. But it was exciting, too. She waited until I was up to her. We shivered from the cold and the thrill of it all. She held out her hand and I grabbed on. It's shallow for ages, she said, like a shelf. I looked back. Mammy was just at the top before it dips down again. She couldn't see us immediately, through the fog. By this time, we were out at least a third the width of the lake and the water was only up past our knees. I threw my head back and laughed. Bridget looked at me. That's it, she said, that's it. She started laughing, too. We clung to each other, soaked, freezing, laughing our heads off.'

Ali's fingers flitter in the air, motioning her on.

'Mammy could see us by then. She was beckoning furiously. I thought I could hear her calling us back. She broke into a run, but it wasn't easy to run there, so many lumps of loose rock. Bridget knew we were in for it one way or the other, so she squeezed my arms, her eyes dancing, thrilling with adventure. Oh, Ali, I remember that look – she really was the fairy on the Christmas tree. No one could resist her. One more little bit out, she said, just another few steps. No, Mammy'll kill us. She'll kill us anyway. Just another few steps. I let her pull me along. And then we both dropped like stones.'

Nell has to take a sip of tea to moisten her throat. Ali sits very still, hardly blinking.

'We plunged in, water over our heads in an instant. I tried to scream and my mouth filled. It was a vortex, pulling us down. The water wasn't smooth and dead any more. Right where we plunged, it was a living, seething thing, turning so that it sucked your legs. Bridget was beneath me – I could feel her hand around my ankle. My hands were flying above my head, trying to touch the side of the ledge we'd fallen off. But I couldn't feel a thing, only water, pitch-black water in every direction. I couldn't swim. Bridget could – she'll get us out any second, I forced myself to think, if I just hold on a little longer, not breathe. Bridget can do anything. But I didn't really believe that. She was still grasping my ankle, her hold getting weaker. I couldn't keep the water out another second. I took a deep breath and my lungs filled immediately. Up there I could just make out glimmers of light. If I could just . . . If I could just . . . kick my way up there. But Bridget was pulling me back down. I'm not sure. I'll never be sure. But I think I kicked her hand away with my free foot. Suddenly, I was moving up so fast toward the glimmering light, I didn't even have a second to think that Bridget was sinking down to the darkness.'

There's a movement on the stairs, a little wraith shifting position. Grace. For a while now, Nell has suspected that she's at last come out of her room. Watching and listening from above, always minding her parents throughout every long, companion-less weekend.

'I didn't know she held your ankle,' Ali says after a long time. 'If you did have to prise her off – you don't blame yourself for that, Nell?'

'Blame. It's such a comprehensive word. Often an irresponsible word. Like guilt. Sometimes I think we luxuriate in guilts we willingly accept, to absolve ourselves of the shabby, scabby ones, as you put it, that don't seem big enough. No, I behaved reasonably under the circumstances.

The instinct to save yourself is perfectly natural. Of course, I went over it and over it in my mind afterwards. Of course, I tried to imagine Bridget's last thoughts, if she blamed me, as she was sucked down. But always, I figured it was like one of Mammy's random, arbitrary events which change the course of history. My particular story, very minor on the scale of things, but that was it decided, I would put my two feet back on the ground, while Bridget, the gazelle, would jump right off the edge of the world.'

Ali hesitates, choosing her words with care. 'So that was the thing between you and Granny. You told her about Bridget holding your ankle, about kicking back to save yourself. I see.' Ali nods several times. 'I see.'

No, darling, you don't see. But you needed a reason. We'll let it lie there.

'It had nothing to do with me getting pregnant. Nothing at all. From the very beginning, even if she was cross with me, she was looking forward to you.'

'Thank you,' Ali says. The grey eyes shine with tears. 'Yeah. Thanks.'

Grace comes downstairs stroking a thin tabby. It leaps out of her grip onto the kitchen floor. Ali holds her arms out and her daughter flies in. Curled up on Ali's lap, gently being rocked back and forth, Grace sticks her thumb in her mouth and crinkles a wide grin to Nell.

There. A thorn or two plucked from the inside.

'I want you to leave.'

'Thought you might say something like that.' Adam stretches and yawns. Framed in the doorway in just his jeans, with the waistband button lying indolently open, he reminds her of a horse she once coveted more than anything in the world. Burnished, in his prime; there can't be too many years of that beauty left to him. Perhaps the very reason for his wanting something more solid beneath his feet than a caravan floor. He glides to the side. 'Come in. Let's talk.'

'No. I'll stay out here, thank you. There's nothing to talk about.'

'Unless I'm mistaken, this is Ali's property now.' He pulls his mouth down expansively, a big shrug as he looks to the left and right over Nell's shoulder. 'Where is she? Not here, that's for sure. Asking me to leave.'

'You should know, I'm having your herbal brew analysed.'

'So?' It takes a while to register. A slow, broad grin cracks on his face. 'I think your imagination's running away with you.'

Their eyes lock, his challenging silently. How confident he is, now that he feels safe enough to drop the diffidence. Certain now that Ali will come to him despite her mother's presence. He gives another little stretch, a ripple of movement beneath the smooth, nutty pelt. The tip of his tongue is pressed between bone-white teeth as if to contain words he will not waste on this redundant exchange.

'And Mrs Simms? Was her imagination running away with her?'

A little frown creases his forehead. He doesn't even remember straight away. There have been so many, probably.

'The Rutland Arms? Mr Simms definitely remembers you. He's not likely to forget the state of his wife after you'd gone. All but broke their marriage up, she said. They've had some counselling and things are much better now, you'll be glad to hear.'

An ugly scowl. It's almost obscene how much she enjoys that scowl.

'I called another place, too. Pretty much the same story. What, they didn't have any land to offer you? Just gullible wives, and a week's takings when you vanished in the night. But here was the real deal, wasn't it Adam? How did it start with Ali? A little brush of your hand against her cheek, those great big tawny eyes, brimming with sympathy? You're good, I'll grant you that. But then you've had years to perfect such a subtle technique. My arrival threw you, though. Ali wasn't quite so anxious to hand over this site. Doubtless you've been threatening to leave. As if.'

He glares through narrowed eyes, not bothering to hide his hostility. Rapid exhalations dilating both nostrils. 'I did plenty to help here, too.'

'From the kindness of your heart? Or investment in your future? Yes, I'm sure you did help a lot. But you've caused damage, too, probably more than you know. No, Adam, don't even think of giving me the sob story. It's over. No goodbyes, please. Just go. Don't make this any harder for Ali. If you're not gone by this evening, I'm calling the police.'

'Nell—'

'Don't. Just don't. How you really care for her? How this time it's different? Please. I may not have been the best mother in the world, but this is *my* chance. Not yours. You were right, I don't trust easily and maybe that is why I'm on my own. Maybe I've left it too late to be any other way. But if you ever come near my family again, I'll make you very, very sorry. Believe me on that.'

Nell turns on her heel, leaving him to his impotent glare. She heads down to the cove. No matter how clinically stripped he tried to present his life, how divested of history, his ego dictated that he had to keep a record. Everyone keeps something, collects something. Though it's unlikely he'll keep a brochure of Hennessy's public house, she thinks with a delicious spurt of satisfaction. No trophies collected here. Except her daughter's heart.

The sky is the colour of pewter, with slashes of blazing white spilling through at intervals. She thinks of that small horse she once came across on a walk with Agnes. Up on a hill, pure white against a milky twilight. The contours of the animal had taken on blurred, blue edges. When it moved, what looked like currents of electricity rippled along the haunches. The head was finely tuned and tapered to a delicate upturned muzzle. It plucked at grass, then lifted its head from time to time to shake, as though the long silky mane was bothering its eyes. Nell and her mother watched in harmonious silence for the longest time, their heads cocked in the same direction. Nell wanted that horse. If she never wanted anything else in her whole life, she wanted that animal. Just to look at every day. Just to know that she could look at that extraordinary perfection, any time she might care to. It didn't matter that he wasn't a gazelle; an iridescent horse would do. They tried to move closer, but his ears twitched and he climbed higher on the slope of hill. Let him alone now, Agnes said. We'll only make him run and he might damage himself, this hour of evening.

Nell wouldn't budge when her mother pressed. Come on. Agnes grew cross. It's only a bleddy horse. But what if he's lonely? Nell asked. Schoolgirl phantasmagoria, Agnes scoffed. Come on, will you. He might be lonely, Nell persisted. Suddenly Agnes was shouting, her face swollen with temper. It's a horse. Horses don't get lonely. She stamped away. He's himself, hasn't he? He has himself.

Yes, Nell thinks, looking back at the willowy figure framed in the doorway, head down in meditative thought. He has himself. At least she has family. At least she has that.

The track is still slippery with rain. A few fat drops bullet the surface of the ocean ahead.

'A child around the place again,' Agnes said. 'I'm sort of getting used to the notion.'

'Yeah.'

'You'll want eyes in the back of your head until the day they—' Agnes broke off abruptly. 'Well, anyway,' she added, tossing a stone.

Nell had joined her mother for a last walk down on the crescent cove. In hours they would leave for the airport. For a week, Agnes had been a distant and brooding presence. She had listened, but said nothing, as Nell went about booking the flight, liaising by phone with Uncle Albie and Mary Kate. Said nothing when Nell had tentatively brought up the subject of money. Later that night, on her bed, Nell found an envelope filled with sterling twenty-pound notes. In the morning, it wasn't mentioned. 'Thank you for the envelope,' Nell ventured around tea time. Agnes gave her a tight, grim smile. Her disappointment clouded the air between them. Nell could hardly catch her breath when they were in the same room together.

'We're doing the right thing. It's a good idea. I'm sure of it,' Agnes continued, skimming a handful of small flat stones.

'What's that?'

'You. Going to Uncle Albie and Mary Kate. I'm sure it's

for the best. A good idea. You'll be looked after there. He's a nice old stick, for all the fancy talk and the bow tie. And Mary Kate'll be useful to have around for the first few weeks with a baby. They'll set you up all right. Between them, they'll have more time to give you than myself.' A perplexed frown. 'What about all the equipment?'

'Equipment?'

'Cots, prams . . . What'll you do? Ship the stuff over ahead of you, or will you hold off and we'll get things here?'

'I don't know.'

'You'd want to start knowing.'

'I don't even know what I'll need yet.'

Agnes pursed her lips. Skimmed another stone. 'No, I suppose you don't. You'll be finding out.'

'I could ship stuff, if I need to.'

'Right. That's how we'll do it so.'

They walked along the water's edge, up to where one arm of the cove slid out into the sea. Agnes kept murmuring something to herself.

Nell tapped her back. 'What?'

'I'm saying, I'm sure it's a good idea.'

Nell wondered if she should have her strealish hair cut the minute she set foot in Oxford. A fringe, maybe, long enough so that if she didn't like it she could wear it held back by an Alice band. She wondered if her clothes would seem very outdated. But if Mary Kate had a sewing machine she could make adjustments to her wardrobe. She could buy some magazines for ideas.

'What'll you say to Paudie and Julia?' she asked absently.

'I'll say to them the same as I'll say to anyone that asks in the pub. I'll say you've gone over to help out Uncle Albie – he needs a hand. I won't say he's sick, but that'll be what they read between the lines. So we'll hide one thing with what the people think is another. I've done that before. When your father first dropped the weight, I took on a cough, to take the attention off him, or he'd have been driven mad with enquiries.'

'And the school?'

'The same. You can repeat the year, can't you? Look, Nell, people only have to know when it's a done deed. I don't want to scare you, but things can go out of kilter. Or you might change your mind, decide you want to give the baby up — I'm only saying, mind. There's no need to look like that, Missy. Right this minute, you don't know. A lot can happen over the next few months. So we'll say nothing until you're back. We'll face the music only when we have to.'

She stood looking out to sea, flicking imaginary dandruff from the broad shoulders of her coat. She knows, Nell thought. She knows I won't be back. Not for a long time. Nell was scuffing at pebbles along the shore's edge. She glanced up and Agnes was gazing intently at her, that curious little half-smile on her lips. *She knows.*

'It's a big responsibility, you know. I wonder that you're ready for it. Your life won't be your own for the longest time.'

Nell couldn't remember a time when, if ever, her life was her own.

'When Da passed away, may he rest, I looked at the pair of you, Bridget and yourself, and I wondered, how in the name of God, will I manage? Will I be able to make a fist of the pub and be a decent mother at the same time?'

'You did grand.'

Agnes shot her a look. 'Did I? Did I indeed?' She twisted a heel of one shoe into silt by the water's edge. 'I wonder.'

'You won't always be disappointed,' Nell blurted out. Tears stung in the corners of her eyes.

Agnes stiffened, as if a thousand volts had shot through her. Her lips clamped into a white, fleshless line. She searched Nell's eyes for a moment, then hastily dropped her own. It hadn't been intentional, but it was as if Nell had just voiced the unspoken, hovering thing between them. She wanted to reach out and clutch it back from the air. Agnes took a while to compose herself. Imaginary dandruff flew off in clouds, where her hands briskly swept. Her cheeks were sucked in tight.

At last, she said, 'Don't ever, so long as we live, *ever* let me hear you say a thing like that again.' And she made to strike Nell, while simultaneously her other arm reached round her daughter's waist, summoning her close. They stood, locked together, for minutes, as seagulls wheeled overhead and the sea lapped meekly round their ankles.

Agnes stepped back first. They both plunged hands in pockets and stared hard at their immersed feet. Agnes broke into a wheezy laugh. 'How'd we manage that?' she asked of the water. But she might have been asking of the embrace. They exchanged an embarrassed glance. Agnes bent over to peer into the clear sea, rummaged among the stones and pulled out an oval grey pebble, covered on one side by a mesh of white. It was quite distinctive, even by her picky standards. She held it up to the light, for them both to examine.

'That'll do nicely,' she said, popping it in her coat pocket. She patted the small bulge. 'Well. I s'pose I'll be talking to myself on my walks, for a while.'

Nell's head shoots up. She was staring down at foam broiling round her shoes, looking for a grey stone with a white mesh of marble, when the first sound exploded. She looks up at the sky, expecting a flash of lightning after a solitary clap of thunder. Another report cuts through air, leaving an echoing whine. This time, she knows instantly that it came from a shotgun.

She breaks into a run, stopping at the break in the ditch, to catch her breath. A third shot rings out, so close that for a moment she thinks it may have come from inside the caravan. Blood surfs in her ears. A mist of rain clings to the tips of her eyelashes, blurring everything in sight. Birds flap high above the trees, screeching indignantly. Her extended foot catches on a branch of one of the crossed alders and she crashes in a sprawling heap to the other side. She stumbles to her feet, but her left ankle gives immediately.

Grace is shrieking, down by the stone wall which bisects the fields, her arms flailing wildly. She stops suddenly, holding her hands to her mouth. Nell has to blink rapidly to clear her vision. Ali is by the caravan. She gets up from a prone position, turns slightly toward Nell. A patch of bright red spreads out on her sweatshirt. Her hands are covered in blood. She appears to be swaying. Adam stands further away, the shotgun high against his shoulder. He turns, following the line of Ali's gaze and the barrel points directly at Nell.

'Ali! Ali!' Nell screams. She knuckles her eyes clear of rain.

Ali gestures with one raised hand to Grace not to come any closer. She takes a few steps forward, head pivoting from side to side, as though in confusion or disbelief. Nell hobbles close enough to hear Ali's guttural moan. Watches as she falls to her knees.

CHAPTER TWELVE

Here was something in her hand that involved all the senses. Watching Uncle Albie swirl the glass, dip his beaky snout to inhale the contents, the way it seemed red velvet clung to the sides, the way he rolled the liquid in his mouth, the sound – all the senses; she got that immediately. He nodded for her to proceed. She lifted the balloon of St-Emilion to her nostrils, breathed in, swirled, then inhaled again. The first sip trickled back her throat, almost going down the wrong way, she was so anxious to emulate him exactly. The second she held for a while, aerating through her teeth, though not as noisily as his exaggerated performance. He was deliberately overdoing it, to show her how it should be done. Most of what he said went right over her head.

He told her about the estate, the best vintages it had produced. He went on about the ripe, juicy aroma of red and black fruit, the bass tastes of earth and toasty oak. He showed her the colour against a background light, how it held its dark, deep ruby hues even through the light. While he waxed on, his face animated as a child's, she watched him, and wondered at his wonder. It was just a pool of red liquid

at the bottom of a glass, for pity's sake. There wasn't much
call for wine in the bar in those days, but she knew as well as
anyone that if you drank enough of it you wobbled when
you walked, same as porter.

Still, his fascination held her spellbound. She took another
sip. But it wasn't the earth he spoke of that she detected. The
dry stone chips they threw on a freshly tarred road at home
were what came to mind. The flinty, triangular texture, a
trace of treacly tar behind, like black syrup. When he mentioned red fruit, she thought of bristly autumn raspberries,
springing out of a solitary bush in her mother's overgrown
yard. Wild rhubarb, she said, as much to herself as to her
uncle. His eyes widened. Down by the ditch, she explained,
where we cross into the road that leads to the cove, Bridget
and myself, we'd suck the sticks of rhubarb till we got stomach cramps. But it was good, green at the base, sour and
sweet at the same time. Go on, he said. She sipped once
more. What black fruit are you getting? he asked. Not black,
she said, brown, the brown *feeling*, a sort of . . . sadness,
which hits you at the end of October, just before winter sets
in.

He looked at Mary Kate, who rolled her eyes and carried
on knitting a baby's matinée jacket. Uncle Albie opened a
bottle of Chablis. He nosed and said he was getting honey
and butter, bluebells perhaps, something spring-like, at any
rate. What did she think? Nell inhaled, flushed a deep pink
and looked away. He persisted. The bottom sheet of her
mother's bed, she responded eventually. He frowned, nosed
the glass again. Sheets? Yes, linen maybe. She did not add:
linen edged with sweat, ammoniac urine and Pond's cold
cream. She could hardly believe that he took everything she
said so seriously. To her, it started out as a game, a couple of

steps above I Spy. She giggled at some of his expressions, the expansive gargling and general hoo-ha, as her mother would have called it. But his undivided attention, his devout concentration, on her, on anything she had to say, was its own narcotic.

She thought of the baby curled up, warm and protected in the fluid of her womb, party to all this exotic talk. Her hand crept down to rub the swelling mound. There was a new person in there, waiting to take their allotment of air. Mary Kate's knitting needles clicked at a whirlwind pace; if the metal pins weren't coated in plastic, Nell was sure that sparks would fly. For the first time, it struck home, what was about to happen. Until she reached Oxford, for all she was aware, she might have been about to give birth to a banana. But that evening she experienced the first thrill of anticipation. She knew absolutely, in her blood, that it would be a girl. Ali, she would call her, after Alison, her father's mother. Once the name came to her, the child became real. She felt ready to battle a herd of wildebeest. She would plunge into a pit of venomous snakes to protect this little thing. Ali would have a clear chart, a blank page, on which to write her own history, unencumbered by the ghostly baggage of her mother's past. She would belong entirely to Nell, and in turn Nell would belong entirely to her. The age gap so minimal, to strangers they might even be taken for sisters.

All night they continued. He made Nell spit the mouthfuls out after a while, so she wouldn't get drunk. Nevertheless, she felt heady, giddy, excited by this new vista opened up to her, the freshness of beginning again through this vocabulary of taste. A beginning which simultaneously incorporated all that had gone before. She tasted

sand, pebbles marled with marble, rank ditchwater. She
tasted beer scum, daisies, a pleated school skirt reeking of
sour, spilt milk; tasted earwax, ink from a leaking school
Biro, rust on the back fender of a bicycle, Bridget's red scarf
after she'd eaten a bag of crisps, the urinal channel that ran
from wall to wall in the men's toilet, a black crust of rime
round the inside of a Morris Minor's exhaust. A Morris
Minor? Uncle Albie interjected. So specific? Yeah, she
replied, at least, I think so. Of course, I'm just imagining,
she added. It's hardly as if I've actually licked an exhaust
pipe, is it? Whatever you say, Uncle Albie said. Whatever
you imagine.

Years later, taking her place in a tasting symposium, she
learned to use one vocabulary for the group, while in her
head she used another. You couldn't convey the specific to
the many. Not what was specific to your own childhood.
Sometimes it might hit a responsive note, but more often
than not it would have left people standing there, shaking
their heads in confusion. While she described an austere,
tear-jerking Savennières from the Loire, she thought of the
slices of lemon, impregnated with black cloves, kept in a
glass bowl in the bar for making hot whiskeys. A syrah-
based Saint-Chinian, almost too concentrated for easy
drinking, reminded her of Julia's blackberry jam, difficult
to spread and peppery on the tongue. And always there
was rain. Light, floral spring drizzle. The salt-laden,
stormy squalls of winter. Drops mixed with Blisteze from
cracked lips. The brackish, peaty taste of freshly fallen rain
blending with the dull waters of a lake, lying in the gourd
of a hill. A good wine could invoke any range of disparate
and often entirely personal experiences. A good wine
unlocked a store of information in the vault of her head. A

great wine was the sum of her collected knowledge. Home, as it were, on the tip of her tongue, any time she yearned for it.

Ali bends over the dead pony, trying to protect Grace from seeing the bleeding holes. Two in his neck and one, finally, in the head. By the wall, Grace weeps inconsolably. Adam slings the shotgun into the back of the car that he's hitched to the caravan. A small malicious smile plays on his lips, but Nell has a peculiar feeling that it is more for effect than anything else, as though he is enacting rites of departure which have become part of his armour. Another place he has failed to call home. Another set of people he must wilfully reject so that their rejection of him becomes subordinate and he can kid himself if this person didn't get in the way and if that person didn't get in the way – this time or that time, he might have been accepted.

'Go to Grace,' Ali says in a quiet voice to Nell. 'Don't let her come down.'

'You miserable bastard.' Nell pushes past him. 'You didn't have to do that.'

'I don't like to leave anything behind.' It shows only for a brief second but Nell catches the flicker of shame. He has had his moment's gratification but he is not inhuman and there is remorse.

'You could have left her the damn pony. What did it matter to you?'

'It didn't. It doesn't.' He pokes the head with the tip of his shoe, perhaps hoping that Ali will look up to take his message fully. She remains bent over Terence. Her head gives a little shake, not quite believing yet what has happened.

'What a small mean person you are,' Nell spits back at him. She retraces a step. 'Maybe it's not your fault to a degree. And maybe you've had really bad breaks. But you know you liked Gracie, and you know she's going through a hard time. You could have forced yourself to remember what that feels like.'

In spite of himself he darts a glance at the sobbing child and quickly looks away again. Shooting the pony was the only way he knew to rip out his feelings for her.

'You'll always be in a caravan, one way or another, Adam. In someone's backyard. Outside. Looking in.'

He blinks back the insult but it's found a home none the less. Small satisfaction, but some. He hesitates a second, speechless and black-faced with impotency. It's all her fault he has to go. To go with nothing is shameful to his personal sense of fair play. A week's takings and the memory of a betrayed husband's haunted expression at the very least, the absolute minimum he deems owing for a lousy, stinking boyhood stuck in a trailer with a violent soak of a father. Another time, another place, she might even feel a pang of compassion for him, but never this time and not in this, her daughter's place. She wills Ali not to look up at him, not to give him that much. And relishes it when Ali turns her stooped head in the other direction.

'Go to Grace, Mum, please,' Ali insists quietly.

There is nothing in the world she wants to do more, but she doesn't want to afford him an opportunity to have a final say with Ali. A last attempt to try to dupe or worse, insult her as a woman, the way she looks, the odious scent of her ridiculous infatuation, how he hated every moment of touch between them. No, it will be hard enough for Ali to recover. She holds his eye until he swings round, then slams into the car. Wheels dig into the soft, wet earth, trying to gain purchase. Nell moves toward her grand-daughter. When she looks back, car and caravan are proceeding in a series of stops and starts until they pass through a gap and onto a rutted track leading up past the house. She presses Grace's sobs against a spot just below her breast, keeping her eyes trained on Adam all the while. He never looks back.

Up in the yard, Nick has just returned with bags of shopping. His head swivels, watching Adam pass by. He leaves the shopping and walks downfield, trousers flapping round painfully thin legs, shabby old flags wrapped round poles.

'Adam murdered Terence,' Grace manages to get out. 'Why? *Why?*' She looks up wide-eyed to Nell. There is no way to explain to a child that the random cruel impulses of other children in the playground carry on with some grown-ups. What hope for her future then? No way to explain that Adam's reward for going empty-handed was the pleasure in annihilating the only good thing he could leave behind. So she says nothing.

Without a word, Nick gently draws his daughter from Nell's arms. Grace hiccoughs between sobs. He rubs the conker head pressed against his side, in tender, soothing caresses, while questioning eyes carry down to the curve of Ali's back, still turned to them. Nell is about to say some-thing but he presses a finger to his lips, a resigned inclination of the pale, angular head. His silent collusion will hold. Hollows under the cheekbones, as light slants across his face, look as if they have been gouged with a spade. He takes Grace by the hand and they slowly walk up to the house.

Nell remains by the wall. Ali shakily rises. Go to Grace, Mum, she said.

'I'm only glad he's gone, even if the poor child's upset about the pony. Bad cess to him, anyway.' Paudie hitches up his shoulders. 'Didn't I tell you he'd a look about him?'

'How many more times now, Paudie, d'you want someone to tell you you were right?' Julia says behind the front door.

'One of these fine days, I'll take a big chunky stick to her,' Paudie mutters to Nell. He looks up at the sagging evening sky, puts a palm out, checking for drops. 'Look it, I'll walk you up if you don't want a lift.'

'It's only a couple of minutes, I want a few breaths.' She steps away.

'It's going to bucket down on top of your head.'

'I don't care.' Nell smiles.

'Nell, you won't go without saying goodbye?'

'No Paudie. I won't go without saying goodbye.'

Once she knows he's closed the door, she stops a little way up, peering through the tangled hedgerow at the distant sands below. No sign of Bola on his evening run. He may have passed already. The sky frowns over a dirty-looking sea. She hugs herself, ignoring the first spits that plink onto her head. Melancholic October evening. The brown feeling of her childhood at winter's approach. A deep feeling of loss overcomes her. All the people who have slipped through her fingers, never to be seen again, never to be *known* again. The random accident of knowing anyone. The accident of outliving anybody. For that matter, of loving anybody. Her phone's remained switched off for the last couple of days.

She hasn't wanted to deal with any calls. But more than that, much more than that, she hasn't wanted to deal with Henri's lack of calls.

The sky rips open, drenching her in seconds. She continues to look until sky and sea merge into one grey veil. Drops beat off glossy wild rhododendron leaves. Runnelling in wet plaits down her face. She thinks about the life she would have lived if she had remained here, the life that lies ahead of her now. It's almost dark by the time she turns for the rest of the walk home.

Someone's playing a fiddle in the pub. High, piercing notes quiver through the rain. Warm yellow light through the window looks welcoming. There's something very grounded, solid, about an inn, yet transitional, too. You visit, you leave — the attraction for someone like Adam isn't all that difficult to see. She has to paw rain from her eyes to see where's she's walking. A figure steps through the pub door, wrapping a raincoat round a slender body, head huddled down under an immediate blast of rain. He runs to a small parked car. About to get in, he stops and turns instead, squinting as she approaches.

'Ah.'

'Ah you,' he says.

She keeps a little distance for a moment, hardly believing this relief which makes her legs tremble. Rain makes tiny upside-down triangles of dark hair mesh across his forehead, pings up from sloping shoulders of a beige raincoat — new, she thinks; he's come prepared. Tiny, glittering beads cling to the tips of the ludicrously long eyelashes, behind which he, the essence of him always, those dark, peaty eyes gleam with schoolboy mischief, with a shade of apprehension, too: what will she make of this surprise visit? They look and smile, top teeth biting down over lower lips to stop smiles turning into inane, cheesy grins. So hot and immediate and *knowing* between them, they have to look away momentarily, expel air, then check one another again. Deep self-mocking grooves on his brow, a crooked, ironic grin: aren't we a bit long in the tooth for this? His head cocks to the side, waiting for her to close the gap. She must make the first move.

'You look like something from an old black-and-white film.' She draws closer.

'Imagine how I feel.'

She steps into the circle of his arms, resting her head against his drenched shoulder. Even through the rain, all the old familiar scents immediately tingle her nostrils. Toasted tobacco, the beer he's just had, cedarwood aftershave. If she could preserve this moment, she would wrap it round herself like a much loved blanket, the edges just touching her nose.

'I could just inhale you. In one breath,' she laughs, nuzzling into that space by his neck she never would have thought possible to miss so much.

'You can try that. Later.'

They kiss, lips wet and gluey with rain, then pull away, a little sheepish, a little embarrassed to find themselves standing here, soaked to the skin, clinging like teenagers.

She looks up at a million silver syringes falling, illuminated by the pub window. 'I suppose this is quite romantic, if I didn't hate that word.'

Of course it's a damn flush, but this once she can pretend it's a blush colouring her cheeks. Because the truth is, funny though it may be, only one thing comes to mind: she feels . . . shy. Awkward and silly and so liquidly overheated, she could jump his bones, right here on the puddled ground. Anticipation makes her breaths rapid and slightly shivery.

'Nell,' he says, a huge beam making little pouches of skin stand out round his mouth.

She traces with her fingertips. 'Let me guess. You're a grandfather.'

'Yes,' he nods happily. 'Jeanne. She fits in here' – hands cupped together. 'Tiny! Unspeakably beautiful, of course, and strong. My God if you could have seen her fight for her life. Two whole weeks – every day we thought, this is the day. She can't fight another. Tubes nearly big as her, sticking out everywhere.'

'Why didn't you tell me?'

'If she hadn't made it, I would have told you. The last time we spoke I was outside the hospital. They gave her last rites that night. I couldn't speak, Nell, I just couldn't. You know when you can't talk because you're holding your breath? Because if you say it, it will happen? She'll be in the premature baby unit for a while, but yesterday, I bought her a spoon, and I can tell you I've never been so pleased to get a lifetime's guarantee in all my life.'

'Oh, Henri.'

'Are we soaked enough, d'you think,' he says, 'or should we stay out a while longer?'

'I don't think it matters. I can't possibly get any wetter.'

'Yes, you can.' He grins, slipping his hand round hers.

Words tumble into the darkness. They talk at a staccato pace, as though they fear daylight will bring with it the old block-ages, the old impediments. Henri tells her that a strange amicability has descended upon himself and Lucienne, that, faced with the prospect of losing their grandchild, they man-aged to pull together like two embattled, war-weary opponents, united by fear and a mutual respect for older battles won and lost. That they managed to find kindness for one another and a degree of sympathy he could not have believed possible only months ago. And that it was the kindness that confirmed, to both of them, that the marriage was irretrievably over.

He speaks of his anger with Nell the last few years, confirming her suspicion that he had noticed every turn of her head away, every irritated little intake of breath when he approached. Each time, he determined to keep away from her apartment for a long period, to give her time to miss him, to give him time to analyse how much he would really miss her. But, like a bee compelled to the next flower and the next flower and the next, he was likewise compelled to her rejection. Had even managed to confuse it in his head with a form of love.

He tells her of his plans for the Domaine, the mechanics of the divorce, speaking in the vital, hushed whisper of a man coming through the first full-on confrontation with his own mortality. His enthusiasm for what remains – a considerable span, he hopes – is infectious. He could be a teenager looking over the parapet at decades of possibilities stretching ahead. He takes care to voice these plans in the singular, omitting any dependency on her for their fruition. In his own way, relieving her of any duty or responsibility she may feel for his future.

Lying in the cradle of his arms, listening, peering into darkness, it seems to Nell as though a great burden is slowly lifting from her shoulders. A great weight she never realized was there. Here, in her mother's bed, in her mother's room, for the first time, or so it seems, she doesn't feel that creeping, insidious compulsion to keep him at a distance. She tells him about the past weeks, her worries for Ali and Grace; Nick, too – she's grown fond of that etiolated but constant man. And when, for once, he doesn't try to provide solutions or offer advice, she delves deeper and it strikes her with considerable force that she has spent her entire life loving at a distance. She has expected others to respect this need in her, withdrawing when the inevitable clamour for more came along. It further strikes her that is the only way she has known how to love. Always in retreat, in backing away, never on her approach.

They make love for the second time with slow, prolonged kisses, more intimate by far than penetration. She wraps her legs round his buttocks and draws him deeper until all the old resistances melt away and she is opened up, turned inside out, a receptacle. She imagines herself as nothing but a warm, sticky vagina, a mouth sucking him in, letting him wander wherever he likes without prohibition. They make little sighing noises, squeezing linked fingers fiercely as if to mark this renewal of themselves as separate entities invading each other. As she approaches climax, she closes her eyes and lets herself fall, completely, no imaginary claws holding her back, into a blissful nothingness.

They fall asleep for a short while. In her dream, Nell thrusts out her hip, just as she used when seeking the reassuring contact of Agnes's body in the bed beside her. Her eyes flutter awake; she has been pressing against Henri. Sleepily, he pulls her closer, draping one thigh across hers. They try to sleep again but there are too many things to say. They chuckle at this almost childlike volubility – words can't come fast enough. As a pearl wash of dawn light creeps across the room, they delight in the fact that they are grandparents, that there is all that joy to look forward to, that they

are indeed blessed and fortunate. And that they can still fuck
like rabbits when the occasion demands.

The message light on her mobile flashes where she's left it.
Yawning, she fumbles for it. Henri is snoring quietly
beside her, smiling in his sleep when she kisses the tip of
his nose. She recognizes the chemist's voice instantly. He
drones on at length. When the message comes to an end,
she gets out of bed and replays it. It could have been there
for days.

Henri sits up, only semi-awake. 'What is it? Nell?'

'It's all right. Go back to sleep. Shh,' she adds pressing a
finger to his lips. He falls back on the pillow.

She's still listening, with the phone in the crook of her
head and raised shoulder, as she steps down the offshoot of
stairs, to knock on Nick's door.

He is standing by the window, squinting through streaming eyes. It's as though he persists in looking out as some
form of punishment to himself. He rubs his eyes with a
scrunched-up tissue and offers a watery smile. The air is
thick with the sickly sweet odour of expectorants. Outside,
a low silvery sky offers a break in the rain.

'Nell?'

'I was worried about that mixture Adam was giving you.'

'The herbs?' His lips curve into a thin smile. 'Well?' He
perches on the edge of the bed, a man waiting for a sentence
to be passed. 'You had it analysed?'

Nell nods, surprised at how quickly he's come to that
conclusion.

'Cyanide? Arsenic?' he continues in a tone laden with
self-mocking irony. Yet there is the ring of real suspicion

there, too. If so, he willingly took the mixture anyway. She sits close beside him on the bed and presses his hand.

'No, Nick, nothing like that. They found cat hairs in the sample.' Nell breaks the gloomy resonance between them. 'The mixture contained a high dose of glycoprotein, which is what causes the trouble. Seemingly cats carry it in their saliva and urine, and because they groom so much their hairs are full of the stuff. They found a number of hairs in Adam's concoction. It's all over the room, on the sheets, the pillows, everywhere, and then you were drinking it as well. The lab technician had a hunch, and called the Allergy Foundation. A severe reaction in some people can manifest itself in all sorts of ways, not just obvious things like hay fever symptoms. Listen – listen to what the chemist has to say.' She presses the phone into his hand. 'At one point, he could be describing you to perfection. The lack of energy, the loss of weight, streaming eyes which of course would be affected by bright light, the mucus, everything. It probably never showed before because you've never been surrounded by so many cats. You might have just had the odd sneeze and thought nothing of it. You say you had tests, but did you mention the bloody cats all over the house?'

Nick listens to the message, holding Nell's gaze all the while. When he's through, he calmly returns the phone and sits with his bony hands crossed limply on his lap.

'I was supposed to go back to the hospital for a series of allergy tests,' he says, a touch shamefaced.

'Why didn't you?'

He doesn't respond for a while. The hands tighten. 'I wanted to stay around here,' he says at last. His head swivels to look at her. 'I think you know why.'

'I see.' Nell returns his stare. 'It was you with the shotgun the night Ali ran down to Paudie and Julia, wasn't it?'

A brief hesitation, and then his head inclines. 'I thought if I could just hang on it might pass.'

'Adam and Ali, you mean.'

'There. It's said,' he says after a while. He seems relieved.

'We were off our heads, Ali and me. I don't deny that. A magic mushroom. I'd suspected for a while, in any case: Ali couldn't look me in the eyes.' His mouth twists, attempting a smile. 'She told me she still loved me. All the usual shit before someone tells you they love someone else more.'

'I'm sorry.'

'Yep.' He swallows hard, waits to compose himself, before continuing. 'I wanted to kill him. Or her. Someone, at any rate. Maybe myself. Yes, it was an edifying scene all right. An Academy Award winner. Ali rushed down to Paudie and Julia's and I sat at the kitchen table with the barrel of a shotgun in my mouth. Isn't that nice? I thought about my whole life, my father the fuckhead, the years of travelling with Ali – maybe it was the mushroom, but everything flashed by, so clear I could almost touch an image of myself as a young boy. I thought, I am useless, I am the fucking failure my father used to call me. Nick, the Failure. And then – maybe the effects were wearing off – I thought about Grace coming down to bits of my brain clung to the ceiling in the morning. I made a cup of tea, and waited for Ali to return. We haven't mentioned it since.' His lips curl into a bitter smile. 'If Ali wants me out of here, I'll have to go.'

Nell opens her mouth to offer some banal reassurance, but he's right: if Ali wants him out, legally he hasn't got a leg to stand on. If he does get better once the cats are gone, things will have to come to a head. Perhaps, in his own way, he's been happy to remain ill. A feeble way to cling on, certainly, but the only option he could see open to him. She lets out a long sigh, starts to wipe cat hairs, thinks better of it.

'Where would you go?' she asks.

'I don't know.' He shrugs. 'I'd have to stay around here, to be near Grace.'

She looks at him then, surprised yet again, by his quiet resilience. 'I'm glad you said that.'

'I don't stay just for Grace. You understand that?'

'Yes, I understand. I'm glad for that, too.'

Nick turns towards the window again, lost in his thoughts. The only thing in the world he has to offer: his constant presence. A presence Ali both wants and doesn't want. It's difficult to know who to feel sorry for in this pleated entanglement. The detritus of other people's lives she's so studiously spent her own life avoiding. She's here now and there's no getting away from it. Rubbing shoulders with mess and fallout and a crazy bag of contradictory emotions. There's nothing pristine about love, she thinks, nothing pure and exalted, like in the novels she read as a young girl dreaming of faraway places. Maybe it starts out white and luminous as a blanket of snow, but it's in the grey, nebulous marshes that love resides. An image of Agnes, another stayer – that ambivalent smile – comes into her mind.

'Strange, don't you think,' she says, 'that someone, a man we know nothing about, has the power to create all this confusion.'

'It's not him,' Nick says after a while. 'I don't even blame him, if that's what you think. The confusion is in ourselves. It's always in here' – he taps his chest – 'just waiting to come out.'

'What can we do?'

'Live with it,' he says, grim-faced. He looks down on the yard, filled with dread at what they both know has to be done. 'Grace will be home in a few hours.'

There are twenty-two cats and kittens in an assortment of boxes and small animal cages, spread out across the floor of Paudie's trailer. Earlier, he'd hitched it to the back of his car when he came with Julia to help. Nell assigned an adult to each room, and all afternoon a mordant procession has moved in and out of the house. A deathly feel to the task, growing stronger with every passing minute, as Grace's home time approaches.

'That's the last out of her room, anyway.' Julia holds a wriggling kitten in her gloved hands. She darts Henri an apologetic glance as if to say, what a time you picked.

Accusing mewls and whimpers from the trailer make them grit their teeth, avert their eyes, each one of them trying to avoid the mirrors of betrayal. A couple of the angrier toms, who put up a decent struggle, glare balefully through metal bars.

'And that's only what's in the house.' Paudie strokes his chin. 'You'll have to get the vet to round up what's in the shed. Half of them are pure wild. I took one look in and I slot the bolt back double-quick.' He casts Henri a shy glance from under his brows. Han-ree, he calls him. 'Now so, Hanree, you could pass me up that last cage there. Thank you. Good man.'

Nick leans by the back porch door. He hasn't been able to help but, as if in deference to Grace, he's served the occasional customer in the bar, then returned to watch the proceedings right through to the bitter end. Ali has skirted round him, avoiding his eyes, handing him mugs of tea in silence. Nell's hired two industrial vacuum cleaners from a shop in a nearby town; the village had nothing to offer in that line.

Her black sweatshirt looks like a mohair sweater. Gloves reek of cat's pee. The litter trays in Grace's room and the kitchen sent her dry-retching to the nearest sink. From time to time, she's heard a solitary anguished sob escape Ali's lips, but they were quickly stifled and she got back to work. Hardly a word has been spoken. They all stopped around lunchtime for a cup of tea; no one could face a bite of food. They stood, circling the kitchen table, sipping in morose silence. Occasionally Julia said, it's for the best, and everyone grunted or nodded. But for the best didn't make anyone feel any better.

One final check, and they're certain every room has been cleared. All the windows have been opened. A drum of disinfectant waits beside the vacuum cleaners.

'I'll start with your room, Nick,' Nell says.

He raises a hand and tries a feeble smile. There is something even more withered about his demeanour, as though the possibility of his health improving conversely heralds the end of his wellbeing. Paudie taps his trouser pockets, checking for car keys. With his failing sight, at eighty-two, he's probably a menace on the road, but Julia whispered to Nell earlier, 'I do the long driving. He only goes local. Everyone knows him, they skip out of his way, but fast, I'm telling you.'

'Right. I'll head away so,' Paudie says. He's going to take the cats to the vet, a friend of his. Homes might be found for a few of the kittens, but when Nell asked him what will

happen to the rest he shrugged, spat to the side. What did
she think will happen to them? The same method that's
been used ever. No sense in wasting that expensive putting
down stuff on the likes of that lot.

'Atlantis, here we come,' he says, getting into the car.

The cats mewl like whimpering babies as the trailer rattles
across the yard's rough flagstones.

'It had to be done,' Nell says to no one in particular.
Henri squeezes her arm. 'No point in prolonging the agony,'
she adds, but her voice is thick. 'Best that they're gone when
she gets here.'

'Of course,' Henri says.

Ali makes her excuses and heads to the bar. As she passes,
Nell can see that she's trembling from head to toe.

Grace senses something's up, the minute she walks through
the back porch door. Already, she may have wondered why
none of her friends were weaving greetings around her
ankles. Nell, Henri and Julia exchange glances: who's going
to do it? But Ali steps in from the bar and gently pulls Grace
into a far corner. Nell strains but she can't hear the words.
Ali stands, stooping, her hands resting on her daughter's
shoulders. Grace doesn't say a word. Her mouth pops open
slightly. A crimson flush suffuses her face, scarlet in an
instant, only the tops of her ears bear a remaining trace of
white skin. She looks across to Nell. There are no tears, but
that flush grows incandescent. The pitch of Ali's voice rises,
justifying and pleading at the same time. They can hear
Nell's words repeated: it had to be done. It had to be done,
Gracie.

Grace removes the rucksack from her back. She wrenches

her shoulders from her mother's grip, firmly not harshly. The sack lies by her feet. She steps over and makes her way to the stairs. Julia makes sympathetic clucking noises with her tongue.

'Don't you want a glass of milk, or a biscuit or something?' Ali calls after her.

At the bottom of the stairs, Grace turns. She looks back at her mother, across what seems a huge distance. Her brown eyes hold the shiny glaze of conkers. She looks feverish.

'No,' she says. But it sounds like a grunt, the stunned emission of someone punched in the gut, aware of pain, but still not fully comprehending the force of the blow. She runs up. They wait for the slam of her bedroom door, it doesn't come – only silence.

The silence continues as they try to conceal surreptitious guilty glances. Ali makes as if to head back into the bar, changes her mind and goes upstairs instead. She returns a couple of minutes later, lost in her thoughts, an ominous shake to her head.

'She's put something against the door. I can't get in. She won't answer me, either.'

'Crying her eyes out, the poor pet, I s'pose,' Julia says.

'No, I don't think so.' Ali seems more perturbed by the silence. 'I couldn't hear a sound. Nothing.'

'Where's Nick?'

'He's gone to see if he can buy a pony.'

'But how will he get it here?'

'How should I know, Nell?' Ali snaps. 'Maybe he's going to ride the damn thing, for all I know.' She draws her hands down her face, expelling a deep, quavery breath. Since Adam's departure, she's just managed to eat enough to avoid collapse, just managed to put one foot in front of the other.

'Sorry, Henri. This is a terrible welcome for you. Really, I am sorry.'

'Don't worry about me.'

'Ali,' Nell interjects, 'look, if he's not back in an hour or so, you go and see if he needs help. I'll do the bar. A pony. A pony would be good. Okay? Okay, darling?'

Ali's lower lip trembles. She merely nods.

The bar remains quiet throughout the early part of the evening. Mostly old men at this hour. It's the strangest feeling, pulling pints, enacting the routines of her childhood, under Henri's bemused gaze. He watches the way she uses the spatula to take the first head off the pints of Guinness, the way she gauges the settling of the liquid in time for the next top-up, the way one hand presses a whiskey glass up to an optic while the other nimbly taps out an amount on the old-fashioned till. There is a little spurt of pleasure at sharing this part of her life with him.

'I'll go and check on Grace,' she says, when there are no more orders.

The bedroom door is still closed when she goes up. It won't budge when she rattles the handle.

'C'mon, darling. Come and have something to eat.' Nothing. She tries another tack. 'You might have a new pony soon. Your own pony, Grace. You'll have to take good care of him.' No response. Nell pounds on the door. 'Look, I know you're very upset. But you want Daddy to get better, don't you? Maybe you can keep a cat out in a shed or something. Come on, darling. You can't stay in there for ever. Grace? Grace?'

She gives up after another few tries. On her way down

the stairs, she calls over her shoulder, 'I'm going to put some supper and a drink outside your door. Okay?'

In the kitchen, she makes some beans and toast, fills a glass of milk, runs out to serve a couple of quick pints, then trudges up again.

'There's a tray outside your door. Beans on toast. I'm going downstairs now, so come out and get the food while it's still hot. I'm going now. Hear? Down I go. Gone.'

At the base of the stairwell, she strains for a sound of movement above, but nothing happens. It's nearly seven o'clock. The four-paned patches of dull sky, beyond the kitchen window, are starting to darken. What's keeping Ali and Nick? Whatever, they'd better come back with a damn pony, now that she's mentioned it to Grace. Better yet, maybe they've tethered it while they take time to talk things through. Oh, wouldn't that be nice! she mocks herself.

There's a loose sheet of paper, folded over, on the table. Paudie's spidery scrawl, though he's printed in capitals, slanting almost horizontally to the left. He must have come in one of the times she was upstairs trying to coax Grace out of her room. It says he's just popping in to let them know the deed is done, is how he puts it. The vet took a couple of kittens but would take no more. After that, himself and a young helper drove up Eagle Rock and dumped the rest. He goes on at length — the page is covered in writing — to explain that they don't like to use the sea any more for such operations because of the tides. There are a couple of crossed-out lines, where clearly he was trying to justify the use of the lake, then thought better of it, most likely, remembering Bridget. He hopes the little girl is all right. He'll come back later for a pint. Paudie.

Nell sits and absently folds the note over and over, until it makes a small square package. The thought of the hapless cats makes her queasy and, for a moment, horribly guilty, but not sufficient to quell the rumble in a stomach deprived of nourishment all day. Reading between the lines and judging by the length of the note, Paudie wasn't exactly over-enamoured of his ruthless commission, either. But he's a countryman, with little time for sentiment as far as animals are concerned. She makes some fresh toast and pours out what's left of the beans. The sound of voices picks up in the bar, food starts to stick in lumps at the base of her throat, from bolting it down too fast. The heartburn of eating in time to the bar, she remembers it well. There's barely time to mop the plate with a spongy roll of toast before Henri peers round the curtain. Not even time for a cup of tea. She motions with her hand, she'll be right there.

Eyebrows up in silent query, she begins to serve along the far end of the counter. People have been waiting patiently, confident in the knowledge that someone would pitch up to serve them eventually. It's a small pub in the middle of nowhere; half the pleasure is in the anticipation. The elderly man who used to play the melodion looks a little unsteady on his stool, but she fills his pint anyway. There has to be a certain brutality to bartending. Her mother would continue to serve until a man virtually blacked out, confident in the knowledge that someone would get him to his door.

Two long-haired, bearded crusties, as Agnes would have called them, one with a banjo, the other a tin whistle, set up a diddledididy chorus in the corner. Just mucking about at the start, gaining in confidence as people turn to look. In spite of herself, her foot begins to tap. She's carried a residual loathing for that kind of stuff, having endured Agnes's ballad sessions three nights a week throughout every summer. None the less, the men are full of music, and it's difficult to resist. It's nice, she thinks, allowing herself a spasm of sentimentality, that the old music still gets played, that there's a place for it in this young, surgent country. When they stop for a break and order pints at the counter, which are paid for by the men on either side, she realizes that the banjo player and the tin whistler are both English.

'This is nice,' Henri says, nodding to the rhythm. 'Traditional.' He's fumbling in a back pocket for something, a camera, she realizes, giving him a baleful look.

'Take that out and you're a dead man.'

'Would they object?'

'I object.'

'But I'm a tourist.'

'Not any more, you're not.' She smiles.

It starts to rain. Spray flies into the bar each time the door opens. Nell looks up, expecting Ali or Nick each time but hours have passed and there is no sign. A couple of young women ask after Ali as usual. Nell tries to engage in a desultory, ongoing chat with them, but it doesn't come easily, not the way it does for Ali, and she senses their strained politeness. Bola comes in, ordering his first of two pints, and she asks him about his daughter. No news, he says with regret. Still, no news. He takes up his usual table and sits alone. By the time Paudie comes in, the melodion man is joining in the music, humming aloud while arthritic fingers play air notes on a spectral accordian. He looks elated and frustrated in equal measure, the parts of him that don't look downright drunk. When there's another break in the music, he sways on the stool, closes his eyes and starts up a comeallye, waving with one hand for others to join in. It sounds as though he's singing out his nose.

Nell tries to have a quiet word when he stops to drain a glass. A young woman rolls her eyes and tells her not to be wasting her time, there's no stopping him once he's started. The banjo player strikes up in the lull, seizing the opportunity, but melodion man throws back his head again and lets loose with a howl, which is the same opening note to his entire repertoire. Ow-ooo, it goes, going downhill from there. Nell thinks her head will split. Henri's shoulders go up and down with suppressed laughter. He gathers empty glasses and steps behind the counter to wash them in the sink. Nell can hardly take her eyes off him, standing there so naturally, so easefully, for all the world as though he might have stood there yesterday evening. He catches her appraisal and gives a sheepish grin.

A noble call, melodion man bellows. Who'll it be? Who'll it be now? Come on, let you give us something from Africa, Nigeri-aaa, he shouts. Paudie blanches. Bola pretends not to hear. There must be mighty songs out of that place. Melodion has managed to swivel on his stool to cajole him. Come on, you're letting your side down. Sing out, there's a man. Tell us how you fought the good fight.

Bola gives Nell a pained look. She's pouring a pint, wincing. The banjo plucks a few encouraging notes, the player looking in Bola's direction. Anything you know will do us. Something from your own country, whatever you like. Now a few murmurs here and there back up Melodion's constant barrage. Bola just sits and shakes his head. Short of breaking a bottle over the old man's head, Nell can't think of a way to stop him. There's an edge developing to his imprecations, an unmistakable challenge, a border of sarcasm for a country that can't produce a decent rebel song. An old man at a bar counter, nursing old wounds, while below on the beaches the raw, recently wounded, run with their gashes still gaping. Bola suddenly rises to his feet. The bar grows hushed. Nell thinks he is going to slam out the door. He takes his time to look around. His giant hands curl into tight fists. His mouth opens.

'I saw the light on the night that I passed by your window . . .'

A few heads turn, shoulders go up in confusion. Bola ignores them, closes his eyes to continue:

'I saw the flickering shadows of love on your blind . . .'

A couple of whoops now and chuckles as people recognize the song. Even Paudie permits himself a grimace of a smile. Nell feels her heart begin to lift after the traumas of the day; she sings aloud while reaching for the optics, imagining a curly haired poppet, Tom Jones, on his mother's knee, a UN supremo in the making.

'Why, why, why, Delilah?' Hands thrum out the corresponding beat along the counter top — da da dadadada dum — 'Why, why, why, Delilah?' He rolls on, ending with an anguished fist to his forehead. 'Forgive me Delilah, I just couldn't take any more.' Everyone roars back, 'Forgive me Delilah, I just couldn't take any mo-ore.'

Ali's head peeps around the curtain. 'What's going on?' she asks Nell. 'I'm not paying him.'

Nell steps back into the kitchen. Nick sits by the table, looking drained and exhausted.

'We got a pony,' Ali says. 'Third place we tried, and it took some persuading. We had supper there once we'd clinched the deal.' Her eyes are red-rimmed and puffy. Nick pointedly turns away when she looks in his direction. 'Where's Gracie?'

'Still in her room,' Nell responds. 'I couldn't get her to come out.'

'She's not there now.' Ali frowns. 'I've just checked.'

'Are you sure she's not hiding under the bed or something?'

'No. The door was wide open. I had a good look around. Anyway, is that her tray on the table?'

The plate has been cleared, the milk drained. An icy hand grips Nell's heart. She circles the handles of the tray.

'Nell?'

She lifts, hardly daring to look underneath, but there it is, Paudie's note, no longer in a tight square but flattened into a smooth plane, by Grace's hand.

CHAPTER THIRTEEN

Once Nell has read the note aloud, there is a wintry silence in the kitchen, a staving-off moment, while the contents are digested from Grace's point of view. They look for holes in the information, gaps she couldn't possibly fill in for herself. But Paudie is a methodical man and his words are comprehensive. Still, they cling to that eerie stillness which comes when you are still clinging to doubt, before worst suspicions are fully realized.

Ali clears her throat. 'How long ago might she have read this?'

'I don't know,' Nell responds. 'Hours, maybe.'

'Hours,' Ali repeats to herself, working out the arithmetic.

Henri steps through, drying a glass with a dish towel. 'Nell, the bar . . .'

'Shit! The bar.'

Nick rises to his feet; he has to lean on the table for support. 'I'll take over. Is Paudie there? Okay, right, he'll give me a hand. Ali, check the house thoroughly, everywhere. Then the yard and . . .' He looks at them hopelessly. 'How long would it take a young child to walk up there, Nell?'

'A couple of hours, maybe. At night, possibly longer. But I believe there's a road now?'

Ali nods. Her face is stretched tarpaulin tight, skin the colour of crushed chalk. She spurs into movement, checking the porch, back to a cupboard under the stairs. She runs upstairs, down again almost immediately. Her breaths come in short, shallow rasps.

'Her wellies are gone. Two jackets, two torches, and she's taken batteries, too.'

Nell quickly steps out to the bar to have a word with Paudie. She returns, keeping her eyes trained on the floor.

'We'd better go.' Her voice sounds strangely calm to her own ears, as if it echoes across a tranquil sea. Though the strain shows on their faces, she can detect the same strange quietude, the suppression, in their voices, too. While they can fear the worst, they must not say it. 'Nick, Paudie's serving. Better if you and Henri stay here, in case she's around the place somewhere.'

'She's not here!' Ali can't contain the first note of panic. 'You know she's not here.'

'I'm coming,' Henri says but stops at Nell's silent plea. Nick is too exhausted to carry out a proper check of the house and yard. She signals with her eyes it's best if Henri does that.

'Should we phone anyone?' he calls after them.

But they're grabbing coats, hats, anything they can find, off the pegs in the back porch. The door swings open after them. Heavy rain immediately thrums on their heads.

'Torches!' Ali shouts, one hand on Nell's car door. She runs back into the house and returns seconds later with a small pocket torch and a kerosene lantern.

'I keep these in the bar, for power cuts,' she says, inside the car.

Nell sets the wipers on full, reverses with a swerve, very nearly hitting the side of the porch. They drive off with an angry squeal of tyres on the rough forecourt.

'Where? Where's the entrance to the road?'

'Left here. We have to go round the back of the rock. Right – *right*, Nell!'

'Sorry. Keep your eyes peeled along the ditch.'

They turn into a snake of a track. A swelling flood gathers at the junction with the main road. Twin waves sluice up on either side of the car as Nell presses through, accelerator to the floor. If this rain keeps up, shortly it will be unpassable. The track winds up in a series of loops. She has to push the gears into first. Even so, if there was the slightest possibility of meeting another car round one of these treacherous bends, they would almost certainly crash. There is nothing to be seen on either side, only darkness, an idea of bushy growth and driving rain. The road, such as it is, is pocked with potholes, a beard of grass all along the middle.

Suddenly Nell slams on the brake and slows the pace right down.

'Keep going. What're you slowing down for?'

'I mightn't see her in time in this rain.'

'You're right.' Ali faces her for the first time. A fixed line where her mouth should be. 'Nell?'

'We'll find her. It'll be okay.' Nell doesn't return the beseeching stare.

The road ends abruptly in a small clearing, widened for a makeshift carpark. Nell drives right to the edge, to point the car lights down into darkness. They can make out the blunted contours of scattered rocks, a path cut through high grasses by walkers. Ghostly limbs of stunted hawthorns, their twisted branches dripping rain. Ali is about to jump out when Nell roughly shoves a coat and hat into her hands. They quickly wrap up in the foggy warmth of the car.

'I'll leave the engine running and the fulls on. It might light us down to the lake. Save the torch and lamp. Have you got matches?'

'Yes.'

'She does know of this road?' The thought strikes Nell. 'I mean, she wouldn't have tried climbing up the other side, near Paudie and Julia's?'

'No. This is the way she's come with me before. C'mon.'

They jump out, coats drenched in seconds. Up here, a high wind screeches round their heads. It folds the rain into layered sheets, grey-white in the headlights. Ali runs blindly down the footworn path in the grass. Nell pants to keep up, just managing to grab the coat-tail ahead.

'Slower. You'll trip over a rock. Slow down.'

Ali grinds to a halt. Nell narrowly avoids bumping into her back.

'I can't see anything. Can you see anything?'

They stand together, looking down. The lights at their backs only reach to the edge, before the path dips down in a steep decline.

'We'll have to use the torch.'

They pick their way along, managing to see only a couple of feet ahead. Ali throws her head back and begins to frantically call.

'Grace! Gracie!'

Their feet sink into squelching mud, despite the makeshift track. It clings in a wet paste to the soles of their shoes. Another hundred yards along, Ali starts to beat back air as her feet slide and she collapses onto her back.

Nell reaches to help her up. 'You okay?'

Ali plunges on, weaving the torchlight left and right into wet blackness. 'Grace!'

With the wind and rain, their hollers carry hardly a dozen yards in any direction. They have to move in single file. Nell reaches ahead and grabs Ali's hand. If the torch goes, they could easily lose one another. She can feel the knobbly knuckles, bony ridges of her daughter's hand, the way her spindly wrist flexes in and out, accommodating their simultaneous twists and turns. The pressure of wet flesh against her own is somehow reassuring. All right? they ask over and over again. Mind your step there. Watch out for that boulder. What a night to be out. It's slippery here, dig your heel in. All right?

The mindless words, spoken trance-like, without pause, give a comfort of sorts, in the way a banal, everyday ritual becomes a focal point in times of stress or grief. Until they get to the lake, they will not refer to their worst fear, the very worst dread. There is even a curious elation, forced by adrenalin, every fibre of their beings focused on each individual moment. The walk, the rain, the dark, each stumble, each breath, heightened by terror of what may lie ahead. Therefore, precious, to be savoured – there may never be moments when the worst wasn't confirmed again.

By the time the track starts to level, they are croaky from shouting. The torch picks out twin red lights, the eyes of a startled sheep about to cross ahead of them. It moves quickly out of their line of vision.

'She'll be terrified.'

'If she's up here,' Nell adds, though there is hardly a trace of doubt in her mind.

Ali stops ahead of her. 'But what could she have been

thinking? That he let them loose around the lake? Or he threw them in? What?'

Nell mumbles something. It's not the time to point out that the cats would have been bundled into weighted hessian sacks, that Grace had overheard Nell talking about the hole in the centre of the lake, that Grace would know Paudie and his helper headed out there. Doubtless she was thinking they would have dropped them in, one by one; in which case, if she could make it in time, she might pick out a few survivors. Nell shivers uncontrollably.

'Are you all right?' Ali asks.

'Fine, just cold.'

'Look!' Torchlight settles in a wavery line on pitch black water. They move down.

'Nell, if anything's happened to her—' Ali's voice breaks off in a choke.

Nell squeezes her limp paw. 'Shh. Swing the torch round.'

There's a sign by the water's edge, over to the right. Another, a good distance to the left. The warnings Julia spoke of, presumably. Would Grace have taken the time to read them? Where they stand, before the first ripple of black lake, the earth sucks their shoes up to the ankles. They have to haul their feet out to take a step closer. Torchlight follows a broken, jagged path of yellow across black until it melts away into sheer darkness again. Bullet-holes of rain score the water's inscrutable surface. Ali abruptly drops her mother's hand and wades out to her shins.

'Ali, come back! You can't just—'

'Hold my hand, then,' Ali shouts back. 'I'll inch forward slowly. You keep a tight hold. If I lose my footing, you can haul me back.'

'It's too risky. Not in this weather.'

'Nell.' Ali turns; Nell can just make out the contours of her face in the backlight of the torch. 'What choice is there? What else can I do?'

'Hang on. Let's put a match to the kerosene lamp, at least.'

Ali hesitates a second, then wades back. They try to form a makeshift umbrella of their bodies as Ali strikes one stuttering match after another. At last, a flame holds steady. Nell swings the lamp out while her other hand stretches ahead, clasping Ali's in a blood-stopping grip. The torch sweeps in wide arcs ahead of Ali. When she steps too rapidly, Nell forces her to slow down. The water creeps up their trouser legs, spreading like liquid on blotting paper, so cold, that it forces involuntary moans from their frozen lips. When the wind lets up at infrequent intervals, Nell can just catch a low, concentrated incantation coming from Ali. A response echoes in her own head: please, please. Bargaining with God, or the elements, or the furies themselves. They inch out until black water reaches a point just under their knees. Rain beats on their faces; it feels to Nell as though it's weighted with prescience, a mourning for all frangible living things.

In that place in a person's head which remains unspeakably calm, irrationally reasonable, throughout the worst crisis – the dark, mysterious spot where the worst is already being tried and tested, analysed, before it's confirmed – Nell can't help but find a strange, a perversely exquisite, symmetry to these moments. It's over forty years since she set eyes on this place. Forty years since her trembling, freezing legs last stood in these dark, unforgiving waters. There is almost a mathematical linearity to the events of the past few hours. One part of her brain saying, what are the chances? How could this happen, here, again? Another part, calmly detached, saying, why, of course, this wasn't finished with at all. Of course we're here in the middle of the night, in the pouring rain, looking for Grace. Her feet are dead weights, trudging in the wake of her daughter's.

What does Ali hope for? What excessive hope is she nursing? That they will come to where the waters grow rough and tumultuous, and Grace will be standing there, gazing down? That she will turn, as though in slow motion, and pull back from the brink just as they arrive? What point in saying she wouldn't have a prayer, if she did step out here? The only point, right this minute, is grasping Ali's hand as tightly as she can, though already her own hand is numb and lumpen. Ali is no Agnes; she doesn't have the weight or strength to fight the suction, the way Agnes did, diving over and over again into swirling waters that threatened to suck her down. No, Ali would surrender like a wood shaving. Nell is overcome with sudden nausea: an image of Grace, thin and brittle as an autumn leaf, taking that final step.

'Look!' Ali points the torch at a spot, some distance ahead. 'There's the drop.'

'Careful. Go easy.'

They inch closer to where the lake suddenly appears to come alive. There are intermittent flecks of white, an undercurrent of movement ripples beneath the otherwise dead surface. Nell tugs Ali's hand. They are only footsteps away from the end of the ledge before the sheer decline. Ali swings the torch in frantic loops, but there is nothing to see, only curtains of rain and, beyond that, impenetrable darkness. She hollers Grace's name until nothing sounds from her throat. They step sideways, drawing their feet in a line parallel to the patch of restless water. Any second, Nell expects Ali to take a plunge. Her hand encircles her daughter's wrist, but the wet and cold make her purchase slippery and unreliable.

'Step back a little, Ali. We're much too close.'

They hug the edge, moving in the other direction. There is a desperate and defeated note to Ali's croaky calls. Back and forth they step, though their movements have taken on a careless, stumbling quality.

'I don't know what to do,' Ali cries, taking a step forward. Nell immediately tenses her hold on her wrist and manages to haul her back.

'We can't stay out here all night.' Nell forces her voice to sound reasonable. 'We're tired and it's dangerous. We'll end up making a mistake.'

'I don't know what to do.' Ali's shoulders heave up and down. 'How can I go back?'

'Come on, darling. We have to go back.'

'No!' But already she is allowing her mother to guide her steps away from the edge.

Nell raises the lantern. It casts flickering, dull light on Ali's angular face. Her eyes are hidden in dark, cavernous sockets.

'I don't know what to do,' she repeats in hoarse whispers, all the way back to the lake's edge.

There was never the slightest possibility that they would find Grace, out there in the darkness. They both understand that perfectly well. Yet while there was something to fixate on, even blind, crazy, illogical impulses, there was still the chance that a simple equation might take shape from the chaos — we search, therefore we find. Ali collapses to her knees in the muddy shallows, the stark concinnity of another equation let into her consciousness: they have searched, and have not found.

'There's every chance she's at home somewhere.' Nell

tries to force a note of conviction to the lie. 'She's probably tucked up, nice and dry, just punishing us for a while. Maybe she wants us to think, she's run away. Maybe she *has* run away. There's no more we can do tonight. Come on, let me help you up.'

Ali brushes her hand away and begins a shaky rise to her feet. Touch is too much to bear, words of hope, which might be thrown back in their faces, too much. Nell holds the lantern high and wide, to shed light on a path for Ali. Something catches her eye, far in the distance, over by one of the warning signs. A small, metallic gleam, reflecting the glow from the lamp. Without a word, she moves quickly along the shoreline. At first, she can't see anything. Perhaps it was just a beam of light against a curled lap of water. She swings the lantern in widening circles. Stifling a cry as she picks up the gleam again, she bends to retrieve the black cylindrical tube with gold markings. A battery. She quickly tucks it in a pocket and returns to Ali.

'What? Did you see something?'

'No. Just my eyes playing tricks. Come on, hold my hand. I'll go first this time.'

They pick the wrong track and end up a good distance from the car. As they round a boulder, they look back and the twin beams of the headlights pierce the gloom, way over to the right. With such poor visibility, moving in halting stops and starts, in a constant battle with a driving, contrary wind, it will take them over an hour to reach the path they should be following. They turn and retrace their footsteps until they reach the point where the carved grooves in the grasses bisect. After a while, the headlights guide them up through the scratching gorse and heathery bushes. Ali practically collapses on the bonnet. Nell half bundles, half thrusts her into the steamy warmth of the car's interior.

Only the sound of Ali's racking sobs breaks the silence, for the longest time. Then as if she has used up all her fuel, she lapses into stunned silence. Their feet and hands are numb; Nell can barely turn the controls on the heating up to full. A blast of hot, stifling air from the fan accentuates the wet of their clothing. Nell begins to peel off her soaked coat, the wool cloche cap that clings like a layer of skin to her head. Ali remains limp and lifeless while Nell leans across to peel off her drenched coat too. There isn't much room for manoeuvre and it takes a long time. Nothing can be done about the wet, clinging jeans. The most that can be hoped is that the wet will grow tepid as the car holds its heat.

'I'm staying here. I'm not going back,' Ali says in a drained voice.

'If that's what you want.' Nell places a hand on one bony shoulder. At first, Ali resists, then her head falls to the side. They huddle together, the bristly head lying in the warm, damp scoop between her mother's neck and shoulder-blade. The car's engine drones on in the silence. There is nothing to say. Nell checks the fuel gauge: plenty to see them through the night. She thinks of the battery in the pocket of her coat, draped across the back seat. A little cry threatens to emerge from the back of her throat, but she swallows to suppress it, and gazes ahead into the dancing, twirling funnels of rain, caught in the headlights. She turns the lights to dim.

Was there a moment, however fleeting and transitory, when Bridget, realizing she was never going to reach the surface again, experienced a strange spurt of joy that her sister had sliced up from the water above her head? Did she

have a second, untempered by terror, to send up whatever
girlish hopes and dreams she might have nurtured, along
with her sister? Or did she, until the very point of blackout,
still believe that a pair of hands would plunge down and
pluck her out too?

An hour passes before their shivering subsides. Ali's
breathing grows more regular, more of a momentary passing
out than sleep. Nell's shoulder throbs with the ache of keeping it raised to support her daughter's head, but she daren't
make a move for fear of disturbing this cocoon-like, temporary equilibrium.

Until the divers hauled Bridget from the depths, an
unspoken, hardly formed hope still kindled somewhere deep
inside her mother and herself. In the parts of them that
defied logic and corollaries, in the vestigial recesses that still
believed in toothfairies and goblins, no less for her mother,
with that constant list of her head toward the back porch
door, than for herself. That disbelief when death strikes.
How could that happen? How could that happen to us? To
Bridget the gazelle? It had to be a trick, one of Bridget's
sleight-of-hand, mercurial, golden moves. For the longest
time there was almost a sense of affront, of having been
duped – that she hadn't pulled it off.

Ali whimpers and rolls her head away. When Nell turns to
check, she's staring out the passenger window with deadened, hollow eyes. In the morning, once they've called on
professional help, she'll pull her aside and quietly tell her
about the battery. No point in adding to her torment
tonight.

'Ali?'

Ali doesn't respond. Nell settles the back of her aching
neck onto the headrest and closes her eyes. She tries to

summon up a sense of Grace, a sense of her out there, huddled, frightened in the driving rain. But nothing comes. Only the wet, rasping breaths of her daughter's despair, fogging up the already foggy interior. A heavy wind rocks the car. Half past four, the digital clock winks into the gloom. Already, hours have passed.

The walk back down the hill was the longest of Nell's life. It seemed that days passed before they could see the roof of Paudie and Julia's house, nestled in a hollow in the distance. It was hours before they set off on the journey home in the first place. Once Agnes came out of the water, streaming like a large, drenched beast, they took faltering steps close to the edge, looking down as though they could conjure Bridget from the murky depths. As though, any second now, she would spring up, eyes gleaming with devilish glee. Got you! I got you there. 'Course I didn't drown, you eedjits.

It was next to impossible to comprehend the suddenness, the finality of what had happened. Nell knew it was the same for her mother, moving back and forth in the shallows, making low whimpers which sometimes peaked to a high, altisonant pitch, but mostly kept to the same steady, almost soothing rhythm. Almost like a lullaby, crooned over and over to lull a baby into sleep. Peculiar jumbled thoughts flitted in and out of Nell's head. She wondered what they would tell the school, if her mother would write an absent note for Bridget. If the red scarf might be hers for ever. She was Arctic cold and hungry in spite of everything. She wondered if it would be possible that they might eat later on, and, if so, what they would eat. She wanted soup and toast. Thick slabs of white toast, soaked with melted butter. She would choose tomato soup. Bridget always wanted mush-room. Doubtless it would be mushroom, because Bridget always won the toss.

In the morning, she could see her sister, standing with her feet apart, declaiming to the whole class, telling them how she died yesterday. Drowned, she'd say, putting on a spooky voice, reliving each unnerving second. She'd tell how the land gave way beneath their feet, the water sucking them down. God it was black as pitch and frrreezing. It got into my nose and ears. I couldn't breathe or anything. Of course I was scared – what a spaz question. Not half as scared as Nell, though. Mammy lit off us. She took a huge stick and—

Agnes was hauling her by the coat collar to the edge of the lake. Her fingers bit into one loop of the scarf around Nell's neck, tightening it so that she was blue in the face and choking by the time they stepped onto dry land. Her mother stumbled to a large, flat-faced boulder, leaning down on to it, her bunched fists carrying her considerable weight. She wasn't crying, just that whimpering which Nell hated more than anything. Nell could hear the chattering of her own teeth. Of a sudden, Agnes moved back to a spot where the black waters licked at her shoes. Her shoulders went up in a giant shrug, hands out in the air, palms raised. This couldn't be. How could this be? She took a step, then stopped as though debating something. She turned and focused on Nell, though Nell thought she couldn't possibly see her through that foggy glaze where her eyes should be. What was she saying? Nell inched closer, shunting her frozen but-tocks along the wiry grass.

'Mammy?'

Agnes's hands fell limply by her sides. Her shoulders col-lapsed. She looked up to the top of the hill, signalling they might begin the journey home. Nell rose to her feet, slinking into place behind her mother's stumbling, weaving footfalls. Agnes reached a hand behind her back, Nell grabbed it.

'Stay in my sight,' Agnes said. 'Stay where I can see you.'

Nell managed to step into a kind of rolling rhythm with her mother's steps. But her mind had closed down. Cold and exhaustion had taken her over. She was walking in her sleep.

A pale wash of light suffuses the car's interior. Nell blinks awake. How is it possible that she slept? The body's imperative, ruthlessly insistent: if sleep is required, sleep must prevail. Ali starts beside her, eyes staring uncomprehendingly through the windscreen for a moment, until she remembers where they are and why they are there. The rain has stopped. A silvery streak bulges through from a smoky cloud overhead, streaming through the windows in the shaft of light that has woken them. A swish of car tyres behind.

It's Nick and Henri with the local Garda. They tried to get up earlier but the base of the road was flooded – it's only marginally better now. They were sure they'd get stuck. 'A hellish night to be out,' the young Garda remarks superfluously. He's trying to be full of blustery cheer, as though this is just a wayward start to a perfectly normal day. Ali steps out of the car, moving towards Nick. He hands her a heap of dry clothing, pours hot coffee from a flask. Their lips make soundless movements. Nell and Ali take it in turns to sip from the plastic mug. The warmth is like a prayer percolating down. 'We'll spread out,' the Garda says. 'No point in us all looking in the same direction.' He points out a different path for each of them. Nell is glad of his studious efficiency. But, behind his pinched little face, she can see their own worry reciprocated.

She doesn't dare catch Henri's gaze. She might break down entirely, and what use to her daughter then? Still, she hears the catch of his breath behind her, senses the tight, rigid back, and because he does not try to offer soothing words, or reach for her as he would usually, almost forcing comfort on her, she knows that he does fear the worst.

Nick can't manage the tracks but insists on staying outside, up where the lip of the hill smooths out before the descent to the lake. He sits on a rock with his hands wrapped round his raised knees. His face is paler than the pearly morning sky, dark grooves scoring his cheeks from nose to mouth. A tiny muscle pulses constantly on one cheek. Ali gives his shoulder a quick, cursory squeeze but he doesn't turn round. Nell resists an automatic first impulse to draw her hand away when Henri grips. Instead she leans on him and lets his shoulder carry her weight.

The Garda leads the way, keeping up a light, steady banter until the point where the tracks divaricate and he shows with his hands the routes they all should follow. Ali is beyond questions or answers. Deep within the core of her being, Nell understands that Ali is already preparing for the long days ahead. If she were harbouring a real tendril of hope, she would say to the Garda that they should start with the lake. Nell doesn't know why she seems so certain of this, but she is certain. In some inverted way it makes sense: you start at points of possibility, you end at the point of most probability.

'Ali?'

Ali swings round. She looks like a skeleton wrapped in layers. Nell opens her mouth to tell her about the battery. She should prepare her, in case Ali happens across any other telltale pieces of evidence confirming Grace's presence. But she can't bring herself to say the words. Instead, she does a ridiculous thing, she blows a kiss. For a second, Ali stands rigid, almost startled. A tiny smile sketches the corners of her lips, they round into a circle, she almost makes it, but her mouth falls slack once more. They turn and walk in opposite directions.

Further along, Nell has to hunker down behind a slab of granite for a pee. Her bladder takes an age to empty. There are specks of blood on the ground: her period, two months late, has chosen this incongruous moment to resurface. She wipes herself as best she can with clumps of brittle, reedy grass. Over on the far side of the lake, she can just make out the slender figure of the Garda beating a path with a stick through marshy growth. Sheep break into startled jumps ahead of him, then stop to pluck at grass, undisturbed, once they sense he poses no threat. In between loud calls of Grace's name, Nell can hear the growl of her empty stomach demanding nourishment. The coffee gurgles and rumbles in the vacuum. She would eat if someone were to hand her something. That she could eat is the most surprising thing. And if it's to be that they end up sending divers down for Grace, she will eat then, too. After a time. The thought shames and soothes in equal measure. She thinks of thick doorsteps of white toast, turned a light shade of gold, soggy and quilted with butter. Tomato soup.

Henri is checking behind huge boulders high above her. He looks down, catches her eye, his head gives a little shake, then he continues.

She is over by the side of the lake, where she first waded in with Bridget. A steep incline, stepped with loose rocks and boulders, leads up to a rim which, in turn, falls in a gradual, softer gradient down to a spot near Paudie and

Julia's house. There's another sign pegged into the water's edge, warning of the danger. A huge jackdaw swoops over the rim of hill and disappears. The bruised sky has melted into uniform silver, the light so sharp it reflects like a ray against a blade's edge. Only the centre of the lake remains dark and obscure. Broken dashes of brilliance shimmer in a halo along the shoreline. Air in her nostrils is spicy, purged by the night's rain, so rich and peaty, it feels as if every breathful fills her lungs with soupy liquid. She checks her watch. Half past seven.

Directly ahead lies the slab of rock Agnes leaned on with her fists clenched into tight knots. Its smooth front face almost reaches into the water. On her way round, Nell bends to select a brown stone, the size of a hand, mottled with spots of black. All the stones at the lake's edge are dun and wren-coloured. She slides it into her jacket pocket and walks on. A few steps along, she turns on an impulse and retraces her steps. At the back of the boulder there is a hollow where the granite tips up from the ground, listing forward slightly. A green wellington boot sticks out. It is empty. She bends down to peer into the gloomy space, less than two feet in height. Grace lies curled into a tight ball. Oblivious of daylight, she shivers in her sleep.

'Just another minute, Henri. I hate this place and I'll never come up here again. But just one more minute.'

Nell sits on the boulder, shivering. It's over an hour since Grace was bundled up, still dazed from the ordeal of the night but not seriously injured. She had stepped into the lake, promptly twisted her ankle and smashed her torch. Terrified in the darkness, she'd managed to crawl back to shore to find shelter under the rock. Nell watched as Nick and Ali staggered through the long grass, carrying their prize between them. Try as she might, she could not find the strength in her legs to follow.

Constantly, her eyes seek out the spot in the lake where the waters turn dark, reflecting no sky.

'What happened?' Henri asks, following the line of her gaze across the water. He pours more coffee from the flask and hands it to her. 'You say you remember kicking back to break Bridget's hold on your ankle. And then you went up in a sudden rush. What else?'

'What I didn't say was that two hands reached in and pulled me up.'

'Agnes.'

'Agnes. It all happened in a blur, naturally. One minute I was inhaling water, the next I was taking huge, choking gulps of air. I couldn't even see her at first. It wasn't easy hauling me out. We both keeled over to the side. I remember her hands on my back, shoving me further along the ledge into the shallows. She was grunting, making little whimpers. When I turned, she was diving down, head first. I could just see her ankles. She came up, took a deep breath and dived again. Over and over – she wouldn't give up. I kept calling to her but I doubt if she heard me. I felt my way along until my hands gripped the rim of the ledge. I was so afraid, each time she went down, that she wouldn't come back again.'

'Nell?'

'Sorry. Sorry . . . It's just . . .'

'Go on.'

'After a while, when she did come up, her whimpering had turned to deep growls. The sort of *uhhhh* sound you make just before a baby comes. She knew she wasn't going to pull her daughter out. She was exhausted by then, exhausted and defeated. She came and rested her head on her hands, like this, on the ledge beside me. That strange sound kept coming out of her mouth.'

'The poor woman.'

'Yes. She was always so big. Broad. So capable. In the water, with just her head and shoulders sticking out, she looked like some tiny, shrunken creature I could barely recognize. Not a word passed between us. I don't think she remembered I was there, to tell the truth. Not for a long time, anyway. I put my hand on hers and that seemed to shock her into life again. Her head lifted; she looked completely dazed. Her eyes travelled up my arm, to my chest, to the red scarf still tightly wrapped round my neck—'

She breaks off, two fat tears gliding down her cheeks. A gulp, and suddenly she is crying noisily, without inhibition, like a child. Henri puts an arm round her shoulders, gently rocking in a sideways motion until she can speak again. 'It was just the briefest moment, a swelling of her pupils, I don't know . . . something. I've never forgotten that look. I've tried, but . . . never.'

'When she realized it was just you and her from then on? That she'd lost a daughter?'

Nell bites down hard on her lip. 'The scarf, Bridget's scarf around my neck. What I was seeing in Mammy's eyes was the moment she realized she'd pulled the wrong daughter out.'

They stroll along the pebbled cove, arms linked, content with silence. Henri skips a few slim stones across the water's surface, deep within his own thoughts. Nell studies his profile, surprised to find herself so surprised by the sheer familiarity of him. Even the tiny black hairs on his fingers, above the joints, seem so much a part of her life that she wonders that she's never remarked them before. She pulls him closer, happy when he jolts out of his reverie and smiles at her. He has made his choice, he has chosen her and that is his right – she doesn't feel a compulsion to challenge that right any longer. She thinks that she may well be good for him and will not cause him harm, after all.

They cross over the alders and walk upfield. Nell waits outside while he fetches his bag from the house.

Before he gets in the car, he turns to make a confession. 'One thing I should tell you before you come back. I've sort of taken over your apartment.'

'Taken over?'

'Yes, well, not me as such, but Jeanne. I went a bit over the top, buying things. Big things. Equipment, toys – big toys. Marie-Louise doesn't have the room. She wants to stay in Paris for now: it's not going to work out with the bastard. So you're the storage unit, I'm afraid.' He's manfully trying to look apologetic, but clearly the idea of Nell returning to parcels of nappies, prams, high chairs and God knows what is too amusing to resist a covert smile.

'Thank you for that. Any room left for us at all?'

'Just about.' He checks his watch, quickly kisses her cheek. 'I'd better go. Next week, then?'

'At most. I just want to be sure that Grace is okay. The pony helps, but she's such a lost little thing. She still talks to the cats, you know, as if they're all around. I heard her last night. I wonder if I could palm Lulu off on her?'

'You don't mean that.'

'No, I don't mean that. Tell her I'll be home soon.'

'Nell? Room for us, you said. Meaning?'

'What do you think?'

'Good. That's settled, then.'

'It's settled. And yes, good. Very very, yes.'

The three ponytails eye Grace's booty with rapacious, narrowed eyes. Grace hangs her head when she leaves the shop with Nell, not even tempted to engage in a little tantalizing. A megachew bar lolls limply from one corner of her mouth like a dog's pink tongue. Not so much as a slurp. The girls are a line of small, impassive Buddahs, only their eyeballs moving.

Right. Nothing for it. Buy the bitches.

Nell fixes her widest smile. She peels open a bar of chocolate, running a fingernail along silver foil, making the squares stand out individually. Next, she delicately breaks off one square and pops it in her mouth. Her tongue makes a sucking sound against the roof of her mouth. Three sets of eyeballs are fixed on her lips.

'Hello, girls.'

''Lo.'

'D'you know these lovely girls, Grace?'

'They're in my class,' Grace mumbles. She doesn't look at them.

'Oh, you should have said. That makes all the difference. Chocolate, anybody?' Nell breaks off three squares and extends on the silver foil. Two ponytails pluck immediately, the one with freckles gives a slight shake of her head. The one to crack, Nell concludes.

'I'm sure we can do better than that,' Nell beams. 'C'mon, girls, let's see what damage we can do in the shop.'

They hesitate a second, but greed quickly overcomes all the warnings they've had about taking sweets from strangers. Grace looks at Nell with her mouth bunched up, eyes wide with disapproval. She has little choice but to follow them all inside. She watches, steaming silently, as Nell gives them each a bag, telling them to choose whatever they fancy. They don't have to be asked twice.

Outside on the pavement again, they're desperate to be off with the loot, wanting to add up, swap, compare, scorn. But Nell, by dint of her own solitary spell in the schoolyard desert, is something of an expert on the mysterious secret codes which little girls must live by, and knows they can't move off until she accepts their thanks and dismisses them. They are forced to walk alongside Grace and herself until she elects to set them free. Grace races ahead, head down, muttering furiously to herself.

'Who are you, anyway?' one of them asks.

'Grace's nan, of course. Didn't she tell you about my visit?'

'Her granny? You don't look like my granny.'

'Don't I?'

'More like my auntie.'

'Must be the magic I sprinkle on my cornflakes. Oops, I'm not supposed to say that.'

'Say what? About magic? You don't really know magic. Only in books people know that.'

'And filums,' another chimes in.

'The circus a few times, too, maybe,' the last adds, more diffident than the other two, less sure of herself.

'Oh, there are lots of things you don't know about at seven.'

'I'm nearly eight.'

'She is. She's seven and four quarters.'

'Really? Anyway, the thing is, if I could do magic, it would only be good. Unless of course, anyone was nasty to my darling granddaughter.' Nell does a little pout. 'I wouldn't like that.'

'What would you do so?' Freckles challenges, making sure the others see her sneer. This woman is talking pure rubbish but she's paid for the sweets and they have to listen till she shuts up.

Nell stops, a finger to her lips, deep in thought. They gaze up at her expectantly. She makes a bulb-going-off-in-her-head face. 'I know. I'd stop the presents.'

'What presents?' they ask as one.

'The ones I'm going to be sending all the way from Paris, every single month from now on. Presents for Grace and three, maybe four, of her best friends.' *Houston, we have landed.* 'Lovely things. Making things and glittery stuff with hearts and stars. Clothes sometimes, maybe. Clothes from Paris, you understand.'

'Every *single* month? Nah.'

'Every month. Because she's so special. That makes her friends special, too.'

'Like when every month?'

'No exact day. You'd have to call to the house for a play, lots of days, to see if anything had arrived. If there weren't lots of days, I'd be inclined to think she should choose better friends, whom she plays with more often. If you see what I mean.'

One of them nudges Freckles to see what she thinks. The quietest of the three, the uncertain flame-haired child with white marble skin, stares up at Nell in awe. She has the greatest potential, Nell decides and gives her a genuinely encouraging smile.

'Why don't you come up to Grace's house now and see her new pony?'

'She has a pony?'

'He loves apples. Maybe you need to check at home first?'

'We're allowed out until five o'clock,' Freckles asserts with a hint of scorn. Really, do they look like babies?

Grace has stopped further along, head cocked to the side, still muttering. Across the distance, Nell can feel the dagger eyes aimed in her direction.

They debate in terse whispers. Freckles makes the final decision. She gives Nell a look as if to say she's no one's fool but she'll play the game, so long as Nell keeps to her side of the deal. A little current of recognition passes between them.

'Grace, wait up!' Freckles hollers. 'Thanks for the sweets,' she remembers, before breaking into a run. The other two follow, ponytails swinging in their wake like gleaming tassels. Grace stands electrified. At first she looks as if she might break into a startled bolt in the opposite direction. Freckles descends on her, says something, runs on waving an arm, summoning her minions. The flame-haired girl slows by Grace, an almost imperceptible nudge of one shoulder against Grace's, urging her into action. Nell has to laugh out loud. She's never seen her granddaughter look quite so flummoxed before. She stares at Nell, turns her head, stares after the girls, the rev of her jiggling shoes apparent, itching to get going. A last look back over her shoulder and she's off. She catches up quickly and falls into line behind them, matching her pace to theirs. The flame-haired girl slips a pace back and says something. Grace throws her head back and laughs far too heartily and far too long, but the other child seems pleased. They walk on, two abreast. Just before they turn a corner taking them out of her immediate line of vision, Nell sees that Grace has scooped her hair into a bundle at the back of her head, holding it firmly as her conker ponytail swings from side to side.

It is late morning when Ali slips into her room. She eyes the packed suitcase on the bed and gives Nell a watery smile. 'I'm going to miss you around the place.'

'Not for long, though. I'll be back soon.'

Ali plucks at the corners of the eiderdown. 'So.' She shrugs, apropos nothing. 'So.' She moves to the window and stares out with her arms folded.

Terence, the new pony, has the run of the lower field. A rectangle of flattened yellow grass marks the spot where the caravan used to be.

'Are you all right?' Nell asks softly. She places the back of her hand to her daughter's cheek.

'Maybe.' Ali attempts a feeble smile. 'Maybe I will be.' She turns from the window as though the emptiness below is too painful to countenence. 'I wish you could just forget people, put them out of your mind completely. But that's not possible, is it?'

'No, that's not possible.'

Over Ali's shoulder, Nell watches Nick walk downfield with a feed bucket for Terence. There's been a marked improvement in his health since they scoured each and every room. He's still rapier thin, prone to fits of coughing, but Nell has sensed an almost angry insistence on his part to be well. To offer that much, at least, to his daughter as a gift, her reward for losing her cats. There's no way of knowing if the runner-up prize of himself will be enough for Ali. The strain between them has been considerable, but there is kindness, too, the gentleness that springs up between people when they have been forced to look over the edge together.

Ali looks down at the lines of Agnes's memory stones, drilled along the floor. Nell tips the remaining stones from the bottom of the stool box.

'I was looking for one in particular.'

'Describe. Maybe I can help.'

'If I remember right, it's flattish, a sort of steel grey on one side, while the other side is covered in a criss-cross of white. It was quite distinctive.'

'This is what you're looking for, I bet.' Ali lifts a stone from the mound. She turns it over. The faded markings of the date and place are just legible on the marbled side.

Nell holds it in the cup of her hands. 'The day I left,' she says, 'Mammy picked it from the sea. It just says the date and the cove.' She shrugs. 'I don't know, maybe I thought she might have written something on it after I'd gone. Just being a sentimental fool, really.'

'Anything on the plain side? Faded into the grey maybe?'

Nell turns it over again, shakes her head. 'No, nothing.' She drops the stone back onto the pile. 'Anyway.'

Ali tips the mound with her foot. They spread out across the floor. Nell absently catalogues dozens of walks. Memories as solid as the stones themselves. The geological foundations of her life mapped out for anyone to see. Nothing can ever eradicate those moments with her mother. The shape of everything to come, marked out by crystal and granite, limestone and shale, black concentric rings on palest marble. Each stone a history lesson, a meandering conversation, an inadvertent grazing of their hands together as they stared out to sea. The first swim, stretched out like a seal calf along her mother's broad back, a mutual turning away when thoughts of Bridget left them breathless with longing. A stack of stones for O'Connell, the Liberator, all to himself. Two white, pearly pebbles for two holy communions. A solitary pink oval for one confirmation.

It's not for nothing, Nell thinks, that the elderly reach back to reclaim their childhood. Their infantile babbling making perfect sense to them. The tiniest of insignificant details, dredged up from decades ago. A pot boiling over, the night a parent died, blackened pap of a banana sandwich, that first day at school. The circular minutiae round the big events that uniquely fingerprint our lives. What can we become, except what we remember? And all that we try to forget.

'What is it, Nell?'

Nell is on her knees, a puzzled frown pleating her brow, fingers rapidly scrabbling through the multi-coloured pebbles, her frown increasing as she turns one after another.

'Nell?'

Suddenly Nell sits back to rest on her heels. She stays like that, needing a moment to compose herself. At last, it's clear why Ali remained so strangely ignorant of Agnes's practice of collecting stones. Why she didn't even realize what they were when she sealed the stool box.

'Look at the dates, Ali.' She puts the cool granite to her flushed cheek, imagining the cushioned palm of her mother's hand. 'Our walks were a comfort to her, not a torment.' She looks at Ali. 'This grey stone is the last. The day I left. There are no more memory stones.'

Hours pass as they sit cross-legged on the floor, surrounded by Agnes's stones, talking about the past, delighting in the different complexions they give to the same rememberances. They hoot at Nell's image of Agnes with her hat on, trying to eat millefeuille delicately in Angelina's. The way she would manage a bite of the flaky pastry, then anxiously look around to see if the whole place was seeing what a mess she was making of it. The way she kept dabbing a napkin to her lips while talking with her face, making conversational expressions, pursing her lips, raising her eyebrows, though Nell wasn't saying anything. The way a great big gob of cream went unnoticed at the corner of her mouth and Nell hadn't the heart to lean across and flick it away: the mortification would have silenced Agnes for the day. The brisk walk in the wrong direction as soon as they stepped out onto the pavement. Turning into exit signs, shuffling past entrances, glancing over her shoulder in confusion. Leapfrogging across busy intersections, head down: if she didn't see the cars, they simply didn't exist.

The evening meals in restaurants. More prolonged agony, every waiter being thanked profusely even when they were serving the next table, Agnes obliged to thank them when she felt the other diners were being too lax in that department. Little glares across tables, throughout the meal, when they didn't act on her blatant hints. Nell darting quick, apologetic smiles. The refusal to take a taxi home afterwards, because Nell's apartment was only a stone's throw away. An hour's trudge through the city later, her bunions on fire – there, that didn't do us any harm.

'And shopping!' Nell explodes. 'Oh Lord, shopping in Paris with Mammy.'

Ali hops up. She stands, imperious expression, addressing

a shop assistant. 'How much d'you say? What's that come to, Nell? But there's nothing in it. A few stitches on a bit of material. I'd expect a suit—'

'A nice blue suit,' Nell chimes in.

'A nice blue suit, for that kind of money. Nell, talk to this girl here. See if she wants to be reasonable.'

'And in Oxford,' Nell wheezes, 'out with Uncle Albie and Mary Kate, the English accent, d'you remember?'

Ali fixes her imaginary hat. 'Thank you so much. Thank you. Thank you vehhy much.'

'I'm most grateful to you,' Nell prompts.

'Oh yes. I'm most grateful to you. Would it be possible, do you think, we might have another one of your lovely bags – no, not one of them with Sale written on it, one of them nice shiny, stripey ones.'

'Thank you *so* much.'

Ali squats again, bright tears of mirth sparkling in her eyes. Her hand slides across and squeezes Nell's.

'She was some woman,' she says.

'Yes, she was. She certainly was.'

It is the sort of afternoon when the light looks like liquified butter. A dazzling October afternoon, a last promise of what will return, after the grey death of winter. Down to her right, the glittering sea seems to have absorbed the sun.

Paudie opens the door before she has a chance to knock. 'Come in, Nell. Come in.'

'Well,' Julia says, wiping her hands on an apron. 'Are we your last port of call?'

'Yes. I'll be heading off in an hour or so.'

'How's the gedleen doing?' Paudie asks, his head nodding

in Julia's direction. 'She's still giving me a scalding for leaving that bleddy note.'

'She misses the cats, of course, but she's excited about the pony. I think she'll be all right.'

'I've made you a couple of brown cakes to take back with you.' Julia fetches a parcel.

'And there's black puddings in there, too,' Paudie says. 'I know the man that makes them. It's good stuff. Nothing like that shop drivel.'

'Thank you both,' Nell takes the neatly wrapped package. 'For everything, I mean. Mammy, too – looking out for her.'

'We're so used to keeping an eye on the house above, I s'pose we'd do it in our sleep.' Julia touches Nell's arm fleetingly. 'We're none of us getting any younger, Nell. Now that you've found your way home, you will stop with us again, won't you?'

'You'll be sick of me.'

'There'll only be the few visits out of myself,' Paudie chortles, measuring his span out. 'But you've shirts racked up ahead of you yet, young woman.'

'Not so young, Paudie.'

'From where I'm standing, you're but out of the cradle.'

They stand huddled in the doorway, waving, as Nell heads off for a last walk along Derrynane beach. 'But out of the cradle' repeating in her head, making her smile with the delicious pleasure a child feels before Christmas. When the bowels and the gut churn with anticipation, when anything might happen, because it can, because there's time and Christmases ahead. She is the future her past child anticipated. What shame at fifty or sixty, or maybe even ninety, in throwing her head back to gloat at a full moon or a stunning

October afternoon. I've made it to the future. I'm here. And when I'm no longer here, nothing can ever change the fact that, once, I was.

As she jumps from the grassy bank, down onto the soft golden sand, it does feel as though her limbs have developed extra spring, or rediscovered an energy which has been lying dormant. How easily she had slipped into the change of life, automatically assuming a change for the worse. Closing in on herself like an animal preparing for hibernation. Shutting down. For all the world, she might have ended up hiding in a white apartment, no less than Adam in the self-imposed exile from humanity of his caravan.

A light wind riffles her hair, teasingly. The sky stretches out to the horizon in one deep blue sheet of unsullied velvet. Tiny, whispering waves lap along the shoreline. The tan sand looks smooth and vacuumed from a receding tide. For a moment, she is absolutely convinced that Agnes and Bridget walk just a little distance ahead. A solid rock, shambling in the dancesteps of a golden mirage. The great hulk of Agnes, turning from her daughters, reaching down to pluck a solitary stone, washed up then abandoned by the retreating waters. Yes, she has managed to keep her alive all these years. A version of her which Nell could live with. And now it is time to let her go. To let her spirit rest, content in the knowledge that, at last, her daughter knows that she was loved, though as she was, flawed and human with the capacity to hurt and be hurt – not as the perfect memory they couldn't help but make of Bridget.

She thinks of Henri, the years he, also, has patiently waited. She will ask him to move Marie-Louise and the baby into the apartment, too. Oh, it's a ridiculous notion!

The kind of mad, irrational promise you make to yourself on jewel-like days such as this. Just for a while, of course, until his daughter decides what she's going to do with the rest of her life. The very idea of soiled nappies, rattles, bottles of milk racked up in her fridge, makes her fold over with a wheezing laugh. It won't work. It will drive her crazy, out of her mind. But she'll give it a try, for as long as it works. She'll try giving the rubbing shoulders, shivery unspoken businesses, the unpredictable transactions, the irresolutions, of other people's lives, a chance to reel her in. The contradictions and complications, so that in the confusion she may one day stare out her window, looking down onto boulevard Raspail, and not even be aware of the background noise, the persistent turmoil of existences colliding with hers. It will just be part of the landscape.

She turns, happy to be part of this wonderful day. To have air in her lungs, sand in her shoes and years of shirts racked up into the distance. Bola covers the gap between them in a few easy strides. He gives her a broad smile, more animated than she has seen him before. Jogging on the spot, he tells her that the papers have arrived for his daughter. She will come next month with his sister. It might not work out, he shrugs, but then again it might. It's a good day, he says, looking up at the blue wash of sky. This will be her country now. He's about to move on again when Nell stops him. She reaches in her jacket pocket and pulls out the dun stone she picked from the lake the morning they found Grace. She curls his fingers round it. He looks curious but doesn't ask a thing.

'For your daughter.' Nell says. 'Let this be the first memory stone. In her new country.'

She walks away. Glad to have known rare moments of heart-stopping beauty, the possibility of more lying ahead in the future. And glad, too, for the shabby, scabby stuff of life that makes perfection more bearable.